C000140524

USA Today bestselling auth[...]
decision to write romance to[...]
a flight delay that engrossed[...]
mind at all when her flight was delayed two more times.
Giving her readers the chance to escape into another world
has motivated her to write over one hundred books for a
variety of Mills & Boon series.

J. Margot Critch currently lives in St John's,
Newfoundland and Labrador, with her husband, Brian,
and their little fur buddies. A self-professed Parrothead,
when she isn't writing, she spends her time listening to
Jimmy Buffett and contemplating tropical locales.

ALASKAN BLACKOUT

JOANNE ROCK

THE WRONG RANCHER

J. MARGOT CRITCH

MILLS & BOON

First Published in Great Britain 2023
by Mills & Boon, an imprint of HarperCollins*Publishers* Ltd
1 London Bridge Street, London, SE1 9GF

www.harpercollins.co.uk

HarperCollins*Publishers*
Macken House, 39/40 Mayor Street Upper,
Dublin 1, D01 C9W8, Ireland

Alaskan Blackout © 2023 Joanne Rock
The Wrong Rancher © 2023 Juanita Margo Bishop

ISBN: 978-0-263-31765-7

0823

This book is produced from independently certified FSC™ paper
to ensure responsible forest management.

For more information visit: www.harpercollins.co.uk/green

Printed and Bound in the UK using 100% Renewable Electricity at
CPI Group (UK) Ltd, Croydon, CR0 4YY

ALASKAN BLACKOUT

JOANNE ROCK

For my middle son, Camden,
a keen observer who gets things done.
Thank you for your ready wit and
inspiring me to have more fun.

One

Quinton Kingsley wasn't surprised when the ride he'd hired dropped him off at least one hundred yards from his destination on Amaknak Island in Alaska.

In the rain.

"Sorry, man. Mud season is vicious here," the young driver called back to Quint over the threadbare headrest of a sedan model that had been obsolete for at least a decade. "This is as close as I can get to the bar without getting stuck."

Of course it is. Quint stuffed his phone deep inside a pocket of his leather messenger bag to protect the device from water damage. To the driver, he lifted his hand in a gesture of acknowledgment visible in the rearview mirror. "I understand. Give me a minute and I'll be on my way."

"Sure thing," the twenty-something driver mumbled from his seat up front, long hair hiding his face as he bent over his phone.

Over the span of the seventy-two hours he'd been in the aptly nicknamed Last Frontier State, Quinton had careened from one travel disaster to the next. First he'd been stuck in Anchorage waiting for favorable winds to fly to the Aleutian Islands. Then he'd bounced through violent headwinds in a prop plane once the weather cooperated enough to allow the daredevil pilot through the storm front. Next he'd been forced to coerce a ride from a local to his destination, since the car service he'd reserved hadn't been able to accommodate the adjusted date of his trip after the Anchorage delay. So he could hardly have expected this last leg of his two-thousand-mile odyssey to go smoothly.

But nothing would stop him from confronting his half brother, Clayton Reynolds, whose last known address was the dilapidated building bearing a generic Open sign in a small front window visible even through the driving rain. Clayton had purchased the place three years ago when he left Silent Spring, Montana, after a blowup with their father. Quint had never known his half brother well, since Duke Kingsley had never formally claimed his oldest son born outside of his marriage to Quinton's mother. Clay had drifted in and out of their lives back in Silent Spring, Montana—a couple of weeks in a summer here and there—spending the majority of his formative years with his mom on the West Coast. But three years ago, Clay had spent a few months in Silent Spring to work things out with his birth father. That attempt at mending the old rift had gone south in a hurry.

Quinton had already been living in Silicon Valley at the time, working on his tech company, so he didn't know the specifics. No one did except for Clayton and their father, who'd died the winter before.

Rain pounded the roof of the car as Quint reached for the door handle. At least he'd stopped off at his hotel before driving on to the Cyclone Shack perched on a muddy rise near Dutch Harbor. He'd been able to change out of his leather loafers and into a pair of boots. The all-weather footwear and jacket were going to prove invaluable on this last leg of the trek.

A journey he was months overdue in making since Duke Kingsley had died months ago and Quinton hadn't been able to locate Clayton to settle some details from the old man's wildly unfair last will and testament. The will had ignored Clayton. But Quint refused to let their dad's prejudice ostracize his half brother.

If only he could locate him to make the situation right.

Now, shoving open the vehicle door with one hand while he yanked up a rain hood with the other, Quinton stepped out into the driving rain. Immediately, the downpour pummeled his head and shoulders through the jacket. Water sluiced around his boots as it ran down the hill while he elbowed shut the car door. Tucking his messenger bag close to protect the important paperwork he needed to have signed, Quinton kept his eye on his destination while he navigated the slippery terrain.

Aluminum sided and one story tall, the run-down structure could have been one of the equipment barns on the Montana ranch where Quinton had been raised. The place was functional looking with a wooden wheelchair ramp next to the steps to the metal front door, a faded sign bearing its name hanging to one side of the entrance.

The soggy ground sucked at his boots as he heard the

sedan drive away, the squeaking of an engine belt loud enough that he could hear it even over the racket of the storm. And the waves. The bays and inlets of the Bering Sea were normally calmer at this time of year, according to the guidebooks Quint had skimmed on the plane. But today, the sea churned against the rocks, the sound carrying across the road and up the hill. Rainy season was just beginning now that they were midway through September, and that meant deluges. Low pressure systems.

Even the occasional cyclone.

With any luck, Quint would be far from Amaknak Island before more severe weather hit.

He had no idea why Clayton hadn't answered his letters, calls or emails, but he hoped confronting Clay in person would allow them to settle things. With that comforting thought in mind, Quint reached the front door of the bar. As he tugged it open, the wind pulled at it so hard he had to wrestle the thing closed behind him.

Eyes adjusting to the dim interior of the metal building with only a few windows, he felt the weight of curious stares from all around him. Twenty patrons, perhaps, populated the bar on a Thursday evening. Modern country music played from an unseen source, the tinny reproduction suggesting an undersized speaker. A handful of no-frills pine booths and high-top tables filled the interior, while the long side of the building boasted a bar illuminated by industrial-looking metal pendant lamps.

The shelves of liquor were the establishment's main decoration, although a bulletin board stuffed full of papers and photos had been nailed to a wall in the far corner near a digital register.

Quinton paused on the front mat to wipe his boots

when a female voice sounded over the twang of steel guitar on the sound system.

"If you're here to eat, take a seat wherever you like," the voice—low and slightly musical—called to him. The words weren't accented, exactly, but there was a cheerful quality in her smoky tone that made him turn around to see the speaker. "I'll be with you in just a moment."

Scanning the space, Quinton glimpsed a hint of copper-colored hair disappearing behind the bar. Since he definitely wasn't standing inside the Cyclone Shack for the purpose of eating, he headed toward the makeshift serving area that looked like someone had built it on sawhorses. Plywood filled the space in front of the stools, though the countertop appeared to be genuine hardwood.

In his mind, Quinton was already calculating what his brother could do to improve the place with his share of the Kingsley inheritance. Just as soon as Clayton could be convinced to take it off Quinton's hands.

With the renewed energy of a man who has finally reached his object after a long journey, Quint waited impatiently for the figure that had disappeared beneath the countertop to reemerge. Because unfortunately, as his gaze swept the gloomy interior of the place once more, he didn't see anyone else working at the Cyclone Shack today. In particular, he didn't see Clay.

Damn it.

"What can I get for you?" That low, smoky cadence hit his ears again, snapping his attention front and center once more.

A copper-haired knockout frowned at him, like something unwelcome that had washed up on the dark rocks that lined Unalaska Bay. Her pale skin and freckle-covered nose were delicately shaped, but those features were the only dainty thing about her. Her bright hair was long and windblown, as if she'd just stepped in from a cyclone herself. As if she couldn't be bothered to primp and preen for anyone's sake. And her mouth was unabashedly sexy. Full and generously shaped, her lips were a deep, rosy pink without any trick of cosmetic that he could detect.

Dressed in a heavy fleece hoodie and bright orange bib waders, the woman held a stack of laminated menus in one hand and a massive tackle box in the other. Assessing, marine-blue eyes narrowed as they took in his jeans and boots. His still-dripping oilcloth jacket, which he hadn't worn since the last time he'd herded cattle. All more suited to a ranch than an Alaskan fishing port.

Perhaps that was why, when he didn't respond to her question right off, she smirked at him. "Welcome to Alaska, by the way."

He couldn't have said why her seeming amusement at his expense nettled. It didn't matter what some stranger thought of his cowboy get-up in a bar at the edge of nowhere.

But before he could inform her that he was the brother of the man who owned the place and that he'd come for business, not a drink, she shoved the tackle box across the bar to a big bear of a guy Quinton hadn't noticed come in. Probably because he'd been too busy staring at the hot fisherwoman-server.

"Thanks for letting me try the gear, Ryker," she said to the grizzled giant, who took the tackle box from her and set it on the floor next to a stool where he lowered himself. "I caught six coho in an hour trolling about two miles an hour using the ten-pound downrigger. Between the four of us we had the coolers full in a few hours."

She slid one of the menus from her stack toward Quinton, then stuffed the rest of them into a wooden bracket beside a digital cash register before picking up a clean rag and wiping down the surface of the bar in front of him. As if preparing for him to take a seat there.

He shrugged out of his coat and laid it on one of the stools while taking a seat on another, waiting to reclaim the woman's attention. She was a blur of movement as she cut limes to refill her supply, the knife blade flashing between swipes along a plastic cutting board.

"This storm rolling in stirred 'em up," the patron with the tackle box at his feet remarked. "And you can borrow my gear anytime. I made twenty bucks off my bet with Fletch that you would have the best haul this morning."

"And Fletch bet against me?" The woman laughed. "I'll remember that next time he tries to sweet-talk me into running a tab for him."

When the lime slices were finished, she shrugged her shoulders out of the straps for her waders, allowing them to droop alongside her hips. Once the neoprene fabric pooled at her waist, she had to fold the material over itself a few times before she could tie the straps into a makeshift belt.

Revealing a narrow waist and standout curves discernible even under the thick fleece hoodie she still wore.

Not that he should be noticing when he hadn't come here for pleasure. He needed to do right by his half brother, who'd been shortchanged by their dad. Nothing could interfere with that.

"Excuse me." Quinton leaned forward to recapture

the server's attention. "I'm looking for Clayton Reynolds. Is he around?"

The woman's flurry of activity ceased as her gaze swung back to him. Her hands fell away from the knot she'd been making as she stepped closer to the bar to face him.

"Who wants to know?" Her chin tilted.

Defensive. Challenging.

And for one unwise second, he wished he wasn't here for business. Because being the center of this woman's notice stirred something inside him that didn't often awaken.

"Quinton Kingsley," he returned evenly, heart pounding harder at her new regard. "His brother."

A smile slid over her features before she bit off a sharp bark of laughter. She tossed her head back, her windblown mass of copper strands dancing along her shoulders as she gave voice to a kind of dark mirth.

"Any particular reason that amuses you?" he asked when she seemed to have recovered herself.

"Yeah, there is, in fact," she shot back, settling her elbows on the bar to face him. Her voice didn't sound amused any longer. "I've been fielding phone call after phone call from you and your family for months, trying to tell you that Clayton wants no part of Kingsley *anything*. Yet here you are in the flesh, the Montana rancher coming all the way to Alaska, fresh from riding the range, just so I can tell you to your face." She leaned closer still, so near now that he could see the details of her irises in her eyes. They weren't just one color. There were dark patches beside light ones, a complex network of shades. "Clayton." She jabbed the bar with her index finger. "Doesn't." Another jab. "Want. To. Be. Found."

Foreboding washed over him at her certainty. Or maybe it was the fact that she seemed to know Clayton so well that disturbed him.

Was this woman—the bold redhead that made Quinton's blood run hot—a wife or girlfriend to his brother? Clay sure as hell hadn't kept the family informed of his personal life.

"How would you know? Who are you to Clay?" he asked in a rush, his pulse surging so fast that he could hear his heart pound in his ears.

The woman rocked back on her heels, elbows sliding off the bar as she laughed again.

"And that right there tells me all I need to know about you Kingsleys." Shaking her head, she picked up her bar mop and began to wipe her way down the counter, with a scrubbing motion that suggested she wished she could wipe him away too. "Do you really expect Clay to take your calls and your meetings when you can't even be bothered to know him?" Straightening, she whipped the white rag over her shoulder, her cheeks flushed with color. "I'm McKenna O'Brien, you dolt. His *sister.*"

Okay, technically she was Clay's stepsister. No relation by blood.

But anger streaked through her that one of Clayton's half brothers would trek all the way to the Aleutian Islands after Clay had made it clear he didn't want anything to do with the family that had never claimed him as one of their own. Hell, in every way that mattered, *she* was far more of a sibling to Clay than any of his biological kin.

Not only would she forever embrace Clay as family, but she would always take his side after the way he and his mom had treated her when she'd found herself married into their world. Clay's mom, Dena Reynolds, had certainly never made McKenna feel like a stepchild when she had entered McKenna's father's life. McKenna had been just twelve years old and fresh from the death of her birth mom from a firearm accident. Clay had been twenty by then, and out on his own working oil rigs in Alaska while Dena settled into life with McKenna and her father in Seattle. Then, even after McKenna's dad drank his way into cheating on Dena, Clay's mother had made it clear that McKenna had a home with her always.

Or, at least up until Dena's death three years before. After that time, Clayton had told McKenna that she would always have a home with him. And he'd made good on his word when McKenna's post college life in San Francisco had turned upside down after a relationship gone bad. She'd fled to Dutch Harbor eighteen months ago to help Clayton run the Cyclone Shack, and he'd taken her in, no questions asked. When he needed to leave town for personal reasons that seemed to have a lot to do with the Kingsley clan, he'd allowed her to take over the payments on his house. His business.

Clayton was the best family she had left considering her father's backslide into alcohol and a whole slew of other vices that did him no good. So she had no intention of sharing Clay's whereabouts with the tall rancher whose chest looked molded of steel and eyes shone the color of summer honey.

Even if there had been a moment when the sight of him had sent a surprise bolt of heat through a body she'd feared wasn't capable of it anymore.

How unfair that her first twinge of sexual attraction

in eighteen months had to be for a guy she already knew was a treacherous jerk. She read enough newspapers to recall that Duke Kingsley had bestowed the entirety of his estate on two of his biological sons—Quinton included—while completely disregarding the others. Luckily, Clay had turned his back on his arrogant siblings three years ago, so being disinherited hadn't cut as deeply as it might have if he'd been expecting to finally be recognized by his father.

"Clayton doesn't have a sister." The dark-haired rancher stared at her like she was the imposter here and not the other way around. Everything about him appeared custom-tailored, from his charcoal-colored button-down that fit his broad shoulders to precision, to the jeans molded to strong thighs.

Not that she could see the jeans anymore with him seated at her bar. Unfortunately, her brain remembered what he looked like a little *too* well. But good looks didn't buy a man a pass in her book. Far from it. All the more reason to be wary.

"You have a hell of a lot of nerve calling yourself family to Clay when you know *nothing* about him." Unwilling to engage in dialogue with a man she'd hung up on countless times in the past six months whenever he'd phoned the bar, McKenna stomped off to wait on patrons who were actually prepared to pay money for her time and service.

She would let Thinks-He's-a-King Kingsley cool his heels by himself for a while since she had no intention of giving him what he'd come here for. And how dare he suggest Clay didn't have a sister?

Twenty minutes later, that last thought still circled a

wounded place inside her, adding to an old ache. Not that she would have ever allowed it to show. She traded fish stories with Ryker, who thought it only fair to spend the thirty bucks he'd won in the Cyclone Shack since she'd been instrumental to his winnings. She appreciated him patronizing her bar. Or what would be her bar, one day soon, when she finished repaying Clayton for the business he'd tried to give her when she'd returned to Dutch Harbor eighteen months ago, broken and alone.

That was what real family should be about, she thought with leftover fury as she cast a glance toward Quinton Kingsley once more. He still sat at the bar where he'd been before. Only now he had company in the form of Angela Forrest, the widowed wife of a fishing boat captain who'd gone down with his ship five seasons ago. Angela, fit and lovely as she entered her mid-fifties, sipped her usual afternoon ginger ale while nodding and smiling at whatever King Arrogant was saying to her.

A woman the locals admired, Angela often took it upon herself to welcome newcomers to the area, the same way McKenna would bet she'd done for years with new crew on her husband's boat. McKenna would bet half the people in the Cyclone Shack right now had sailed with Captain Forrest at one time or another. And while Captain Forrest had made them feel at home on the sea, his wife would have made sure crew members families felt at home back on land.

McKenna reminded herself to let Angela know Quinton Kingsley would not be staying in Dutch Harbor for long. Furthermore? Quinton wasn't the kind of people they wanted in their close-knit community.

"You got eyes for the new guy, McKenna?"

The question, spoken quietly and conspiratorially by Ryker as he opened his second bottle of a local craft brew, snapped her out of her meandering thoughts.

"Of course not," she hastened to set the record straight as she dragged her gaze away from Quinton and hurriedly cleared empties from the bar stools on Ryker's other side. "Since when do I have eyes for outsiders when the best men I know live right here?"

Ryker's hoot of laughter suggested he didn't buy that. "Best men? Is that what you called young Billy Jenkins when you tossed him out on his ear last weekend?"

McKenna cringed to recall her loss of temper Friday night when the bar had been full to overflowing and a rowdy table of young guys kept hassling some female tourists. It wasn't just bad for business; it was offensive to her as a woman.

Nevertheless, her tirade about it had probably been over the top since the kid's harassing comments about the ladies had sparked hurts of her own from harassment of another kind. She hoped news of that hadn't spread too far around town, but that was probably wishful thinking.

"Come on, Ryker." Methodically, she carried empty bottles to the recycling container and dishes to a plastic tub destined for the kitchen. "Billy and his followers are still knocking on the door of manhood. Talk to me after they weather their first full fishing seasons on the sea."

Ryker's smile slid away as he lifted his bottle to acknowledge her point. "No doubt that'll put some common sense in their heads and fear of God in their hearts."

Hurrying away with her dirty dishes, McKenna refused to allow her eyes to stray toward the place where Quinton Kingsley still sat. If Ryker could discern something in her expression when she looked at Quinton, then clearly she wasn't hiding her curiosity about the man well enough.

But after a year and a half of working in Alaska, through the cold and wet months where the sun didn't rise until after 10:00 a.m. and set again just seven and a half hours later, McKenna had learned to be stronger. Tougher.

Mentally, emotionally and physically.

She could dig her heels in with the best of them. She would resist the lure of the stranger she needed to be wary around.

So she wasn't concerned about Quinton Kingsley's arrival. Because whatever a Lower 48 man could dish out, she could handle. She *had to* after the way one of them had nearly crushed her.

Putting blinders on herself, she managed to get through one hour after another with Quinton sitting in the middle of the bar. The rain stopped eventually, but the weather remained windy and cold, whipping through the front door anytime anyone new entered the Shack. She'd even managed to take Quinton's order at one point since she couldn't very well allow him to sit there without buying a damned thing. She was a businesswoman now, first and foremost.

During that brief exchange, Quinton had been as brusque and efficient in their interaction as she'd been. But now, as the night wore on and the bar began clearing out while she wiped down the tables, she could see that Clay's stubborn half brother wasn't about to give up and leave anytime soon. He'd quizzed two of the locals on Clay's whereabouts already, but McKenna knew he couldn't have learned anything concrete about where his half brother had gone since Clay hadn't told a soul besides her.

But obviously, Quinton wasn't going to limit his questions to her alone.

Why had she thought he might give up when these Kingsleys were—by all of Clay's accounts—entitled by birth into believing they deserved the wealth and good fortune that came their way?

When at last the bar was empty, save for Quinton and her, McKenna walked briskly to the stereo behind the counter and snapped off the music. For the first time since Ryker had pointed out that she had "eyes" for Clay's half brother, she allowed herself to look her fill at the Kingsley heir who'd strode into her bar late that afternoon.

"It's closing time," she announced, peeling an elastic hair tie from her wrist and using it to gather the ends of her wind-tossed mane. She'd barely had time to breathe since walking into the Cyclone Shack after her early fishing outing, let alone run a brush over her head. Not that she cared what she looked like in front of this man. "That means even entitled ranchers need to make their way home for the night."

Rounding the bar, she flicked off one set of lights that illuminated the bar and reached for her coat from one of the pegs on the wall. She left her fishing waders there after finding a second to peel them off halfway through her shift.

Behind her, Quinton made a low whistle.

"Are you always this tough on people?" he asked as he stood. His height and breadth suddenly taking up more space than she'd remembered. "I mean, yes, I should have recalled that Clay had a stepsister. But considering I never spent much time with him since he rarely returned to Silent Spring after he turned eighteen and neither did I, I'm not sure you can hold that against me."

And whose fault was it that Quinton didn't know Clay at all? Although his words reminded her that Quint was the brother who'd moved to Silicon Valley as soon as he'd graduated high school and started a tech company while he was in college. He probably hadn't lived that far from her when she'd been in San Francisco.

She hated to think about that time in her life. And she wasn't going to argue with this man about his lack of effort to know his own family. Her throat had gone a bit dry at the sight of him looming over her and she hated herself a little for that. She returned her attention to her fleece jacket, punching her hands into the sleeves.

"I don't. But I also don't appreciate that you don't take no for an answer." She yanked the zipper as high as it would go, almost pinching her chin in the teeth. "You called here enough times to be aware that I wasn't about to give up your brother's whereabouts to the likes of you. So why come all the way out here just to make me tell you the same thing in person?"

"So you admit that you know where Clayton is?" Quinton's low voice circled around her as he took a step in her direction, his long, oilcloth duster slung over one arm, a leather bag—like a portfolio for papers—tucked under the other.

Had she done that? Admitted something Quinton hadn't known?

"What does it matter if I do? You'll never find Clay unless he wishes to be found." She yanked a red wool scarf from one of the pockets of her jacket and wound it around her neck.

"Are you sure those are his wishes?" One of Quinton's dark eyebrows cocked in question. "Or yours?"

A shiver ricocheted through her at this man talking about her wishes in a space that suddenly felt far too intimate with just the two of them.

McKenna forced a grim smile, but probably only managed to bare her teeth. "Doesn't matter, since you're not finding him either way."

For a long moment, he only studied her in the dim light.

"A tough break for me," he said finally, lifting his coat and shrugging his way into it, his big shoulders flexing. "But since you're my only hope of finding him, it looks like we'll be seeing a lot of each other until you change your mind."

His movements stirred a scent that was smoke and leather. And male.

The subtle notes of it distracted her, making her brain stutter as she tried to take in his meaning.

"Excuse me?" She stuffed her hands in her pockets now that she didn't have anything left to do with them. The wary anxiety that filled her didn't have an outlet.

"I'm not leaving Alaska until I find my brother," Quinton explained slowly, emphasizing every word. "So you can count on me being here every day until either Clay gets in touch with me himself or you help me find him."

Her stomach dropped a little.

Not that he intimidated her.

But damn it, this day had been stressful enough having

him in her bar. What would it feel like, day in and day out, if he were to really follow through on that?

"That's not happening," she said finally, edging past him to head for the door.

She needed to put this argument—and him—far behind her.

But Quinton beat her to the door somehow, opening it for her so she could step outside ahead of him. She hesitated only a moment at having to pass beneath his outstretched arm. Then she darted past. Thank God the rain had stopped.

"In that case, I'll see you tomorrow, McKenna O'Brien." He nodded at her as he stepped into the damp air swirling around from the storm's aftermath.

She stared at him, stone-faced, before turning to lock up behind them. When she pivoted back toward him, a truck was pulling into the muddy parking lot.

"This is my ride," Quinton explained, sliding his phone into a breast pocket of his coat. "Do you need a lift home?"

"From you? Not a chance." She marched toward her own vehicle, telling herself that Quinton Kingsley wouldn't last a week in the Aleutian Islands, far from his rich family and fancy home. She shouldn't care one bit what he said about returning to the bar indefinitely.

"Good night then, McKenna," he called good-naturedly, sounding far too amused for her liking. "See you tomorrow."

Not if she could help it.

As she slid into the driver's seat of her four-wheel-drive SUV, she noticed that Quinton's ride didn't leave the parking lot until she was safely inside her vehicle. Yet the small display of gentlemanly instincts didn't diminish the fact that he was a man used to having his own way.

This time, however? McKenna planned to show the Kingsley interloper that no amount of money or influence could budge her into betraying the one person she still called family.

Two

Three days into his standoff with McKenna O'Brien, Quinton sipped a late-afternoon cup of coffee while he worked from a corner booth at the Cyclone Shack. With a wireless device in his ear, he was able to converse with the main office of his tech company in Sunnyvale, California, to make sure the business remained on track in his absence. Not that it required much overseeing this quarter. He'd been away from the main office for months since his father had died and work had still been accomplished efficiently and on time. Punching the button to put his screen in sleep mode, Quinton slid the earpiece off and set it on the wooden table. The sound of classic rock hit his ears, the bar stereo tuned to an AM radio station that played a lot of seventies music.

By now, he had a routine for visiting the bar, establishing himself by the dinner hour at the booth in the back so he had a clear view of the front door to scope out newcomers and potentially find locals he hadn't yet asked about Clayton.

Most of those conversations came to nothing as customers scratched their heads to recall the man whose name had been on the deed for the place for three years. By all accounts, before McKenna took over the business eighteen months ago, Clay had simply hired locals to staff and run the place, rarely ever setting foot in the bar himself. A couple of folks remembered meeting him but couldn't say where he called home.

By this point in his quest, Quinton didn't hold much hope for that route to finding his brother. The private investigator the Kingsley family had hired months ago had hit a wall in his search too.

Now, Quinton needed McKenna's help.

His gaze found her as she shoved through the door from the kitchen to breeze around the tables and check in with her patrons. Today she wore her burnished auburn hair in a loose ponytail secured by a scrap of white nylon rope. Black jeans and an oversize gray hoodie with the name of a locally based fishing trawler screened on the back were variations of what he'd come to recognize as her everyday work attire. Dark colors and warm layers were the norm for her in the drafty bar. Yet the idea that today's hoodie might belong to a man in her life— because it was too big for her, because he didn't think she'd ever worked on a trawler herself—made the taste of his coffee turn sour on his tongue. He set aside his empty brown mug and stared at her, willing her to stop at his table next.

As if she felt the weight of his stare, she glanced up from where she leaned over Ms. Weatherspoon's table, reading aloud the list of ingredients in the fish stew to the gray-haired retiree who'd shown up every afternoon at the Cyclone Shack along with Quinton.

He had already gotten to know a few of the regulars in the days he'd been a fixture in the bar. Ms. Weatherspoon had proved the most talkative of the bunch, perhaps driven by the fact that she lived alone and counted on the daily outing as her social time. Quinton had overheard McKenna counsel her on everything from which fish would be freshest at the local market to how to recover a lost password for one of the woman's apps.

McKenna narrowed her blue eyes at him before she returned her attention to her customer. After jotting something on a pad of notepaper she carried, she moved in his direction. All day long she hustled to meet the needs of patrons. Except for him. Because whenever she headed his way, those normally efficient steps slowed considerably. As if she wasn't willing to get any nearer. Was that because she genuinely didn't want to interact with him? Or did she feel the same zing that he did when they were near, and she was simply treading warily around that?

"I noticed your Royal Kingsley-ness staring." She tucked her pen behind her ear and the notepad in the kangaroo pouch of her sweatshirt. "Can I assume you'd like to order something else from the menu? Or is this another attempt at an information shakedown in the middle of my workday?"

He whistled low between his teeth as she stopped short in front of the booth.

"Looks like you're in razor-sharp mode this afternoon," he observed, closing the screen on his laptop and sliding it farther from him. "And possibly jumping the gun to blame me for something I'm not doing. I've been careful to save my questions about Clay until the end of your shift."

Her full lips flattened. Thinned. "There's a first time for everything. More coffee then?"

Glancing down at his empty cup, she reached for it.

At the same moment, Quinton laid his hand over the rim to keep the mug on the table. Effectively putting their fingers on a collision course. And for a brief instant, McKenna's cool palm brushed the backs of his knuckles.

Electricity coursed through his veins, a leap of something hot burning his chest as her eyes darted to his.

Oh yes, she felt that zing too. He could see it in her gaze, in the spots of color on her cheeks.

"No. Thank you." His fingers curled against the ceramic sides of the cup as the front door of the place swung open and a boisterous crowd of young guys walked inside, laughing and jostling one another.

The group of men were of little interest to Quint, aside from the fact that he hadn't asked them about Clay yet. However, as he turned his attention back to McKenna, he noticed her shoulders were tense. Her chin jutting as she watched them.

Protectiveness surged through him just based on her body language.

"Are they bad news?" he asked in a low voice as the group slid into a booth a few tables away. The spillovers dragged chairs from another table to join their friends.

Snapping her head around to face Quint once more, she pulled her lips into a mulish frown. "No worse than you, Cowboy."

And then she was gone, returning to her high-speed

work pace as she grabbed menus for the newcomers and slapped them down on their table before taking drink orders.

Quint followed the interaction until a cry of dismay from closer to his table distracted him.

Pale faced, Ms. Weatherspoon shook her head as she peered at her phone screen, eyebrows scrunched as one weathered hand covered her mouth. Sensing trouble, Quint rose to his feet and closed the space between them.

"Everything okay over here?" he asked, taking in the remnants of a barely touched chicken salad sandwich.

"I think I made a bad mistake," she answered in a hoarse whisper, never taking her gaze from the screen. "An embarrassing mistake."

Glancing down at the object of her attention, Quint saw flashing red-and-black graphics—a hooded skeleton head interspersed with a symbol for poison.

"Did someone send you that?" He pointed toward the screen. "Do you think you opened a message that contained a virus?"

The images could have been associated with some kind of game she'd been playing online. But considering his line of work in digital security, his brain went to a worse scenario. The graphics were amateurish, the sort of thing a kid might attach to an early hacking attempt.

"It's much worse than that," she confided, smashing her phone facedown onto the table so she didn't have to see the screen any longer.

Empathizing with her obvious distress, Quint lowered himself into the seat across from her just as McKenna reappeared at the table, her eyes full of concern for Ms. Weatherspoon.

"What's wrong?" McKenna shifted focus to him as she dropped onto the booth bench beside the older woman, who'd begun to sob quietly. She laid an arm over her shoulders and gently squeezed as she asked Quint, "What made her so upset?"

Quint pointed to the pink-and-white-daisy phone case lying discarded between the chicken salad sandwich and a sweating glass of iced tea. "Something on her phone, I think," he explained before diverting his attention back to the retiree. "Ms. Weatherspoon, let us help—"

"You can't!" she wailed softly, lifting a tear-strewed face. "I was deceived by someone who messaged me that my grandson was in trouble."

As soon as the words were out of her mouth, Quint's stomach dropped for her sake. He knew the grandparent scam well. A simple, much replicated ploy that often targeted seniors who might be fooled into thinking they were talking to a grandchild in trouble. Julie Weatherspoon's tale varied a little in the details, but in the end, she'd wired money that she believed was to bail her grandson out of jail.

"I can't believe I fell for it," she sniffed as she wound up her story, her heavily ringed hand squeezing McKenna's wrist. "But it sounded just like Jeremy's voice. And he begged me not to tell his mom and dad that he was in trouble, which just tore at my heart."

McKenna offered soothing words, her manner with the woman bearing none of the cool hostility she seemed to reserve for him.

Something shifted in his chest as he watched her tip her forehead toward the other woman, her long copper ponytail slipping forward as she gave her a quick, fierce hug. A rogue emptiness yawned inside him as he witnessed the exchange. Swallowing down the feeling, he focused on the practical.

"It's important to secure all of your devices as soon as possible," Quint counseled while the nearby table full of young guys erupted in laughter. "Want me to give you a hand with that?"

"Would you?" Julie Weatherspoon's expression was so grateful and relieved that he wished he'd offered sooner. "I didn't even realize what happened until my screen froze just now and I got the message that I'd been hacked."

Ah damn it. He hated the thought of anyone getting scammed this way and he had a bad feeling her computer woes weren't over yet. How could he not lend a hand?

"We should get to work then," Quint suggested, taking the phone just as McKenna shot to her feet.

"I'd better get back to my customers." McKenna lingered a moment at the table, her stormy blue eyes fixed on him as she withdrew her notepad from her hoodie pocket once more. "You'll take good care of her?"

The words weren't quite a challenge issued. More like a demand he didn't dare refuse.

Not that he wanted to. Yet what did it say about McKenna's view of him that she thought she had to hold his feet to the fire in order to ensure he gave his assistance to this person in need of a hand? For the first time since arriving in Dutch Harbor, he wondered what exactly Clayton had told her about his family.

About him.

Obviously, he had a long way to go to earn a scrap of trust from her.

He held her gaze for a long moment, willing her to read the sincerity in them. Then, in all seriousness, he assured her, "You have my word."

Humming along to a rock and roll classic playing on the bar stereo, McKenna dried the drinkware as the clock ticked nearer to closing time. All the while ridiculously aware of the last patron in the Cyclone Shack.

Again.

Her gaze stole over to Quint once more at his seat at the bar where he tapped out something on his phone, his laptop long ago packed away for the day. He'd left the booth table a few hours ago to take up his late-day post at the bar—a move he'd repeated each day after his arrival. There was something methodical about that. Some part of him that must appreciate a routine. Order.

Surprising from the Kingsley son who'd left the Montana family ranch at a relatively young age to pursue a vastly different direction for himself. In the few times over the years that she'd conjured visions of Clay's half brothers, she'd always imagined this one would be more of an upper class elitist who ate avocado toast and wore flannel even though he worked in tech.

Okay, maybe that was just her ill-informed stereotype of anyone employed in Silicon Valley, and that was on her, not them.

But either way, she hadn't pictured Quinton to embody her idea of a Montana rancher with his boots and duster coat that looked like he'd just come off the range. On the two days it hadn't been pouring, he'd worn a Stetson. And then, there was that regimented aspect of him that conducted business for a certain amount of time each day and then turned his focus to quizzing Cyclone Shack patrons about his brother.

Her brother, damn it.

She wasn't giving up her claim to Clay.

Now, sliding a spotless wineglass into the rack where it belonged, she allowed herself another glance at her last guest. His square jaw and high cheekbones looked carved from granite as he sat under the stark light of a pendant lamp. His long lashes hid his eyes as he worked, the intriguing contours of his face and rough-looking texture of his stubbled cheek making her palm itch with the curiosity to touch him.

And if that sounded like she'd been observing him far too closely for the last twenty minutes since the previous patron had left the building, well, that would be because she had.

"You did a nice thing for Ms. Weatherspoon tonight," she mused aloud, surprised to hear herself converse with him after the days of restricting discussions to taking meal orders and warning him away from Clayton.

Yet images of Quint helping Julie Weatherspoon had circled her brain all evening. Especially when Julie had called her over to gush about Quint's patience and smarts as he guided her through resetting her device and passwords after helping her download a software product— his company's apparently—that would help protect her privacy and data.

In light of the ways McKenna's digital privacy had been utterly decimated by the cruelest of exes imaginable, she couldn't help a fractional softening in her attitude toward Quint.

"In spite of what you think, an act of human decency

isn't all that out of character for me." Laying the phone on the bar, he folded his fingers together as he studied her in the dim light of the pendants.

She took her time drying the last of the glasses and putting it back in its place before she walked to the stereo and switched it off for the evening. It wasn't quite closing time, but she knew her customers' habits well enough to recognize that no one else would be entering the bar in the fifteen before she locked the front door.

Also, the excuse of shutting down the music had the benefit of bringing her closer to Quint, and she wanted to be able to read his expression for this conversation, a new curiosity burning inside of her about him. Not just because he was hot and one look from him made her blood run faster. No, this new awareness came from a need to understand him.

"So you use your tech superpowers for good when the mood strikes you?" she needled him, filled with the urge to see beyond the strong jaw and the laconic talk to the man beneath.

Who was Quinton Kingsley, and why was he really here?

Why did he need to see Clayton so badly in the first place?

Those questions kept her awake at night.

"I gladly help deserving people if it's in my range of capabilities to do so." His low voice seemed to vibrate on a special frequency calibrated to make her body come alive.

It wasn't fair.

She shifted on her feet and rested her elbows on the bar, positioning herself directly across from him. She refused to back away from the chemistry even though it sparked and hissed the nearer she came. Tonight, she would learn more about him.

"Why? To impress me? Do you think being kind to people I care about will convince me to tell you more about Clay?"

"I built a global business dedicated to digital security, McKenna. Helping someone clean up from a small-time hack took very little effort from me." His golden amber eyes tracked hers. "I wouldn't dream of leveraging my professional skill set to impress someone who seems hell-bent on believing the worst of me for reasons that remain a mystery."

"I wouldn't call it *hell-bent*—"

"What is it that you think I've done to Clayton exactly? You know when he left Silent Spring that last time it wasn't because he argued with me or Levi or Gavin. He argued with *Duke*." The way he spoke his dead father's name revealed more of his feelings about his family than she'd observed yet. "It's our father he never wanted to see again. And for that, I definitely do not blame him."

She tucked that away to reflect on later. At home, when she wasn't so close to him, where they didn't breathe the same air.

Her belly fluttered at the realization of their proximity and she levered herself away from the bar a few inches. Telling herself to stick to safer subjects, she ventured another question. "Julie said you recovered the three thousand dollars she wired to a third party?"

"Not me personally," he clarified, his lips quirking in wry amusement. "But yes, we contacted the FBI Internet Crime Complaint Unit quickly enough that they were able to intervene. That's not always the case, but it worked this time."

Her belly fluttered again. And not just because she felt deeply for people who were tricked and scammed. Quint's quick thinking meant Julie would be able to pay bills this winter. It meant the woman could hold her head high without feeling like she'd been duped.

There was simply no denying that Quint had behaved like a stand-up guy in this instance.

"Thank you for that," she said softly, deciding she'd had all of the personal fact-finding about this man that she could handle for the day. "I'd like to close up early tonight since you've already paid your tab and your drink is long gone."

He bought a few beers a night to justify taking up a seat, but he always offered them to whoever he questioned about Clayton. For himself, he drank one coffee before 5:00 p.m. and water after that.

"Sure thing." He rose from the bar stool, pulling the bag with his laptop onto his shoulder as he moved toward the door. "But you know I have to ask you one more thing."

The same thing he'd asked every other night.

She made no answer as she shut off the lights over the bar and followed him toward the wrought iron hooks that held their coats—his oilskin duster coat, her waterproof jacket. In silence, she slid her arms through the sleeves of the outerwear and flipped the cotton hood from her sweatshirt outside the jacket.

"Is that your sweatshirt?" Quint's question was as unexpected as his gruff tone.

"That's what you want to ask me?" A surprise laugh

huffed from her as she peered down at the gray hoodie with the name of a Dutch Harbor fishing trawler on the front. "It belongs to Clay, actually. Not only do I tend the bar that he bought before he left town, I also live in his former house and have access to the clothes he left behind."

Briefly, she wondered if that meant Quint would angle to try and see the house. To snoop around and look for clues so he could find Clayton and get on with his life. But oddly, he merely looked...relieved?

A sigh whooshed out of him, his shoulders slackening a fraction as he slid into his jacket.

"Right. Clay's," he muttered to himself with the shake of his head before he dropped the Stetson into place. "Care to tell me where I can find him?"

They stood illuminated under a buzzing recessed lamp near the entrance while McKenna's fingers hovered by the light switch. Her forehead came to his chin. The scents of damp leather and salty air that permeated the walls drifted around them. Her heart hammered too loudly.

The way it rattled her chest offered a welcome reminder that she had no business softening toward him.

"I most certainly do not," she retorted before flicking off the switch with one hand and reaching for the front door with the other. The darkness, inside and out, enveloped them. "Good night, Cowboy."

Three

Shortly before sunset the next day, Quinton arrived at the port in Dutch Harbor. He parked the rental SUV he'd obtained now that he was committed to being in town indefinitely. His mood was as gray as the forbidding Alaska sky as he stalked toward the rows and rows of fishing boats. Choppy waves splashed against the seawall and rocked the vessels in port while gulls and other seabirds squawked overhead. He was on a mission to locate McKenna after she'd failed to show up at the Cyclone Shack that afternoon. Upon quizzing the other customers, he figured out what all the rest of them already knew—that McKenna would be out on her boat on her day off.

Not that she'd made any mention of it to him the day before when they'd said good-night. The oversight—certainly deliberate since she knew that he would be at the bar every day—rankled him now as he walked past stacks of the commercial-grade crab pots that outnumbered people around the town. Would it have killed her to give him a heads-up that she moonlighted at another job on her days off from the bar?

Apparently she took groups out on the water to fish, sightsee or bird-watch according to whatever tours would pay her for the escort. But that too he'd gleaned from the other patrons at the Cyclone Shack, after which he'd even found her tour services on Trip Advisor. He'd toyed with the idea of booking one for himself so she had no choice but to spend time with him. Of course, he had no guarantee she'd answer his questions then either.

Now, he searched for the numbers on the boat slips as he ventured down one of the weathered gray docks. Quinton followed the directions someone in the harbormaster's office had given him over the phone earlier. He was on the hunt for a space that held a thirty-two-foot fishing craft.

Clayton's Hewescraft vessel, to be precise. The *Un-Reel.*

Reaching the empty spot a moment later, Quinton paused on the damp dock to breathe in the salt-and-fish-scented air. A wet breeze blew in his face as he scanned the harbor for a glimpse of the *Un-Reel*, a functional offshore watercraft with an Alaskan hull and room for six anglers. Or so he'd read in the description of the vessel from a purchase receipt in the file compiled by the Kingsley family's private investigator.

Even as he thought about the stalled search for Clayton, Quinton remembered he owed his brother Levi a call. Levi had left two messages for him earlier that week, asking for an update on his search for Clay in Dutch Harbor, but Quint had yet to contact him. Withdrawing his phone now as he waited for a glimpse of the *Un-Reel* in the harbor, he figured speaking to his brother would help him pass the time until the tour boat returned home for the evening.

Maybe talking to Levi would lessen the urge to confront McKenna about her need to thwart him at every turn. Why couldn't she understand that he only wanted to give his brother a hand? Hell, he wanted to give him a small fortune. It's not like Quint was in town to borrow the guy's car or ask if they could be besties. He simply wanted to sign over the portion of the Kingsley estate Clay deserved.

When Levi's voice sounded in Quinton's ear a moment later, he didn't mince words.

"About damned time you called," Levi began, not bothering with a greeting. "Have you found him?"

"No. I found his stepsister living in his former house, running his old bar and keeping all his secrets though. It might have been nice if the PI we hired gave me a heads-up about her." He recalled the impact of her words that first night when she informed him, *I'm his sister.*

The guilt he felt over his immediate attraction to her still dogged him. Would he have been able to ignore it better if he'd been prepared to see her when he entered the Cyclone Shack that night?

"McKenna, right?" Levi asked, the noise of ranch life clear in the background. Cattle mooed and bellowed, snorted and grunted. Whoever thought farm life was quiet hadn't spent much time with a thriving herd. "The PI's report mentioned her. He discounted her as a source for information since she refused to speak to him on multiple occasions."

Hearing the cows in the background made Quinton glad he was in Alaska rather than at Kingsland Ranch. After the dark memories he associated with the place and the day his mother died, he looked forward to unloading his share of the estate.

"Sounds about right for McKenna." He suspected the notes about her must have been buried in the sections of the report he'd skimmed. "But since she may be the only person who knows Clay's whereabouts, I'm sticking close to her."

"What's she like?" Levi asked right before he gave a shrill whistle. "Sorry about that," he panted, as if he were running. Or, more likely, on horseback. "I'm out on the north pasture trying to get the herd into the next grazing field and it's just me and Gunner out here."

Quinton had worked with Levi and his border collie plenty of times moving the cattle from field to field, so he could envision the process. Knew it was tougher to manage singlehandedly.

Empathy for Levi didn't make him any more inclined to regret not being in Montana. Quinton had lost his love of the Kingsland Ranch the day his mother died in a trampling accident that should have been avoided. Twenty-six years had passed since then, but that wasn't nearly enough time to reconcile his past with the ranch.

"McKenna is as tough as they come," Quinton admitted with equal parts regret and admiration. "She refuses to talk, but I'm hoping once she sees I only have Clay's best interests at heart, she'll change her mind."

"Meaning you're staying up there?" Levi asked, curiosity evident in his voice while his dog barked in the background.

"I'll be here until I locate Clay." Quinton glared out over the waves as the sun sank lower over the water. He wouldn't return to his hotel today until he'd seen McKenna.

Asked the question he planned to ask her every single day until she gave him the answer he needed.

"You don't need to do that. We can try a different PI," Levi suggested. "See if someone else has better luck with her."

The idea of anyone else hassling her made Quinton's hackles rise.

"No," he bit out the word brusquely. "I'm staying."

In the distance, he heard a burst of feminine laughter carried on the wind and he swiveled on his boot heel to find its source.

Scanning the rolling waters, he spied a gray hardtop fishing vessel making its way through the harbor toward the dock where he stood. A few figures stood on the deck, their animated voices audible though the words were indistinct.

And before Levi could talk him out of staying in Alaska, Quinton made his excuses and disconnected the call. His phone was in his pocket by the time the name of the approaching vessel—the *Un-Reel*, painted in red letters on the bow—came into view.

Even in the gray light of early evening, Quint could discern McKenna's features at the helm through the windscreen. She had her navigation lights on as she slowed the engine to steer into the slip, her attention focused on the berth. Six passengers stood around the open deck, canned beverages in hand as they chatted easily, unconcerned with navigation or helping their captain tie off.

Quinton was about to ask one of them to toss him a spring line so he could help secure her, but a couple of young dockhands ambled past him to take care of the job themselves.

"Looking good, McKenna," one of them shouted as he reached toward the stern where a rope awaited just above a fender on the port side.

While the one dockworker secured to a cleat, the other called for a passenger on board to toss the bow line. The process was quick and painless, the maneuvers clearly well choreographed after ample practice. There was nothing for Quinton to do but remain out of the way while the *Un-Reel*'s passengers departed. The group finished their drinks, retrieved camera bags and extra jackets while thanking their captain for the outing.

The dockhands disappeared as quickly as they'd arrived. Soon, there was only McKenna aboard the boat while Quinton stood on pier watching as she shut off the lights and flipped a few other switches. He had no doubt that she'd spotted him earlier, but she didn't acknowledge him until she stepped away from the bridge and out onto the open deck of the craft.

"I'm surprised to see you here." She met his gaze briefly while she gathered the life vests, her face illuminated by the security lights at regular intervals down the dock.

Dressed in jeans and a simple black sweater with a bright yellow rain jacket over it, she wore her auburn hair in a low ponytail that rested on her shoulder. Long bangs brushed her brows as she bent forward to stow the life vests in a deck locker.

"No more surprised than I was to learn you weren't

coming into the bar today." He leaned against the light post closest to her boat, unwilling to step aboard without an invitation.

A rueful grin tugged at her full lips. "As committed as I am to making a success of the Cyclone Shack, I do give myself a day off now and again."

The sight of her smile, the sound of it in her voice shouldn't have made his dark mood brighten so fast. What would it be like to meet this woman under other circumstances? If she wasn't his brother's stepsister, for instance.

His dark mood returned. Redoubling.

"You might have shared that with me yesterday. Saved me the trouble of interrogating your customers." He watched as she latched the cabin doors and set the alarm before grabbing her keys, her movements around the watercraft as swift and efficient as when she worked at the bar.

"It's the weekend," she reminded him, tucking the keys in a gray canvas duffel she then looped over one shoulder. "Maybe I thought you'd have other plans."

Seeing she must be about finished shutting down the vessel for the night, Quinton stepped closer to the boat to extend a hand to her.

She glanced from his face to his offered palm, then back again. As if she hesitated to touch him.

"When I said I'd be at the bar every day until I had an answer, I meant it," he reminded her, holding her gaze while he waited for her to take his hand. Not abandoning the small nicety while a breeze ruffled her hair against her neck.

Of course she didn't need his help off her boat. But would she ignore the gesture? Ignore *him*?

When her cool fingers wrapped around his and squeezed, Quinton felt it more keenly than a kiss from any other woman. Especially because her dark blue eyes locked on to his and held. As if she was very aware that the touch reached past the boundaries they'd been keeping with each other.

Maybe that's why he failed to release her as she stepped onto the dock beside him. For a charged moment, they held hands in the gray evening, breath mingling in the salty air.

Getting lost in Quinton Kingsley's honey-colored eyes, McKenna told herself she would back away any second now.

She didn't need the hassle of a man in her life now that she'd finally made peace with her solo existence in Dutch Harbor. She'd carved out a place for herself here after the shitshow that had been her life in California, and she wouldn't allow anything to mess it up. Especially not someone who bore the Kingsley name. Loyalty to her brother demanded as much.

Even if she'd dreamed hot, sexy dreams of Quinton every night since he'd arrived in her life.

Part of the reason she hadn't bothered telling him she wouldn't be at the bar today was in a misguided effort to not think about him for a full twenty-four hours. Except he'd been a recurring theme in her mind all throughout the eight-hour bird-watching tour she'd conducted. Even as she steered her boat into rough waters to find the birds her group had sought, pointing out the best sighting grounds for Alaska's much-sought-after bird, the whiskered auklet—she'd also been wondering what Quinton was doing back on the mainland.

"You're wasting your time," she reminded him now as she withdrew her hand. The rasp of his skin along hers, however briefly, sent a shock of awareness tingling through her. "You can visit the bar all you like or join all of my adventure tours. But I'm not spilling Clay's secrets."

She edged the strap of her duffel bag higher on one shoulder and then headed down the wharf toward the main pier, needing to put distance between them again. It was safer that way. She waved to a few dockworkers and fishermen she knew, the community of locals close-knit.

Quinton fell into step beside her. "It's my time to waste. And since it's the weekend, how about if we call a truce for the evening and I buy you dinner?"

Her belly did something perilously close to a flip and she cursed all those feminine instincts that had only led her astray in the past.

"Maybe precisely because it's the weekend, we should retreat to our own separate corners so we can return to the battle on Monday." She walked faster past the stacks of crab pots, as if reaching her truck would somehow magically deliver her from the appeal of the man keeping pace beside her.

He wore a Stetson well, even here where the preferred hat was a beanie. The long black duster that had surely seen plenty of cattle rides wasn't a bad choice for the persistent wet winds. But even though he looked one hundred percent Montana rancher, she knew from too much internet searching that he spent most of his time on the West Coast. That his tech company was holding its own among the giants of the industry, and that his digital security was sought after by major financial institutions.

And yes, she'd spent too much time wondering if a man like this would know anything about the kinds of digital harassment she'd experienced in San Francisco.

"McKenna, please hear me out." His low voice slid around her like a lover's touch, his tone low and appealing.

It slowed her steps faster than any touch could have.

"I'm listening." She gripped the strap of her duffel with two hands, as if holding it tightly would keep her from wrapping herself around the relentless rancher who refused to give up on finding his brother.

Their brother.

He stepped in front of her to look her in the eye. "If I've offended you in any way, I'll head back to my hotel right now and stay out of your way until Monday, when I'll most definitely be back at the bar long enough to ask you again about Clay." He gave her a moment to process his words before continuing. "But if you're only keeping me at arm's length because you think I'll pester you about Clayton tonight, I can promise you that won't be the case."

Her throat went dry at the earnestness in his voice. The sincerity in his eyes. He hadn't offended her. Far from it. He attracted her so thoroughly she could swear she canted closer to him even now. Her heart beat faster.

"I suppose I do need to eat dinner," she admitted finally, knowing it probably wasn't wise. Then, shrugging awkwardly, she tipped her face into the cold fall breeze whipping off the water. "Plus, as the old saying goes, keep your friends close and your enemies closer."

Which was how, twenty minutes later, they were seated inside a pizzeria that was one of the Cyclone Shack's main competitors. She'd left her truck at the pier, knowing she could easily pick it up the next day by getting a ride from one of the dockworkers who lived a stone's throw from her house. Tonight, she would kick back. The pizzeria sat next to the only hotel on Amaknak Island, so it did a brisk business with visitors. More locals came to the Shack, McKenna believed, because the bar's more remote location allowed them some breathing room from the out-of-towners.

She'd chosen this place deliberately, unwilling to let Quinton talk her into one of the more upscale offerings available in nearby Unalaska. Once their server settled a simple Margherita pizza in front of them along with two beers, Quinton went to work serving her a slice before sliding one onto his own plate.

"It sounded like your tour group really enjoyed themselves today," he observed mildly, sticking to his word that he wouldn't ask her about Clayton. "Is that something that keeps you busy this time of year?"

Their booth, near an unused dartboard, made it easy to converse in a space that would get more crowded as the evening went on. McKenna had visited enough times to know what made locals and tourists alike stop by the place. In her less charitable moments, she wrote it off to the location close to the port and the only hotel on the island. But the fact that the owner was a third-generation Alaskan with ties to the fishing community helped too.

"As busy as I want to be through the summer, though it slows down in the fall." She took a small sip of her beer, a craft brew out of Anchorage that she carried at the Cyclone Shack too. "Lots of birders visit to check out the wildlife refuge areas, so I take them out when I can since they don't require much from me and they always leave the boat the way they found it."

Quinton looked at her as he folded his slice of pizza in half for eating. "Is that not the case with most groups?"

"Well, I really like to take fishing groups out when they're serious and focused. But sometimes people say they want to fish when they're really just looking for a chance to get on the water and booze it up." A couple of tours like that had soured her on taking out parties she didn't know personally. "The Bering Sea isn't a place to get distracted."

"I'll bet not." His expression hardened. His jaw clenching before he spoke again. "My time on the ranch taught me at a young age that accidents can happen to the most experienced people."

She wanted to ask him about that, but something in his tone warned her to steer clear. "How about your work? Are you able to accomplish most of what you need to on the road or is this trip hurting business?"

"I'm not sure how much Clay has told you about our family," he began, and she shook her head.

"Very little. You know Clayton. He's not much of a talker in the first place." She added red pepper flakes to her pizza slice. "Add to that the fact that he's eight years older than me, that I didn't come into his mother's life until he was twenty and out on his own, and it's easy to see why I was never a confidante when he was still spending time in Montana."

Clayton had been there for her when she needed a

friend most, however, and it had solidified an unbreakable bond.

"I'm envious of the relationship the two of you forged. But we don't have to talk about Clay or any of the Kingsley clan this evening. I just wanted to enjoy your company one-on-one."

Seeing no hint of guile in his expression, she deemed it harmless to discuss Clayton's past. "It's fine. Go on."

"Clay never spent much time in Montana," Quinton clarified. "Even during the years where he visited every summer, he only spent a couple of weeks with us."

More jaw clenching followed that remark, making McKenna wonder what life had been like in the Kingsley household for them as boys. She only knew the basics. That Clayton's mother had gotten pregnant with Clay around the same time that Duke Kingsley's first wife was pregnant with her son Levi. Clayton had been born first but was never formally acknowledged by the Kingsley family as a son. Had that been Duke's wish? Or the first wife's?

Yet even after Duke's first wife died—the woman who would have been Quinton's mother—Duke still hadn't welcomed Clay into his home as a son. As far as McKenna was concerned, that told her everything she needed to know about Duke's character. It also made her wary of the two sons he'd raised exclusively.

"He visited Silent Spring often enough a few years past," she recalled aloud between bites of her dinner. "That last time led to the big argument he had with Duke before he moved here full-time three years ago."

"That argument remains a point of much speculation for my brothers and I since we weren't there and don't know what happened." He waved away the server who'd stopped by the table to offer another round of drinks. "But as for your original question about my work, I get enough done here. I can afford to linger."

His gaze met hers across the table and something fluttered in her belly. How long would he stay in Dutch Harbor?

The pizzeria was getting more crowded now, the volume by the bar increasing, and a group had arrived to use the dartboard near their table. Which was just as well considering she didn't want this evening with Quinton to feel too intimate. It didn't help that she had the sneaking suspicion she would like him if they'd met under different circumstances.

"Wait until you experience some of our real weather," she cautioned him, though she feared the dark, cold and storms might not scare him off as quickly as she'd once hoped. "My bar isn't called the Cyclone Shack for nothing."

While they finished their meal, Quinton kept the conversation light, asking more about her experience on the sea and what it had been like learning to navigate open water like the Bering Sea offered. Despite all her better judgment, she found herself warming to the topic and the attention.

By the time they finished their meal and stood to leave, she was remembering the last time she'd been out with a man for the evening. Her last date.

It had been over eighteen months ago.

No wonder she'd enjoyed the attention after so many months without romantic companionship. Yet the memory brought a darker thought with it as she accompanied Quinton back outside to his rental, a four-wheel-drive SUV.

Because it had been during that fateful evening that she'd learned the news that derailed her whole life. Instead of standing beside her through the hellish turn of events, her date had cut ties altogether, dropping her off at her house to rage her way through the aftermath alone.

"Everything okay?" Quinton asked as he held the passenger side door open for her on the sleek black SUV. His keen gaze must have caught something in her expression because he studied her with narrowed eyes.

A cold wind blew off the water, moist air chilling her.

"Yes, thank you," she replied automatically. Because she *was* okay. She'd gotten through the worst of that time in her life, hadn't she?

Sliding into the SUV, she was grateful to escape the wind. Her heart pounded faster as she buckled her seat belt while Quinton rounded the vehicle to take his place in the driver's seat.

When he joined her, he switched on the engine to warm up the car but didn't flip on the lights right away. Instead, he shifted in the driver's seat so he faced her across the console. His eyes were troubled.

"Are you sure nothing is wrong? Because if my presence here is truly a problem for you—"

"I promise you, I'm made of tougher stuff than that," she shot back, unwilling to let him think she couldn't handle a few questions. "Tonight was—" What? Unexpected? Welcome, even? She couldn't deny sitting beside him tonight had made her body remember what it felt like to ache for more. "Nice," she finished lamely.

"So why did you look like you were ready to wring someone's neck with your bare hands on our way out of the restaurant?"

Her lips twitched briefly at the image. Then, sobering as she recalled the moment that had put the expression on her face, she huffed out a sigh, her breath a white cloud since the heater hadn't warmed the interior sufficiently yet.

"I was recalling the last time I had an evening out with a guy," she told him honestly, more than ready to spill the story. She'd been toying with the idea of sharing it just so she could ask his professional opinion as a tech expert. "It didn't end so well."

Briefly, she outlined the main points as dispassionately as possible to avoid falling down the rabbit hole of anger and bitter regret. She explained how she'd been in an unwise relationship three years before. How it had ended badly. How the guy had filmed them together without her knowledge during the time they'd been a couple. Then, after the breakup, she'd received a text from an unknown number with a thumbnail image from the video and a link.

Blinking back the hot moisture that had formed in her eyes at the retelling, she realized that at some point during the story Quinton had taken her hand. He held it between both of his now, one palm smoothing over the backs of her knuckles while the other provided a resting place for her fingers.

"So that was bad enough," she wound up the tale, needing to be done with it. "But when I received that text, I was in the middle of a date with a new guy I was actually kind of hopeful about. Except the moment he discovered that I was the subject of some other dude's revenge porn video, Mr. So-Called Nice Guy couldn't pay the check fast enough so he could take me home and dump me."

Just that much of the story had taken enough out of her. She wasn't ready to share how the video had also cost her a job. Friends. It still amazed her how *she'd* been judged when she'd been the victim of someone else's crime.

"McKenna, I'm so damned sorry that happened to you." Quinton's voice was rough. As if he was struggling with some emotions too. "Thank you for trusting me enough to share your story with me."

The wealth of sincerity in his voice touched her. Soothed—just a little bit—the wound that had been torn open repeatedly during the last eighteen months. How different might her experience have been if she'd had anyone in her life a year and a half ago who'd said those same words to her?

A rush of gratitude for his simple human goodness made her squeeze his hand tight. "I appreciate you saying that."

Staring down at their joined palms, McKenna took in the size of his wrist next to hers, his fingers all but concealing hers where they wove together. The dark hairs visible on his forearm where the sleeve of his jacket had been pushed up. There was something so undeniably masculine about him. Something that made everything feminine inside her sit up and take notice.

Her breath quickened as she glanced up at him in the muted glow from a streetlamp. He'd angled toward her to give her his full attention, one shoulder brushing hers. His face so close she could feel the warmth of his breath on her cheek.

And suddenly, the need to thank him for listening—for caring—overwhelmed her. In her experience, that was no small thing.

Leaning closer, she allowed herself to do what she'd done every night in her dreams since they'd met. She slanted her mouth over Quinton Kingsley's.

Then kissed him like he was the last man on earth and the future of the human race depended on the two of them.

Four

Quinton wasn't a man who surprised easily.

Yet he'd never seen this kiss coming. Maybe if he had, he could have steeled himself against the soft give of McKenna's lush mouth on his, or somehow prepared for the unexpected taste of cinnamon lip gloss she must have slicked on after dinner.

If he'd had his faculties about him, maybe he could have made a smarter decision about kissing her. Because he knew better than to take advantage of a woman who'd just allowed herself to be vulnerable with him. But the sensory overload of McKenna's cool fingers sliding around his neck, her warm body straining closer as she leaned over the SUV console while sexy sounds of pleasure hummed from her throat, were too much for Quinton to ignore. His body responded long before his brain caught up.

Already, his hands were on her. One arm wrapped

around her shoulders to draw her near, while the other hand angled her face so he could taste her more thoroughly. And his tongue explored her like he was making a map, seeking out the places that made her shiver and squirm.

How many times had he imagined this? In the space of less than a week, it was too many to count. And not once had he guessed sampling her mouth would wreck him so completely. Or that a few minutes of her lips traveling on his skin, trailing cinnamon-scented kisses along his jaw and down his neck, would have him calculating how fast he could take her home and undress her.

Except he wasn't supposed to caress or kiss her. Because this was Clayton's baby sister.

Breaking the contact, Quinton edged back, panting like he'd just finished sprinting. The sight of McKenna with her eyes still closed, lashes fluttering against her cheeks and her lips glistening, was enough to make him question his sanity. What kind of man would leave her alone and wanting when it was his touch that had ignited her?

He wrestled down his worst instincts with an effort. Swiping his hand across his face, he attempted to blot out the images of the things he craved scrolling through his head.

And failed. Miserably.

"Does my kissing technique need work?" she asked a moment later, her voice sounding bemused.

Quinton dragged open his eyes to see her staring at him with a mixture of curiosity and wariness in her blue gaze.

"If your technique got any better, I'd be driving like a bat out of a hell to take you home with me," he told her sternly. He needed to get himself under control, but it wasn't easy when the taste of her lingered on his tongue.

The sight of her slightly tousled ponytail reminding him that he'd tunneled his fingers through it when he'd urged her against him.

A mischievous smile curved her lips. "And that's a problem because…?"

"Because you're Clay's *stepsister*," he reminded her of the obvious. The relationship that made anything between them impossible. "And that makes you strictly off-limits."

Her auburn brows crinkled together, lips pursing in confusion. "You're no relation of *mine*," she reminded him.

As if he didn't understand the dynamics all too well already. Hell, sitting in the vehicle that had fogged up while they were kissing was only tempting him to kiss her again and again. He needed to drive her back to her place, then go back to his hotel alone so he could take the coldest shower possible.

Flipping on the defogger, he activated the windshield wipers and prepared to back out of the parking lot.

"I'm aware of that," he answered slowly, willing reason to return. "But that doesn't make it right for me to touch someone my brother considers family."

Deeming the window visibility safe enough to drive, Quinton wrenched his seat belt across his lap and jammed the buckle home.

"Is this some weird bro code thing?" she asked, her voice sounding less amused and more irritated now.

Irritated he could deal with.

"Hardly," he scoffed, wishing things hadn't gone so sideways between them tonight. He'd enjoyed their meal together. Appreciated that she'd confided in him. "I should be looking out for you because you're someone important to Clay." Which reminded him of what he really needed to discuss with her. "But I can promise you this. I will scour the internet for copies of that video so I can get them taken down and find the source of the original copy."

That was always the sticking point in prosecuting digital harassment. But Quinton was nothing if not relentless. He would hunt down copies of that footage like the grim reaper hunting souls. At the mention of her harasser, the air in the car chilled between them.

"You really think you can do that?" she asked as Quinton turned out of the lot onto the main road along Margaret Bay.

"Without question." Quinton didn't normally brag about his tech skills, but McKenna's tormentor had no idea who he'd crossed when he'd hurt this woman. The man would pay. "I can walk you through the channels to prosecute the bastard criminally, but with any luck we'll gather enough evidence to make a civil case too."

"I don't know that I want to have it all brought up again."

She retreated to the far side of the SUV, one shoulder pinned to the window as she slumped lower in the seat. Then, peering out her window, she asked, "I suppose you already know where I live?"

As much as he wanted to argue her indecision about bringing legal action against her harasser, Quinton didn't want to push at a time when she might be a bit raw from what she'd already shared. Leaving it for now, he focused on the road as he answered her question.

"I made it my business to know as much as possible about Clayton's life here before I bothered you with questions." He regretted that he'd been short with her after that kiss.

What if she shut him out completely?

The possibility stung more than he would have anticipated.

"And yet here you are. Bothering me so much I thought it was a good idea to kiss you."

The dark sarcasm in her voice would have made him chuckle if he didn't fear how easily he could get caught up in the attraction he felt toward her. Even now, glancing over at her pale profile in the moonlight, made him want to pull her into his arms and finish what they'd started in the parking lot.

"I wasn't happy to hear the PI we hired pestered you so much that you stopped talking to him altogether." He hadn't read the extensive reports word for word, but he did recall that much.

The rhythmic sound of the wipers scraping the windshield was his only answer for a long moment.

"He seemed to think I would be moved to spill all my secrets if I knew he wouldn't get paid without producing Clay." She shook her head as the arc of Quinton's headlights swung toward the narrow driveway that led to her house. "I wasn't impressed."

"That's blatantly untrue. He made his fee structure clear before he began, and he sure as hell collected a check." Quinton made a mental note to speak with the PI about his tactics as he dodged potholes on the steep gravel embankment. "Are you sure you didn't want to pick up your truck tonight?"

He regretted not asking her when they left the pizza place, but she'd said earlier that a neighbor worked on the docks and she could catch a ride with him to retrieve it. Scanning the hillside for signs of life now, however, he couldn't imagine the neighbor resided very close to her.

"No, thank you. I'm wiped after today and Big Mac owes me a few favors." She straightened in her seat, as if ready to bolt the moment he stopped the SUV.

Regret for how the evening had turned out—with them at odds even after a kiss he would be replaying in his head all night long—weighted his limbs. He put the vehicle into Park as he stopped in front of the saltbox-style two-story with a detached garage.

The place was no-frills simple with no landscaping or outdoor furniture, just a white utilitarian front entrance and four dark windows in the blue frame house. He wondered how she handled the isolation of life in a place like this. Had she sought out this existence because of that damned video? The idea of her feeling like she needed to hide herself away in the Last Frontier State because of some asshat former boyfriend made his blood boil.

"Thank you for having dinner with me." He unfastened his seat belt at the same time she did, needing to walk her to the door. For more than just safety. But also because he wasn't ready to say good-night. Not yet.

"I can see myself in," she told him pointedly, holding up one hand to stop him from accompanying her. "Bad enough that you wrote off my kiss as a mistake because you see me as 'off-limits.'" She made air quotes around the words. "I might have reached my quota of alpha male nonsense for the day."

"McKenna, wait." He hovered between stepping outside of the SUV anyway and doing as she asked. Both things had been drilled into his head as part of being a gentleman.

But the slam of the car door in his face helped him to decide. He heaved a resigned sigh as she rounded the vehicle and withdrew her keys from her bag.

Quinton lowered his window to say good-night through it, keeping the headlights on so she could see her way inside.

When the lock turned for her, she glanced up at him, gave him a little eyeroll as if to communicate that he was being absurd to sit there watching her, then disappeared inside the house.

The moment she vanished from sight an ache panged inside him, his first indication that some dynamic had shifted between them. Stuffing the thought down deep, he headed back to his hotel room, where his laptop and a VPN connection awaited him.

Because right now, he had a cybercriminal to catch.

Two storms were brewing the next day as McKenna unboxed specialty beers to restock the walk-in cooler.

As she shoved six-packs onto the lower shelves, she couldn't decide which storm was worse. The one predicted for the Aleutian Islands, which was already battering the Cyclone Shack with high-speed gusts of wind, or the one raging inside her as she recalled her evening with Quinton.

That makes you strictly off-limits.

His words after their kiss—a kiss that had been damned good, she believed, even to a man who surely had tons more experience than her—had circled around in her brain all night long. At first, they'd just ticked her off.

She wasn't *his* stepsister after all. There was nothing in the world to keep her from kissing him if she wished. Then, later that night, she'd gone from miffed to downright mad. How could Quinton write off that lip-lock because of some inflated sense of loyalty to Clay when he had no relationship with his half brother in the first place?

And seriously, how dare he shut her down as if he hadn't been sending his fair share of hot looks her way for days? Those eyes of his told her he wanted her. Badly.

Emptying the first box, she moved onto the second. She found her box cutter and sliced through the tape with a little more force than necessary, the pent-up feelings from the night before needing an outlet. Before she could start unloading the contents, the back door blew open with the force of a particularly nasty gust of wind.

"Damned latch," she muttered as she went to resecure the handle that was on her personal to-do list of fixes that needed to be made around the bar.

Papers from a small workstation swirled around her until she relatched the door. The skirt of her long red dress brushed against her legs, the jersey garment fancier than she normally wore for work, but she'd had a meeting with one of her suppliers earlier in the day. Now, she drew the dead bolt for security's sake as the cook wouldn't be coming in today anyhow. McKenna had given her the day off since business would be negligible with the storm blowing in. Experience had taught her that locals were wise enough to stick close to home when low pressure systems rolled close to the islands. The few tourists who might have ventured into the bar on another day would be too spooked by the weather, already dark and gray in the early afternoon.

Even now, the place was empty. Not that she ever did much business until close to the dinner hour. Two people had stopped by to tell her the storm was worsening, implying she ought to just shut down and go home for the day. But with her emotions so stirred up after the dinner with Quint, she needed the outlet of work.

As she gathered the papers the gust of wind had scattered, she recalled his indignation on her behalf when she'd shared her story. And later, his vow that he'd scour the internet to find the original source, which was the piece she'd need to prosecute her bastard ex. Just hearing Quinton say the words—a promise to help that she knew he would keep—had unlocked defenses she'd kept sky-high for eighteen long, lonely months.

That promise also made it tougher for her to stay mad about the way he'd shut down the kiss.

Papers retrieved, she set them on the small workstation desk and flipped on a light switch in the gathering gloom. As she did, a familiar voice sounded in the front half of the bar.

"McKenna? Anybody here?"

Awareness curled in her belly at just the sound of his voice. Today, she would ignore it, her defenses firmly back in place.

"I'm in the back," she called, raising her voice enough so he would hear her through the door separating the kitchen from the food and bar service area.

Picking up her box cutter, she went to work on the rest of the boxes that needed unloading, grateful for a task to keep her busy. The last thing she needed was more one-on-one time after the way she'd thrown herself at him, and yet here they were again. Alone in her empty establishment.

The noise of the blade ripping through packing tape must have masked the sound of him entering the back room, because a moment later his boots came into view as she hefted another box onto her growing stack.

"What are you doing here?" he asked, voice stern.

The interruption made her pause long enough to take in his dark hair, damp in the front as if his hood or hat hadn't kept all the rain off him. He must have shed his coat up front because his gray flannel shirt and the partially buttoned white tee underneath were both dry. Her gaze paused at the column of his throat. The bristly edge of his jaw that he hadn't shaved in a couple of days.

"I could ask you the same thing." She propped her elbow on the stack of open boxes almost as tall as her. "Considering this is my bar, and not yours, it makes far more sense for me to be here than you. Don't you think?"

His scowl deepened.

Did it make her a bad person that she enjoyed getting under his skin all the more today?

"Have you heard the weather report? Or bothered to look outside?" He shook his head. "I came over because I worried you might be stuck here if you got a ride to the bar without retrieving your vehicle first."

She might have been touched at his concern if it didn't reek of big-brother-style protectiveness. Just thinking that might be his motivation riled her all over again.

"I don't need a watchdog, Quint." Straightening from where she'd been leaning against the boxes, anger vibrated through her. "Just because I was foolish enough to share something personal last night doesn't mean you get to be my self-appointed guardian, okay?"

His expression shifted. The fierce glower softening as something like real concern crossed his features.

"Don't regret that. Please." He stared at her for a long moment, as if weighing his next words.

She was grateful when he broke the stare to pace around the back room, stuffing his hands in the back pockets of his jeans as if he were too restless to know where to put them. It was a strange feeling to see him in a space she considered hers. His tall height and broad shoulders made everything else around him feel diminished. Small.

"I'm aware of the weather," she assured him, her own temper deflating now that he'd backed off. "When I came in early today, the predictions were still fairly benign. I'll just finish up stocking the cooler and then I'll head home."

Quinton ceased his pacing. He turned to meet her gaze again.

"Can I give you a hand? Speed up the process for you in any way?"

Her first instinct was to bristle. To remind him that she could manage her work just fine on her own. But she swallowed back the words in an effort to smooth things over. Quinton had been kind to offer his help. Not just today, but in his efforts to locate the source of the mortifying video and in his kindness to Ms. Weatherspoon.

"All right," she acquiesced a moment later. "If you want to unload some of the boxes into the walk-in refrigerator, I'll break down the empties."

She knew she needed to keep him at arm's length no

matter how much she might yearn for something more. Still, the tension between them spun out for a moment while she waited for his answer. When he gave a nod, the air rushed out of her lungs, the moment broken.

A few minutes later, they worked in tandem. Quinton had been more than willing to take instruction for where to put things, and McKenna had been grateful for a break from standing in the thirty-seven-degree unit.

While she flattened the cardboard into manageable squares for recycling, she couldn't help but notice Quinton's arms flex as he worked. Even through a layer of flannel, the ripple of muscle was evident in his shoulders and back. A visual she wouldn't have guessed would be so distracting just two weeks before when her body had seemed immune to men.

For better or worse, she couldn't deny that Quinton's presence had been the catalyst to awaken her senses.

As she bound a stack of cardboard with twine and cinched the knot, her phone blared and vibrated with an emergency notification. Quinton's did the same, the sound of his device carrying through the cooler's insulated walls. He was quicker to shut his off than her, stepping out of the fridge as she read her alert from the National Weather Service.

Her eyes scanned the message while Quinton spoke them aloud.

"Hurricane-force winds and fifty-foot waves predicted within the hour." He shoved his phone in his back pocket while he came toward her. "Are you sure this is the safest place to be during this kind of storm?"

Her stomach dropped as she read more details of the message. Cyclone. Record low pressure system. Yes, she'd been through both before, but these storms could be scary as hell, the weather far different from anywhere else in the world, including mainland Alaska. The Bering Sea had a dramatic effect on the Aleutian Islands weather.

Outside the rain seemed to pummel the roof of the metal structure even harder, the wind whipping louder.

"Definitely not. And I have pets at home who need me." She'd been careful to crate her Havanese, Loki, before coming into the bar today, but she knew he would worry if the weather worsened. Then there was her cat, Freya, who liked to act tough but always came to McKenna's bed in a storm. "I have to get back to my house before this gets any worse."

Berating herself for leaving the house in the first place, she reached for the heavy yellow coat she'd left flung over a chair near the workstation. She couldn't bear the idea of anything happening to Clayton's house. Or his bar. Or his boat. All things he'd generously given into her care, and she worked her butt off to maintain while he was away.

"I'll drive you," Quinton was already charging through the door to the front of the bar.

McKenna followed, picking up her purse on the way. "There's no need—"

"Yes, there is—" he began, shoving his arms into the sleeves of his oilcloth coat.

It was the last thing she saw before the lights in the bar went out and everything went black.

Five

All the storm advice he'd ever heard cycled through Quinton's brain as his eyes adjusted to the dark. But a cyclone? The weather up here was stormy and unpredictable at best. At worst... He didn't want to know.

The sounds of the storm raged on, but in those moments after the power clicked off, his ears were most keenly attuned to McKenna's breathing. Rapid. Shallow. Raspy?

"Are you all right?" He reached for her, concern blotting out every other thought.

His hands found her arms, and he smoothed his way up the soft knit fabric of her dress. He could feel the echo of the fast, vaguely wheezy breaths in her shoulders as they moved up and down.

"I'll be fine," she spoke with slow deliberation, at odds with her quick exhales. "I have stress-induced asthma and the storm must be triggering it." She paused to gulp air. "My inhaler is in the glove box of my truck."

Worry for her spiked the anxiety already at a peak because of the winds picking up speed outside. That weather alert had said they could see hurricane-force gusts of well over one hundred miles per hour.

The outline of her became more visible as his eyes adjusted to the limited amount of gray daylight that found its way through a couple of small windows on the far side of the bar. Even though it was only midday, the sky was dark enough to pass for twilight.

"I'll get it for you. Do you have your keys?" He'd noticed her truck out front when he'd pulled into the parking lot.

Since they were the only ones in the place, both vehicles were just steps from the front entrance.

"They're right here." She withdrew the ring from her dress pocket and passed it to him. "I just really need to get home."

Quinton recognized her easy agreement as a testament to how she must feel. The woman had crossed swords with him at every turn, so for her to give up those keys that quickly told him all he needed to know about the importance of that inhaler.

"I'll get you to your house as quickly as I can. But for now, wait here and I'll be right back with your medicine," he promised.

He could feel her body vibrate with the force of her shaky nod, grateful she hadn't wasted words when breathing proved difficult.

Clutching her key ring in his fist, he yanked up the deep hood of his jacket as he moved toward the exit. A moment later, he was in the rain making the dash toward her vehicle. Water pelted his head and shoulders while he unlocked the passenger door and stood rifling through the contents of the glove box. Digging past fishing lures, a flashlight and spare wool hat, he found the inhaler. He didn't spare the time to put everything back where he'd found it, instead just locking up the truck before jogging back to the entrance.

No sooner had he stepped through the door than he delivered her medicine. His eyes hadn't yet adjusted to the dimmer light inside the bar when he heard the distinctive sound of the aerosol puff and McKenna dragging in a deep gasp.

Holding it.

He waited in silence, anxiety spiking as he remembered the last time he'd been by a woman's side, listening to labored breaths. The memory of his mother's death blindsided him, rocking him when he needed to think clearly.

McKenna had gotten under his skin too deep and too fast for him to make that connection. He did his damnedest to shove aside the dark thoughts and anchor himself in the moment instead. To just focus on McKenna. He didn't want her to try speaking until her breaths came easily again.

"That's much better." She still spoke slowly, and there was a little crackle in her airway, but he could hear the overall improvement for himself. "We should get going."

"Do you have a gas line you need to shut off here? Or any other prep I can take care of first?"

"No. I flipped off the main power when we left the back room, and I don't have gas service up here." She headed toward the door and Quinton followed. "And before you ask, I don't care if we take your SUV, just get us there in one piece."

Relieved they were on the same page, Quinton unlocked the rental from the fob and moments later they were on the main road, driving toward her place. He kept his speed low, mindful of potential flooding and poor visibility thanks to the downpour, but their route was empty of other vehicles save a rescue truck moving in the other direction. At the base of the hill that led to McKenna's place, he needed to swerve around a crumpled piece of aluminum that might have been part of a roof at one time. He had just enough room for him to navigate past the bent metal.

All the while, he kept one ear tuned to McKenna's breathing just in case her condition worsened. She still sounded raspy and she looked tense when he caught glimpses of her in his peripheral vision. Sitting straight in the leather bucket seat, she braced one hand on the center console and the other on the door's armrest, as if she needed to be ready to bolt at any opportunity. He hated that he'd added to her anxiety, but he couldn't dial back the urge to keep her safe. Not with memories of his mom gasping her last breath pummeling him every time McKenna's airway made a painful rasp.

"I'm coming inside to make sure the house is safe," Quinton warned her as he parked outside the compact blue two-story. "You should take it easy for a while."

She hesitated for a moment before she nodded, her blue gaze fixed on the structure. "The storm is only getting worse. You shouldn't be driving in this anyhow."

Together, they exited the SUV to make a dash for her front steps. With no overhang for shelter, they got doused as she unlocked the door. A minute later they entered the home. It was cold and dark inside, but McKenna flipped a nearby light switch anyway.

"No power here either," she confirmed around a small wheezing breath. For a moment, she fumbled in the drawer of a small cabinet near the door and produced two mini flashlights. She clicked one on and passed it to him before switching on her own. "Loki's crate is in the kitchen if you want to follow me."

Quinton absolutely wanted to go with her. He also wanted her to sit still and catch her breath while he took care of everything, but he wasn't sure how well received that request would be. No doubt she was out of her comfort zone already between the storm and the asthma attack. She'd even said it was stress-induced, so he'd be damned if he'd add to that stress.

Torn about how to proceed, he only vaguely noticed the details of the darkened home. The living and dining areas were in the front of the house where they'd entered, both simply furnished with pale wood pieces. There were no rugs or artwork. Yet as he walked deeper into the house, passing a staircase and small bathroom to find the kitchen, there were more signs of life.

Photo after photo of fishing expeditions were hung on the walls in the hallway, most of them taken on the *Un-Reel*. He scanned them with the flashlight briefly, pausing only long enough to see there were a few of Clay. Quinton hoped he could return to look at them more closely once he'd helped her secure the house for the storm. But most of the images were of McKenna holding huge fish beside people he assumed were tour guests.

Before he could comment on them, he heard her exclaim in a high-pitched voice he'd never heard her use before, "You sweet, good boy! Of course I didn't leave you in this scary storm. Would I do that to you?"

Hearing the warmth in her tone—and better yet, the lack of wheezing—made him hopeful that just seeing her pets would go a long way toward soothing the stress that brought on the asthma. He didn't think his heartrate would return to normal anytime soon, however.

"Is he okay?" Quinton asked as he stepped into the utilitarian white kitchen, just in time to see her withdraw a black-and-brown ball of fluff from a kennel tucked between the refrigerator and a utility sink that looked to be an extension of the laundry room. "And I thought you mentioned you had more than one pet?"

He glanced around the dim kitchen for signs of another kennel while McKenna cuddled the little furball. The dog was flailing its paws excitedly, scrabbling to get closer while a gust of wind blew against the house so hard something thumped the roof. More blowing debris, maybe? The Aleutian Islands didn't really have trees, just a handful of new plantings from efforts to reforest the land.

McKenna exchanged a worried glance with him.

"My cat, Freya," she explained as she moved into the hallway, still carrying her pup. The skirt of her red dress swirled around her legs, her calves bare now that she'd shed her boots. "She won't come to a stranger, but if you want to unplug the appliances and make sure all the exterior doors are bolted, I'll go look for her."

Quinton was already tugging cords from the outlets as her voice retreated up the stairs. He could hear the steps creak beneath her light step even as the winds howled around the house.

Finishing the tasks, he checked his phone for weather updates and noticed his connectivity had disappeared completely. He pulled open a few cabinets and drawers until he found a flashlight on the same shelf as a few candles and matches. He spotted an emergency alert radio on the refrigerator and switched it on. Thank goodness it had full battery power.

By the time McKenna returned downstairs holding a calico cat in one arm and the Havanese pup in the other, he was inspecting the flue in the living room fireplace.

"Is it safe to start a fire?" he asked as he knelt in front of the grate. "Or will it aggravate your asthma?"

Setting her pets on a cushion of the small leather sectional that faced the fireplace, McKenna nodded as she replied. "I think my asthma will be more triggered by the cold than by smoke. And the fireplace is definitely safe. I just had the flue and chimney cleaned a few weeks ago to prepare for colder weather."

Her breathing still sounded normal enough, slow and steady if a little raspy at times. He hoped that meant she was feeling less stressed than she had at the bar earlier. He also hoped she would allow him to give her a hand while the storm raged on so that she didn't have to overtax her lungs. What if she got into respiratory distress?

Because while he couldn't deny he wanted to spend more time with her, what was most important was for her to be okay.

"That was good thinking." He took a couple of small logs from a cast-iron wood stand and placed them strategically in the hearth, then repeated the procedure with three more logs, determined to help. "I brought in some supplies from the kitchen, figuring this would be as good of a spot as any to ride out the storm."

He stuffed some kindling beneath the logs and held a match to it. In the growing flicker from the flames, he could see McKenna's blue eyes on him.

Wary? Curious?

He couldn't begin to detect her mood.

"I'd better get us some blankets," she said finally, her tongue darting out to lick her lips. "Even with the fire, it's bound to get chilly in here."

As she hurried away to retrieve them, Quinton tried his best not to envision himself sharing a blanket with McKenna before the night was through. That wouldn't happen, of course. He couldn't allow something like that to happen.

And yet, if the temperature really did drop significantly in the house with no power, would they have any choice?

While the storm raged on outside, McKenna reread the directions for her inhaler, using a small flashlight to see the tiny print from the drug insert she kept in the medicine cabinet upstairs. But the instructions for taking the prescription were just as she remembered. She wasn't supposed to use any more for four to six hours after the previous dose.

Tell that to her burning lungs. Or the thready panic that had gone through her at the thought of something happening to Clayton's boat while the *Un-Reel* was under her care. Had she followed all the right safety precautions when she'd left it last time? For that matter, had she secured the bar well enough? The house? Clayton had allowed her to step into the life he'd made here, and she couldn't bear the idea of being responsible for damage to any of it.

Now, shoving the paper back into the old-fashioned mirrored cabinet, McKenna told herself to get a grip. She needed to calm down first and foremost if she wanted to get her respiration under control. She closed the door of the medicine cabinet and exited the bathroom to retrieve quilts from a linen closet at the top of the staircase.

Blankets she would be using side by side with Quinton Kingsley. In a darkened house. While they rode out the storm together.

A small throb of excitement tripped through her, even though she shouldn't want anything to do with the man coaxing a blaze from the hearth downstairs.

He'd rebuffed her after their kiss for one thing.

For another, he was a Kingsley. Enemy to Clayton and therefore no friend to her. Except it wasn't easy to remember that when Quinton did kind things like help Julie Weatherspoon recoup her lost funds or made sure McKenna got home safely during a blackout.

Or promised to make her ex-boyfriend pay for the vile way he'd filmed her without her knowledge or consent.

That Quinton wanted to help her heal that wound melted her heart. What woman wouldn't be romanced by a man ready to take down the villains in her life?

She paused before descending the steps again, taking a moment to breathe in the scent of fragrant cedar logs as they burned. The orange glow from the flames was visible even on the second floor, reminding her how dark it had grown outside from the storm.

Right now, it felt like they were all alone in the world

with the unnatural dark that had fallen, the wind roaring around the house and the rains battering the windows from every angle depending on the gusts. Then, in the middle of all the noise from the storm, she could hear Quinton's voice float up from downstairs as he crooned encouragement to her dog, telling Loki he was a very good and brave boy.

Her breath hitched in her throat as she listened, awareness heating her body at the thought of spending more time with Quinton one-on-one. A moment later she realized that when her breath caught in her throat it didn't burn.

Because her inhales and exhales had quieted. Her respiration close to normal. Was it the effects of the inhaler finally kicking in almost an hour after she'd taken it?

Or could there be an inverse relationship between her anxiety and her hunger to touch and taste the man downstairs?

Ludicrous, she chastised herself. That made zero sense. And this was probably her brain doing serious mental gymnastics to justify what she really wanted—a hot and sexy night with Quinton Kingsley.

Another gust of wind rattled something outside the house before a thumping noise against the exterior made her jump. McKenna rushed down the steps, hugging the blankets to her chest at the same moment Quinton appeared in the hallway to look up toward her.

"You okay?" he asked, his dark eyebrows knitting together at whatever expression he saw on her face.

Her lungs burned again, her airway closing at the thought of the severe weather wrecking the house that Clay had left in her care.

"It sounds like the siding is peeling off the walls outside," she managed between ragged inhales as Quinton took the blankets from her. The words burned. Her airway tightened. Resentment at her condition made her eyes sting. "I hate this."

"The storm?" he asked, tucking her under his free arm and guiding her toward the living room, where he'd pulled the small gray sectional closer to the hearth.

She didn't protest him shepherding her around. Maybe a piece of her appreciated that anchor at a time where it felt like she was coming unmoored. She'd worked hard to carve out a life for herself here after she'd left San Francisco and she couldn't afford to let Mother Nature rip it out from under her.

"No." She shook her head, just that one word taking too much air. "Stress asthma again," she clarified, prodding aside Freya from the middle couch cushion so that she could take a seat there instead. "Hate that I can't control it."

"That only makes you human like the rest of us," he observed dryly, shaking out one of the wool blankets she'd brought and draping the heavy blue fabric over her lap.

Then, taking the seat beside her, he dragged a red quilt over his own legs. Now they sat just inches away from one another. Her pulse quickened.

But her lungs eased a bit more, and she wondered if it had to do with that anchoring sensation Quinton inspired.

Definitely not! her inner critic admonished. It just helped to sit down and stop thinking about worst-case scenarios.

"But I guide tourists through the Alaskan wilderness,"

she explained softly, unwilling to tax her lungs to speak too much. "It ticks me off that a storm like this one—the same kind of low pressure event that happens all the time in this part of the world—is sending me into an asthma attack."

In the quiet moments that followed her admission, the fire crackled and spit a shower of orange sparks onto the flameproof mat in front of it. Loki leaped up onto the couch beside her then turned not just once, not twice, but three times before finding a perfect spot to lie next to her. He settled into a sleepy dog lump and seemed to fall into a snooze state almost immediately.

"Plenty of people have fears they never recover from," Quinton observed, propping his feet on the stones of the hearth. He'd left his boots by her front door when they'd entered, so by now he only wore a pair of black socks with his jeans.

"Not you," she shot back, tugging the wool closer to her chin as she peered over at the man seated beside her.

His eyes were dark in the dim light of the living room. A fathomless brown. "I've got one of the worst possible fears for a man born into a ranching family."

His expression had blanked. His gaze faraway.

An uncomfortable feeling pinched her belly, signaling to her she'd trod into awkward new terrain with him. And yet she couldn't *not* ask him for more, curiosity about this man outweighing her better instincts.

"You do?"

His jaw flexed as he peered into the flames. Then he began to speak quietly. "The fear started the day I wandered into the pasture of an unbroken stallion when I was a kid. I was playing some kind of game with my older brother, Levi. Hiding from him, maybe."

Something cool and detached in his tone made her regret asking for the story, as everything about his body language told her this wasn't easy for him.

McKenna reached to touch his arm where it rested on top of the red wool blanket. She squeezed his wrist, offering silent comfort until he continued to speak.

"I think I had it in my head that Levi would be impressed if I rode the horse. I must have known even before the accident that the animal had a reputation for being temperamental." He gave a stiff shrug before shaking his head. "I just remember becoming aware that I was ticking him off because he was snorting and prancing away from me. Kicking a little bit to warn me—"

McKenna moved closer to him, sensing something terrible was coming. She could hear it in his voice, which was growing less detached with each sentence. See it in the clenching and unclenching of his hand. Unsure how else to offer comfort, she tipped her head to his shoulder and took his hand in hers.

"Did he kick you?" she asked softly, tracing circles on the back of his strong hand, her own fears forgotten for the moment.

"No. I must have started shouting because Levi heard me and so did our mom." Quinton's shoulder went tense beneath the place where her forehead lay. "My mother ran into the pasture to get me out of there, but she was kicked in the temple in the process. She died in my arms."

The words were stark, the cool detachment returning to his voice at the horrific end of his story.

"I'm so sorry—" she began, lifting her head from his shoulder to face him.

But Quinton pivoted in his seat to place one gentle finger over her lips. "Thank you. But I only shared the story with you to tell you that I've fought a fear of horses every day of my life since then. Every. Effing. Day."

The pain of that—managing a fear that he had to deal with constantly—revealed a layer that she would have never suspected lurked inside this self-contained and capable man.

The howling wind faded while the realization of what he'd just shared—and why—touched her heart. He'd wanted to comfort her. To assure her that a fear didn't make her weak.

"My fear is a small thing by comparison," she acknowledged, half wishing she hadn't spoken about her anxiety at all so that he hadn't felt compelled to share something that must have caused him some residual pain.

And yet, she was also grateful to understand him better. To know that he'd trusted her with an important part of himself.

"Is there such a thing as a small fear?" Quinton asked, lifting a hand to smooth her hair from her face. "I know in my head that horse bore no blame for something that was my fault entirely, but it didn't make me any less scared that it could happen again. Not to me, but to someone else I cared about."

She felt herself being pulled into that honey-colored gaze of his. Felt the full force of her attraction to him. With every heartbeat she seemed to lean closer to him, as if that throbbing pulse pushed her in his direction.

In the warm glow of the fire, she realized she wasn't

the only one moving closer, however. Quinton had shifted nearer to her.

His hands cupped her face. Tilting her where he wanted her.

And when he kissed her, she didn't have a thought in the world of denying what they both needed.

Six

McKenna was a fever in his blood.

Quinton couldn't escape the heat that had been building inside him from the day he'd first walked into the Cyclone Shack and laid eyes on the sultry redhead. He'd tried to outrun the attraction. But telling himself to avoid her hadn't worked. Breaking off that last kiss hadn't helped him to stop thinking about her. And then, he'd gone and dredged up a story from his past he never shared with anyone.

Any. One.

Yet hearing McKenna's struggle to take a breath had torn open a wound he'd thought had been scarred over enough that it was protected. Sharing that piece of himself had left him raw.

Besides, Mother Nature herself had conspired to put him in McKenna's path. With the storm raging and the electricity out, he knew it wasn't safe to return to his hotel. Rescue workers didn't appreciate having to save people who were simply too foolhardy to stay put.

Then, there was McKenna herself. Hotter than any flame he'd coaxed from the hearth, she pressed herself against him as if she couldn't get close enough. Her hand roved over his back and shoulders, nails lightly grazing the fabric of his shirt.

Was it any wonder he tried to concentrate on the way that felt instead of thinking about her soft breasts flattened against his chest, or her hip grazing his? His blood ignited like she'd pumped an accelerant into his veins.

"McKenna." He growled her name against her lips while the clean scent of her skin made him hungry to taste her everywhere.

He tunneled his fingers into the mass of red waves spilling down her back. Then, wrapping the length of hair around his hand, he tipped her head back gently so he could look into her dark blue eyes.

"Quinton Kingsley, if you're going to tell me you're having second thoughts, save your breath." The whispered words were spoken with a fierceness that belied the volume. "I'll retreat upstairs if you want, but I won't listen to a spiel about why you can't be with me."

Regret weighted his shoulders at the possibility that he'd offended her the last time they'd touched. But he suspected that's exactly what he'd accomplished when he'd voiced his concerns about her connection to his half brother.

Needing to soothe away the damage he'd done—any sense of rejection she'd felt—he traced the delicate curve of her jaw with his hands. "No second thoughts. You're all I've thought about since that kiss."

Right or wrong, this woman had infiltrated his dreams and every waking moment too. With his emotions ripped raw, he needed her too much to walk away.

"Good." Her eyes fluttered closed as his hands skimmed down her throat to her collarbone, her head tipping back against the couch cushions. "We can finish what we started last night."

The clear offer of her words, of her body, undid the last of his restraint. Quinton feasted on her neck, tasting her everywhere he'd touched. Then, slipping his fingers into the wrap-front vee of her knit dress, he palmed the fullness of her breasts. Taking their weight in his hands, he molded and squeezed the soft flesh until the tight points of her nipples were an enticement he couldn't ignore.

With more hunger than finesse, he nudged the straps of her bra from her shoulders so he could free her breasts from the cream-colored satin that shielded her from him. He spared a moment to take in the sight of her, back arched toward him, her auburn hair spilling everywhere while those taut pink nipples practically begged for attention.

Unable to refuse, he fastened his lips around one pretty mound, drawing her into his mouth while he teased the other nipple with his thumb. McKenna's fingers fisted in his hair, holding him in place with the same fervor that she did everything else in her life.

Just thinking about that intensity of hers drove his need higher. He knew their connection would be unforgettable. Out of this realm.

"Are we okay to stay down here by the fire?" He

paused to check in with her before he undressed her any further. "Would you rather go—"

She covered his lips with her fingertips, her blue eyes homing in on his as she sat up straighter to meet his gaze. "There's nowhere I'd rather be."

All right then.

Her eyes slid closed once more as he untied the bow at her waist and unfastened her dress, revealing her whole gorgeous body. Her breasts still spilled over the bra cups since he hadn't undone the clasp yet. At her hips, a narrow triangle of cream satin barely covered her sex, the small panties held in place by thin elastic straps.

He tucked his finger under one strap to test the material, tugging it upward gently so the rest of the panties rubbed between her legs. Her eyes shot open again, pupils dilated as her fingers scrabbled against his chest. She gripped the fabric of his shirt, squeezing it in her fist while he worked the satin back and forth over her most sensitive places. The sultry sounds emanating from her throat encouraged him, making him want to sink himself inside her then and there.

But he wouldn't rush this, no matter how much he hungered for her.

Outside, a gust of wind slammed something against the side of the house, distracting them both for a moment and making Loki jump off the couch to investigate. But when no other sounds followed save wind and rain, Quinton returned his attention to the gorgeous woman next to him on the sofa.

Needing a better hold on her, he lifted McKenna onto his lap, splaying his thighs to cradle her better. The dress was already falling from her shoulders, so he peeled the fabric the rest of the way off. Laying it aside, he undid the clasp of her bra to free her breasts.

When she reached to remove her underwear, he gripped her wrist to stop her.

"Leave them." He spoke the words against her ear while he returned to the elastic straps himself. "Just for a little longer."

Repeating the seesaw motion with the satin, he was rewarded with a throaty moan of his name.

"*Quinton*. Please." She squirmed against him, sending a bolt of heat straight to his erection and making it damned near impossible for him to ignore her plea.

However, ignore it he did. Because he craved the sight of her coming undone in his arms. He needed that even more than his own finish.

He'd dreamed about it too often.

Still, a moment later, she was too at the mercy of her own desire to argue with him. She clutched at his shoulder, her mouth gone slack as he worked the material between her thighs. Slowly. And then faster.

Friction decreasing as the fabric grew damp.

He was tempted to maintain the pace until she found her peak that way, but a part of him couldn't resist touching her any longer. When her breathing went shallow and quick, he let go of the panties and nudged aside the satin, making just enough room for him to touch her wet heat.

When he slid a finger deep inside her, her breath caught. Her body arched. And then, in one glorious cry of completion, she came against his hand, her body pulsing with the force of it. Again and again.

He held her tightly to him with the arm he'd braced around her back. His other palm he let curve around her mound. Her heart pounded wildly just beneath her breast. He could feel the force of it against his cheek as he held her.

And in spite of the heat burning through him, he felt a satisfaction of his own, knowing that he'd taken her there.

He splayed his hand against her spine, wanting more but very willing to wait for it. He'd earned every throaty sigh, every lush spasm of her body, and he would enjoy each second of her completion.

"Quinton." She edged away from him so she could peer into his eyes. "They have a saying where I come from about turnabout and fair play." She dragged her fingertips slowly down his chest, her blue gaze tracking the progress of her touch until she unfastened the first button of his shirt. "Maybe you've heard of it?"

The fire that he'd managed to bank before blazed up again at her provocative touch. At the heat in her eyes.

Against her hip, his erection throbbed an answer she had to feel.

A damned good thing since he didn't trust his voice to speak right then. Especially not when she slid off his lap to kneel in front of him.

And slowly lower his zipper.

McKenna only sort of knew what she was doing.

Her sexual experiences had come to an abrupt halt after her scumbag ex had shared her then-twenty-five-year-old self with all the internet. And it's not like she'd gathered a wealth of sensual knowledge prior to that.

For her to climax so fast with Quinton and then feel compelled to pay him back in kind? All that was new terrain for her. Not just the sex acts. Also, the whole "unselfish" approach was new and delicious. Every nerve ending she possessed was on fire for this man, even now after he'd driven her to incredible new heights.

So yeah, she was willing to put herself out there in a big way to please him. And the best way seemed obvious. She just hoped she delivered for him the way he had for her.

From behind Quinton's shoulder, her cat Freya opened one skeptical eye to stare down from the back of the sofa, echoing McKenna's doubts.

Or maybe she was projecting just a bit.

Once she'd freed Quinton's cock from his boxers, she forgot about everything else but him. Stroking him with one hand, she leaned closer to take an experimental taste.

The ragged noise that issued from his mouth was all the incentive she needed. Licking her lips, she hovered just above the crown and gathered her courage. Then she lowered her mouth onto him.

"McKenna." He chanted her name amid a string of soft curses that assured her she was doing something right.

Shifting her shoulders between his thighs, she took more of him, licking and tasting. Sucking and—

He lifted her by the shoulders, pulling her off him when she'd just found a rhythm. But her confusion lasted only a moment. Seeing the harsh look on his face told her all she needed to know.

"It's too good. I need you." Standing, he reached for one of the quilts she'd brought and laid it on the floor between the couch and fireplace, then added a second on top of it.

While she wriggled out of her panties, he divested himself of his clothes in record time, producing a condom from somewhere. She was grateful he'd thought of it since she'd been too caught up in the hunger for him to think about practicalities, which wasn't like her.

Tossing the condom on the blankets, he stalked toward her, his naked body a thing of masculine beauty. Firelight cast him half in shadow, half in bronze. Muscles rippled in his thighs and arms. And his abs... She could have stared at him for days. Could have used her mouth on him for days just tracing the paths between the ridges with her tongue.

"I like what I'm seeing too," he assured her, his words bringing home that he was getting the same kind of unfiltered view of her that she was enjoying of him.

For an instant, a hot wave of panic threatened as she recalled how many other people had seen her naked without her permission. Fury over the unfairness of that rose in her chest, but before it could rattle her, Quinton was there, his arms around her. His mouth possessing hers and blotting out thought of anything else but him. His body against hers rewired her nerve endings so they were all attuned to him.

Reminding her that what she was sharing was for him alone.

Breaking the kiss, he drew her down to the blankets with him. He cradled her head as he laid her down, his expression serious.

"Are you still with me?" he asked, fingers stroking into her hair as he waited for an answer.

Had he spied some of her momentary misgivings in her face? She wouldn't allow her past to rob the present. Not for Quinton. Not for herself either.

"One hundred percent," she vowed, taking his hand and moving it to her breast. Needing to lose herself in his touch again. "I just…haven't been with anyone since the whole ordeal that brought me here in the first place."

She didn't share that she hadn't even felt the slightest sensual urges. That her libido had been in deep hibernation after the humiliation of the video.

Or that everything inside her had woken up and taken notice when Quinton arrived in town.

Quinton propped himself on an elbow as he looked down at her. He left his hand where she'd placed it but didn't move to touch more of her. Instead, his thumb traced circles on the swell of her breast while he spoke.

"Eighteen months is a long time. Are you sure you're ready?"

Rolling to her side, she pressed her hips to his.

"Hell yes, I'm ready *because* a year and a half is a long time." She could have told him that her desire had more to do with him than any time frame, but she'd shared enough of herself with him for now. He already knew too much about her when she was used to keeping the world at arm's length.

He waited for what seemed like an eternity, his intense gaze probing for the answers she didn't want to give. But finally, that big, capable hand of his began to move on her breast. Cupping. Lifting. Tweaking the taut peak that already ached for his mouth.

"In that case, you should get the condom ready," he

informed before his head dipped to lick a path down her neck.

Relief mingled with pleasure and hunger, her emotions all over the place. Yet as she ripped open the condom packet and rolled it into place, there was no room for anything but the hot desire threatening to burn her from the inside out.

She wanted this man like she'd never craved anyone else. Maybe that should have been a portent. But if it was, she planned to ignore it, because nothing was going to stop her from savoring every second of this night with him.

Every one of those eighteen months of abstinence felt like a lifetime of deprivation right now. And with the rain driving against the windows a few feet above where she lay, the moment felt precious. Like everything important to her could get ripped away in life's next storm.

So when Quinton gripped her hips, lifting her slightly, she was all in. Her gaze locked on his, their breathing syncing up before he edged his way inside her. She steadied herself by gripping his forearms, her whole body trembling.

"You feel so good." He nudged deeper, filling her. Stretching her.

She wrapped her arms around him, getting used to the feel of him. Her heart pounded wildly and she tucked her chin against his shoulder, clinging to him while too many feelings washed over her.

When she caught her breath, she wrapped her legs around him, locking her ankles behind his back.

A gasp hissed between Quinton's teeth, and she hoped

that meant he was reeling from this union too. For now, all she could do was simply hold on as he began to move inside her. Slowly at first, then picking up speed.

Her back slid across the blanket, her hips rocking with his every stroke. She would have slid right off the quilt, but he planted one arm behind her head, mooring her in place as his hips worked.

McKenna's lips parted, but no sound came out. Incredibly, the tension of another orgasm coiled inside her, teasing her each time Quinton gripped her hip to guide her where he wanted.

Cracking open one eye to look up at him, she watched the tendons of his neck strain with his movements and she could almost see him grappling with his own release. Knowing that he was close spurred her on, enticing her to wriggle against him, providing a new friction that made them both groan from how good it felt.

"I can't last." His hoarse words wound through the haze of desire surrounding her, reminding her that she wanted to push him to the best possible release.

If it came sooner rather than later, it didn't matter. She just wanted him to feel better than he ever had before.

"Me either," she admitted, squeezing his hips with her thighs. "I'm so close."

His eyes cranked open, taking her in as they moved together in the glow of the firelight. When he reached between them to touch her right where she needed, her body simply...unraveled.

Pleasure burst through her, waves of it rolling over and over her. She sank her fingers into his shoulders, holding on to him while the release had its way with her.

She wished she could have held it back so he could experience his finish first, but instead, the hot throb of her body around his seemed to spur him on. A moment later, he went taut, all his muscles tensing. And then he was right there with her in all that lush pleasure, his hips jerking from the force of his release.

McKenna couldn't have said which one of them quieted first. In the aftermath, they held each other for long moments. Quinton dragged the blue wool blanket down from the couch to cover them at some point. And McKenna felt the silence grow thick with the magnitude of how things had changed between them.

She didn't know what to say about that. She only knew that being with him had been inevitable. Unavoidable. Necessary.

As for what came next?

"We'll figure it out," Quinton assured her as he stroked a hand through her hair. "Let's just enjoy tonight."

Too sated to concern herself how he'd known precisely what she was thinking, she laid her head against his chest while a log slipped in the fireplace, sending a shower of sparks onto the stones in front of the grate.

Loki had resettled on a far corner of the quilt on the floor, his little black-and-brown body curled into a ball. Freya remained on the back of the couch, unimpressed by the storm or the coupling, her long tail giving a slow swish as she licked a paw clean.

Tonight, while the storm raged outside, they were safe. At least the storm that had been brewing inside her had quieted.

For now.

Because McKenna knew that what they'd done just now changed everything between them. There would be no going back to the way things were. The thought sent a prickle through her like an omen.

Rattling her.

And if she felt unsettled about breaching the barrier that had been between them before, she could only imagine how Quinton was feeling when he'd been adamant about not touching her.

For now though? They had the whole night ahead of them before they had to grapple with what happened when the sun came up.

Seven

Quinton couldn't sleep knowing he'd betrayed his half brother's trust.

He lay awake staring at the living room ceiling, his fingers idly combing through McKenna's hair as she slept. The storm outside had quieted shortly before dawn, but the blackout was still in effect as he tugged the blankets higher on them both. He'd only had one condom in his possession, so they'd found other creative ways to pleasure each other after that first incredible time.

He should be exhausted, but guilt kept him awake in the small hours of morning. The cat mewed quietly at having her corner of the blanket disturbed before resettling herself on a new section of the quilt. The calico tucked herself close to McKenna, casting Quinton a censorious look before closing her eyes again.

Clearly Quinton wasn't the only one who saw himself as a villain. Before now, he had no cause for misgivings about facing Clayton when he found him. McKenna might believe that Clay wanted nothing to do with the Kingsley family, yet Quinton knew that he personally hadn't done a damned thing to earn his sibling's enmity.

Until tonight.

Had it been blindly self-indulgent of him to remain in Dutch Harbor all this time, knowing the tremendous draw he felt toward McKenna? Probably. And no matter how much he wanted a repeat of the night they'd shared—many, many repeats—he couldn't allow himself to remain in a situation that would only tempt him again and again.

Since McKenna had no intention of revealing Clay's whereabouts anyhow, it was a fool's errand to remain in town. Yet, without a concrete lead for where to search next for his brother, what choice did he have but to stay put? Up until now, Quinton had resisted utilizing his digital skills to locate Clay, knowing those methods skirted ethical boundaries. But were they any worse than touching Clay's stepsister?

He would hole up in his hotel room and get to work on his computer to find his brother. Right after he found the scumbag who'd posted the video of McKenna. Quinton had narrowed the search considerably the night before. A few more dedicated hours and he'd locate the bastard. There'd be no leaving this town until he at least put that situation right for this woman.

Gently, he smoothed a long lock of copper hair between his fingertips, admiring the color in the dim firelight. He couldn't imagine how he'd ever say goodbye to her after what they'd shared. A fact that made it all the more imperative he leave soon.

A light clicked on overhead, momentarily blinding him.

Loki woke up to bark twice, tail thumping expectantly. McKenna stirred next to him.

"The power is back on," she murmured sleepily, closing her eyes tighter against the sudden glare.

"I'll shut the lights off," Quinton assured her, sliding out from under the blankets to tug on his pants. "I'm going to take a look around outside to make sure there's no serious damage done."

By the time he plucked his shirt from the couch, he noticed McKenna watching him.

"I'm going with you." She slipped from the covers and rose to her feet.

Quinton told himself to avert his gaze but didn't fully manage the task until she wrapped the red jersey dress around her body. Walking away from this woman wouldn't be easy.

Frustrated at his lack of restraint, he headed toward the side door he'd noticed in the kitchen earlier, grabbing one of the flashlights left out on the island during the blackout.

She padded close behind him, pausing to step into a pair of waterproof boots by the back door while she took a dog leash from a hook on the wall. "There's a pair of Clay's boots in the closet that might fit you—"

"No. Thank you." He answered abruptly, and more harshly than he'd intended. He stopped himself when he spied the surprise on her face. "That is, my brother already thinks ill of me for reasons I don't understand. I'm not here to take anything that belongs to him."

She seemed as if she might speak, and the last thing he wanted was to invite more talk of his brother with all this guilt hanging in the air. Reaching for the door handle, he turned the knob to exit just as the first rays of light were streaking over the horizon. The rays painted the wet grass a damp rose-colored hue.

"Oh no." McKenna's murmured words caught his attention as she stepped out of doors behind him, her gaze focused upward on the house. "Some of the siding came off."

Loki ran out beside her, darting toward a clump of bushes off to one side of the house. As Quinton's eyes adjusted to the muted light of morning, he took in the details of the yard. Strips of crumpled siding that had formerly been on the house were now scattered around the yard. A black-and-white utility shed rested on its roof against the front of the house. Other debris littered the lawn from what looked like the hard top of a fishing boat to a porch awning from someone else's dwelling. A section of white wooden fencing lay in the middle of the driveway, two pickets missing. At least there was no broken glass to contend with, which meant McKenna could give Loki a little more room to explore.

Besides the signs of damage, the morning seemed eerily quiet. The air was warmer than the night before and the wind had calmed too, leaving a damp, oppressive feel behind.

"I can work on the siding once it's a little lighter out," Quinton offered, recognizing there would be hours of cleanup tasks to be done and unwilling to leave McKenna on her own to tackle it—and yes, maybe he was grasping the reason to stick around a while longer.

"Why would you do that?" she asked, her voice cool as she let Loki sniff around some of the new objects on the lawn. "So you feel less guilty about walking away today?"

His head snapped around to take her measure. Her arms were folded across her chest, the leash clipped to her jeans with a carabiner. She looked incredibly beautiful in the pink light of morning, her hair an untamed mass around her head, some waves pressed into the locks from the way she'd slept.

Her blue eyes were as chilly as her tone, however.

"Who said anything about walking away?" He wondered how she'd read him so easily when she had only just opened her eyes a few minutes before.

"You didn't have to *say* the words. Not when every aspect of your body language is practically screaming it." She huffed out an exasperated sigh. "I knew you were backing off two seconds after I woke up."

He couldn't very well argue the sentiment since her assessment was correct. That didn't make him feel like any less of a heel. Burdened by a mixture of remorse and regret at the knowledge that he couldn't ever be with her again, Quinton used the pent-up frustration to begin picking up the storm-tossed debris closest to him. The wooden pickets. A piece of siding.

He started a pile near the driveway in case her neighbors came to claim the bits that belonged to them.

"With the exception of last night, you've made it very clear to me every day that you didn't want me around," he reminded her as he worked. "And you have no intention of telling me where Clay is, do you?"

"None whatsoever." Her chin lifted as she unclipped the dog leash from her belt loop to hold the end in her hand. "Your retreat was one hundred percent anticipated, so no need to draw out the awkwardness by sticking around to rehang siding, okay?"

He moved faster to scoop up more debris, wishing he could clear away his own mess half so efficiently. Because something about this parting felt all wrong after the night they'd shared. As he gathered a couple of empty plastic planters, it occurred to him that he'd shown McKenna a side of himself that he never gave to anyone. Had it only been because he'd thought he'd never see her again once he found Clay?

The explanation didn't sit quite right, and yet he'd be damned if he could think of any other reason why he'd let his guard down so completely with someone he never should have touched in the first place.

Dropping the planters onto the growing pile, he stopped working to meet her gaze. "I'm still going to find the evidence you need to prosecute your cyber harasser."

He wanted her to know he hadn't been talking smack about that. It was important to him that she not lose a second's worth of worry about that asshat ever again.

For a long moment, he thought she might argue the point, but she at last she gave a nod while Loki circled her ankles. "Thank you. Any help on that score would be appreciated."

His throat felt tight at the soft tone of her voice and the vulnerability it hid. He couldn't imagine how much it rankled this strong, proud woman to have to deal with the juvenile bullshit her ex-boyfriend had put her through.

"I'll send you the information as soon as I have it nailed down." He dragged a couple of pieces of aluminum siding over toward her house, still antsy but unsure of his next move. He didn't want to leave her. Although he sure as hell couldn't stay and perpetuate a relationship that shouldn't have started in the first place. His gut burned with guilt even as the rest of him yearned to take McKenna back in the house and kiss every inch of her the way he'd done just a few hours ago. Fearing that was a real possibility if he stuck around, he wiped his hands on his jeans.

"Do you want a ride into town so you can retrieve your vehicle?" he asked, not wanting to leave her out here again without her truck. "Assuming the roads are navigable."

"I would like that." She unwound the leash from around her legs and then headed for the house. "Just let me settle Loki and grab my purse, then we can go."

Quinton told himself he was doing the right thing to leave. To put some distance between them. But in his gut he knew the damage had already been done. He'd betrayed the brother he wanted to reconcile with, and he'd no doubt hurt a good woman in the process, based on McKenna's stiff shoulders as she strode into the house.

The sooner he uncovered Clay's whereabouts and got out of Dutch Harbor, the better.

Men.

Not for the first time, McKenna thought the word like an epithet three days after Quinton had vanished from her life.

She taped the Closed sign to the front door of the Cyclone Shack, along with a note for her patrons to let them know she'd reopen in thirteen days. That done, she hitched her rucksack onto her back and headed to her truck to make the short drive to the harbor, where she would take an impromptu trip of bird-watchers out to Attu. It was a thirteen-day venture that had fallen into her lap after a tour group based on Adak Island had lost their chartered boat to the recent storm. When the desperate guide had contacted McKenna to take over the trip in tandem with a larger trawler yacht, she had jumped at the chance to get out of town.

This way, she would get some fresh sea air to clear the cobwebs in her brain and give her some perspective on her situation. She would provide tender services for the bigger boat and take smaller groups around the islands that were harder to reach with the yacht. It was a makeshift approach for the tour company to deliver the birding trip, but considering they were in a pinch after the storm and McKenna had enough birding knowledge to act as a second guide, the arrangement would suffice. McKenna would make a nice paycheck, all while avoiding Quinton.

Because… *Men*.

Dumping her sack into the cargo bed of the truck, she tried not to think about how much his disappearing act had hurt. Even though she'd told him after their night together that he was under zero obligation to stick around, a part of her had wondered how he could stay away when the chemistry between them had been amazing. Well, for her it had been. Was there a chance that Quinton always worked that kind of magic with women? She'd assumed that it was because there'd been a connection between them. But with her limited—and crappy—past experiences, what did she know?

Cranking on the truck engine, she carefully but deliberately pulled out of the Cyclone Shack's parking lot, unwilling to spend any more time missing him. Each day that she'd worked at the bar after the storm, she'd held her breath every time the door opened to admit a new customer. Every. Single. Time.

And in each instance, she'd been disappointed that the newcomer hadn't been Quinton. It had been a pathetic display of feelings for a man who hadn't given their night half as much thought as she had. She hammered on the gas as she hit the main road, very ready to let the sea take her mind off her problems. She'd asked a neighbor to care for her pets, and she'd nailed up heavy plastic sheets over the places on the house that were still missing some siding. She'd covered her bases. With any luck, maybe Quinton would be far from Dutch Harbor by the time she returned home.

Unfortunately, the thought gave her no comfort.

Four days into his self-imposed hotel room isolation, Quinton finally had McKenna's cyber harasser nailed.

With the damning evidence in hand to share a hard copy with McKenna, Quinton drove to the Cyclone Shack after four interminable days without seeing her. He'd told himself that the time spent apart would help cool the fire between them, and it was satisfying as hell to have the evidence needed to prosecute the bastard who had betrayed her trust.

Although, as he steered the rental SUV onto the road that led to the Cyclone Shack, he couldn't deny a big part of his satisfaction in tracing the origin of that original video upload had been that it meant he could see McKenna again.

Because of course she deserved to know.

He'd been outraged on her behalf that her privacy had

been invaded that way, so he could only imagine how hurt she'd been to discover what her ex had done. Quinton hadn't made any more progress on tracking Clayton these last few days, but at least he'd done this for McKenna.

Now, pulling into the empty parking lot of the Cyclone Shack, he wondered if she was even here. Normally, the lot was at least half full by midafternoon. Today, there wasn't a single vehicle. Not even her truck in its normal spot far off to one side.

Was she ill? Guilt nipped at him for not checking in with her these last days. Her asthma could have returned. Or she could have fallen off the ladder trying to replace that siding on her own. His mind whirred through a hundred possibilities in an instant, making a lie of all his attempts to put distance between them.

He was about to drive around to the back of the building to see if her truck was parked there when he noticed a white piece of paper taped over the window beside the front door. After shoving the SUV into Park, he stepped out onto the pavement and charged toward the building.

Closing the gap between him and the note, he could make out crisp, bold handwriting in black marker.

Closed For Two Weeks.

His stomach dropped as he absorbed the import of the words while the bottom edge of the white paper curled in the breeze. Quinton smoothed the paper with one hand to better read the rest. Beneath the headline, in a lighter hand, McKenna had written, "Took a group of stranded birders to Attu when another tour guide's boat sustained storm damage. Your first drink is on me when I return and sorry for the inconvenience."

Her name was signed in a feminine scrawl beneath.

Not that there could have been any doubt who'd penned it. But what date had she pinned the note there? Had she just left this morning? Or four days ago?

Leaning against the side of the building, he berated himself all over again for not staying in touch. Memories of the way they'd parted circled through his head now, chastising him for the way he'd retreated. They'd shared an incredible night together, yet he'd withdrawn the moment reality had set in the next morning. Was it any wonder she'd jumped at the chance to leave town for a couple of weeks? Because he had to wonder if her motivation for leaving had really been to help a fellow tour guide.

Or, more likely, had McKenna been very ready to head anywhere to escape him?

Withdrawing his cell phone from the back pocket of his jeans, he tapped out a message to her and hit Send, knowing the chances were slim to none that she'd respond.

Attu was the westernmost Aleutian Island on the other side of the International Date Line. He'd studied enough maps of the area the day he'd been stuck in Anchorage waiting to fly out here. No doubt cell coverage on her boat would be intermittent at best.

Then again, she could just as easily be ignoring him after the way he'd left her place.

Damn it.

Turning on his boot heel, he peered into the window beside the front door, taking in the darkened bar where McKenna normally served up drinks and fish tales. He didn't know what he was hoping to find. Traces of her, maybe. The sense of loss kicking through him now told him how deeply she'd gotten under his skin.

While the wind blew around him, still rattling the note she'd taped up, Quinton's gaze took in the neatly arranged liquor bottles behind the bar. A few fishing nets hanging from the ceiling for decor. The digital register. Behind that, the bulletin board crammed full of local ads and a few photos from McKenna's trips.

He'd seen them all before from the hours he'd spend seated in his usual evening spot. Well, all except one.

A postcard hung in the bottom corner of the board, in a place almost hidden behind the bar. Quinton held a hand up to shade his eyes so he could see into the glass better, curious about the new addition.

Curious about McKenna.

The card featured an image of a gray wolf padding through the snow. Nothing unusual. Yet something about it made him wish he could take a better look at it, if only because it hadn't been there before.

Quinton knew better than to think the card was from Clayton. McKenna guarded her stepbrother's secrets so thoroughly, she wouldn't make a mistake like that. Still Quinton couldn't shake the sense that the image had some relation to his half brother.

Or else he was seeing connections that weren't there because he hadn't come across a single lead on Clay's location.

Turning away from the Cyclone Shack in disgust with himself, Quinton knew he'd have plenty of time to dig deeper in his search for Clay. Because there was no doubt in Quinton's mind that he wasn't going anywhere for the next two weeks.

Eight

Aboard the *Un-Reel* two weeks later, McKenna breathed a sigh of relief to be safely docked back in Dutch Harbor.

Home at last.

Flipping off the navigation lights as she killed the power to the motor, she thanked the dockhands who'd helped her secure the vessel as twilight had turned to dark. The pair hustled off to help another latecomer to their boat slip, a pleasure watercraft based out of Vancouver that she'd spotted two other times on her trip to Attu and back.

Bone weary, she scarcely had the energy to finish her checklist of duties to secure the Hewescraft for the night, but she followed the steps mechanically, eager to return home. Her thirteen-day planned venture had been delayed overnight for weather, keeping her away even longer than scheduled. At least she was alone now after seeing the birding group safely back to Adak Island to catch their flights to Anchorage. The trawler yacht and her crew had set anchor there as well, so McKenna had been on her own to continue the rest of the way to Dutch Harbor.

After the two weeks surrounded by other people, she didn't mind being by herself again. Although, as she locked the cabin door behind her for the night, she couldn't help but recall the last time she'd pulled up to the same boat slip, Quinton had been there waiting for her.

Quinton.

Her fingers paused in the middle of locking the hatch where she kept spare life vests, thoughts of him rolling over her like a rogue wave. Memories of their last encounter were never far from her mind during the trip. Especially during the latter half of the journey when a missed period had sent her into a panic. At the westernmost end of the Aleutian Islands, there had been no place to run into a convenience store for Plan B birth control since Attu was uninhabited.

The possibility that she could even now be carrying Quinton's child staggered her. By the time she got back to Adak Island, the window for Plan B effectiveness had passed and the thought of buying a pregnancy test was too daunting. She'd thought they had been careful that night they'd been together. So maybe the stress of the storm and carrying Clay's secrets around had simply made her period late.

Thinking of her brother reminded her she hadn't spoken to him in weeks. The number for his satellite phone had shown up in a missed call recently, but the spotty tower coverage on her trip hadn't allowed her to even message him back. Sinking to one of the built-in benches that circled the stern of the *Un-Reel*, she withdrew her cell from the waterproof waist pack she kept it in while on the water. The night air was cool and damp against her face as she dialed a number she knew from memory. The wind—about sixteen miles an hour all day according to the anemometer gauge on her display panel—blew strands of hair free from a ponytail she'd already reworked a few times.

The number rang twice before a familiar masculine voice sounded on the other end. Her stepbrother.

"McKenna." Her name rushed from him like a gusty sigh. "I've been worried about you ever since the storm. Is everything okay?"

A burst of love for Clayton made her eyes burn. There wasn't another soul in the world who would be concerned if something happened to her, since her father didn't even bother to keep track of her.

Although, at least for the duration of the storm, Quinton had worried about her too. She tamped down the thoughts of him that would only derail her when she wanted to focus on Clay.

"Everything is fine. Sorry I didn't check in sooner." She leaned a shoulder against the built-in refrigerator unit that only saw use on fishing trips. She drew her feet up onto the bench to make herself more comfortable. Around her, a few of the other vessels had their interior lights on, as some of the folks docking for the night weren't locals and would bed down aboard their crafts. The smatter of lighted crafts made the harbor feel sort of homey. In fact, she felt a far deeper kinship with these Alaskan adventurers who could tough out any storm than she ever had with the neighbors she'd had back in San Francisco. "High winds took off some siding on the house, but other than that, damage was minimal. Both the boat and the bar were untouched."

Thank goodness. After all Clayton had done for her when her life went off the rails, giving her a safe place to land, she couldn't bear the idea of his property coming to harm on her watch.

"Screw the boat and the bar, Kenna," he scolded, using his old nickname for her. His breath huffed heavily and she could hear intermittent crunching noises that made her guess he walked through deep snow. "I was worried about you. For all I knew, you could have been out on the water when the worst of it hit."

She smiled at his tender concern for her while her gaze wandered to a young family playing cards at a table inside their cabin cruiser in a slip across from hers. Two little girls and an older boy. The warm tableau was a far cry from her conversation with her brother—her on an open deck in the wind, on the phone with a sibling deep in the Alaskan Interior—but the sense of family was the same. And she was deeply grateful for it.

If she really was carrying Quinton's child, she would need the emotional support of family more than ever. But she wouldn't think about that now. Not until she knew for certain.

"Thankfully, I was safely back at home during the thick of the bad weather." She'd been oblivious to most of it, in fact, taking shelter in Quinton's arms and wondering if she'd ever again feel as good as he made her feel.

If only it hadn't ended with his rapid retreat the next morning.

"So what kept you from returning my call? Is everything else all right?"

Loaded question. Her hand went to her belly even though she had no intention of sharing news of a pregnancy she hadn't even confirmed yet. But she couldn't hold back the other news from Clay. It would be disloyal to the person who'd been her rock when she'd arrived in Unalaska humiliated and furious about the video and all the ways it had torpedoed her life. She'd lost her concierge job at a ritzy hotel after her boss had heard about the video, claiming McKenna had become a distraction to the other employees. She'd lost friends over the stupid thing too.

"Your brother is in town," she confided in a low voice, even though there were no people around. Darkness had fallen full over the harbor, but the dock lights allowed her to see there was no one visible on the closest wharf. "Looking for you."

For a moment, he didn't speak. The crunching noises halted on his end of the call, though his breath continued to come heavily. "Which one?"

"Quinton." She knew there were two others—Levi, who was close in age to Clay, and Gavin, the youngest. But she'd never met them, her sense of the Kingsley family limited to what Clay had told her and her own impressions of Quinton. "He showed up at the Cyclone Shack since that's the last good information he had regarding your location."

"Ah damn. It would have to be Quint, wouldn't it?" Clay let out a harsh laugh.

A sense of warning prickled over her skin at his tone. She straightened in her seat and then stood, scooping up her keys. "What do you mean by that?"

"I mean it's only a matter of time before he finds me," he said dryly. His steps had resumed. Faster now.

The conversation made her edgy. She paced the open deck, knowing Clayton had his reasons for wanting to avoid his family, but she'd never been clear on why. "Why would you think that? He'll never find out from me."

An ache went through her at the thought of being disloyal to him. Had she betrayed his trust by sleeping with Quinton?

"Of course he won't," Clay said so quickly that she knew he must mean it. "I know you'd never do anything to give me away. But Quinton is—I don't know what you'd call him. A technology savant? The guy could probably hack a bank if he wanted to, so if he's set his mind to finding me…"

Not finishing the thought, Clay cursed instead.

Guilt weighed heavily on her.

She bit her lip, unable to squelch the memory of Quinton's kindnesses to her. His promise to help her prosecute her bastard ex. "Would that really be so terrible?"

She understood why he'd hated his father. But why would he resent his siblings so deeply that he wanted nothing to do with any of them?

"For me? Right now? Yeah, it really would be."

Anxiety made her shoulders tense. "Is there anything I can do?"

"Yes. Don't talk to him. And I'm going to ditch this phone, so it might be a week or so before I can call again."

Her nerves tightened more at the thought of seeing Quinton again. Maybe he wouldn't want to talk to her anyhow. But given the news that she might have to share once she picked up a pregnancy test…

"But Clay—"

"Kenna, I've got to get on top of this," he said quickly, no room for interruption. "Thanks for the heads-up and I'll call as soon as I can."

A moment later, the call disconnected.

Leaving McKenna worried and alone on the deck of the *Un-Reel,* an uneasy feeling stirring faster than any wind. She retrieved her rucksack and dumped her keys into it, knowing she needed to pick up a pregnancy kit before she went home, no matter how weary she felt. But just as she was stepping off the deck and onto the dock, the sound of footsteps echoed in the darkness before a familiar tall form stepped beneath one of the pier lights.

Her mouth went dry as Quinton came into view a few yards away, walking toward her.

"Hello, McKenna."

His voice stole her breath, the sound reminding her of all the times he'd whispered or shouted her name during the unforgettable night they'd shared. A shiver tripped through her.

And for the first time in her life, she knew she wouldn't be able to follow through on something her stepbrother had asked of her.

She couldn't *not* talk to Quinton.

Then again, until her suspicions about a pregnancy were confirmed one way or another, she didn't have any intention of broaching the subject that was very much on her mind.

So she pasted on her best placid smile and told herself to play it cool. After all, he *did* practically leave tracks in his rush to leave her the day after the storm.

"Hi yourself, Cowboy." She didn't bother slowing

down to speak to him though, no matter how much she'd missed him.

No matter how much she'd ached for him during the long two weeks and three days apart.

Pointing her feet toward the parking lot, she kept right on walking.

Standing under the buzzing fluorescent streetlamp at the end of the quay, Quinton supposed he shouldn't be surprised at the decidedly lackluster reception from McKenna.

He'd been the one to put the brakes on their relationship after the night they'd spent together, so maybe it was no wonder that she breezed right past him after two and a half weeks apart. Was there a chance she didn't feel the same staggering draw between them that rocked him back on his heels even now? Breathing in the salty damp air and hoping for a hint of her scent after she'd walked past, Quinton wanted her so badly it hurt.

Grinding his teeth against a surge of possessiveness that he'd never experienced for any other woman, he told himself to pull it together. Because there was a whole lot that remained unresolved between them no matter how she felt about him now.

"McKenna, please wait." He caught up to her in a few steps, dodging a couple of teens taking photos of themselves holding huge crabs from their day's catch.

Shifting a black rucksack on her shoulder, she slowed her step as she turned toward him. In dark jeans and a thick gray fisherman's sweater that didn't hide her curves, she was windblown, makeup free, and drop-dead gorgeous. Her thick auburn hair had been braided with a bright pink ribbon, the silky fabric weaving in and out of the plaits.

"I'm surprised to see you here." Her face was half in shadow as they moved away from the last streetlamp and headed toward the parking area. But her blue eyes were shrewd, missing nothing as they ran over him. "I had the sense you would be leaving town when we last spoke."

A light mist of rain began to fall as he recalled the uncomfortable conversation the morning after the blackout. He'd never said he was leaving Dutch Harbor in so many words, but he could understand why she'd thought as much given his behavior. He'd been quick to assure her he would still send her the information she needed to prosecute her cyber harasser, hadn't he? No wonder she'd assumed he wouldn't be in her life by the time she came back to town.

"I have too much unfinished business here to think of leaving yet." He halted as they reached her truck, not sure where to begin with all he wanted to tell her. All he wanted to ask. But he wouldn't launch into any of those topics now, when the soft mist of rain made a hazy curtain between them. "I stopped by the harbor last night, but the dockmaster told me you'd been held up a day because of a weather delay."

He'd been worried. Even knowing she was strong and capable as hell. The more time he spent around Unalaska and the people who carved out lives in the Aleutian Islands, the more respect he had for this place where the Pacific met the Bering Sea.

Just seeing her now, safe and whole, made him want to kiss her. Hold her. Savor the fact that she had returned to him unharmed. He wished he had that right, but he understood he'd been the one to sever the brief bond they'd experienced together.

"We waited out the bad weather on shore." Her words were clipped as she pulled a key ring out of her rucksack and unlocked the truck cab. "The tour groups know that's a risk they run with outings up here. I won't endanger anyone for the sake of a schedule."

A rumble of thunder underscored her words and reminded him that this wasn't the best time or place for a conversation.

"I'm relieved to hear it. I won't keep you when you must be tired after your trip." By the gold glow from the dome light, he could see violet shadows beneath her eyes he hadn't noticed before. From exhaustion? Stress? He hoped that he hadn't been the cause of any worries on her part. "But we need to speak. Would you let me take you to dinner Friday?"

Something in her manner made him think she was going to refuse him. The way she moved her shoulders, perhaps, or appeared ready to shake her head as if to say no. But then she seemed to stop herself. Biting her lip, she hesitated for a moment before nodding.

"We probably should talk," she agreed finally, her chin notching higher. "I should be able to get someone else to cover for me at the bar on Friday."

The rush of pleasure he felt at her agreement seemed out of proportion for the news he wanted to share. To tell her what he'd learned about her harasser and to reveal his next steps for finding Clayton, which would inevitably take him away from Dutch Harbor. Yet, just knowing they would have time alone together sent a ripple of heat through his body hot enough to make the falling rain steam right off him.

"In that case, I'll pick you up at seven." His heart pounded faster at the prospect of being with her.

How would he go back to their former boundaries with one another now that he knew what it felt like to hold her? He fisted his fingers and shoved them in the pockets of his jacket to keep from reaching for her. The need to tug her against him and kiss her burned brighter with each passing moment.

If he thought McKenna might cave to the same hungers as him, however, he couldn't have been more wrong. She stepped up onto the running board of her pickup and slid into the driver's seat. He had the urge to plant himself in the vee of the open door, to hold it open and stand close to her until she acknowledged she felt the same fire in her blood that ran in his. A fire that had only grown the longer she'd stayed away.

Instead, he watched her turn the key in the ignition and flip the switch for the heater. Giving him the silent treatment? Well, he could fix that at least.

"Besides the weather, how was your trip?" he asked, genuinely curious. He'd read more about the kinds of tours she led. Had spent some time envisioning her out there on the open sea.

For the first time since she'd stepped off of the boat onto the pier, he saw her features soften. An almost-smile curving her lips.

"I spent hours watching seabirds screaming and circling islands where no human ever walks." Her eyes took on a distant look as if she was still hundreds of miles away. "I saw whales playing in the fog. And when I wasn't tracking marine life, I was darting around islands with smoking fumaroles and glacier-covered volcanoes." She swiped the sleeve of her sweater across her forehead to dry the rain from her skin. "It's nice to escape our so-called civilized society sometimes."

His stomach cramped at the idea that the world had ever given this woman a reason to want to escape in the first place. Tenderness toward her caught him off guard, making his throat burn.

"I'm glad you had that experience." He knew he should let her leave. She had a life and home to return to, none of which involved him. "It sounds incredible."

"I would have never even known that world existed if not for Clay." She turned a switch on the dash that cranked the heater fan to a higher speed.

He could feel the still-cold blast of air from the closest vent as he told himself to back away.

"He's been a good brother to you," Quinton agreed carefully, wishing he'd had the chance to know him better during those infrequent weeks Clay had spent at Kingsland Ranch. No doubt he'd failed Clay then. And he didn't even want to think about how much he'd violated the bounds of brotherhood by touching McKenna in the first place. "See you Friday."

Stepping back, Quinton shut the driver's side door for her so she could head home for the night. As he watched her taillights blur in the rain that started coming down harder, Quinton knew he needed a strategy for their date night.

Because no matter how much he still wanted her, he couldn't afford to remain in Unalaska any longer. He owed it to Clayton to hand over his portion of the Kingsley inheritance. Quinton wouldn't allow anything to stop him from performing the task that would be his last official act as part of the Kingsley family.

Once he'd given his own portion of the family holdings to Clayton, Quinton wouldn't have any reason to return to Kingsland Ranch. He'd be free of the place forever so he could return to his home in Sunnyvale, California, where he could run his tech business away from the complicated family ties that had strangled him for years.

It had been his goal to escape Kingsland ever since his mother died.

So there was no good reason why it seemed like an empty one now as McKenna's red taillights slowly faded out of sight.

Nine

Squinting one eye, McKenna stared in her bathroom mirror, her hand trembling a little as she brushed on mascara for her date with Quinton.

Frowning at the telltale sign of her agitation, she jammed the makeup wand back into the tube and told herself to get a grip. She'd survived the abject mortification of having her naked body broadcast to the world on the internet without her permission. Surely she could survive...

Motherhood?

Agitation redoubled at the memory of those two pink lines on each of the three pregnancy tests she'd taken since returning from the Attu trip. How could she possibly be expecting a child after a single sexual encounter with the first man to turn her head in a year and a half? And they'd used protection. Could the universe honestly have that sense of humor?

She tipped her forehead to the cool glass of the mirror and thunked it gently against the reflective surface. "McKenna. McKenna. McKenna."

Doubting the process was drumming any sense into her, she straightened and peered back at her own image. She'd cleaned up well after the last few days of angst over her situation. She'd found a long-forgotten little black dress in her closet for the evening with Quinton, and the fabric hugged her curves without being too overt. The cut was simple but flattering, with long sleeves and ending just above her knee. A swath of fine black merino wool wrapped around the middle and tied at the back, a small feminine detail that gave the dress interest. She hadn't fashioned a bow but had made a simple knot so the two ends hung long behind her.

With the addition of diamond earrings—a gift from Clayton for her twenty-first birthday—she looked almost like the woman she'd been before the Great Flight into Alaska to escape the world's judgment. Almost. Because that woman was gone forever.

The McKenna staring back at her now was a ghost of that naive girl.

Scratch that. She wasn't a ghost. But a stronger iteration. McKenna 2.0.

Soon to be a mother.

She was saved from falling down another spiral of worry by Loki's bark. At her feet, her two pets were seated on either side of her while she finished getting ready for her outing. Glancing down at them, McKenna gave the furry pup a scratch on the head to soothe him, knowing the cat had a knack for winding him up.

Stroking the Havanese's silky fur had the added benefit of calming her nerves a little too. Or at least it did until the doorbell rang and Loki darted away from her to run down the stairs, yapping excitedly to greet a guest.

Quinton.

She met her own worried eyes in the mirror one last time before turning on her heel and heading for the stairs. Her high-heeled black boots tapped along the tile as she wondered how on earth she was going to tell him about the pregnancy. She had no game plan for tonight, other than a deal with herself that she would spill the news before she landed back on her doorstep.

And if the thought of sharing the news with Quinton seemed daunting, how would she ever tell Clayton? He hadn't wanted to ever see any of his brothers again and had gone to great lengths to keep his whereabouts a secret. Yet this news would inevitably bring Clay and Quinton together.

Wouldn't it? Her heart ached at the thought of hurting her brother.

Pausing on the waterproof front mat to let out a breath, McKenna braced herself to see her date. The father of her child.

She yanked open the door with more force than she intended, causing Quinton's brown eyes to widen slightly as Loki barked a greeting. An amused smile played about the corners of Quinton's lips. He stood on the front step in a dark suit and gray overcoat, a bouquet of dark purple orchids and calla lilies in his hands.

"I hope that greeting means you've been looking forward to seeing me." He extended the bouquet as his gaze slid over her. "You look beautiful, McKenna."

Her throat went dry as his eyes locked with hers. She hadn't been prepared for romantic gestures like flowers and compliments. Hadn't he been ready to bolt after the blackout?

Yet her heart rate responded favorably to his attention, her traitorous body remembering how much she liked his focus on her. The last time he'd been here, they'd ended up naked in front of the fireplace, wringing pleasure from one another as easily as if they'd been lovers for years.

"Thank you." Her words rasped a little, her emotions all over the place as she took the blooms from him, her fingers brushing his warm hands. Desire stirred inside her, quickening her pulse still more. "Please come on in while I find something to put them in." Then, bending toward her dog, she made sure to include him in the invitation since his training had taken a step back while she'd been out of town for two weeks. "Loki, come."

Happily, her pet followed her into the farmhouse-style kitchen while Quinton took off his coat and left his shoes by the door. She appreciated his thoughtfulness since the outdoors were perpetually damp these last few days.

Although something about having him pad across the plank flooring in his socks felt intimate. Like he belonged here.

She shook off the thought and calmed her nerves with routine.

While she gave Loki a treat for his good behavior and then found a vase for the bouquet, Quinton stood near the entrance, his attention fixed on the photos in the hallway.

For a moment she stiffened, recalling that she'd brought home the postcard that Clayton had sent to the bar so she could enjoy looking at it here. Clay hadn't written on it or anything. But there was a postmark on it that she didn't want Quinton to see.

Her heart pounded hard as she watched him, wondering if he'd noticed the card with a picture of a wolf. The height and breadth of Quinton seemed to fill the room even when he moved around the perimeter.

But he walked right past the postcard with the wolf. Relief whooshed through her.

"I noticed these the day of the blackout but didn't get a chance to ask you about them," Quinton mused aloud, looking every inch the successful tech CEO that he was in his bespoke suit. He tapped a knuckle against an image of her and Clay on the *Un-Reel*, a massive Chinook salmon in her hands. "Have you always had an interest in fishing? Or is that something you took up once you moved here?"

Her fingers faltered on the kraft paper around the flowers. "I've fished since I was a little girl," she admitted slowly, thinking back to spring mornings on Cedar River with her dad while she unwrapped the arrangement of exotic purple flowers. "My father taught me at a young age. He's an alcoholic, and we don't speak anymore. But our time on the water together was always fun. It gave me at least one happy memory of him."

Quinton turned around to face her, walking deeper into the kitchen. Freya circled his feet, warming to him with unusual speed. But then, both of her pets had spent some time with him during the storm. Maybe they'd grown attached to him then.

The same way she had.

"So your father married Clay's mother?" Quinton asked as he scooped up the cat to pet her, winning bonus points in McKenna's book for not minding a little fur on his sleeve.

The calico, who normally kept to herself around strangers, purred contentedly to have her face scratched.

"That's right. When I was twelve, my mother died in a hunting accident." McKenna had spent a long time trying to come to terms with her senseless death. "My father wasn't around much for me, so to his credit, he quickly married a woman more capable of raising a child than he was."

"I'm so sorry about your mom," Quinton said quietly, setting down the cat as he reached McKenna's side. "It's a terrible thing to lose a parent so young."

She glanced up at him while positioning the stems in a heavy stoneware vase, recalling that he understood all too well what it was like after the way his mother had died. "It was awful. Mom had gone out hunting with her brother and his gun went off accidentally."

McKenna understood rationally that the incident hadn't been intentional in any way, but she'd never been able to fully forgive her uncle for his carelessness either. To this day, she didn't have anything to do with her mother's family.

Not that they'd ever tried to reach out to her either. Her maternal grandparents had never liked McKenna's father.

"That must have been terrible to go through." Quinton's hand palmed the middle of her back between her shoulder blades. A touch of compassion that really did comfort her. The urge to lean into him was so strong she had to turn away from him in order to fight the impulse.

She folded the kraft paper to fit it into a recycle bin under the sink.

"Yes, but the bright light to come out of a horrible year was Dena Reynolds." McKenna smiled, remembering her stepmom's relentless good humor. Her refusal to let life get her down no matter what was thrown her way. "She was one of the best people I've ever known. Even after she and my father split, she made sure I understood that I always had a home with her."

That she was loved and wanted. In the end, that kind of selfless love had been a great gift. One that McKenna would pass on to her own child, no matter the circumstances of this baby's birth.

It was the first thing she knew for certain about her pregnancy. Her child would always feel loved.

Her hand went involuntarily to her flat belly, as if her touch could convey that love already. She and Quinton had both maneuvered complicated blended-family dynamics growing up. Would they be able to navigate those waters effectively to help their child feel secure? McKenna blinked through a swell of raw emotion, hoping she could keep it together long enough to get through this date.

To share the news with Quinton in a way that would free him from any obligation toward her or this baby.

"Are you feeling all right?" Quinton asked a moment later, making her realize that she'd been lost in thought.

Her hand still on her abdomen.

She relaxed it now and pasted on a smile, determined

to get through the evening. They had a lot to discuss even before she got to revealing her secret.

"I feel fine." Physically, at least. "I'm ready to go whenever you are."

Quinton escorted McKenna down the Dutch Harbor pier twenty minutes later, enjoying her reaction to his surprise choice for a dining experience.

They strolled together on the opposite end of the harbor from where she moored the *Un-Reel*. They'd bypassed the commercial fishing boats to access the larger pier used for cruise vessels. One of which was docked overnight during an extended itinerary that included stops in Australia and Asia. Facts he knew after thoroughly researching options for their date night.

The ship in question loomed large in front of them now, a 550-foot craft with a hull painted navy blue, sleek and imposing. There were no passengers milling about the boat at the moment, since it had docked earlier that day, but a side entrance was still staffed by two employees to monitor anyone who came aboard. The pair sat on high stools beneath a small canopy that protected them from the misty rain in the air.

"Um, should I be worried that we're boarding a cruise ship?" McKenna asked, hugging her black windproof jacket more tightly around her as a damp squall blew around them.

She looked stunning tonight in her simple black dress that showed off a bombshell figure normally hidden under layers of clothes. And she'd left her long copper hair to hang in waves that hugged her shoulders. The auburn mass was tucked under a wide hood now because of the weather, but he looked forward to seeing it again once they were seated inside.

"No need to worry." He greeted the ship's representative who walked down the temporary gangplank to meet them. Handing over the paperwork he'd prepared in advance, Quinton turned back to McKenna while the crew member reviewed it. "We're only here for a meal and we'll be back home long before the ship departs."

Long enough for him to tell her what he'd learned about her cyber harasser and to let her know he was leaving Dutch Harbor for good. He looked forward to the former and dreaded the latter. Probably because he couldn't imagine never being with her again. Yet he wanted to give her one night that wasn't tainted with stress about the blackout. One night to remind her that she didn't need to hide out in Alaska just because of one jerkoff in her past. She was a good woman who deserved to be treated well.

Now, the liveried cruise ambassador passed the paperwork back to Quinton and held out an arm to usher them inside the open doors to the interior of the ship. "Very good, sir. The restaurant is on the fifth deck if you take the elevators straight ahead."

"Thanks very much." Quinton tucked the papers into the breast pocket of his jacket before settling his hand on the small of McKenna's back to guide her inside ahead of him.

"We can dine on board a cruise ship even though we're not passengers?" She looked back at him suspiciously, her blue eyes narrowed.

Even though the question was light and playful, Quinton suspected that there was a small amount of worry and distrust beneath it. He had the sense that she wasn't a woman who would ever give her trust again to anyone who hadn't worked damned hard to earn it. A reminder that Quinton could never be a good choice for her considering the scars his upbringing had left.

"I'm friends with the chef," he told her simply, steering her into the first empty elevator cabin and pressing the button to take them to the fifth deck. It hadn't been easy to arrange, but it helped that his company had done some time-sensitive IT work for the cruise line. "And they like to call this an expedition ship, by the way. Less emphasis on cruising and more on the on-shore adventures."

"I see," she mused, swiping off her hood now that they were indoors. "I can hardly begrudge tourists access to the Aleutians since I earn half my living from guiding groups myself. But selfishly, I hope this part of the world never becomes overrun with visitors."

"With this weather? I doubt it," he said as the elevator doors opened outside of a softly illuminated dining room. "For tonight, I hoped you might enjoy the kind of creature comforts you give up by living far from the mainland."

The scents of spices and roasted meats mingled in a savory aroma while uniformed staff moved among the diners. Real white candles burned on every table beneath clear glass hurricane shades.

"Oh wow," she murmured as she took in the elegant space. A bank of windows overlooked the darkened harbor on the far end of the room while the back of the restaurant was ringed with yellow-and-gold-lighted wall tiles. "This place is gorgeous."

Pleasure filled him at this small approval.

"Apparently, it is the only Michelin-rated restaurant in Alaska right now." He would have hired a chopper to fly them into Anchorage if there'd been a better option there. "I hope you brought an appetite."

A wry smile curved her lips that he couldn't quite read. "I'm definitely hungry."

An hour later, they were midway through a perfect evening. He'd gotten to see another side of McKenna, learning about her degree in hospitality and her brief stint as a concierge in San Francisco. He knew the hotel where she'd been employed, an excellent establishment that he wouldn't frequent again unless they did something about the small-minded supervisor who'd fired her when she'd been the victim of someone else's malice.

But the conversation had provided a natural segue for him to share everything he'd uncovered about the origin source of footage that had caused untold harm. He'd already emailed the information so she had digital files to provide the authorities, but tonight he'd explained her possible next steps over the most perfect lobster thermidor he'd ever eaten.

McKenna had ordered the same since it came recommended by the chef, though she'd refrained from the wine that would have been an incredible pairing with the dish. He might have thought the instinct was born out of being the daughter of an alcoholic, but he recalled she'd had a beer the night the last time they'd gone out.

Not that it mattered. Quinton was enjoying the evening far more than he ought to, considering he needed to tell her that he would be leaving town soon. He delayed saying anything about it since they seemed to have reached an agreeable impasse tonight, where they simply relished the time together without confronting the deeper issues.

That she wouldn't tell him anything about Clayton.

And the fact that he'd betrayed Clay by sleeping with his half brother's stepsister.

A thought that threatened to wreck an incredible evening with a woman he still desired more than anyone he'd ever met. She told him stories about fighting hundred-pound fish as easily as she shared anecdotes from the time she was a concierge and found ways to fulfill special guest requests—like filling a guest's hot tub full of white rose petals or importing a guest's favorite mustard, which was only made by hand in small batches in the south of France.

While Quinton was busy trying to envision the McKenna he knew standing behind the concierge desk of a metropolitan city hotel, indulging demanding guests, their waiter returned.

"May I bring you dessert?" the server asked while discreetly using a silver table crumber to remove a few bits of bread from the white linen cloth. "We have a Meyer lemon meringue tart that is not to be missed, but I'm also happy to bring you a menu if you'd like to review all of the options."

Quinton looked to McKenna, but she shook her head. "I couldn't eat another bite. Everything was fantastic."

His gaze stuck on her for a long moment after he asked the waiter to bring the bill. He tried to pinpoint what made her look so lovely tonight. Her color was high, her beauty so fresh she glowed. Perhaps her long trip out to Attu had been good for her.

Or maybe he was just making excuses for not telling her he needed to leave Dutch Harbor. He already had a flight booked for Sunday.

But how could he get on the flight when he couldn't even envision how to leave her alone once he dropped her off at her place tonight? The need to kiss her again was a hunger their meal hadn't begun to sate.

When McKenna stood after he'd settled the bill, she allowed him to help her on with her jacket. Quinton took a moment longer than necessary, sliding his hand beneath her hair so he didn't trap it under the coat. He thought he heard her intake of breath. A sharp inhale.

But then she cleared her throat and turned to face him. "The dinner was extraordinary. Thank you so much."

"I'm glad you enjoyed it. I will confess I worked hard to find something special that you probably hadn't done before." Once more, he allowed himself to touch her waist briefly, just enough to escort her toward the exit.

His fingers tingled with the need to touch more.

"I definitely haven't tried my luck to board a cruise ship while it was in port," she said dryly. "Leave it to a Kingsley to think of something so decadent."

He wondered if she viewed him as entitled, like one of the guests she used to indulge as a concierge. But almost immediately, she shook her head and halted her step, turning to look back at him.

"I'm sorry. That came out wrong. The evening was special and I appreciated it. I only meant to say that people around here wouldn't think to do something like that. To go to great lengths to show a date something unique."

It surprised him that her blue eyes appeared sincerely worried that she'd offended him. Which was a far cry from her usual attempts to keep him at arm's length.

The urge to cover her lips then and there was almost more than he could tamp down. Instead, he curved his palm around her hip in a gesture more possessive than he'd allowed himself all evening.

"I'm glad you enjoyed it," he told her sincerely, his voice going deeper at the thought of being with her again.

Because he couldn't deny that's what he wanted more than anything tonight. Not to worry about telling her he was leaving. He really just wanted the chance to experience that incredible chemistry between them one last time.

While he debated if it would be a mistake to make the most of their last hours together, McKenna removed all doubt about what she wanted by turning into him and placing a hand on his chest.

"Come home with me, Quinton."

Ten

McKenna refused to question her passionate instincts as they drove toward her house after dinner.

Shifting restlessly in the leather passenger seat of the luxury SUV, she wanted Quinton with a hunger unlike anything she'd ever felt before. She'd thought she'd known attraction to other men in the past, but those experiences didn't even compare to the desire that crawled all over her skin tonight. The need had been building all the days they'd spent apart. Then, his obvious efforts to provide a truly memorable evening for her had gone beyond the physical. He'd touched her heart.

Not only had he devoted hours of his time and talents to tracking the misdeeds of her bastard ex-boyfriend, but Quinton had also provided evidence the police would need to bring charges. All of which he'd shared during an incredible evening out.

Seated across from him over a meal cooked by a world-renowned chef, McKenna had felt special. As though she mattered.

Was it foolish of her to be swayed by that kind of attentiveness? Perhaps the gesture that had felt so unique to her was commonplace enough for him. No doubt Quinton Kingsley could afford to dine at exclusive gourmet establishments every night if he so chose. But McKenna wanted to believe there'd been more to the date than just a Kingsley using his fortune to dazzle a woman of far lesser means.

Quinton had earnestly tried to give her a special shared memory. Something she would keep with her long after he left Dutch Harbor.

And he *was* leaving Unalaska soon. His inevitable departure came through in every word and action since he'd arrived on her front step. Tonight was obviously a goodbye that he meant to do well.

The thought caused a pang in her heart as they cruised the dark and windy road toward her house, a light rain continuing to mist the windshield. There would be an emptiness inside her once he left. Not just because she would miss him, but also because she understood that if it wasn't for the baby she carried, she would almost certainly never see him again. She would never know if he stuck around because he craved more time with *her*. Was she delaying telling him that she was pregnant because she wished to see how the evening would play out before revealing the news that would change everything between them forever?

Maybe that was a part of it. Was it wrong to want some part of him that was just for her and not because he felt duty bound to their child? But she wouldn't think about that now when they still had a whole night ahead.

By the time he steered the SUV into the driveway in front of her house, she was so keyed up she fumbled to get the seat belt unfastened, her hands awkward. After switching off the engine, Quinton reached across the center console to help her.

"I can get it for you." His voice rumbled low and deep in her ear as he inserted a finger between her hip and the lap belt.

Her skin tingled under her dress where his knuckles grazed her. Longing pooled low in her belly. Her breath came in shallow pants. But this wasn't anything like the asthma attack.

Her breath had simply been stolen by this enigmatic, sexy man who'd been a stranger to her just a few weeks before.

"Thank you," she murmured distractedly, her attention snagged by the smoking look in his eyes as their gazes collided.

Her heart raced when his focus shifted lower, settling on her lips. He dragged the pad of his thumb across the lower one, a touch that set her on fire.

"Do you have any idea how much I thought about this mouth while you were away for two long weeks?" The rough edge in his voice thrilled her as much as his words.

Did the desire that consumed her plague him too?

"No, but I sure hope you came up with some ideas about what to do with it during that time," she challenged him, very ready to act on the needs bottled up for too long.

Tonight might be the last opportunity they ever had

to be together this way. And she couldn't bear for him to walk away without touching her again. Without experiencing the thrill only he could deliver.

"I've got no lack of ideas," he promised, tipping her face up toward his so that his breath huffed along her lips when he spoke. "Starting with this."

When his mouth covered hers, she went light-headed. For a moment, she simply let him kiss her, soaking up the sensation of having his tongue slide over hers. His hands gripped her shoulders to steer her. Steady her. She'd never felt so thoroughly kissed by anyone else. Quinton focused on her like there was nothing else in the world except for her. Except for lavishing attention on her lips.

He tasted and nipped, licked and explored. Taking his time and making her crazy for more. She wanted his mouth everywhere at once, but at the same time, she never wanted the kiss to end. Her fingers clenched at his chest, holding on to him before she melted right into him.

In the end, she only stopped for a moment to catch her breath. Because honestly, when he was kissing her that way, she forgot all about breathing.

They stared at one another across the front seat of the SUV while the windows fogged. Dazed from that toe-curling kiss, McKenna gripped the lapel of his jacket harder, needing to anchor herself.

"We should take this inside," she suggested, even though she had her doubts about whether or not her legs would carry her that far when her whole body tingled pleasantly.

Was it anticipation that made her feel that way? Like all her atoms shimmied and danced?

"You know what will happen if I start kissing you

again," he warned in a voice that bordered on a growl, his pupils so dilated they were almost black.

As if the vision he conjured would have a prayer of discouraging her.

"I certainly hope so." She wanted to lure him into her house and seduce him into kissing her all night long. "Come inside and show me."

Not giving him time to answer, she opened the passenger door and stepped out into the drizzle. Yanking the hood of her rain jacket over her head, she hurried toward the front door easily visible thanks to the porch light she'd left on.

From inside, Loki barked a greeting before she even got the key in the lock. McKenna heard the other door of the SUV slam shut and Quinton's steps sounded behind her as she unlocked the house.

Moments later, they dripped together on the front mat, peeling off boots and outerwear while Freya and Loki watched the flurry of activity with interest. Normally, McKenna greeted her pets with ample praise and scratches for good behavior while she was gone. Right now, however, her every thought was about having Quinton's hands and mouth on her again.

She didn't have long to wait.

His shoes off and his coat hung up, Quinton took her hand and led her through the house to the stairs. Her heartbeat went wild, pounding so hard as if clamoring for attention. Her whole body one restless ache. And all the while, he steered her where he wanted her to go.

Her bedroom at the top of the stairs.

They hadn't made it there during the night of the blackout since they'd wanted the heat the fireplace had to offer.

Now, he stepped over the threshold of the darkened room, tugging her along. Not that she needed any encouragement to go there with him. Just being close to a bed with Quinton was enough to make her skin feel too tight, like she was ready to come right out of it.

When he paused beside the queen-size mattress covered in a blue-and-yellow quilt her stepmother had made with her during her senior year of high school, McKenna almost couldn't believe he was here with her. That a man who affected her this way was even real.

Was she really going to just lose herself to the attraction when she had something of monumental importance to tell him? She turned toward him, almost thinking she wasn't being fair to ask him for one more night in his arms.

Then, she saw the look in his eyes. Heard the rasp in his breath. That raw male need *she'd* inspired. And she didn't have a chance in hell of ignoring it. Not when she craved it so badly.

They fell together in a frenzy of touching. Her hands roamed all over him, underneath the jacket of his suit so her fingers could climb up the muscles of his back. Then down his chest to splay over his abs through his dress shirt. Except she didn't want any barrier between them, so she tugged the tails of the shirt free from his pants until she could trace the ridges of his abdominals. His skin was hot and her touch made an involuntary shiver go through him. She savored that moment of feminine power over him, wanting to feel the exultancy of it again and again.

Only how could she focus on that when his hands roved all over her too? He'd already lowered the zipper on her dress so that it spilled off her, sliding down her body in a way that turned her on as much as any other touch. How was that even possible? But she was past the point of reason, her senses attuned to every feeling so that even a light breeze on her skin threatened to drive her closer to her sensual peak.

"I need to see all of you." His words were warm against her ear while he unfastened her bra and discarded it. Then, glancing down at her in the dimness broken only by a sliver of hallway light from the partly open door, Quinton made a hungry sound in the back of his throat. "Have to have my mouth on these."

Shamelessly arching her spine, she offered herself to him, eager to feel his lips fastened around the aching peaks of her breasts.

He obliged within moments, and the ache there only migrated to the empty place between her thighs. She writhed and whimpered as he teased a nipple between his teeth, rolling it over his tongue until she thought she'd come from the exquisite pleasure.

Except she wanted to savor this. Savor him.

"Please, Quinton." She unfastened his belt with one hand so she could lower the other into his pants. Stroking the hard length of him made her all the more frantic to feel him inside her. "I need this. Now."

Quinton was hanging on to his restraint by a thread.

With McKenna peeling her clothes off, her red hair haloing her body like a copper nimbus and her breath coming in sexy little sighs, it was all he could do to take his time with her. He wanted her underneath him, on top of him and all around him.

Then, once she wrapped her cool fingers around him

and feathered silky strokes up his shaft, he was teetering on the brink after not being with her for weeks. All the hunger he'd built up for her roared through him with fresh ferocity.

"We need protection first," he reminded her with his last functioning brain cell, knowing he needed to keep her safe.

Letting go of her with one hand, he dug in his pocket for a condom. Before he'd picked her up tonight, he'd berated himself for putting it there in the first place, certain that he wouldn't need it on a date when he was telling her that he'd be leaving Dutch Harbor for good. Yet here they were.

Half-naked, desperate for one another, and he still hadn't told her he'd booked a flight for the day after tomorrow. Guilt stung, but only for a moment considering the way McKenna was touching him. She shifted on her feet, her thighs rubbing against one another in a way that made his mouth water. She rolled her hips against his as if she couldn't get enough of him.

He knew the feeling all too well because he couldn't get enough of her either.

Raking off his shirt and pants with impatient hands, he found a condom through a haze of lust. McKenna's room smelled like lavender and vanilla, a fragrance that he'd occasionally caught on her skin and that he hadn't been able to identify until tonight. He liked seeing this softer side of her that she hid from the rest of the world, from the feminine clothes to the quilt on the bed that was a hand-stitched work of art.

Most of all, he loved knowing he wreaked the same havoc on her body that she did on his. That his touch made her breathless and needy. That his kiss could make her ready to peel off her clothes so she could lie with him.

Even now, she hooked her wrists behind his neck and guided him closer. She'd wriggled out of her underwear while he undressed, so there was no barrier left between them. Nothing to diminish the sensation of her silky skin against his hot flesh. She fit him like she was made for him.

By the time she tugged him down to her bed, he'd almost forgotten about the condom in his hand. She plucked it from between his fingertips, however, and stared at it for a moment.

Her eyebrows furrowed. Troubled?

Since he couldn't interpret the expression, he took the protection back and opened the packet himself, rolling the condom into place. By the time he did, McKenna rained kisses along his shoulders and chest, her eyelashes fluttering closed while she concentrated on the task.

Tenderness and possessiveness streaked through him in equal measures, demanding an outlet. He kneed her thighs apart, making room for himself there before he covered her. He kept his weight on his elbows, mindful of her and wanting to bring her solely pleasure.

The first deep stroke inside her stole his breath. Her body was a tight fist all around him.

"McKenna." Her name was a hoarse croak while he struggled to adjust. To acclimate to how incredible she felt so he didn't lose it then and there.

But she was having none of it.

She bucked underneath him, demanding friction. Pressure.

Sweat beaded along his back while he waited another

moment. Telling himself to get a grip. Then, as if sensing that she was already driving him wild, she locked her ankles around his waist, her thighs snapping closed around his hips. She arched her back, a mischievous smile on the full lips he couldn't get enough of.

"Do you like that, Cowboy?" Her husky words teased the response he knew she wanted.

He pushed deeper. Harder. Filling her so that her eyelids drooped closed, a feminine hum of satisfaction making him desperate to hear that sound again and again.

"Damned right that's what I like." He spoke into her ear, then ran his tongue along the rim, all the while working his hips faster. Harder.

McKenna stopped teasing then, her fingernails sinking into his shoulders with just the right amount of sting to keep him from getting lost in the pleasure too soon. He rolled her on top of him, wanting to see her from that angle. Even in the shadowed room she was a sight to behold, all tousled hair and ripe curves, her head thrown back as she got closer to her breaking point.

Seeing that, knowing she was close now, gave him the last push that he needed to quit holding back. He reached between them, circling her swollen clit with his finger until she went still. Her mouth fell open, making a perfect, round O.

Then her body was convulsing around his, squeezing him and reminding him that no other woman had ever made him feel this good. His hips pistoned back and forth, taking every last ounce of pleasure that he could before he found his own release.

So. Damn. Amazing.

His thoughts splintered, his world fracturing while

McKenna shouted his name. For long moments, he could only manage to draw breath, his heart slugging hard enough to drown out everything else. She slumped on top of him, her hair a silky blanket over one of his shoulders. Her breath fanned out over his chest, while her hand lay over the rough throb of his heart.

He wanted to stay that way with her for hours. At least until the dawn broke. But he knew that remaining tangled up with her like this would only lead to him wanting her over and over.

Then how would he ever tell her that he needed to leave Unalaska?

Stroking his fingers through her hair, he waited until she'd settled alongside him, repositioning herself on the bed so she could lay her head on his chest, one leg thrown over his. Then she pulled up an afghan from the bottom of the bed to cover them.

He dragged in a long breath, owing it to her to explain.

But she spoke before he had the chance. "I know you're going to be leaving soon."

She sounded serious. Not sad, exactly. But her voice had a grave note he'd never heard from her before. Instead of focusing on that, however, he couldn't help but ask, "Am I that transparent?"

He kept stroking her hair, perhaps needing to soothe himself as much as he wanted to soothe her. Because no matter how wrong it might have been to betray Clayton by sleeping with his stepsister, Quinton couldn't regret what had happened between him and McKenna. Not anymore.

"I knew from the day you arrived that you were only here to find out about Clayton," she explained before levering up to one elbow. "It makes sense that you'd take off once you understood that I wasn't going to share his location with you."

He could feel her eyes on him even though her face remained in shadow.

"It's important that I find him, McKenna. I have a legacy to share with him, and I need to heal whatever it is that made him cut himself off from my brothers and me." He hated that he was such a sorry excuse for a sibling that he didn't know what it was that Clay held against him.

But he would make it right one way or another.

"I understand." McKenna sounded more serious than ever. "For what it's worth, I really hope you are able to make peace with him." She hesitated, her words stopping abruptly as if she debated what to say next.

Quinton almost spoke, debating asking her one last time to share whatever she knew about Clayton so he could start brokering a truce as soon as possible.

But then she continued in a rush. Her words almost incomprehensible as she said, "Because, um, to my complete shock... I'm pregnant."

Eleven

Quinton felt the ground fall away from underneath him. McKenna's words simply didn't track in the aftermath of sex so good it had rearranged his atoms. He'd barely recovered himself.

She was pregnant? A vein throbbed in his temple, keeping time with his suddenly pounding heartbeat.

"I don't understand," he managed finally, knowing that his whole future might very well hang in the balance of what he said next. He needed to proceed with care. "So soon? And we were careful…"

His words trailed away. They were meaningless and he knew it. A pregnancy could happen at any time. No matter how careful they might have been. He'd attended sex ed in high school. The mechanics hadn't changed since then.

"I'm aware that I'm in the very early stages, but I skipped a period while I was on the tour to Attu." McKenna righted herself to sit up straight in bed, holding the pale blue afghan to her chest. Her blue eyes had a worried look. "If I'd been anywhere close to civilization I would have tried to hunt down some Plan B contraceptives, but by the time we neared a village with a store, I was well past the time for that to work."

Quinton realized he'd sat up at some point too, his back pinned to a headboard padded with heavy gray twill. The afghan still covered his lap and legs, the loosely woven yarn a fragile shared connection between them.

"I'm glad you told me," he assured her, the words coming on autopilot since he knew what he needed to say. He would never be the kind of father that Duke Kingsley had been, only recognizing half of his children. "Since the news has a great impact on us both."

McKenna's brow furrowed, her lips compressing into a frown. "Actually, I wanted to talk to you about that as well. There's no reason for you to feel obligated when I'm perfectly capable of raising a child on my own."

He felt his brows shoot up. Wariness replaced his earlier shock. "Excuse me?"

"There's no need to rearrange your whole life for a pregnancy you didn't want—"

"Wait." He had to halt that line of thinking immediately, concerned about the message she might have misconstrued from his surprise. Shifting to face her on the bed, he took her shoulders in his hands so she could see his expression. Hear his sincerity. "This baby might be unexpected but it is most certainly wanted."

In the quiet aftermath of his declaration, McKenna's calico cat leaped onto the bed, winding her way between them as if brokering a peace. She settled on one of the pillows and proceeded to lick a paw.

McKenna's fingers strayed to Freya's head, where she stroked through the long, multicolored fur.

"I understand what you're saying. I only meant that you're under no obligation to remain here because of this." Her chin tilted up. Defensive.

What had he ever said to give her the impression he was the kind of guy who would cut and run in a situation like this?

"McKenna, there is every obligation." He lifted a hand to her face, willing her to understand. "I wouldn't walk away from my child any more than you would."

She seemed to weigh his words, her struggle to trust evident in every line of her tense shoulders. Finally, she nodded. "Fair enough."

Quinton felt a weight roll off his shoulders, thankful he'd made himself clear on that point at least. But he knew it was only the beginning of everything they needed to work out between them.

The next point was one of considerable importance. He took one of her hands in his, shifting closer still. Freya mewed a protest that they'd intruded on her space before resettling on the foot of the bed.

"If this baby continues to grow and thrive in the coming months," he began, his throat so dry he needed to clear it. Tension strung his muscles tight. "I hope you will consider marriage to me."

He could hear the wooden cadence in his tone as he pushed the words free but didn't know how to fix that. It had been tough enough framing the life-changing words he hadn't expected to speak this day.

This year, even.

McKenna withdrew her fingers from his. Her tone had cooled when she spoke again. "Don't be absurd. You don't want to be married to me any more than I want to be married to you."

A knife twisted in his gut that he was wrecking this. Possibly hurting her in the process. Yet how could he pretend to be ready for marriage? He hadn't even accomplished his primary goal in coming to Dutch Harbor, so it wasn't like he was in a good position to stick around now. For that matter, the woman who carried his child had dug her heels in so hard to defy him she'd forced Quinton to continue his search another way.

Unless that postcard downstairs held a clue to Clayton's whereabouts after all. He hadn't thought about it during the course of their date or the amazing encounter that had followed it. But now, he thought back to the wolf picture that had appeared randomly on the Cyclone Shack bulletin board. Then reappeared in McKenna's home. In his gut, he felt sure there was a connection to Clay. Right now though, he needed to allay McKenna's concerns for the sake of their child.

"I want whatever is best for this baby," he clarified. "After seeing my father fail to claim all of his offspring, I can tell you with one hundred percent certainty that I won't follow in his footsteps."

McKenna appeared only slightly mollified by the explanation. His eyes had grown accustomed to the dim light in the bedroom by now, and he could see the slight relaxing of her shoulders even as her teeth continued to worry her lower lip for a long moment while the night wind howled outside.

"I don't want that any more than you do," she said at last, hugging her arms tighter around herself. "But I'm not sure the best answer is to race into a union based purely on convenience."

The weight of the future shifted squarely to his shoulders, the need to protect the mother of his child as important to him as giving any child of his a secure home life. Memories of his mother breathing her last gasp in his arms was a rough kick to his chest. The loss still left a big hole in his life. Quinton wouldn't abdicate the responsibilities of family for anything.

"Thankfully, we still have time to think about the future." He rearranged the pillows behind her, hoping he could convince her to lie by him once more. "That's the gift of finding out about this baby so early. We can sleep on it for now, can't we? You must be exhausted."

He suspected it was long past midnight by now. She had to be tired. The stress of the pregnancy news must have weighed on her. What's more, he recalled hearing somewhere that the first trimester was the most taxing.

"Maybe a little." With a reluctant nod, she relaxed into the place he'd made for her, allowing him to tuck the covers around her. Quinton's mouth went dry at the thought of the new responsibilities and what it meant for his future. But for now, he simply lay beside her, hoping she would sleep.

He wanted her to feel well while carrying his baby, for one thing.

For another, he intended to take a look at the postcard in her downstairs hallway and see if it contained any clue to the whereabouts of his missing half brother. Because now more than ever, he needed to find Clayton. With no more hope for Quinton of hiding his affair with McKenna, the chances of reconciling with Clay were worse than ever. This was his last window of opportunity to heal the rift.

In the name of family, however, he needed to try.

As for Quinton's dream of distancing himself from the Kingsleys forever once he located his brother? That hope had died the moment McKenna revealed her baby bombshell.

Now he had no choice but to maintain some connection with his family, if only for his child.

The next morning, McKenna awoke to a nose bump from Freya. It took a few moments to gather her bearings in the bedroom that was too bright for her normal waking hour. The spot beside her on the mattress was vacant, the pillow still dented from where Quinton had lain.

Quinton. Her hand gravitated to his side of the bed, testing for warmth lingering to the sheets…but found them cool. Had he left her house while she slept? Was he downstairs even now? She thought she heard some noises from the kitchen. And the fact that Loki wasn't on her bed, wagging his tail and licking her face to obtain his breakfast, suggested Quinton had probably stuck around.

Their amazing date and the night together that had followed stirred a wealth of tender feelings for him that she shouldn't indulge based on his reaction to her baby news.

Memories of the wooden, unfeeling proposal still chilled her in the light of day. When she'd accused him of rushing into a union purely for convenience's sake, he hadn't denied it. Hadn't suggested there might be more between them than some shared genetic material, even though they'd spent some extraordinary hours together. Hours that had meant something to her—enough to believe that she was falling for him.

Only to find out that those feelings were hers alone and nothing Quinton shared. While her heart ached over that, the cat mewed softly, a feline complaint perhaps that McKenna had slept in. When she'd pushed away his offer of marriage, she'd half hoped he would persuade her, give some indication of growing feelings.

Rising from the bed to wash her face and brush her teeth, McKenna tried to envision her next move now that the night of passion was done and cold reality stared her in the face. She didn't want to think about Clayton's warning to her not to talk to Quinton. Clay had called his half brother a technology savant and suggested he could hack a bank if he chose. Did that mean Clay didn't trust him?

McKenna dried her face, worry making her steps heavy. She should have questioned Clay more about what he meant. About why he refused to see any of the Kingsleys again, even going so far as living off the grid to avoid them. What would he do when he discovered McKenna carried a Kingsley baby?

Now, dressing in a pair of black leggings and a long-sleeved white sweater she liked for lounging, McKenna inhaled the scent of coffee wafting in the air. While she padded down the steps in a pair of striped wool socks, she heard the jingle of Loki's collar right before the front door of the house opened and closed.

She gave a relieved sigh. Some of her worry eased knowing that Quinton would take Loki for a morning walk so she could sleep in. He hadn't run out on her during the night at least. Chances were good that he had only remained at her home to discuss next steps for sharing custody of the baby she carried since he'd made it clear he wanted to be a part of the child's life.

But they could build on that, couldn't they?

Somehow, she would hide the deeper feelings that had already taken root inside her. After her disastrous track record with men, she shouldn't be surprised that Quinton didn't harbor the same tenderness toward her that she did for him. Yet it hurt just the same.

Now, she stepped into the kitchen with Freya circling her feet. McKenna was in the act of reaching for a stainless steel teakettle when the brightly lit screen of Quinton's open laptop caught her eye. The device sat on the opposite counter, an island where McKenna took most of her meals.

Respecting his privacy, she normally wouldn't have given it a second glance. Except even across the kitchen, the monitor's display showed a clear image of a map. The shape of the land mass clearly identifiable as the state of Alaska.

Everything within her went still as she realized the outline of the Frontier State contained one red oversize pin pointing to an area that McKenna recognized well. The top third of the state, in the very middle. A place she knew was at the farthest edge of the Arctic National Wildlife Refuge and part of the Alaskan North Slope.

How did she know?

Because the red pin pointed to the precise spot where Clayton had been living off the grid for over a year.

Her heart hammered in her breast, all thoughts of her morning cup of tea forgotten. Feet moving in the direction of the laptop, she stared at the bright screen, blinking cursor and the undeniable accuracy of the location pin.

How could he have possibly discovered Clay's whereabouts? She had been so careful. Her gaze scanned the island, as if it could produce clues. But there were no notebooks or papers to see, nothing that would give away her half brother's hiding spot. Just a bowl of apples sitting beside McKenna's truck keys and her closed laptop.

The guy could probably hack a bank...

Clayton's warning words about Quinton's tech skills came back to her as she stared at her computer sitting so close to his at the kitchen island. Could Quinton have accessed her device? Remembering how he'd tracked down her cyber harasser, she knew firsthand how skilled he was in that arena. Had he hacked her computer the way Clay had implied Quint was capable of? Memories of betrayal at the hands of her ex-boyfriend scorched a hot streak through her at just the thought.

Her legs turned to water beneath her and she had to plant her hands on the cold white tile to keep from swaying.

The door from outside swung open, admitting a rush of damp wind along with two sets of footsteps—one light, four-legged patter and the other slower, heavier and very much human.

Her stomach dropped as she turned to face him. Needing to confront him about a betrayal so devastating it was difficult to even form words. Hurt and fear twined inside her so tightly she couldn't even make sense of her thoughts.

"How could you do this?" she blurted, pointing a shaking finger toward his laptop sitting so close to hers.

Quinton paused in the middle of unhooking the leash from Loki's collar, his big hands making the brown and black bundle of fur appear even smaller.

"How did I do what?" His voice was quiet. His dark eyebrows crinkled, confusion scrawled on his features. "Narrow down Clayton's location?"

Her heart pounded so hard the sound of it seemed to echo in her ears. The volume of everything else seemed muted by comparison. She watched Quinton finish unhooking the leash before hanging it on the coat rack near the door.

"So you don't even deny it." She thought she'd known what betrayal felt like before. But this? Having Quinton stab her in the back was a hurt beyond anything she'd ever imagined. Because unlike with her ex, this time she had actually cared. Deeply. "How convenient was it for you to sleep in my house—to sleep with *me*—so you could have access to information about Clay?"

"McKenna." He walked toward her, hand outstretched, and she backed up a step, her butt hitting the kitchen island. Frowning at her, Quinton halted in his tracks, as if he was surprised that she was so rattled. "I promise you, it never occurred to me that I'd be able to put two and two together about Clay's location when you and I went out last night."

Pain pierced her chest at the thought of how vulnerable she'd allowed herself to be with this man. She carried his child. To her horror, her eyes burned.

She would not allow herself to show him how much he'd hurt her. Blinking back her feelings, she folded her arms across her chest.

"So you didn't think of hacking my computer until *after* I fell asleep?"

Quinton reared back as if she'd delivered a blow, his surprise evident.

"Hack your computer?" He shook his head as if in disbelief. "McKenna, I don't know where you got that idea, but I promise you I would never violate your trust that way."

A doubt slithered into her brain. He appeared sincere. And genuinely shocked at the conclusion she'd drawn.

Still, she couldn't afford to believe a man on blind faith anymore. She needed to be stronger than that for the sake of the child she carried.

"Your laptop is next to mine," she murmured, rethinking the chain of thoughts and fears that had slid through her mind this morning. "I know you're a tech genius. And suddenly, after asking me for weeks where Clay is, you have the answer all figured out today when you've had the opportunity to spend time in close proximity with my computer."

Quinton shook his head slowly. He held up both his hands, as if in a show of surrender.

"I realize you have every reason to battle trust issues

when it comes to men, McKenna." He dropped his hands to his sides, his broad shoulders sinking. "I guess I'm still rocked that you would think I could do something so blatantly underhanded after everything we've shared."

A pang in her midsection made her question herself. Of course she wanted to believe him. But could she trust her judgment when it had steered her toward the wrong people in the past?

"How did you find him?" she found herself asking, needing some plausible alternative explanation.

His jaw flexed and tensed, turning to granite. She recognized she'd offended him. She scooped up Loki from the floor, needing the comfort of her dog when she didn't know what to think.

"I spotted that postcard in the Cyclone Shack before you left for your trip." He nodded toward the corridor where she'd hung framed pictures, most of them from fishing trips. Of course, he did not refer to the framed photos but the wolf postcard with no writing on it that she'd stuck in the corner of one of the frames. "And something about seeing it here too made me take a closer look at it this morning."

Yeah, she'd been foolish to bring it here. Foolish to leave it out anywhere at all when it had a postmark on it.

Quinton hadn't hacked her computer after all.

"I'm sorry, Quinton." Her hands floated briefly over her belly. As if she could protect their baby from the unhappiness between its parents right now. A gulf had opened between her and Quinton, spreading wider with each awkward moment of this conversation. "I shouldn't have been so quick to jump to conclusions."

He gave a nod. Agreement? Or accepting her apology? She couldn't be certain. His face appeared like set in stone.

"No doubt we have a lot to figure out between us in the next nine months," he said finally, his gaze as cold as his words. "We don't know each other after all."

Stalking past her to the island, he folded down the top of his laptop and scooped it under his arm.

Her throat went dry. The magnitude of all that had passed between them in the last few weeks weighing heavily on her. Or maybe it was this morning's mistake that sank her heart the most.

"Do you have to leave?" she asked, hating the tentative note in her voice.

Then again, she sort of deserved this tentativeness by thinking the worst of him, didn't she? Regret over how she'd treated him bubbled to the surface of the roiling soup of her emotions.

"I need to speak to Clayton. Face-to-face." His grip tightened on the laptop, his knuckles almost white. "I'll check in with you when I get back so we can work out a custody agreement. This morning doesn't change the fact that I still want to be a part of this child's life."

She noticed he hadn't repeated his offer of marriage. Not that she would have accepted it now any more than she'd been ready to the night before. However, the realization that she'd damaged their relationship to this degree still hurt.

Her temples throbbed. Her heart ached.

"All right. Thank you." Her gaze went to the postcard of the wolf in her hallway, an idea occurring to her. "Do you have enough information to find him?"

She hadn't wanted to betray her brother, yet she also couldn't bear the idea of Quinton wandering around the North Slope unsure where to find Clay.

"I'll figure it out," he assured her, picking up the keys for his SUV. "Goodbye, McKenna."

Her heart broke.

As she watched him put on his coat and walk out the door, the hollow feeling in her gut told her what she had feared all night long.

She had fallen for him. Just in time to lose him forever.

Twelve

Buckled into the passenger seat of a 1950s era de Havilland Beaver aircraft specially adapted to fly the harsh northern landscape, Quinton studied the Brooks Range out the windscreen.

The seven-hundred-mile stretch of mountains included the world's highest Arctic Circle peaks. Quinton had been immersed in maps for days after leaving McKenna's house to pinpoint his brother's potential dwelling on the edge of Alaska's North Slope. Narrowing down the location had been slowed by thoughts of McKenna and all the missteps he'd made after learning about her pregnancy.

Part of him still couldn't believe he'd walked away from the woman carrying his child. But he'd been upset and hadn't wanted to say something he regretted. He had to think of her health and the well-being of their baby, after all. So he'd taken a breather to settle things with Clay. Even knowing he and McKenna weren't going to have a relationship, he couldn't afford to have her hide out like her brother had done. Not with his child. But he missed her more than he'd ever thought possible. Even more than when she'd left for her trip to Attu.

She'd texted him an apology in the cool aftermath of their argument, and Quinton knew he should accept it. Yet even the night before their argument, she'd shoved him away with both hands when he'd suggested they wed. McKenna had blatantly refused to consider his marriage proposal.

Admittedly, his offer might not have been the flowery kind that some women dream about, a fact that troubled him in hindsight. Could he have dressed up his appeal to her in a way that would have made her say yes? He'd been rattled by the baby news at the time. Plus, he figured McKenna's practical nature would appreciate a union based in honesty and laid out in black-and-white.

He'd misjudged everything, however. Making it tough for him to focus on the inevitable meeting with Clay once the plane landed. Regret about how he'd handled things with McKenna burned away thoughts of anything else.

"We're almost there." The bush pilot's voice sounded through the headset Quinton wore as the aircraft banked toward the east. "The coordinates you gave me will put us down close to a campground near Galbraith Lake. You will see the water up ahead to your right."

Unease roiled.

If his information had been correct about Clayton, Quinton would be confronting him all too soon. There'd been a time when he looked forward to this meeting with his half brother. Quinton planned to gift him all his shares of the Kingsley inheritance, including his portion of Kingsland Ranch. Plus the one-quarter of the inheritance that Clayton deserved by birthright.

All of which would make Clayton Reynolds a very wealthy man.

Now, however, when Quinton also had to tell Clay that his stepsister carried Quinton's child? Cold dread filled him at the thought of facing a man who had already made it a point to distance himself from the Kingsleys.

A distance he took very seriously judging by the barren tundra of the subarctic climate that reached in every visible direction of the ground below. What had Quinton and his other brothers done to warrant this level of estrangement? But he owed it to Clay to have this conversation after all the ways their father had mistreated him over the years.

Lost in the old memories of their father Duke Kingsley's dysfunctional household, Quinton forgot to scour the ground for possible sightings of a temporary dwelling. So it came as a surprise when the pilot's voice sounded in his ears again, momentarily muting out the dull roar of the Beaver's engine.

"That could be the place you're looking for." The pilot, a full-bearded guy named Dave, who looked well suited to the north in his waterproof gear and neck gaiter, pointed to a white-and-gray travel trailer at one end of the lake where the water narrowed.

Instantly alert, Quinton double-checked the GPS coordinates on his satellite phone.

"Close enough." He gave a thumbs-up to Dave. "Let's give it a try."

When Quinton had contracted with the air taxi company to fly him into the Alaskan bush, the pilot had been apprised of the fluid itinerary to find a missing man. Dave had agreed to circle the area for as long as daylight and weather permitted, including waiting on the ground for Quinton to conduct his business so that he had an exit strategy.

Based on how few temporary dwellings they'd seen in the last two hundred miles, Quinton felt good about their odds of this being Clay's. The postmark for a tiny Alaskan village on the wolf postcard at McKenna's house had been the most important piece of the puzzle. Once he had that information that placed Clay on Alaska's North Slope during the past month, Quinton was able to focus his search efforts. He'd pulled up records of Clayton's work history when he'd been employed by the Alaskan oil rigs over a decade ago, triangulating places where Clay would have familiarity and access. Without a plane of his own, Clay was more limited in his movements since many of the settlements weren't linked by roads.

Moments later, Dave landed the single-engine prop plane on a stretch of open ground less than fifty yards from the RV. There was no truck in sight capable of pulling the travel trailer. However, a small off-road vehicle sat to one side of the camper next to a long strip of reflective panels for solar power. Quinton took it all in as he removed his headset and unfastened his seat belt, stepping down to the ground a moment after the pilot. Cold air hit his face, the damp weather making the wind all the more biting with the temperature hovering around freezing.

While Dave stretched his legs on one side of the aircraft, Quinton walked toward the sleek RV that didn't appear as though it had been used through many harsh Alaskan winters. The fifth wheel looked new, the paint bright.

What were the chances Clay would be inside, even if this was his current home base? Then again, what would the guy do every day outside of the trailer in this remote part of the world? There was no other sign of civilization as far as the eye could see.

Just when he began to despair of having to scour the landscape from the air, however, the door of the RV popped open, a yellow glow from within spilling out momentarily into the gray Alaskan day.

His long-missing half brother stepped outside.

Tall and muscled like a lumberjack, Clayton Reynolds had the square jaw and carved cheekbones of their father, a gift of Duke Kingsley's Eastern European heritage. Levi and Quinton had inherited the darker coloring of their Spanish Creole mother, but Clay's eyes were leaf green and his hair a lighter brown that had been blond when he'd been a kid.

He'd always been built differently too, with a long torso and powerful arms that had made a young Gavin dub Clay "Paul Bunyan" when they were kids. A memory that Quinton had completely forgotten about until this moment.

"Hello, brother." Quinton greeted him with a nod instead of a hug or even a handshake, uncertain what his reception would be.

Especially since Clay's features betrayed nothing of his mood or reaction. He regarded Quinton with a cool green gaze.

Silent. Stony.

Quinton sucked in a breath to take another angle. To tell his brother why he'd come. But just then the hinges of the trailer door squeaked, the insulated metal frame opening once more.

McKenna stood framed in the doorway behind her stepbrother. Shock squeezed Quinton by the throat as he took in the sight of her. She looked even more petite beside Clay. Dressed in ivory-colored joggers and a matching sweatshirt, she looped her arm through his and tipped her forehead to his shoulder. Her copper-colored ponytail fell forward as she peered at Quinton through her lashes.

"McKenna?" One hundred questions tripped through his brain as he tried to make sense of her presence. Of how fast she would have had to leave Dutch Harbor to beat him here.

Then again, she'd known where to find Clay all along. She could have flown straight here whereas Quinton had needed two more days after the flight to Fairbanks to plan his search route.

"Clayton already knows everything," she explained, her fingers curling around her stepbrother's elbow.

Protectively?

Or was it possible she was…restraining him?

The thought had only pieced together in Quinton's brain once he observed the tense flex of Clay's jaw. The color in his face rising.

Yeah, no doubt that Clayton was royally pissed off at him.

It was Quinton's last coherent through before a fist came flying toward him. Because he knew the blow was well earned, he didn't do one damned thing to evade it.

"Clay, no!" McKenna cried, lunging for her brother's arm too late. She'd purposely stood on his right side to prevent exactly this scenario.

But he'd outmaneuvered her by clocking Quinton in

the jaw with his left. She wasn't sure what surprised her more. That Quinton made zero attempt to defend himself. Or that he remained standing after the force of the impact while Clay strode a few steps away as if to get himself under control.

Now, staring at Quinton, who still stood close enough for her to touch, McKenna craved nothing so much as to launch herself at him. Cradle his face in her hands and breathe in the scent of him after days spent apart. She'd missed him. Ached for him. But what good would come of her acting on that impulse when Quinton had purposely placed this distance between them?

Yes, it was partly her fault for not trusting him when she should have. Yet Quinton was also to blame for the new chill between them. He didn't share the deeper feelings for her than she felt for him.

The love.

Because no matter how much she wished she hadn't fallen for him, she couldn't deny that what she experienced right now filled her heart. She knew it because she hurt for him when he hurt. Almost as if Clayton had taken a swing at *her*.

"Are you all right?" she asked Quinton quietly, no longer caring what Clayton thought of her regard for his brother. She'd trekked all across the state to reveal her baby news in person because she wanted him to hear it directly from her. "I can get some ice from inside."

"I'm fine," Quinton bit out between clenched teeth, his eyes never leaving Clay's. The red imprint of his brother's fist remained on his jaw. "Perhaps it would be best if Clayton and I spoke alone."

Hurt carved a new hole in her, just when she thought she'd erected her defenses from this kind of sting.

"This baby is my business too," she retorted, reluctant to leave them together with no one to run interference. She'd arrived at Galbraith Lake almost twenty-four hours before Quinton, and she'd given Clayton a no-holds-barred account of her relationship with Quinton.

She'd felt guilty that her carelessness with a postcard had led Quinton to Clay for one thing. For another, she had hoped to frame her relationship in a way that would reconcile the brothers. For her sake and her child's, if for no other reason. But Clayton remained unmoved. Neither of them had been surprised when they'd heard a prop plane land out front and Quinton had come striding toward the travel trailer. Yet her efforts to run interference for the men had come to nothing.

"I understand that." Turning his attention toward her, Quinton softened his voice as he spoke. "I welcome the chance to discuss that with you too. Yet the original reason I sought Clayton still stands."

Her gaze darted to her brother, who had strode toward the prop plane to talk with the pilot. Once she was sure Clay was out of earshot, she shifted her full attention to Quinton.

"The inheritance." She spoke with more bitterness than she'd known was inside her. But then, she'd absorbed a lot of Clayton's frustrations with his father over the years. Maybe she just was also scared of the changes the Kingsley legacy would mean for him. "You want him to go with you to Montana, don't you?"

That would mean she wasn't just losing Quinton. She would lose her stepbrother too. Suddenly the life she'd built for herself in Alaska that had been so fulfilling just a month ago, now loomed lonely in front of her.

Quinton frowned, finally rubbing a hand along his jaw where Clay had hit him. "I'd like him to, yes, but he doesn't *have* to go anywhere. Either way, I need to tell him face-to-face what is his by right."

A multimillion-dollar share of a cattle ranch thousands of miles away. Would Clayton's resentment of the Kingsleys prevent him from accepting the legacy he deserved? Her conscience shouted that she couldn't allow her own interests to sway him in any way. After everything Clay had done for her, she was duty bound to encourage him to accept his birthright.

"In that case, I'll leave you to it." She moved to return to the RV so she could retrieve her jacket. A walk in the cold air would be welcome about now. Maybe the near-freezing temperature would chill some of the raw hurt she felt over this unhappy meeting with Quinton.

"McKenna, wait." He touched her elbow briefly. Then, seeming to think the better of it, he snatched his hand back. "Are you feeling well? You're not too tired from the trip?"

The obvious concern in his eyes made her heart hurt more. He was a good man, and he would make a good father to their child.

She only wished she hadn't alienated him so completely with her trust issues.

"I'm doing well," she assured him, her hand gravitating to her abdomen as she looked up into the honey-brown eyes of the man she'd come to know so well these last weeks. "I hope you understand why I had to come here ahead of you. It was important to me to be the one to tell him."

Without her permission, her fingers gravitated toward the dark red mark on Quinton's jaw. She stroked the stubbled skin gently before realizing she'd lost that right.

Quinton didn't move as she pulled away.

When he spoke again, he said only, "We'll talk more afterward."

She didn't bother telling him how much it would mean to her for them to reconcile. She'd lost any power to influence him when she'd accused him of hacking her computer. Instead, she used all her willpower to keep from touching him again. To keep from thinking about what they'd lost.

Withdrawing to retrieve her jacket, she left the two most important men in her life alone to sort out their rift.

"Can we talk rationally now?" Quinton reached Clay's side where his brother walked near the edge of a bright blue glacier lake. "Because you already got your one free swing at me."

Clayton had stalked away from the RV after speaking to the bush pilot for a while. Now, his half brother stopped and faced the water, his arms folded across his chest. Quinton joined him, and together they watched while McKenna followed the shoreline in the opposite direction, her auburn hair easy to track in the treeless tundra.

Between them, he could see a few caribou lying in the grass, but nothing that would give her any trouble.

"We can speak now," Clayton affirmed, tearing his green eyes from his stepsister to glare over at Quinton. "I already gave you the punch you deserved."

"Glad we got it out of the way," Quinton admitted, working his jaw back and forth to make sure the hinges were working properly.

"You were lucky it wasn't my right hand." Clay reached down for a handful of rocks and used his right arm to send one skipping into the lake.

A musk ox rose from a spot in the long grasses downstream, then lumbered closer to the water, not paying them any attention.

"Don't I know it," Quinton agreed, recalling scraps from their younger years.

Clay remained quiet a moment before he asked in a low voice, "So did you seduce my sister to find me?"

Fury shot through him. All of his hopes for a rational conversation died.

"You bastard." He got in Clay's face, his fist clenching. "Even if I was that much of a degenerate, how dare you think for a second that McKenna would sell you out."

"You sure about that?" Clay prodded, his eyes narrowing while Quinton seethed.

He paced away from his brother, angry huffs of his breath streaming from his mouth in the cold air. He jammed his fists in his pockets before pivoting to face him again.

"Are you kidding me right now? Do you have any idea how defensive she is of you? How protective?" The vein in his temple throbbed. He could feel his frustration beating there along with his pulse. But he wasn't done yet. "Your property was her main concern during the blackout. Clay's boat. Clay's house. Clay's bar. She would have gotten swept off in a cyclone herself before she let something happen to anything of yours."

"I see." Clayton nodded, his face impassive as he chucked another stone into Galbraith Lake. The guy had been a reserved loner for as long as Quinton could remember, rarely letting his guard down during the weeks he'd spent at Kingsland when they'd been kids. But this was taking reserve to new, infuriating levels.

"Do you? Because McKenna read me the riot act when she thought I might have used foul means to locate you. You won't find a more warm-hearted, generous—" Quinton broke off as he saw a sly smile spread over Clayton's face. "What?"

"You love her," Clay said simply. "That's what."

Did he?

The howling wind in his ears quieted as Quinton's whole world rearranged. The pieces re-sorting themselves as he tried to make sense of the words and his brother's turnabout. Had Clayton been playing him to get a read on his feelings?

"She's important to me," Quinton said carefully while his logical brain tried to turn the clues into something quantifiable. Something shifted in his chest. "And special."

Clayton waited for a couple of long-tailed ducks to swim past before he skipped another stone. As if the world hadn't just tilted sideways. "Call it what you want, brother. But you've got it bad whether you know it or not. Since when does the family tech genius cool his heels for two weeks in the Aleutian Islands to wait for a woman while she's out to sea?"

Quinton frowned, answering by rote. "I couldn't leave without saying goodbye."

Yet that was only half the truth, wasn't it? He'd shared

the deepest secret of his heart with her that night of the blackout, telling her about his mother's death. That had been a piece of his soul and something he didn't share with anyone. Ever.

Had he been falling for McKenna even then? No doubt he'd always struggled with relationships after the way he'd lost his mother. But the memories he had of her—vibrant, independent, happy—made him think she wouldn't want him to live without love.

"You've got an answer for everything," Clayton muttered, heaving the last of his rocks before dusting off his hands and shoving them in the pockets of his navy jacket.

"No, I don't." Quinton stared into the distance where McKenna's red hair was only just visible. He willed her to turn around and come back so he could share some of what Clayton had helped him see. "You've just shown me that I don't have an answer for anything. But I'm going to do my damnedest to fix that."

"Good. Kenna deserves someone smarter than you're being lately." Clayton grinned, the first sign of the brother Quinton remembered from long ago. From the years before Duke Kingsley had bullied Clay into being someone that his son didn't want to be.

Which reminded Quinton of the mission he'd come to Alaska to complete.

"Fair enough. I'm going to work on being the right man for her. But in order to do that, I need you to get your ass to Silent Spring, Montana, for a few weeks to accept your portion of the Kingsley legacy. I'm also gifting you my shares of Kingsland Ranch, which you know I have good reason to leave forever."

The shock on his brother's face was visible beneath his

usual reserve. Clay's dark eyebrows furrowed as he visibly struggled to make sense of the gift. Then, an instant later, the brief visible evidence of his emotions vanished as if it had never been. Something about Clayton's obvious efforts to mask his real feelings made Quinton decide not to ask him why he'd gone to ground after their father's death. Why he'd made it a point to evade the private investigator Levi had sent to Dutch Harbor to search for him. Because if he pushed Clay now, he might lose any hope of getting him to come to Montana. He'd allow Clay to share more when he was ready.

Right now, Quinton was just a messenger for the rest of the family. And he'd delivered the news he'd come to share.

"I have plenty of reasons not to want to go back to Silent Spring too." Clayton's shoulders tensed. His face serious as he stared out over the water. Clouds had moved in over the surface, making the daylight more muted.

"So don't stay once the paperwork is settled," Quinton suggested, sensing he was near closing the deal. "But Levi, Gavin and I are all in agreement that Duke's will was bullshit and it needs to be righted."

Clayton scrubbed a hand over his bare head, his close-cropped dark hair hardly moving. "I'm in the middle of a research project up here," he hedged.

"So finish it up first." Quinton shrugged, anxious to get back to McKenna. To work things out with her. To tell her he loved her and was willing to put in as much time as it took to heal their relationship. "If you give me your word you'll come to Montana once you're done, that's good enough for me."

"Will you be there?" Clay asked, one eyebrow raised.

Quinton glanced back in the direction where McKenna had disappeared, the urge to see her now all but overwhelming him.

"I'll be wherever McKenna wants to be." He recognized that with absolute certainty. "But I'll travel to Montana for a week or two while you're there so we can all sign the paperwork."

Studying him through narrowed eyes for a moment, Clay finally nodded. "Deal."

Relief rocked him.

The two men shook hands while the mist settled lower on the lake. From a hundred yards away, the pilot shouted down to them, suggesting they needed to get underway before worse weather blew in.

"I'd better go get McKenna." Quinton backed up a step, ready to pursue the woman he loved to the ends of the earth if necessary. "I'm going to try to convince her to fly out with me."

"You do that, and I'll get her bag packed," Clayton agreed easily. He jabbed a finger at Quinton. "Just remember to treat her right or I'll know about it."

Quinton's chest squeezed again. This time he recognized the ache for what it was. Love.

"Deal," he parroted back at Clay before taking off down the beach to ask McKenna for another chance.

Thirteen

Strapped in the back of the bush plane Quinton had hired to fly him out to Galbraith Lake, McKenna braced herself for landing. Her gaze flicked toward the cockpit, where the father of her baby sat beside their pilot. Quinton's handsome profile was visible from her seat of cargo netting, his headset in place as they approached Coldfoot, Alaska, about 250 miles north of Fairbanks. The engine rumbled too loudly for any conversation except through the headset, so she'd been saved from any discussion about where things stood between them.

For now, at least.

With the aircraft descending after a flight of less than an hour, the time for a conversation with Quinton rapidly approached. Would he accompany her back to Fairbanks and put her on a plane alone for Dutch Harbor while he returned to his tech company's base of operations in Silicon Valley? Or would he head straight to Montana to meet up with Clayton in the weeks ahead? There hadn't been time to ask either Clay or Quinton questions when Clay interrupted her walk along the frigid glacier lake to bring her in his off-road vehicle directly to the plane. The cloud cover had been getting denser, according to their pilot, and he'd urged her to hurry aboard to beat the weather before the Brooks Range was completely hidden in fog.

McKenna hadn't been able to read Clay's expression when he'd handed over her already-packed duffel bag, but when he'd hugged her goodbye, he promised he would phone her the next day.

Did that mean he'd settled things with Quinton, who'd boarded the plane before her? Certainly Clayton trusted Quinton enough to allow her to fly home with him. But had they made peace? And if so, where did that leave her? Would Clayton forsake his life in Alaska for good to start over in Silent Spring?

The lonely ache inside her at the thought of saying goodbye to her brother was a pale echo of the loss she felt over alienating Quinton, but it still hurt. Had part of her determination not to share Clayton's whereabouts with Quinton been born of a desire to keep Clayton close? She really hoped not. She hoped her love for others was more giving than that. But she'd sure undermined two important relationships lately—with Quinton and with her brother.

Whether that had been a subconscious impulse or not, McKenna recognized the time had come to let her brother go with a full heart. When he phoned her tomorrow, she would tell him why he should travel to Montana. Why he had to accept a legacy he deserved.

The Beaver plane touched down smoothly, jostling her

only a little. McKenna gripped the seat restraints more tightly as the aircraft slowed and then halted altogether. Out the window, she spied a rustic, one-story cabin lit by a single floodlamp over the main entrance. A picnic table sat outside near a four-wheel-drive pickup truck she didn't recognize.

Was Quinton staying here?

Her heart stuttered. She tried to recall what had been said about their destination when they'd taken off back at Galbraith Lake. She'd been frazzled about having to hop directly into the aircraft without even returning to the travel trailer, her brain too full of questions to process much more than Clay telling her she should "head back" with Quinton.

Now, she unstrapped herself from the jump seat while the pilot opened the cargo door. The cold wind of early evening rushed in, stealing the air from her lungs. She'd been better about carrying her inhaler with her since the panic-induced episode of the blackout, however, so she was able to breathe just fine despite the drop in temperature and the stress of the impending conversation with Quinton about their future apart.

A moment later, Quinton stepped out of the plane, coming around to her side of the aircraft. Their eyes met, the weight of all uncertainties between them a tangible presence. They needed to figure out what happened next. But not in front of Dave, who was pulling their bags out of the back of his plane.

"That should do it." The pilot planted the bags on the picnic table. "It's been a pleasure flying you."

Quinton shook the man's hand while McKenna wished him a safe flight home. Apparently Dave's air taxi service was based out of Coldfoot until winter set in, so he only needed to fly another twenty miles to return to his home.

They waved a goodbye to him in the growing dark as they watched the navigation lights fade out of sight. The weather had changed considerably once they reached the other side of the Brooks Range, the sky clear and crisp now. The wind still gusted, however, lifting her ponytail from the shoulder of her down insulated jacket.

While she waited for Quinton to speak—to inform her of what would happen next for them—she shivered a little. Tucking her chin into the vee of her zipper where she hadn't pulled the fastening all the way up, she folded her arms across her chest.

"Are you hungry?" he asked at last, turning warm brown eyes her way, his whiskered jaw illuminated by the sole outdoor lamp. "I left some food in the fridge inside."

"I'd rather talk first. I'm honestly too nervous to eat with so many questions between us." She would face whatever came her way head-on, determined to handle it for the sake of her baby. Their baby. Admittedly, she would be devastated if Quinton wished to leave. But she wouldn't allow him to chain himself to her for life for the sake of their child. "How did things go with Clayton? Are you reconciled? Is he leaving Alaska?"

Perhaps it had been cowardly of her to start there— with topics that were far afield from the most important question of her heart. But she needed to work up the nerve first.

"Should we go inside where it's warm first?" Quinton reached for the bags. "There are two beds inside and I don't want to try making the drive back to Fairbanks in the dark."

Had he mentioned two beds because he didn't want her anymore or out of respect for her boundaries? Either way, they had time to talk and for her to find the answer. The Dalton Highway, which had been built for the Alaskan pipeline, wasn't paved the whole way, with long stretches of gravel between the smoother areas. She didn't blame Quinton for not wishing to drive such a dangerous stretch of highway at night. But she wasn't sure she was ready for the intimacy of that small cabin yet. Not when she needed answers about what lay ahead for them and the child they shared.

It hurt just thinking about going their separate ways.

Besides, it was easier to hide her emotions out here in the dark, with a stiff wind to cool her burning eyes.

"Would you mind if we just sat here for a little bit?" She pointed to the picnic table. "I could use the fresh air after everything that's happened these last few days."

"Of course." Quinton was already shifting their bags around to clear a spot for them. "Let me grab a blanket out of the truck."

She climbed up onto the warped bench to sit on the flatter surface of the table while Quinton retrieved a plaid wool emergency blanket from a bag inside the silver pickup truck.

Even now, when he had every reason to want to distance himself from her, he was thoughtful of her. Caring. Her throat constricted as he took a seat beside her, shaking out the wool throw so that it lay over her lap and his too. An outsider looking at them might think they were a couple, that Quinton was solicitous.

McKenna knew, however, that he behaved that way because she carried his child. Also because he was just that kind of good person. He protected the people around him, a quality she'd observed in him from the very beginning when he'd gone out of his way to help Julie Weatherspoon after she'd been scammed. McKenna's heart swelled with feelings for him as Quinton's voice rumbled in the darkness beside her.

"To answer your questions, I'm not sure if Clayton and I are reconciled, but I can tell you I feel a whole lot better about where things stand between us now." Quinton turned toward her, his expression clear in the soft glow of the exterior light on the cabin. His lips curved up on one side. "I have the feeling I made out better with him because you broke the news about the pregnancy. Thank you for that."

"Seriously?" McKenna reared back a little, surprised that he would suggest such a thing. "Considering he punched you in the face, I'm not sure I helped one bit."

She wondered if the spot was still sore, but she didn't see a bruise yet.

"He could have done a whole lot worse." Quinton shook his head, as if contemplating what else might have happened. "And he agreed to come to Montana for a couple of weeks to hear us out and sign the paperwork. That's a far better outcome than I expected when I arrived."

Her heart dropped like a stone in her breast. Not that Clay was leaving. But because Quinton had just made it clear that he would be too.

"That's good then," she forced herself to say, fingers digging into the edge of the wool blanket. She bit her lip for a long moment to try and get her emotions under control.

In the silence that followed, she listened to the call of

a far-off loon. The closer hooting of an owl. Sounds that seemed to echo the loneliness she already felt at being left here alone.

"I don't know that he'll stay in Silent Spring for long," Quinton continued, pointing out the green haze of the aurora borealis lights taking shape in the darkest section of the sky. "But I'm grateful for the chance to right some of the mistakes our father made."

Her eyes blurred a little as she stared at the small smudge of green that would probably turn into a far more impressive display as the night wore on.

"I'm pleased for you both." She knew the words didn't sound pleased, but then it took every ounce of her restraint not to let Quinton see the hole in her heart at the idea of him departing. "How soon will you leave for Montana?"

Quinton turned his eyes toward her, his intent gaze seeming to see right into her soul. "I'll wait until after your first doctor appointment. Do you have a date yet? I want to be with you for all of them if you'll let me."

Blinking the blurriness of an unshed tear from her eye, she refocused on him. "You do?"

The owl that had been hooting flew closer, its call growing louder and more insistent.

Whoo-whoo-whoo.

"My God, yes." He laid a warm hand on her knee through the blanket, the weight of his fingers making her heart beat faster. "I'm sorry that I was too stunned to react to the pregnancy news with the enthusiasm it deserved. I was caught by surprise, which is no excuse, but please know that I am fully committed to you and this child, McKenna." He hesitated before continuing, his touch squeezing briefly before he released her. "Or, at least, as committed to you as you will allow me to be."

Hopeful emotions sparked to life from the embers of their affair. McKenna told herself to proceed with caution. To wait until she understood him better.

Perhaps he was only referencing the marriage of convenience he'd once proposed.

"You will make an incredible father," she told him honestly. Because he deserved to hear that after the rough childhood he'd weathered. Perhaps he didn't recognize the amazing qualities he possessed. "A caring, protective, wonderful dad any child would be lucky to have."

Reaching across the space that separated them, she touched him the way he'd touched her, laying her hand on his knee. Did it affect him half as much as his touch had stirred her?

His gaze lowered to where her fingers rested a moment before he laid his palm on the back of her hand. Her heart pounded so strongly, she wondered if he could feel it reverberate through the veins around her knuckles.

"I will do everything in my power to make those words true," he vowed in a low voice that told her how much it meant to him. His throat bobbed with a long swallow before he continued, "But I want to be more than just a father to our baby, McKenna."

Her mouth went dry at the look in his eyes as the moment spun out between them. She didn't allow herself to guess what he meant. She needed to *know* if the future he wanted included her in a more meaningful role than as a wife of convenience.

"In what way? I can't settle for a marriage in name

only, Quinton. I just…" She felt the lump in her throat and took a moment to swallow the emotions. "I can't."

Carefully, Quinton folded her fingers between both his hands, his body swiveling toward her so that his knee brushed hers under the blanket.

"I love you, McKenna. I realize you deserve a more flowery declaration, but I'm a man of science and words sometimes fail me—as was clear during my botched proposal. But I want you to know that I mean every word. I. Love. You."

Shock sent her reeling. Her ears rang, her pulse speeding.

"But you said—" she began, ready to remind him that he'd already told her a union would be based on practicality alone.

Quinton laid a finger lightly over her lips. "I was wrong about so many things. About what I was capable of, for starters, because I've never committed to anyone to the point where I might have to fear losing them."

More green lights appeared in the sky, an otherworldly glow that made the moment feel timeless. Like they were alone in the world under this fuzzy green streak in the heavens.

"You couldn't lose me if you tried," she promised him, already imagining what it might be like to be in this man's life forever. "Living up here on my own these last months has taught me how resilient I am. That I can handle what life throws my way." She remembered with a pang the way she'd jumped to the worst conclusions with him, letting her fears undermine what she knew to be true about him. "And I swear that if you give me another chance, I will never doubt you again."

"You already apologized for that," he reminded her, letting go of her hand to wrap his arms around her, enfolding her in his warmth and love. "And it's already forgotten."

Relief might have knocked her over if hope hadn't been there to bolster her back up. The promise of a future together gleamed brighter than the ghostly green that shimmered above their heads while she savored the feel of his strong arms around her. Anchoring her.

Accepting her.

"Just like that?" she asked, a mixture of wonder and love for this man making her voice crack.

His forehead tipped to hers, his breath a warm stirring of air near her nose.

"Of course. You think I don't understand how surprise and confusion might make someone say something they didn't mean?" He shook his head, a movement she felt more than saw with their faces pressed so close together. "I was so stunned by the baby news, I said all the wrong things too. Things I didn't mean. Because I want more than just a marriage of convenience for our child. One day, whenever you're ready, I hope you'll build a real life with me, based on love."

She edged back, needing to see into his eyes to measure these words that seemed too impossibly good to be true.

"Me? An Alaskan bartender with the most sordid internet fame imaginable?" As she said it aloud, the idea seemed all the more out of reach. "I love you, Quinton, but you're a Kingsley. Famous in your own right for your tech company. I would never fit into that life."

"There is nothing remotely sordid about you, McKenna." Quinton's brown gaze never wavered. "I want to be with you, wherever you are. I don't care if that's in Unalaska or Silicon Valley or Coldfoot." He gestured to the cabin in front of them in this remote town of about thirty residents. "Hell, I'd even go back to Montana if that's what you wanted. Nothing matters to me as much as being together."

The possibilities of their future rolled out in front of her eyes, tantalizing her with new opportunities. And the offer to relocate for her touched McKenna's heart more than she could have dared imagine, healing a corner of her soul that still ached from a childhood of abandonment.

"I do love it up here," she admitted slowly, realizing that Quinton meant every word he said. That he'd given his heart to her and would go anywhere she chose. The thought humbled her. "And I would like it if our child could spend at least some time in Alaska just to see this world that helped heal me."

A sigh of relief shuddered through him so tangibly she felt it. "I would say that it's been healing for me too, but I have the feeling that it was meeting you that changed everything." He stroked his thumb over her cheek, sending a tingle of awareness through her. "Changed me."

"Maybe part of the year in California," she suggested, her gaze dipping to his lips. She wanted a kiss. Needed it. "And part of the year here."

"We don't have to decide tonight." Hauling her onto his lap, he wrapped her closer to him before raining kisses along her jaw, ending at the corner of her mouth. "We could think about it in the morning, after we've settled more important questions."

He hovered just above her lips and her eyelashes fluttered in anticipation of his kiss.

"Such as?" She clutched the lapels of his jacket, not even noticing the spectacular display overhead now that Quinton was this close to her.

Loving her.

He licked along her lower lip before dragging it between his teeth. When he let go of it, she wanted to weep with frustration.

"Such as how many times are you going to scream my name tonight once I get you inside that cabin?" His voice was so rough her thighs shifted restlessly in anticipation.

"I'm not sure, Cowboy, but let's go find out."

He swooped her up and off the picnic table before charging across the frozen tundra toward the tiny log structure. McKenna held on tight, ready for their forever to begin.

* * * * *

THE WRONG RANCHER

J. MARGOT CRITCH

This one is for anyone who turns to romance
for comfort in a tumultuous world.

One

Piper sat back in the buttery-smooth leather seat and sipped from her champagne flute. She looked out the small round window of the private plane that had been sent to Chicago to take her to the small Texas ranch town of Applewood. "Ms. Gallagher," the flight attendant said, collecting Piper's now-empty glass from the table next to her. "We'll be beginning our descent now. Touchdown on the Applewood airstrip in just ten minutes."

"Thank you. For everything." Piper had never experienced such luxury before in her life. In just forty-eight hours, her normally modest life had done a full one-eighty. If her trip to Applewood worked out favorably, this was something she could get used to, but she wasn't going to count her chickens too early on that one.

"It was a pleasure having you on board. I hope you have a great time in Applewood."

Piper smiled at the woman, who turned to walk back to the galley. *Applewood*. Piper mused over the word. It was a town she'd never heard of before two days ago, and thanks to the network of billion-dollar ranches in the town per capita, it one of the wealthiest in the country. Seeing as how a private jet was her first introduction to the community, she believed it. She smoothed a hand over the arm of her chair as she felt the plane decreasing its altitude.

A few minutes later, the plane landed at the Applewood airstrip, and Piper found her luxurious ride over far too soon. She disembarked and saw that the tarmac was lined with small white luxury planes. She'd previously wondered why Applewood had its own airstrip and regional airport, but now it all made sense to her.

She was led into the small airport, where she was to wait until her bag was unloaded from the plane and brought to her. The walls of the small building were made of glass and she took the opportunity to check out the environment around her. From the air, she'd seen the large swaths of rolling hills and ranchland that broke up the dense forests and comprised much of the town. The sun was high in the sky, casting a warm glow over everything in sight. It was a stunning sight, so tranquil, so quiet, so far removed from her crowded, bustling neighborhood in Chicago.

She pulled her phone from her purse to take a photo. Her eyes were still on her screen when she turned away from the glass wall and crashed against something hard and quite warm.

"Oof," she said as the air compressed from her lungs at the impact, and she looked up to see the amused smile of possibly the sexiest man she'd ever seen. "I'm so sorry," Piper told him, feeling an embarrassed flush rise in her cheeks. "I really should be looking where I'm going."

He put a steadying hand on her upper arm. "It's quite

all right, ma'am," he said in an irresistibly slow drawl. "Are you okay?"

"I'm fine, thank you."

"I noticed you looking at the scenery," he noted.

She took the opportunity to look up at him again. He was the classic tall, dark, and handsome type, with a stunning smile, strong jaw and high cheekbones. The thick waves of his black hair were brushed back, and she was tempted to push her fingers through them.

"Yeah, I just landed and was killing some time while I wait for my bag," Piper overexplained. She did that when she was nervous, and for some reason, this man made her nervous. She tore her eyes away from him and back to the glass. The sky was a stunning cerulean blue. "It's gorgeous here."

He was wearing a black T-shirt and jeans, a leather backpack slung over one shoulder. His square jaw was covered in a short dark beard. *Speaking of gorgeous sights.* She covertly looked him up and down through her dark sunglasses. He was handsome, and from the way he filled out his clothing, she could tell he was strong. Piper was absolutely transfixed.

"Is this your first visit to Applewood?" he asked her.

"Yes, it is. I don't know just how long I'll be here, yet," she explained. "But I'm looking forward to getting out there and exploring." And maybe crossing paths again with this mysterious hunk. "Do you live here in town?" she asked.

"I do. I guess my plane must have landed just after yours."

His plane. So he was another rich person in Applewood. And she didn't bother to correct him about her own status. "Yeah, perhaps."

They watched each other for several beats before he

smiled and shook his head, clearly embarrassed. "I'm sorry, I've forgotten my manners." He stuck out his hand. "Maverick Kane."

She shook his hand. "I'm Piper Gallagher. Nice to meet you, Maverick. Or do you go by Mav? Or Mr. Kane?" She was having fun flirting with him. She'd been on Texas soil for all of ten minutes, and she was already smitten.

"Whatever you want to call me is fine by me. I'm sure I've heard worse." He laughed, and the warm chuckle vibrated throughout her body. "So, you're staying in town then?"

"Yeah," she told him, even though she wasn't entirely sure where she would be staying. That was one of those little details that Piper was certain, one way or another, would work itself out. "For a while, at least. I don't quite know for how long yet."

He hooked a thumb over his shoulder. "You know, I've got my truck out there in the parking lot. Why don't a give you a ride?"

"My mom always told me to never accept a ride from a stranger."

He smiled at her. "Of course—you're right."

At that moment there was nothing Piper wanted more than to spend time with Maverick Kane. He was charming, sexy, and she wouldn't mind getting to know him better. "It's okay," she told him. "I have a ride coming. Thank you for the offer, though. I appreciate it. I just hope everyone else in town is as friendly as you."

He leaned closer, a slick grin on his face. "Don't let that get around," he told her. "I wouldn't want it to affect my reputation." He straightened. "Enjoy your stay," he told her. "Maybe I'll see you around."

Piper smiled. She really hoped she would cross paths with Maverick Kane again. "Yeah, maybe you will."

He returned her smile and, for a moment, their eyes connected, and if they had been better acquainted, Piper was sure that he would have leaned over and kissed her. But they were strangers, and that wasn't how things worked in real life. Instead, he cocked an eyebrow and smiled at her, showing off his straight, white teeth. "Well, you shouldn't be too hard to find," he commented, letting his eyes roam over her.

Before Piper could respond, Maverick turned on his heel and walked away. Her eyes stayed on him and even when he exited through the door, her eyes stayed on the exit.

"Your suitcase, Ms. Gallagher."

Startled, she turned to the voice. It was the baggage handler who had brought her bag from the plane. "Thank you," she said absently as she dug into her purse for her phone. "I appreciate it."

"Do you need me to call you a car?" he asked.

"No, thank you," she told him, scrolling through her text messages. "I have someone coming for me."

"Very good, ma'am," he said, tipping his hat at her. "You have a nice day now."

"I will. And you, too," she added. In her hand, her phone vibrated and the screen lit up with the notification of a text message.

Right outside, it read.

Again, Piper looked toward the door and hesitated. *Right outside* was Elias Hardwell, successful rancher, one of the richest men in Texas, patriarch of the well-known Hardwell family. And—oh, yeah—her father.

When she walked out of the airport and into the parking lot, Piper looked around and saw a black luxury SUV parked in the middle of the small lot, with an older man standing beside it. He raised his hand. It had to be Elias. She released the deep breath she'd been holding in her lungs and took the trepidatious first steps toward him and rest of her life.

As she got closer, she was able to take in the features of the man. He was tall, broad and his tan-colored cowboy hat covered silver hair. He wasn't a man who looked to be the eighty years he was. It was, without a doubt, Elias Hardwell—her father. He removed his hat and smiled at her. "Piper," he said, his voice holding an awed quality.

She extended her hand, keeping some measure of physical and emotional distance between them. "Mr. Hardwell."

He paused for a moment but shook her hand. "I understand if you're reluctant to call me Dad, but I'd appreciate if you call me Elias."

She nodded. "I think I can do that."

They went around to the rear of the SUV and he waved his hand over a hidden sensor, which opened the hatchback to the trunk. With strength that she wouldn't have guessed an older man would possess, he lifted her suitcase and hoisted it into the back of the vehicle.

He opened the passenger's-side door. "Thank you for responding to my email," he told her.

"How could I not?"

Piper recalled how, only two days ago, her life had been turned completely upside down. She'd started her day in what she'd thought was going to be a typical Monday-morning pitch meeting for the fashion magazine she worked for—well, *used to* work for. There was news of a takeover, a larger publication consuming their brand, and apparently Piper's services were no longer needed.

So, newly unemployed, she'd packed her desk and returned home, where she'd put on her sweats, piled her hair into a messy bun, ordered cheesecake from the place around the corner and worked on her résumé. When she'd opened her email, however, those plans had been scuttled when she was greeted by an unexpected letter from a man named Elias Hardwell. Her eyes had focused on several key phrases—*Private investigator. Found you. Birth father. Please call me.*

A quick internet search had told her that Elias Hardwell had owned one of the largest cattle ranches in the country, which also bred and trained race and show horses. He'd since retired and stepped down from operations, leaving the business in the hands of his grandson, Garrett.

"Thank you for the ride down."

"I trust the plane was comfortable."

She laughed. "I guess it's been a while since you've flown commercial. Any flight where I don't feel like I'm being herded like cattle is comfortable. The plane was downright luxurious. I've never flown private before."

"It's a good way to travel." Elias checked his watch. "I guess we'd better get going. I want to show you around Applewood, but only for a little bit. We don't want to be late."

"Late for what?"

"Family dinner."

"Family dinner?" she asked, reticent. She had been hoping that she and Elias would have some time to get to know one another without other people. She had thought he would suggest lodging in town, giving her a chance to get acclimated, but she was starting to think that Elias may have a flair for the dramatic. "Like, a dinner with the whole family?"

He chuckled. "What do you think 'family dinner' means? They're a great bunch."

"Who all is going to be there?" she asked, feeling nervous. A big family was something she'd always craved; she'd always wished she'd been a part of family dinners, celebrations and holidays. And since she'd lost her mother, the feeling had been compounded. But to be thrown into a big family gathering a stranger to everyone wasn't exactly the way she'd expected it to happen.

"Well, you have a brother, my son, Stuart, and his two sons will be there, Garrett and Wes, along with their wives. And of course, my own bride-to-be, Cathy, will be there, and a few select family friends."

"Your bride-to-be?" she asked, intrigued that, at his advanced age, he was getting married.

"Yes, I met Cathy a long time ago, after my first wife died. We've finally settled down and will be getting married in a couple of weeks." He slid his gaze across the center console to her. "I hope you'll still be sticking around until then."

"A wedding? Well, I certainly didn't pack for a formal event."

"There are shops in town and I'm sure we can find something you like."

"Why don't we see how this evening goes?"

"I understand." He took his eyes off the road to briefly look over at her. "And I'm sorry if I'm pushing things. Just tell me to back off if you want."

"Thanks. And it's okay. This is a strange situation for both of us."

After spending some time showing her around Applewood, as she'd expected, it was a beautiful little town, and the surrounding area, with its sprawling ranches, was magnificent. Just now, Elias was driving them down a winding dirt road, presumably to his own sprawling ranch.

"So, what does everyone think about me coming?"

Elias chuckled, but she didn't like the sound of it. "Cathy and I have talked about you. She actually urged me to find you. But everyone else?" He shook his head. "They don't know squat."

"What?" she exclaimed, sitting up straight and turning to face him. "They don't know?" Her earlier estimation of the man was apparently correct. *Drama, drama, drama.*

"I thought it would be a fun surprise for everyone," he finished.

Piper opened her mouth, trying to find the words. "Are they…a group that generally enjoys surprises?" she asked.

This time his laugh was hearty and filled the cab of the SUV. "I wouldn't say they do."

She wondered what other *surprises* he'd arranged for his family in the past. "This is unbelievable," she said, shaking her head. "I feel like you're setting me up for something."

"No, my dear," he said. "I'm not setting you up. But I figured that this might be the best way for you to meet everyone. So no one has the time to get their backs up."

"You think they'll get their backs up?" she asked. But she should have realized that, of course, they would. She was walking into a family as the long-lost daughter of one of the richest men in Texas, and they would likely be thinking about their inheritances or whatever it was that rich people cared about when strangers walked into their lives.

"No, of course not. But there will be questions," he told her.

"That's to be expected. I have questions myself."

He nodded. "All in due time," he said.

As they crested the top of the hill, a large ranch house and its expansive grounds came into view. "There she is— home."

"You still live on the ranch?" she asked.

"Cathy and I moved to Arizona a while ago. I left the ranch operations to my grandson, Garrett, and he's newly married and I thought it would be a good idea to give him some room. We love it in Arizona. It's a good change of scenery, but I miss the ranch. There's nothing quite like it."

As they got closer, a nervous energy tore through Piper. This was it. She took a deep breath. Her life was about to change. She was on her way to meet her new family. She hadn't forgiven Elias for springing this on her, and all of them. It would be awkward as hell, probably tense, hopefully not hostile, but this was her chance to get to know her family, and she was going to take it.

Two

Piper could feel her heart pounding as the SUV came to a stop in front of the ranch house. *House* was obviously a misnomer, as the building was immense, but it still looked warm and inviting. There were other vehicles parked there, high-end trucks alongside luxury cars, and she stilled. For the first time since the moment she'd spoken to Elias, just a couple of days ago, before she'd started this journey, it felt like the bad idea that it was. They both sat in the SUV, looking straight ahead for bit. Her confidence waned as she considered pulling the old man out of the vehicle, sliding behind the wheel, putting the gear in Reverse and stealing Elias's SUV to make her escape back down the winding gravel road and the hell out of Applewood.

"Are you ready?" Elias asked her, interrupting her daydreams of making Grand Theft Auto a reality. "We have to go in at some point."

She looked at the older man, his eyes kind, and the same chestnut-brown as hers. Whereas she'd thought him manipulative and dramatic before, he now looked nervous, and she wondered if he was feeling like she was. This was just as emotionally tense for him as it was for her, even though it was a situation he'd created. "Yeah, I guess so.

"Do you think this will all be okay?" she asked. They were sharing a quiet moment together, their first one. "Will they be okay?"

"I like to keep my family on their toes. They'll tell you all about it, I'm sure. But I now realize that this involves someone else's life—yours. They're good people in there, but I honestly don't know how they'll react to this news. I'm sorry I didn't tell them first," he said, looking back at the house as if he were trying to buy time. "I don't know why, but I thought this way would be better for everyone. Why don't you let me go in first and then lay the ground-work?"

Piper didn't know the man next to her—her father—very well, but he seemed to be a great departure from what she knew of him. "Really, I want to turn around and run," she confessed. "You can come with me, if you want." They laughed together. It surprised her that that she could feel vulnerable and comfortable with him already. She met his eyes and she knew they shared a special con-nection. They'd had a fast-tracked DNA test a few days ago, and even though they were still waiting on the result, she didn't need it to know that the man beside her was her blood. "Let's go in."

Elias opened his door and Piper wished that she had the courage to do the same. This was a big deal. She had no idea how his family—*her* family—would react to her pres-ence. She knew there would be confusion, at best, abject anger and hostility, at worst. She closed her eyes and took several deep calming breaths, got out of the SUV and followed Elias to the door.

They entered the house. The inside was just as grand as the outside. High ceilings, shiny, although scuffed, wood floors, expensive leather furniture that looked so plush she could probably sink into it. She followed Elias to the back of the house, where a wall of glass greeted them. She could see about a dozen people milling outside on the patio. They were all talking, laughing, enjoying each other's company, as a family would. Several moments passed before anyone noticed the two of them standing inside.

Elias approached them first. He greeted his clan with hellos and hugs, and they responded in kind, respect shown, as she'd expected, for the family patriarch. The first to turn his attention to her was a younger man with light hair—unlike hers, she'd inherited her mother's red hair—and he regarded her with blue eyes. "Well, hello there," he said, extending his hand. Piper recognized him from her internet searches. It was Garrett Hardwell, the current majority owner of the ranch. Elias's grandson.

She shook his hand. "Hi." Her heart thundered in her chest as she stammered out the word. Everyone was watching her, and her eyes went to Elias as she hoped for guidance on how to proceed.

"And you are?"

"Piper Gallagher," she told him dumbly as every person on the patio turned to look at her questioningly.

Elias moved forward, realizing that he would have to step in. "Everyone, this is Piper. She's—"

"A journalist," Piper blurted out. It wasn't a lie, of course, but she thought that the words *Elias's daughter* wouldn't be a welcome announcement. Elias's head whipped to her and he looked as confused as everyone else.

"Okay," Garrett said with a nod. He pointed to the woman beside him. "This is my wife, Willa." She shook Willa's hand. "My brother, Wes, and his wife, Daisy. If you haven't met her yet, Elias's soon-to-be wife, Cathy. And my own father, Stuart." She shook hands with everyone. She could tell they still had many questions.

"It's so nice to meet you all."

After a beat of silence, Garrett cleared his throat. "What exactly brings you by here?"

Faced with her new family, and their expectant, confused faces, Piper's heart pounded in her chest. This suddenly felt like a terrible idea. She had to think of something, so she went with a lie. "I'm here to write a story," she told them. "About your family."

Their faces remained in their confused state.

Elias turned to her. "Piper," he said, gently, before stepping forward. "There's something you all should know," he told them. "Piper is my daughter." He turned to Stuart. "She's your sister."

A stunned silence fell over the group as Cathy took Elias's hand, offering him support. Piper wished she had the same in this room full of strangers.

She looked at Garrett and Wes. "And I guess that makes me your auntie."

"Aunt," Wes said, bewildered.

Willa cracked a smile. "So, there's no big story about us?" she asked playfully.

Piper exhaled. Elias had already dropped the bomb, but now it was her turn. "Probably not. I am a journalist, that part was true. I came here with Elias to tell you the truth, but then I got nervous." She swallowed. "I didn't know that Elias hadn't told any of you." She narrowed her eyes at her father. "Maybe that would make a good story, after all."

Wes crossed his arms, his jaw hard and his eyes narrowed in a glare. He turned his attention to his grandfather. "Why didn't you tell us?" He gestured to Piper with a wave of his hand, but he didn't look in her direction.

"Why didn't you tell us before you brought her here?" he asked.

"Wes," Elias said with an edge to his voice. "No matter what, Piper is a member of this family and a guest in this house. You'll remember your manners and treat her as such." He put his hands on his hips. "Neither Piper nor I handled the introductions well, but she's here now, and we're all together."

Despite the many people on the patio, all was quiet as everyone was digesting the bombshell announcement.

Willa spoke first. "Where have you been all this time, Piper?"

"Chicago," she answered. "I was born and raised there."

Willa turned her attention to Elias. "And what's your answer to that question?"

"Yes, this is my question to answer, as well," Elias said. "I met Cassandra over thirty years ago. We—" he cleared his throat uncomfortably "—became acquainted, and we parted ways after a few weeks. Cassandra told me she was pregnant, and then she disappeared. We parted ways, but I never forgot about her, or stopped wondering what ever became of the child. Cathy convinced me to reach out to a private investigator."

Willa turned her attention to Piper again. "And your mother?" she asked carefully.

Piper felt her eyes fill with tears as she thought of her mother. "She passed away a few years ago." With the exception of the people standing in front of her, her mother had been her only family. That was why connecting with the Hardwells was so important to her. When it came to family, she was alone in the world.

"I'm so sorry to hear that," Willa said. Her gaze shifted to Wes, who looked rightfully chastised.

"Thank you. And I'm so sorry for just crashing into your lives like this."

Looking at her curiously, Garrett moved forward and stood in front of Piper. He was looking intently at her face. "I see the resemblance, you know," he said. "The eyes, the nose, the cheekbones. You look just like Elias, and the traits he passed on to all of us." He moved back.

"Really?" She glanced around and noticed that Garrett was right. Based on her looks alone, she looked like this entire family. It was enough to make her eyes tear up again.

"Yes," Elias said before extending his arms to her. She hesitated at first because the move was unexpected. But the emotions bubbled up within her and she went with it, moving into the hug. Until now, she and Elias had kept a distance between them, each waiting to see how their complicated relationship would play out. When they pulled apart, she saw that the rest of the family was still watching them. And that was fair. She and Elias had both dropped huge news on them. They needed and deserved some time to come to terms with it.

Stuart came to her first. "Welcome, Piper," he said, extending a hand. The formal gesture was a far cry from Elias's hug, but she shook back.

Elias looked at her. "Why don't we go out on the porch and talk? I think we need to catch up." Elias turned to Garrett and Wes. "One of you go out and get Piper's bag," he ordered. "Set her up in the eastern wing."

"She's staying here?"

"Yes, of course. We welcome everyone here at Hardwell Ranch."

"That isn't necessary," she told the group. Piper hadn't thought she would be staying in the family home. "I'll make arrangements to stay in town." Even if she'd told them she was his daughter, it hadn't been her intention to stay with them. Talk about too much too soon.

"That's ridiculous," Elias told her. "You'll stay here."

"I don't know," she said. "This has been a lot for everyone. If I stay somewhere in town, at least we can all gather our thoughts." Piper handed over her card, and Garrett took it. "Elias has my contact information, but it's on there, too. Call me and we can set up a time to get together."

"Okay, I will," he said.

She nodded awkwardly. "Great. I guess I'd better be going." She paused. "If someone has any idea of a good place to stay…"

Willa, Garrett's wife, stepped forward. "If you don't have a reservation anywhere, I'd suggest the Applewood Inn. I'm the owner."

"Oh, really?"

"Yeah. I know we just so happen to have a vacancy tonight. When you check in, tell Amy at the registration desk I'm giving you the family rate."

Piper's eyes widened at Willa's words. She supposed she was family now, but that idea would take some getting used to. "Thanks. I appreciate it."

She and Elias left the house and walked out the door to the front wraparound porch, which overlooked part of the ranch. They each took a seat on a rocking chair. "So, how do you think that went?" she asked Elias.

"It went as I expected."

"Wes and Garrett don't seem so happy."

"Give them time." They sat quietly, and each watched the sun as it began its descent on the horizon. She heard Elias take in a breath. "I'm sorry I wasn't involved in your life."

"For a long time, I wondered why I didn't have a father. I always wondered about you. But I never asked. My mother gave me a good childhood. I was a happy kid. But she was so adamant about doing it on her own, so I kind of understand why you weren't around."

"I wish I could have found you," he told her. "I thought about you all the time. I wondered who you were, if you were happy."

"I'm here now."

He nodded. "I can't turn back time," he told her. "But I can be involved in your life now."

"I'd like that. Thank you for reaching out to me. I'm glad you did. Although, the family might disagree."

"This is your family now, too."

"Honestly—" she took a look back at the house "—it's a bit too early to say that yet."

"Well, let's ease into it. I'm glad you came. I just regret that we've wasted so much time."

"Me, too."

"But if you're open to it, we can use the time we have and get to know each other now."

Happiness and relief watered her eyes. She felt a tear breach the corner of her eye then roll down her cheek. She quickly wiped it away. "Yeah, I'd like that."

Elias put his hand over hers and he smiled at her before removing it again. "So, why not stay at the main house?"

She looked back at the closed door of the house. The family as a whole hadn't been exactly welcoming, so it was probably not a great idea to stay with them just yet.

She wanted to give them their space and the opportunity to get to know her. She turned back around to face Elias. "I just don't think now is the right time. And I wouldn't feel right imposing on the family dinner. I think they all need time to process the news. Dinners can come later."

He nodded solemnly. "They'll come around," he promised. "Don't forget, this is your family home, too. You have just as much claim to the space here as anyone else in the family."

That made her sit up straight. She hadn't thought about the vast amounts of money and assets that belonged to the family. She wasn't looking to make a claim on any of it—that wasn't why she'd come to Applewood. She just wanted to meet her family, to have the chance at a big, loving family that she'd always wanted.

There was certainly room at the large ranch house for her to move in and stay out of the Hardwells' way if they wanted that. At least if she stayed at the ranch house, it would force her to get to know her family. Maybe she would stay there someday soon. "I should probably get going," she said. "Is there anyone I can call for a ride?"

"I can arrange a ride, or if you'd like to drive, you can use one of our cars," Elias offered.

"That would be great, but do you think it'll cause any problems between y'all?"

He nodded. "You're already getting the lingo," he said with a grin. "No—like I said, they'll get over it." He began to walk away and gestured for her to follow. "Come over here with me."

He led her to a nearby garage and when he opened the door, she was surprised to find that, besides being a successful rancher, the man also collected cars. There were ten cars of different makes and vintages, sporty, classic and luxury, but her eyes landed on the cherry-red convertible near the door. "Wow. I don't know a lot about cars, but this one's a beauty."

"Yeah," he said, coming to stand next to her. "She is." He went to a small locker on the wall, spun the dial on the combination lock and opened the door, exposing a set of keys for every car. He casually tossed one to her. When Piper caught them, he nodded at the convertible. "You like 'er? She's yours."

Piper's mouth dropped. "I couldn't."

"It's the least I can do for not being in your life. You deserve it."

She couldn't argue with that. If Elias felt she could use a classic car, then who was Piper to tell him no?

"Why don't we both sleep on it?" Elias suggested. "Drive it around a little bit, and when you get settled in, come back and get to know the family. They know better than to be anything but welcoming."

She nodded. "Okay, thank you."

Elias left, and Piper got in the car and sat behind the wheel. She smoothed her hands over the leather of the steering wheel. She was disappointed that the evening hadn't gone perfectly. While the Hardwells had been responsive to the introduction, there would be a lot of work and getting to know each other ahead of them. A wave of delayed embarrassment washed over her. She'd felt awkward as hell standing in front of them, and she hoped that it would pass by the time she saw them again. Hopefully, someone would call her tomorrow to get together.

Finally, she started the car and turned on the radio. As she drove away, Piper tried to recall the road they'd taken to get to Hardwell Ranch. But the road was winding, built on old horse paths, no doubt. She took several turns and, as she was losing daylight, Piper realized she was lost. Pulling over, she picked up her phone to look up a map, but the directions provided were extremely sparse. She had to figure out where she was headed before night fell.

The trouble was, all of the scenery looked the same.

Three

The evening was always Maverick Kane's favorite time to ride. The sun had just started to set, casting a yellowish-orange hue over everything in sight. He'd spent the day traveling and he was glad to be back on the ranch, where he was truly happy. Around him, he could feel the environment settling in for the evening. Flowers were closing their petals and daytime wildlife had started to head back to their nests and dens, making room for their nocturnal counterparts. It was a good time of day to be alone. That was exactly what Maverick wanted. With the exception of the clip-clop of his horse's hooves on the gravel road, the air around them was silent. Or it should have been.

The music reached him first, and Maverick cocked his head to the side to discern what it was. And then he was struck by the melody; it was a familiar song, the notes loud, synthesized, auto-tuned, from a pop starlet he'd known almost twenty years ago. One he'd spent nights partying with in Los Angeles, before they'd poured themselves into waiting limos and Town Cars under the blinding flash of paparazzi cameras. His horse picked up speed, bringing him closer to the offending noise, which shouldn't be on his land. That symbolized another life for him, and he didn't want to dwell on the mistakes of the past. He crested the hill then saw the red convertible parked on the side of the road that led back to his. He hadn't been expecting company—Why should he? Why would anyone visit him?—so he knew that, whoever they were, they didn't belong there.

He snapped lightly on the reins and, at an increased speed, headed for the car, his mood worsening the closer he got. Maverick didn't take kindly to strangers on his land. The townsfolk in Applewood generally kept their distance, and this stranger was surely there because they wanted something from him, or worse, to talk about the years he'd spent on Hollywood Boulevard, paparazzi capturing pictures of him barely functioning, going in and out of nightclubs. He frowned, the shame and regret of his past rolling through. He had to remind himself that that wasn't him anymore.

Maverick came up behind the convertible, old pop songs still blaring from the stereo that had to have been updated since the car had been manufactured in the 1960s. The car itself was a thing of beauty, vintage, cherry-red, somehow still shiny despite the dust she'd surely kicked up on the gravel road. But as he pulled his horse to a stop next to the driver's side, he noted that the beauty of the car paled in comparison to its driver. Her light brown hair was skillfully knotted in a braid over her shoulder and, while her large, black sunglasses obscured most of her face, he knew from her high cheekbones, delicate nose and heart-shaped lips that he'd already encountered her once before that day.

She was the woman from the airport—Piper. He'd had a feeling that he'd be seeing her again.

But that didn't excuse her from being uninvited on his land. "Are you lost, ma'am?"

She glanced up from her phone, and raised her dark sunglasses. Her hardened expression softened as she looked at him, recognition in her eyes, like she was glad to see him. "Maverick Kane."

"The one and only. Nice to see you again, Piper. Everything okay here?" he asked.

Her full red lips were turned down at the corners. "No," she said at first but then she sighed. "Yeah, I guess I am lost. Kind of."

He dismounted and leaned against the door of her car. "Where are you trying to go?"

"I just left Hardwell Ranch, but I'm trying to get to town. I thought I was going the right way—" another look at the map on her phone "—but I must have taken a wrong turn somewhere."

She'd been at Hardwell Ranch? He briefly wondered why. Was she connected to the family? The mention of them left him with a bitter taste in his mouth. What would someone connected to the Hardwells be doing on his land? He glowered at her as she manipulated the map on her phone.

Every time he crossed paths with Elias and Garrett, there was negativity between them. They never stopped reminding him that he didn't quite belong in the area. Despite the fact that he'd never done anything to the old man, he didn't seem to have any sort of time for him. Maverick's grandfather, Harlon, the original owner of his land, had done whatever he could to ruin the Kane name in town. And, given how stuck in their ways those people in town seemed to be, Maverick knew it was useless to try to counter it. The damage had been done, and all Maverick could do now was to spend his time living quietly on his land, building up his own ranch and keeping to himself.

Maverick forced himself to relax. Piper might not have anything to do with his family's rivals. However, the Hardwells owned one of the most successful and well-known ranches in the country. She could have been a guest of the ranch or visiting the equine training facility, which also fell under the umbrella of Hardwell's operations. But no matter the reason she had been visiting the ranch, it had nothing to do with him. It was none of his business. "You sure did take a wrong turn." He pointed at the route on her phone screen. "You should have carried on down the main road for another couple of miles. Just turn around here, and when you come to a fork in the road, you're going to want to take a right. Then you'll take the next left, and you're in Applewood proper. You can't miss the sign."

She consulted her map again. "I see it now. Thanks. I probably shouldn't tell a strange man where I'll be staying—most of Applewood doesn't even seem to be on my map—but how do I get to Applewood Inn?"

"You're right, you probably shouldn't be telling me that, but I promise I won't stalk you."

"Thank you. I left the ranch in such a hurry that I never confirmed where exactly I was going."

A hint of fruity perfume floated over the air between them, just like it had at the airport earlier that day. And, again, it smelled as delicious as he imagined she would taste. Before Maverick got too caught up in his fantasy, he leaned back slightly and cleared his throat. "It's always a good idea to get your bearings before setting out in these parts."

"Where exactly are we now?" She pointed at the gravel road, where, if she'd traveled forward on it, would have led her to his home. "Where does this road go?"

"It goes to my ranch." To his home. To his bed. He extended his hand and she took it. No matter what business this woman had with the Hardwells, his mind had no business going *there*.

"Oh, really? Earlier today I wouldn't have pegged you as a rancher."

"Pray tell, how would you have pegged me?" he asked, his voice laced with innuendo.

By the way her cheeks colored, he could tell that she hadn't missed the double entendre.

"Your name is Piper, right?" he asked in an attempt to put some distance between them. Even though he'd remembered her name, he still tried to play it cool, as if she hadn't affected him so greatly during their first meeting.

The corners of her lips turned upward slightly as she nodded. "Yes. I'm Piper Gallagher. Nice to see you again, Maverick. Or should I say 'cowboy'?"

Not many of the townspeople considered him to be a cowboy, or even a real rancher, and he smiled down at her. "Like I said earlier, you can call me whatever you want."

She grinned. "Is that so?" she asked, keeping her hand in his. She leaned back, giving him an appraising look. He stood there, his palm flattened against hers, for several beats too long. When the song on her radio changed and started up with a blistering auto-tuned beat, he remembered himself and pulled back.

She grinned and turned down the volume. "Sorry about that."

"It's quite all right," he told her. "We just don't get a lot of loud music around these parts. The horses don't like it. Unless it's of the country-western variety, of course."

She scrunched up her nose as if she thought the idea of the music to be distasteful, and he agreed that she might be right. "Thanks for your help," she told him. "I should be going."

He was sure he could have stayed on the side of the gravel road, talking to the woman into the night. But the sun was starting to set and she should be getting on her way. Applewood was one of the safest towns in the state, but if one didn't know where they were going—and she clearly didn't—its dark, winding roads could prove treacherous. "Yeah, you'd best do that. It's getting late. You don't want to be stuck out here on your own."

"Thanks for the tip." As he felt her gaze through her large sunglasses, he wondered about the color of her eyes, the depth of them. "Maybe I'll see you around town again, cowboy. Looks like we'll be neighbors for a while."

That caught him off guard. Was this sparkplug of a woman, in this flashy, vintage convertible, with her loud pop music, going to be staying in Applewood for an extended period of time? "Really?"

"Yeah."

"You've got business with the Hardwells?"

"I guess you could say that."

He didn't know what she'd meant by that, but he didn't pry. What she was doing in town was none of his business—especially if she was connected to the Hardwells, the sworn enemies of his family.

"Well, thanks for all of your help," she said. "But I should probably be going before it gets too dark."

He stepped back from her car. "Drive safe now," he told her.

She nodded, and when he led his horse a cautious distance from her car, she sped onto the road, kicking up dust with her tires. The woman was a whirlwind, and she'd entered his life like one.

Four

Following Maverick's directions, Piper finally made it to the Applewood Inn. Elias was right, the drive did allow her to gather her thoughts, and she got to see some more of the town before she lost the light. Her short drive confirmed what she'd seen of Applewood with Elias: it had modern luxuries but still maintained a small-town feel. She saw quaint coffee shops and restaurants with updated but still-rustic storefronts. People milled on sidewalks and came out of shops as storekeepers turned over signs, signaling that they were closed for the evening. She was looking forward to getting back out there to explore in the daytime.

She parked outside the Applewood Inn. It was a two-story building, white with black shutters. It looked grand, like a place she could never hope to afford—but also homey, with bright flowers and a manicured lawn. She pulled her small rolling suitcase from the trunk and entered, dragging it behind her on the stone walkway.

Inside, she walked up to the counter and was greeted by

the desk agent, who smiled pleasantly. "Hello, welcome to the Applewood Inn. I'm Amy, how can I help you?"

"Hi, I don't have a reservation. And I fear I'm a little past check-in time. Piper Gallagher."

She smiled. "Oh, yes, Ms. Gallagher. In fact, I was just talking to Willa. She mentioned you would be coming by, and she said to give you the family rate."

"So she said," Piper said with a nod while she fished her credit card from her wallet and slid it across the desk. "I'm just curious, can I ask what the family rate is?"

"Oh, it's free," Amy said with a laugh, pushing the plastic card back toward her.

"Free?" She had expected a discount, but she hadn't realized that she wouldn't be charged. Piper made a mental note to thank Willa for the room and offer to pay for it when she saw her tomorrow.

"Yes, ma'am," the woman said. "Willa's the boss, and that's what she said. She does that for family and some special guests."

Willa wondered which category she fell into. "I can't argue with that, I guess."

"Nope," Amy told her. She handed over a magnetic key card. "You're in room six. It's just up those stairs and to the right."

"Thank you," Piper said, taking her bag and heading for the stairs.

"I can arrange a porter for your bags," Amy called after her.

Piper shook her head. She was already staying at the inn for free. She didn't want to be any more trouble for anybody. "That isn't necessary. I can handle it from here."

She found her room with little work. When she got inside, she was pleasantly surprised. It was a corner room, which featured a large window on one wall and French doors that looked out onto a manicured back garden and the wooded land beyond it. She kicked off her shoes, dropped her purse on the table and looked around. The room was comfortable, large and tastefully decorated. She unpacked the few things she'd brought with her. She hadn't intended on staying in Applewood long, but she now wanted to stay there as long as it took to get to know her family. And with the way they'd reacted to her earlier, she had no idea how long that would take.

Piper retrieved her phone from her purse on the table and fell onto the bed next to it. She tapped the screen to open the video chat app one, then dialed her best friend Cynthia's number.

It rang once before her friend picked up. "I was waiting for you to call," she scolded.

Piper winced. Cynthia had asked her to call when she landed in Applewood, but, with finally meeting Elias, she'd forgotten, even though she'd known that her friend would be worried. "I know. Sorry. I got caught up."

"How did it go? Did you meet your family?"

"I did," she said, not sure what else to say.

"And?" Cynthia asked carefully.

"My father's an interesting man. If a little eccentric."

"How did the family take it?"

She blew out a heavy breath. "Well, I didn't get thrown out on my ass."

Cynthia laughed. "Sorry. But what happened?"

Piper sighed. "I wasn't sure what I was expecting, but Elias hadn't told them I would be arriving, or even that I was his daughter."

"Wow. Seriously?"

"He's got a flair for the dramatic, that's for sure." She

rolled her eyes. "So, we get to the ranch, and the whole family is gathered there for dinner. Elias tells them who I am, and everyone freezes up. Some reactions are better than others. But all completely understandable. I didn't even stay for dinner. When I got Elias's email, it was a shock to me, too."

"So, what's your plan now?"

She looked around her room at the Applewood Inn. "I guess I'll stay in town for a bit. Get to know my family, if they're interested in that."

"What? For how long?"

Piper shrugged. "For a while, at least. And plus, since I lost my job, I don't have anything to return to Chicago for—"

"Excuse me?"

"Except for you, of course." Her eyes landed on the large glass window. She stood from the bed and opened it up. The sky had turned dark, the stars and moon on full display. She looked out on the inn's lighted manicured grounds. She couldn't see anything beyond the trees, but the silence of the scented night air had a soothing effect, and she was excited to check out the town in the morning. "But, you know, this place is nice enough. I'll have to show you over a call in the daylight. It'll be a good change of pace, for a while anyway."

"And who knows, you might meet a hunky cowboy before too long."

Piper said nothing and her mind shifted from the embarrassment she'd felt at the Hardwell Ranch to the man who'd been the first to welcome her to Applewood, and who'd later helped her when she'd taken a wrong turn. Maverick Kane was classically handsome and hadn't seemed rugged enough to be the owner of a ranch. His smile had been white, his jaw strong, cheekbones high and chiseled. His broad shoulders had been…well, he looked more like a classic actor playing the part of a rancher in a movie.

"What's that look for?" Cynthia asked, watching her over the video.

Piper grinned at her. "You seriously wouldn't believe the guy I met."

"Ooh," her friend said, interested. "Tell me everything."

"Well, I didn't really meet him. We ran into each other twice. I mean we only exchanged names, and he gave me directions."

"Okay, spill."

"That's pretty much it. He was gorgeous, but then he promptly told me how to best go about getting off his land."

"Well, it's a small town, isn't it? Maybe you'll cross paths again. You already have twice in just a few hours."

When Piper thought about Maverick, the tingle she'd felt in her palm when his hand had grasped hers returned, and she smiled. No matter how the Hardwells responded to her presence, perhaps she could find other things to occupy her time, like gorgeous cowboys named Maverick who did things to her hormones. "Maybe we will cross paths again," she told her friend. "I'll tell you if we do. But for now, I'd better go and get settled in."

"Okay, hun. Call me later, okay? Keep me updated."

"I will," she said, ending the chat.

Piper opened her laptop. Telling herself that it was solely due to her journalistic curiosity, she typed *Maverick Kane* into her search bar.

The first hits she pulled up shocked her, driving a small, surprised scream from her throat. They were pictures of a teenage Maverick, on celebrity gossip blogs, stumbling out of clubs he'd been too young to enter, with starlets and heiresses hanging off his shoulders. One blog referred to him as the heir to Kane Energy, an oil company, and, despite the fact that he hadn't turned twenty-one by the time of the photo, a hard-partying kid. As Piper scrolled through the paparazzi pictures and the blogs, she saw a young man who was a far departure from the quiet, serious, ruggedly handsome—*understatement!*—man she'd encountered on horseback.

She finished up her research with a look into Kane Energy, the company once owned by his grandfather, Harlan. Oil deposits had been discovered on the land, which had built the man's company and brought the family massive wealth. The oil on the original land had dried up, but Kane had already moved on into other energy sectors, leaving the land empty. Now, apparently, Maverick lived there.

She pulled up a more recent photo of Maverick, the caption saying it was taken at an Applewood gala. *Of course, Applewood is the type of town to host galas,* she thought with an eye roll. In his black tuxedo, clean-shaven and his hair gelled back, Maverick looked so different than he had in his jeans, T-shirt and cowboy hat. But he was no less attractive.

Piper thought back to their initial meeting; she hadn't missed the spark between them, and she knew that he hadn't, either. Between working at the magazine and her freelance writing, she had been so busy that it had been a while since she'd had the time to seek out a man. She may be in Applewood for a while, getting to know her family, so she might as well have a little fun while she was there.

Five

It was only morning, but when Maverick walked out of the supply shop holding a sack of chicken feed over his shoulder, he could already tell the day was sure to be a scorcher. He'd flung the heavy bag into the back of his truck when Wes Hardwell pulled up next to him.

While the Hardwells had always hated him and his family, he and Wes had become friends when Wes had moved to Applewood in high school. They both knew that it had been typical teenage rebellion pushing them together back then. Jointly, they'd raised hell before his move to Los Angeles and Wes's to London. Since Wes had returned to town, however, they'd managed to maintain a tentative *acquaintanceship*, as much as their deep family rivalry would allow.

"Hi, man, how's it going?" Maverick asked Wes.

"Not too bad," Wes answered, sizing up the sacks in the truck. "You've got chickens now?"

"Yeah, I just added a few to the ranch," he said, putting a hand on his stomach. "I like eggs."

Wes laughed. "How is everything going over there?"

"Pretty good. It's a lot of long hours. I've been taking on one section of land at a time. Restoring it back to how it used to be before my grandfather started in oil is a long, expensive process."

Wes nodded approvingly. "It's good work, though."

"If only your grandfather would see it that way."

Wes grinned. "You know how he is. If it helps, he's only here whenever he gets tired of Arizona."

Maverick laughed. "That does help." He thought of his own stubborn, hardheaded and downright mean grandfather and cast his eyes upward. "I know all about opinionated grandfathers, may he rest in peace." *The bitter old bastard,* he finished silently.

Harlon Kane had been a hard man to live with. He and Elias went back decades and had once considered themselves to be friends, but years and differences in opinions had driven them apart. Whereas Elias had embraced the land, respected it, grown it, added to its betterment, Harlon had used the land, stripped it of its oil and destroyed a large part of it, all for money. The Kane family business grew to a multibillion-dollar corporation. Maverick couldn't dismiss the fact that he'd greatly profited from that money. It had given him a privileged life and he was aware of it, and grateful for it. But after his grandfather passed away, all Maverick had wanted was the acres of land his grandfather had started with. He was cleaning up the land to use it for himself.

Most of the townsfolk respected the work he was doing, but because he was a Kane, Elias Hardwell couldn't see past it. Hell, Maverick could uncover the cure for cancer on his land and share it with the world, and Elias would still think he was the same as the man he'd feuded with for decades.

"How are things on Hardwell Ranch?"

"You know I'm not supposed to be discussing business matters with the enemy," Wes said with a subversive grin.

Maverick laughed again. "Yeah, I might just steal all your ranching secrets." In the distance, he heard the roar of an engine and looked up in time to see the same cherry-red convertible drive by at a higher speed than would be appreciated by most of the people in town. Piper Gallagher was still around, it seemed. He watched as her red hair blew in the wind.

"And there she goes," Wes muttered, shaking his head.

"What's that?"

Wes suddenly looked nervous. "Um, that woman. She came to our place yesterday evening."

Maverick had been curious what sort of business Piper had had with the Hardwells. Maybe Wes would shine a little light on it for him. "Oh, really? What's her deal?"

Wes shook his head. "She's a journalist and she's Elias's—she's my… She wants to get to know the family, maybe do a piece on us. That's it."

Maverick grimaced. A journalist? He was trying to keep a low profile in Applewood. The last thing he needed was a reporter coming to town and blowing up his spot, telling the blogs what he was doing. Plus, he couldn't shake the feeling that there was something Wes wasn't telling him. "Did you mean to keep it so vague?"

Wes laughed. "You know we like to keep people guessing. But I think it's something we'll be keeping under our hats for a while." He touched the brim of his Stetson.

Interesting. "I met her yesterday," he told Wes. "She was lost near my place. I gave her directions back to town."

Piper. He said her name to himself, as if savoring the word on his lips.

"Yeah, and apparently she's sticking around," Wes supplied. "For a while, anyway."

Maverick nodded. Even though the idea of having Piper in town was an appealing thought, he knew that he couldn't afford to get close to a journalist who might be all too happy to dredge up his past and embarrass him. "If that's the case, I'd better stay the hell out of her way. I'm not too interested in spending time with any journalists."

"I don't know, I'm sure your stories are much more interesting than anyone else in this town."

"And I won't be telling them any time soon," he said, shaking his head, thinking about the nights he'd spent carousing with starlets in nightclubs. Piper may not be in town to do a deep dive into his life, but he wasn't being egotistical to think that the minute she found out he was Maverick Kane, heir to the Kane oil fortune, former Hollywood club kid and paparazzi fodder, she would see a story. He couldn't let that happen. "Those days are long behind me." And he was going to keep it that way. He stared down the road to where Piper's convertible had disappeared around the corner.

"Wait, wasn't that one of Elias's classic cars she's driving? I thought I recognized it last night."

Wes nodded, with a frown on his face. "Yeah, um, after bringing her here, he just handed over the keys to one of his favorite cars." He shook his head. "It's been a pretty wild day."

"Really?" That was strange. Even Maverick knew how much Elias thought of those cars. There was definitely something odd going on when it came to the woman. He knew for a fact that Piper Gallagher was trouble, and he'd best keep his distance.

* * *

As she drove through the small town of Applewood, Piper checked out the shops and other businesses that lined Main Street. It was your typical small town, but it was obvious from the high-end shops, luxury vehicles and large homes she'd seen so far, that its townsfolk were some of the richest in the state. In her research, she'd learned that many high-profile families and ranchers lived in the area, and the air of opulence in the town confirmed it.

Posters advertised the Applewood Days Festival, and crews seemed to be hard at work setting it up. She'd have to check it out while she was there, however long that would be.

Thanks to careful saving, and a small severance payout from the magazine, Piper had enough money in the bank to last her a while before she decided to head back to Chicago, if she even wanted to return to the city. She certainly didn't have an end date in mind, but until she found her next path, she might need something to keep her busy. As a journalist, she could pick up some freelance gigs online, but a temporary job of some kind in town would really give her an excuse to stay in Applewood, and the time to get to know the Hardwells—her family.

But first... Feeling the need for caffeine, she pulled into the gravel parking lot of a café, her tires kicking up dust. She got out of the car and saw that the café was situated next door to the local newspaper office. A sign in the window said Help Wanted. She stood in front of the door for a moment. She might as well check inside to see if they had any leads on freelance jobs.

She walked into the office and it felt as if she had stepped back in time. It was a small, beige, dark, dusty space. The blinds were drawn in an effort to keep the Texas heat out of the un-air-conditioned building, she assumed.

It clearly wasn't working, she thought as she breathed in the stale, stuffy air. Each corner held a small desk with communal office equipment. The office of the *Applewood Tribune* was certainly a far cry from the modern, bustling bullpen she was used to in her former job.

"Can I help you?" the man closest to her asked, exhaustion and irritation coloring his voice. His desktop was covered with scattered papers and what looked to be story and advertisement copy.

Piper hooked her thumb over her shoulder. "Hi," she said, raising her hand self-consciously. "My name is Piper."

"You here for the editor job?"

He'd been so abrupt that it had caught her off guard. "I'm sorry?"

He looked at her over the rim of his glasses. "You have any experience, darlin'?"

"I guess," she told him. She didn't have any editorial experience, but she might be able to talk her way into a job as a reporter there, if she wasn't a good fit for the editor's job. It was worth a shot, at least. "For five years, I worked for a fashion and lifestyle magazine in Chicago. I can email my résumé." She pulled out her cell phone to retrieve it from her cloud storage.

He held up his hands. "No, don't bother. I've heard enough. You've got the job."

She widened her eyes. She'd gone in looking for leads on freelance stories, but was now outright being offered the editor job—no résumé, no interview. "Really?"

He threw down the papers in his hand before standing from the desk. He plucked his cowboy hat from the wall and slipped it onto his head. "Yup. Now that you're here, this is my last day."

She looked around at the other three people in the room,

and she could see their amusement as they glanced up from their own work and smiled at each other. "Are you serious?"

"As a heart attack." He took her hand and shook it vigorously. "Welcome to the team. Have fun." He waved to the others in the room. "It's been nice working with you all, but thirty years in this office is more than enough. I'll see you all at Longhorn's for my retirement party."

He left and the other three people returned to their work, not offering any sort of welcome to her, or an explanation behind what had just happened.

"What—who was that?" she asked.

"That was Bill, our former editor," a woman responded. She stood and extended her hand. "I'm Paula, I cover society events and the municipal politics beat." She pointed to a man across the office. "This is Jorge, announcements and obits." He waved, and Piper waved back. "And that's Carl."

"What do you do, Carl?"

"Breaking news."

Piper dipped her chin at him. "'Breaking news,'" she repeated after him. "In Applewood?" She'd only been in town since the day before, but she didn't see how much breaking news could come out of a place so small.

His smile was large. "I didn't say I was busy."

Piper laughed. "Well, I'm Piper. I'm here from Chicago, and I guess I'm your new editor. That was the strangest job interview I've ever had."

"Bill's been trying to retire for more than a year now, and that sign's been up just as long," Paula explained. "Let's just say that Applewood has a small candidate pool."

"And none of you wanted the job?" she asked. In response, they all laughed at her before returning to their work. "Lucky for me," Piper muttered. She went to the window and pulled down the Help Wanted sign before taking a seat at her new desk, behind the mess and stacks of papers that Bill had left behind.

Her phone vibrated in her bag. She checked the display. It was a message from Garrett, suggesting that they get together the day after tomorrow, when they finished with work. She frowned. She'd been hoping to get some time with the family earlier than that. But she had to let it happen on terms that worked for everyone. She and Elias had sprung her appearance on them, and she had to be gracious enough to give everyone time to come around. To the Hardwells, she was a stranger who'd crashed their family dinner. As long as she had a job in Applewood, she had time to get to know them.

When she'd landed in town the day before, she hadn't imagined that she would be landing a job, let alone gaining a new family and meeting a handsome stranger. She wondered what other surprises life in Applewood had in store for her.

Six

Several hours after his day started, Maverick finished up his chores in town. He'd made several stops between the feed shop, the hardware store and the grocer. He'd been busy and skipped lunch. So he pulled his truck into the full parking lot of Patsy's Diner.

Patsy's had been a mainstay of Applewood for decades. Back in the day, the diner had been the number-one date spot in town, and he'd spent many evenings there hanging out with his friends, dining with girls on dates, but he hadn't stepped foot in the place since he'd returned home the previous year. After having only a mug of coffee for breakfast this morning, he figured today was a good day for a juicy burger and an icy-cold Coke.

He entered the restaurant and, just like back in the day, the place was full. Patsy's and its delicious offerings were as popular as ever, untouchable by fad diets and changes in consumption over the decades. He looked around and, not seeing any free tables, he opted for a seat at the far end of the counter and started in the direction of the empty stool.

"Maverick, hi," he heard a familiar voice call to him. Stopping, he turned and looked around. It was none other than Piper Gallagher. She looked as tempting as she had been the day before. Her lips still wore a cherry-red shade similar to that of Elias's car, but this time, he could see her large brown eyes, which had been previously shielded by her sunglasses.

"We meet again," he said, looking down at her.

"Yeah, I have to grab a quick something and then head back to the *Applewood Tribune* office. I've got a story to write, and I'm still trying to organize the mess that Bill left me with," she told him hurriedly.

That took him off guard. "Wait, what was all that?"

She laughed. "I accidentally got a new job as editor of the town paper today."

He knew almost nothing of the woman, but it was clear that Piper Gallagher was full of surprises. "How does one *accidentally* get a job?"

She shrugged. "When I find out what actually happened, I'll tell you."

The stool next to the one he'd selected for himself opened up. He gestured to it. "Well, to celebrate, why don't you let me buy you dinner?" he asked. The words, out of his mouth before he could stop them, were completely out of sync with his commitment to stay away from her. "You can tell me about your new job."

She seemed to think about it for a several seconds, but then her lips turned up in a grin, and her eyes crinkled at the corners as she looked up at him. "Twist my arm, why don't you? Let's grab a couple of seats before they're filled. But I insist on buying my own burger."

Maverick was suddenly glad to have the company, but he had no intention of letting her buy her own meal. He dropped his hand to her lower back and ushered her to the far end of the counter. When they sat, the waitress handed them each a menu.

They both perused the menu in silence before selecting their orders—a burger for him, chicken fingers for her. When their drinks arrived, Maverick turned to her. "So, tell me all about your new job."

She laughed. "It was surely an experience," she told him before launching into the telling of how she'd been looking for freelance story leads but had stumbled into becoming the editor for the *Applewood Tribune*.

"So, are you planning on moving here?" he asked. He couldn't help but ask questions about her. He still had no idea what had brought her to Applewood, and Wes had been vague about what he knew, but he needed to know if he was on her radar for a story.

"I can see myself staying for a little while, at least," she told him. "Permanently? Probably not. I've got a comfortable room at the Applewood Inn for now, a new job and the flexibility to settle here for a while. Short answer—I guess I'll just see what happens."

"I've never met anyone who could just uproot and settle new within a day."

She shrugged. "That's kind of been my life, though. Being a journalist makes it easy to change gears. I've never wanted to stagnate in one place for too long. Switching it up keeps me fresh, keeps the words coming and I never get bored."

"And what about the story you're writing on the Hardwells?"

"Story?" she asked, looking confused, which he found odd.

"That's what Wes told me."

Her eyes widened, but after a beat, she seemed to recover, and again looked sure and confident. She shook her head. "Geez, word sure does travel in this place."

"You might be the big-city journalist, but I have my sources, too. It's a small town—word doesn't have far to go." He gave her an appraising look, up and down, taking in her short denim skirt and tank top, her long hair tied in a ponytail with a bright pink scarf. "But a woman like you, driving around in Elias Hardwell's car—" his eyes settled on hers "—you're the news."

Her gaze connected with his, and in the loud, bustling diner, they shared a quiet moment. She turned back to her drink, and Maverick focused on the way her plump lips closed over the tip of her straw. Still drinking, she slanted her eyes in his direction, catching him staring. She smiled at him, and the rest of the world fell away. Uncomfortable with the scrutiny, Maverick looked away first, turning his attention to his own drink. He didn't say anything. And, luckily, before he felt the need to talk, the waitress appeared with their food.

They both ate several bites before Maverick put down his burger. He had to find out what had really brought her to Applewood, and he had to make sure it had nothing to do with him. She'd ignored his question previously, so he thought he'd try a more direct approach this time. "So, I've got to know—what's your deal with the Hardwells?" he asked.

Her head tilted to the side at the question and he knew that he hadn't exactly being covert in asking it. "Why exactly do you need to know that?" He noted a hint of hesitation in her voice.

"I'm just trying to get to know you," he said with a shrug and an easygoing smile, trying not to put her off completely.

"Like I said before, I'm just always looking for new stories, new leads," she told him. "I thought about coming down south, and that led me here and to ranching as a topic. This led me to the Hardwells, one of the most successful ranching families in the country."

To Maverick, it sounded a little far-fetched, and he knew she was holding back about something. He'd be interested in learning what that was. "That's a pretty random topic, fairly removed from Chicago. Do you write much about the industry?"

"Not really. I just like learning about different things."

"And now you're the editor of the town paper." She may have been in town to interview the Hardwells—even though that didn't ring completely true to him. Was the Hardwell story interesting enough to bring a woman to one of the smallest towns in Texas? Or was she here to find the former bad boy of Hollywood Boulevard? Something about it didn't feel quite right.

"Weird how some things work out, right?" He didn't respond and she popped a French fry into her mouth. "So, tell me about yourself, Maverick. I met you for the second time yesterday while unintentionally trespassing on your land. You're a rancher, too? One with a private plane, as well?"

"Are you interviewing me?"

"No. We're just making conversation, right?"

The vibe had shifted between them. It was heavier, moodier, but from the way she looked at him, he knew it was just as flirty.

"You had a lot of questions for me," she pointed out. "You can't handle the same? Does something about innocent questions make you feel like it's an interview?" She leaned closer. "Why so sensitive about it?" she said, lowering her voice. She looked at him closely and he felt his temperature rise under her gaze. "You look familiar, Maverick."

He looked away. "No, I just have one of those faces."

She hummed and shook her head. "No, I definitely know your face. Maybe you look like a guy who used to be famous for being rich tabloid fodder about twenty years ago."

Maverick maintained eye contact but leaned in. He could feel his heart rate rising as sure as he could feel the heat increasing in his cheeks. He stilled and knew then that she knew who he was. "No. You must have me confused with someone else."

She shook her head. "No, I don't think I have."

"I didn't take you for one to be reading celebrity gossip rags."

"Hazard of the job, I guess."

"Is that why you're here?" he asked outright.

She drew back, clearly surprised by his question. "What? No. Of course not. Try getting over yourself. Me being in Applewood has nothing to do with you."

Maverick realized that he was being egotistical. He watched her carefully. "It was stupid of me to ask. I know the world doesn't revolve around me."

"Glad you realize it," she said with a smile, which he returned.

"But you wouldn't be the first person who has tracked me down here."

"Really?"

"Yeah, a few reporters, some *fans*—" he used air quotes on the word "—any time one of my old friends was in the news, the old, embarrassing photos and stories would be dragged to the surface, bringing people out of the woodwork."

He pinned her with his gaze so there would be no mistaking his meaning. "I'm not interested in being one of the subjects of your writing."

"Well, that's good. I'm not interested in writing about you. We all have things that we may want to keep quiet."

He watched her and caught the lonely, forlorn look on her face, wondering what sorts of things she was looking to keep quiet. He realized that he was being overly suspicious. He raised his palms to her. "You're right," he said. "I'm sorry I was so sensitive. I see you've done your research, but I'm not that guy anymore. I try to keep to myself since I've moved back here. I don't socialize much, and it's been a while since I've had a friendly conversation with a beautiful woman." Knowing he'd played his hand a little too much, he looked away from her and drank from his glass. He cleared his throat. "You asked if I'm a rancher. The answer is that I'm trying to be. I've got a few horses so far. A couple of herds of cattle. And I recently got some chickens."

"That sounds like a fairly small operation for a piece of land big enough for me to get lost on."

"Yeah, it's a lot of land, but I've got plans for every acre."

"How'd you start out?"

"Now this is feeling like an interview." Maverick toyed briefly with what to tell her, but he settled on the truth. "I inherited the land from my grandfather," he explained. "He'd used it for oil, but now I'm cleaning it up and restoring the land."

She nodded. "That's interesting. If you've got some time soon, why don't I come by your place? You can show me the work you're doing."

That hadn't been his intention. He didn't need a journalist, no matter how attractive he found her, coming to his ranch and getting into his space. That was the opposite of keeping a low profile. Even if they didn't necessary like him or his family, the people of Applewood were typically content to let him live a quiet life in the small town, and he was grateful for it.

When he didn't respond, she must have gotten the hint. "You know, never mind. Forget I asked," she said, raising her hands and turning back to her plate.

"It's okay. Like I said, I'm just a private person. I don't want that kind of attention anymore."

"I get it."

They both ate their food and the break in conversation gave Maverick the chance to think about Piper. Even though he knew he should keep her at a distance, he wanted to know more about her. He turned to her again. "You know what, forget everything I said. I'd be happy to show you around sometime."

She smiled. "Thanks. I'll probably take you up on it. But I understand that, being a private person. There are things about me that people don't know, and I wouldn't want them getting out until the time is right." That was the second time she'd mentioned something like that, and he wondered what those secrets of hers were. Did it have anything to do with Wes's odd behavior when he'd run into him? It wasn't his place to ask, but it made him curious.

Piper broke the moment first, pulling back. "Well, thank you for the meal, but I've got to be getting back to the *Tribune* office."

"Yeah, you've got a paper to get out, and I've got to be going. I need to get back home." He reached into his wallet and pulled out a fifty-dollar bill to pay for their meals. "It was nice seeing you." It was true, now that he knew his past wasn't the reason she'd come to Applewood.

"Likewise." She paused expectantly in front of him, looking up at him.

"Allow me to walk you out."

"Quite a gentleman," she said. "Lead the way."

He cupped her elbow in his hand and, together, they walked outside.

She was a beautiful woman, but that wasn't all. Piper's dark eyes were sharp, and the ever-present, knowing grin on her face told him that she was more aware of the attraction between them than he'd realized. She intrigued him, and he wanted to get to know her better. He wanted to learn everything about her; her secrets, her dreams, what made her laugh, what made her cry. A bolt of lust shot through him as his eyes drifted lower to the soft cleavage revealed by her low-cut shirt. *What turned her on?* "Maybe we can get dinner again," he suggested. "Sometime soon, and not at a noisy diner counter."

She grinned up at him. "Are you asking me out on a date?"

"Only if you say yes. Otherwise, we can forget it happened."

"Well, I'd better not embarrass you." Her grin became a full smile. "Yeah, I'd like that."

"Great." He couldn't remember the last time he'd asked a woman out on an honest-to-goodness date. Since moving back to Applewood, he'd enjoyed a quiet life, and there hadn't been any woman in town who'd caught his eye quite like Piper had. They stared at each other for a while before he leaned down and placed his lips on her cheek.

Of course, he would tell himself that he meant it as a friendly goodbye, but when her head tilted and her lips met his, he was feeling anything but friendly. Her full lips were soft and smooth, but firm, and he found it nearly impossible to pull away. They were in the parking lot of a busy diner and they were clearly visible to anyone who looked out the large front windows or passed by on the street. Maverick didn't care about that. All he could think about was tasting her, touching her. He pulled her closer and, as her lips parted, he took full advantage, swiping her tongue with his own. Piper moaned into his mouth and he felt his entire body go rigid with need. Given no other option, besides taking her there on the hood of Elias Hardwell's classic car, he broke the contact.

She breathed heavily and a rosy flush colored her normally fair cheeks. "Well," she said softly.

"Yeah," he said, trying hard to steady his own breathing. He glanced toward the diner and saw that there were, indeed, patrons he recognized watching them, blatantly, as they brought French fries to their mouths. He waved and they looked away.

"Anyway, about that date," he said, opening his wallet again and passing over one of his cards. "Text or call me for a day that works for you. Also, your visit to the ranch. I'll show you around."

She plucked the card from his fingers. Her hand brushed his for a moment and, again, their eyes connected. "Thanks. I will."

He gave her another cursory once-over and tried to hide the way his body stiffened in response to her lush curves. "I'm looking forward to it," he told her.

Maverick watched the swing of Piper's hips as she walked away from him, and he grinned, even though something told Maverick his world was about to be turned upside down.

Seven

The day after her impromptu dinner with Maverick, Piper made her way up the gravel road to Hardwell Ranch again. This time, she felt just as nervous. When she'd come the first time, at least she'd had Elias at her side, but now, with Elias back in Arizona for a few days, she was going to meet with the other Hardwells alone.

She parked her car in front of a large stable where Garrett had asked her to meet him. She got out of the car and closed the door as he, Wes and their father—*her brother*—Stuart, came out of the building. Garrett raised his hand in greeting.

She waved back and pushed her sunglasses to the top of her head.

"Piper, hello again," Garrett said when they were closer. He extended his hand to her.

"Hello," she said, shaking his hand and then Wes's.

Stuart, however, pulled her into a hug. "Let's not do any of that formal stuff," he told her. "You're family."

She pulled away, smiling. Stuart's acceptance sent

warmth coiling through her. She blinked the tears away. "Thank you, all of you, for meeting me."

"We're glad to," Garrett told her. "And I thought it would be a good idea if Dad and Wes came along, too. We all might as well get to know you, I figure."

"That's great."

"How has your stay in town been so far?" Garrett asked. "Is the inn comfortable?"

"It is," she told him. "It's an incredible place. So comfortable and luxurious."

Garrett's smile was a proud one. "I'll let Willa know."

"Please do. Though, I'll be staying in town a little longer than I thought," she said. "I started working at the *Applewood Tribune*. I might need something a little longer term."

"I think you can work that out with her, but I'm certain that she'll want you to stay at the inn no matter how long you need it."

There was silence as the awkwardness set in. They each looked from one to the other, unsure what to say next. Then she thought of her dinner with Maverick. It, too, had been awkward at times, but she'd turned on her professional charm and instincts. She didn't want to interview her family, but she knew that if she used her experience as a journalist, she could get to know them. It was imperative that she keep an emotional distance from the Hardwells. At least until she knew they wouldn't reject her.

A rapid text tone filled the air around them and Stuart pulled out his phone. "Oh hell," he muttered. "That's one of the nurses at the clinic. There's an emergency I need to attend to," he told them. "I'm a doctor in High Pine," he explained.

That disappointed her, but an emergency couldn't wait. "I understand," she told him. "We'll have time later."

He dropped a hand on Piper's shoulder. "Let's meet up again soon, okay?"

She nodded. "Absolutely."

When Stuart was gone, Garrett shoved his hands into his pockets. "So, where should we start?" he asked.

"I don't know." Her professional instinct was to begin interviewing them, much like how her dinner with Maverick had turned out, so she went with that. "Why don't you guys tell me about yourselves? What was it like for you growing up?"

"We grew up in High Pine," Garrett started. "That's the next town over. I spent a lot of time here on the ranch. Like he just said, our father is a doctor and has a clinic there, so he didn't really get into the ranch or the business side of it. The clinic has always kept him busy enough. It's not for everyone, of course. But when I was a kid, I spent every spare moment here in Applewood with Elias. He's the one who showed me the ropes around here."

"What's your relationship with Elias like? You must be close."

Garrett laughed. "Elias is a tough man, but he's always been there for his family. Family is everything to him."

Piper felt a short stab in her chest. Elias was her father and hadn't been there for her. It was understandable, given that he hadn't known of her existence, but still, it hurt.

Garrett must have clocked her frown and the way she looked away. "Oh, hell, I'm sorry. That was a stupid thing to say."

She waved him off. "No. Don't worry about that. It's nice that you all have that. You're all really close, right?"

"Yeah, especially now that Wes is back in the fold, we really are."

She turned to the older brother. "Wes, you were away? Where were you?"

Wes rubbed the back of his neck with his palm. "Yeah. It's embarrassing to talk about now. But I was a bit of a rebel as a kid. I got into trouble all the time and Dad sent me here to straighten up."

"Did it work?" she asked Wes. "Did you straighten up?"

Wes laughed. "Hell no. I came here and caused even more trouble. After college, I moved to England and started a telecom company."

"So, what brought you back home?"

"The desire to reconnect with my family and my roots brought me back. My wife, Daisy, however, is what made me stay."

"Elias's inheritance demands didn't hurt," Garrett muttered.

"His inheritance demands?" she asked. "I'm sorry, what are you talking about?"

"It's pretty unbelievable," Garrett said with a chuckle. "Last year, at Elias and Cathy's engagement party, Elias announced his retirement, and it was a surprise to all of us. We all thought he'd be working the ranch until his last day."

"But more surprising than that," Wes interjected, "was the part that came next—in order for his grandchildren to be entitled to any of his inheritance, they would have to work the ranch for a period of six months."

"You can't be serious," Piper said with a laugh. The old man was just as eccentric as she'd read. She thought about that. She didn't want anyone to think that she expected the inheritance to extend to her. Piper didn't care for money from the family. But would they think that was why she was in town?

"As a heart attack." Wes shook his head. "And, meanwhile, Garrett is the only one of us that has any actual ranch experience."

"So, you came home and became a rancher?"

"It was a long process, but now I couldn't imagine going back to my regular life or doing anything else. Of course, that requirement pales in comparison to what Garrett had to do."

Piper turned her attention to Garrett. "What did you have to do?"

Garrett sighed. "In order to receive controlling share of the ranch, I had to get married."

Piper's eyes widened. Between Garrett's and Wes's requirements, apparently, she wasn't the sole recipient of Elias's shenanigans.

"It worked out well for me. That's how I came to be with Willa, and it was the best thing that ever happened to me, but how he went about it was definitely a point of frustration for me."

"Yeah, I'll bet." They walked past the stable and Piper almost gasped when she looked up and saw the rolling green hills of Hardwell Ranch, which went on until they met the blue sky of the horizon. The wide-open space made her feel small, insignificant. From their vantage point, she saw herds of cattle in the distance, and a pair of horses running across the field. She could see the appeal of this lifestyle—the Hardwell Ranch was a small slice of heaven. "Wow."

"It's great, right?" Garrett asked.

"Really something," Wes added, also struck by the beauty of the land. "It's not something you get used to."

"You must be glad to be back."

"I am."

"And what about your youngest brother, Noah?" she

asked. "Did he come back to work on the ranch?" Piper was quickly losing interest in the pretense of doing an interview, but was instead enjoying talking to the men and learning about the family.

Garrett rolled his eyes. "He hasn't come home yet. It was surprising enough that Wes came back, but I don't see Noah coming home any time soon."

"He's an artist. He currently lives in the Florida Keys, enjoying the beach-bum lifestyle."

She had seen some of Noah's art online. A master with a paintbrush, his main subject was the open ocean, white-capped waves, sandy coastlines. Not many spoke of his Texas roots. "It's strange—you're brothers, but the three of you are so different."

The day went on. As Garrett and Wes shared stories of their upbringing and the connection to Hardwell Ranch, Piper was riveted by their tales. Every time they asked a question about her own life, she easily deflected back to the ranch. Her upbringing had been so regular, so average, she wanted only to hear about their stories of Elias and her siblings, and everything she'd missed out on. It made her sad. They seemed like such a big, tight, close-knit family. It was what she'd missed as a child, and she felt sad that, biologically, she could have been part of it had she not had the bad luck to be the child that Elias hadn't known about.

After walking around the ranch and the horse training facility, Piper found herself impressed. She looked at her cell phone and was surprised to see that several hours had already passed. She'd wanted to cover so much ground, to learn all she could about the Hardwells, and learn how she belonged. She'd had so much fun talking to Garrett and Wes and hearing their stories. "Look at the time," she said. "I can't believe how late it's gotten."

Garrett smiled. "Yeah, it was a great afternoon."

"I think so, too," Wes said.

"I hope I didn't monopolize too much of your time."

"Don't worry about that," Wes told her. "Garrett employs enough people so that he doesn't really do anything day-to-day."

Garrett gave his brother a shove. "What's your excuse then?"

Piper laughed at the brothers' back-and-forth. "It was nice getting to know both of you."

"You don't know anything yet," Wes told her. "But, over time, you will."

The fact that they were including her in future plans made her smile. She was finally on her way to being accepted by a family. Her family. "I'm looking forward to it."

"Yeah, we are, too," Garrett agreed. "Why don't you come by sometime soon and we can get you on a horse. Do you know how to ride?"

She shook her head. "No. I'm a city girl born and raised. I've never ridden a horse."

"Well, you came to the right people. It's like we knew how to ride before we could walk. Like it's in the blood or something." He paused. "So that means you'll be fine."

Piper thought about that. She and men in front of her shared the same blood. But there was no way she would be able to show any sort of prowess on the ranch. They wouldn't expect her to, of course, but she didn't want to make herself look like an uncoordinated klutz. "That sounds great. I look forward to it."

"How have you been finding the town?" Wes asked. "People treating you right?"

"Yeah," she said with a smile. "Small-town hospitality really is a thing. But I haven't gotten to know many people yet." She paused. Maverick had mentioned to her that the Hardwells weren't exactly his biggest fans. This was the time to ask. "I've met Maverick Kane a few times. He's been nice to me." She caught Garrett's eye roll, while Wes's face remained neutral.

"What was that about?" she asked Garrett.

"Maverick Kane is trouble," Garrett said simply.

"Come on." Wes gave his brother's shoulder a shove. "Mav's not that bad." That intrigued Piper. *Mav* apparently had a friend in Wes.

"The Hardwells and the Kanes have never gotten along," Garrett told her.

It was Wes's turn to roll his eyes. "Forgive Garrett's dramatics—he gets that from our grandfather—but that's not entirely true. Our grandfather and Maverick's grandfather used to be partners and, together, they owned all of the land. But back when they were young men, there was a falling out. So they split the land, separated their business interest. Harlan Kane went into the oil business and Elias stuck to ranching. Both got rich in different ways. But they never spoke again."

"If you listen to Elias," Garrett continued, "he'd tell you that Harlan tried to run us out of business more than once, stole our livestock, poisoned his own land for oil and tried to take ours."

Piper mulled that over and wondered if Maverick's family was truly that bad. "Is any of that true?"

"I'm sure part of it may have been exaggerated but, either way, the men made each other's lives miserable for as long as they were both there."

"And what's that have to do with Maverick?" she asked. Garrett narrowed his eyes at her and she wondered if her tone conveyed any more than a passing interest in the story.

Wes then stepped in. "Maverick and I were close when we were young. Neither of the families liked it. We got in a lot of trouble back then. We were both responsible for it, but Elias always claimed that he influenced me. That wasn't the case. We still talk, but there's no changing Elias's mind on the family," he warned her.

"Bad blood runs deep," Garrett said. "Maverick normally keeps to himself, and that's the way everyone seems to like it."

Piper nodded. She wondered if there was something more to it than that. But she decided not to push it. "Yeah, I've heard that."

Now she had another problem. She thought back to that kiss, the one that still made her entire body tingle. She liked Maverick, was *very* attracted to him. But if what Garrett and Wes had told her about Elias and his thoughts on the Kanes was true, it didn't bode well. And how would they feel about her if it was apparent that she was into their sworn family enemy? She checked the time on her phone again. "Wow, now I'm really late." She didn't have a lot of time before she had to be back to town. "Thanks for the interview. I had a lot of fun today. I'd like to do it again soon. I feel like we've only scratched the surface of the Hardwell family secrets."

"Yeah, pretty much," Wes responded. "I think there are still some secrets to uncover." He gave Piper a funny look and she was curious about what was behind it. They'd had a pleasant afternoon together, but she wondered if he wasn't convinced by her and her sudden appearance in their lives. It surprised her, and she didn't want to do anything that would put doubt in their minds of her intentions. "You're welcome back anytime, Piper."

"What are you up to for the rest of the day?"

"I'm going to Main Street for the Applewood Days Festival. Today's the charity pie Bake-Off. I'm covering it for the *Tribune*."

Garrett laughed. "You're covering the big pie Bake-Off."

"Why is that so funny?"

"The Bake-Off is a holdover from a simpler time. Now, it's basically a social event where people bring in pies that were made either by their housekeepers or bought at the high-end bakery in High Pine."

"Then they socialize over champagne and compare their latest six-figure luxury purchases," Wes added.

Piper laughed. "For real?"

"Yeah, the wives of the town founders would roll over in their graves if they saw what's become of it, but you know how it is. Times change."

Garrett laughed. "I'm sure you didn't cover many pie Bake-Offs in Chicago."

"I definitely did not," she said with a laugh as she picked up her bag.

"Well, enjoy your time here. It's a great town. And for the most part, the people are good."

"There are some bad apples in every bunch," Wes said. "Or pie, I guess."

She wondered who they were referring to. Everyone she'd met so far in Applewood had treated her well. "Just like any town, I guess—small or otherwise. I haven't gotten to know a lot of people yet, but I'm sure I will."

She couldn't help but think of a certain resident cowboy she wanted to get to know better—family feud or not.

Eight

As Maverick walked through the crowd gathered in the softball field, he felt as out of place as he ever had. He'd never been one to take part in community events, but he'd been bored and decided to head into town to see what all the fuss was about. It had nothing or little to do with the potential to see Piper Gallagher there... *Right?*

Not seeing her, or anyone else he was interested in talking to, he ducked into the pop-up bar that had been built in the town square. It didn't just serve as a place to get out of the heat or to get a drink, it was where the town's movers and shakers gathered during the festival for informal meetings and discussions about how they could help each other in the coming year.

Maverick ordered a beer and, when he turned around, he saw that several people were watching him, likely wondering what he was doing there. But he didn't mind the attention. He'd already cut a check to the fundraising committee. In Applewood, if you had money—as most people did—you were welcome in any of the town's social circles, whether they liked you or not. And that—the phoniness, the shallowness—was why he avoided many of the town's events and its people. The bartender placed a frosty, brown bottle in front of him, and Maverick, feeling as if he was on display, headed back outside.

He was glad he had when he took several steps toward the crowd at the front of the field and saw Piper standing by the pies, taking diligent notes in her notebook. She was the only person paying any attention to them, however, as, he learned, was the custom of the festival. The pie Bake-Off contestants all mingled at nearby high-top tables, gossiping and drinking champagne from glass flutes, their finest new jewelry, diamonds and platinum catching the sunlight.

The Applewood Days Festival was one of the social highlights of the year. However, as the average net worth of the citizens grew drastically, it had taken on a haughty air, far removed from its humble beginnings. The same folksy events were still held, but they were now used to celebrate status. But who was Maverick to talk about others flaunting their wealth? His family's oil money had all but started the town on its present course of prosperity and, at times, he wasn't much better.

Maverick was still watching Piper and, likely feeling his eyes on her, she looked up from her notes and in his direction. She excused herself from the women nearby and walked to him. "You know, I really didn't expect to see you here."

He waved his hand over the crowd. "What, I can't come out here and support the culinary arts?"

"Word around town is you're normally too grumpy to come out for stuff like this. I know you like to keep to yourself, but what, are you a recluse or something?"

"Grumpy?" he asked.

Her nod was earnest. "Insufferably so," she said. "As per my sources."

"Who are your sources?"

"I'm afraid I can't disclose that."

"Of course, you can't," he said, with a nod of his own. However, she wasn't wrong. Maverick liked to keep to himself, but something else in what she'd said caught his attention. He narrowed his eyes at her playfully. "You're asking around town about me?"

"You got me," she said impishly. "I'm using my new position of power as editor of the paper to check up on you."

"I thought so. But, no, I'm not a recluse. I just prefer my own company most of the time." Before he'd come back to Applewood, he'd spent his share of long nights filled with crowds, loud music and bright lights. He enjoyed the quiet and solitude of the ranch now.

"It all makes sense now, though," she said thoughtfully. "That's why you kicked me off your property the other night when I got lost."

"I didn't kick you off my property."

"You just showed me promptly how to leave."

"Maybe I don't like strangers."

"Well, you do know what they say about strangers, right?"

"That you shouldn't talk to them."

She laughed and pushed him lightly on the chest. "The saying goes 'there are no strangers here, only friends you haven't yet met."

"Who said that?"

"I don't know," she said with a casual shrug. "Yeats? Or maybe it's just something I heard on TV."

He laughed. Was Piper a stranger or a strange woman?

Either way, she was smart, funny and quick, and he really enjoyed talking with her. "We're friends?"

"Maybe not yet, but I'll have you know that people think I'm pretty fun to be around."

"I'd believe that."

"In fact, most say I'm pretty irresistible."

Maverick considered it and found he couldn't refute that. Since he'd laid eyes on her just a couple of days ago, she'd stayed on his mind. She intrigued him. But it wasn't just her looks—shiny red hair, lush curves, the confidence she had in showing them off—that made his body react positively. What really caught his attention was her humor, the energy she radiated. And there was the matter of that kiss. He couldn't forget that. His blood sizzled thinking about the softness of her lips, her taste, and craved another one. "I can't disagree with that."

Their eyes connected for a beat before he cleared his throat awkwardly and managed to drag his gaze away from her. He looked around the fairgrounds. "You're here on official business for the *Tribune*?"

"Yeah, I guess so. I never knew that a blue-ribbon pie competition would go above the fold, but here we are."

Maverick thought about his own days in the news. The news site he'd been featured on ran a little racier than that, as well. But this was the life he preferred. "That's how we do it here. It's a slower pace. I'm sorry to say, but you're probably going to get bored soon."

"I have to learn how to ride a horse," she said, changing the topic, seemingly pulling the thought out of nowhere. "Garrett and Wes Hardwell invited me for a ride."

Again with the Hardwells. "Well, that'll keep you busy, I guess." He nodded, and the idea of seeing her on the back of a horse or doing any of the unglamorous ranch chores turned his lips up in a smile.

Her cheeks flushed. "Don't laugh at me."

"Who's laughing?"

"I'm a journalist. I can read people better than that. So, what is it? Do you think I'm going to embarrass myself in front of the Hardwells?"

"I don't claim to know that, ma'am."

"I'm *ma'am*, now? Oh, please. I'm not some old maid." She slapped him on forearm.

"I never said that, either." He chuckled. Even though he knew he should stay away from Piper, he enjoyed talking with her. Problem was, he wanted to do *more* than talk with her.

"If you think I'm going to look like an idiot in front of them, you should help me."

He narrowed his eyes. "Help you how?"

"Teach me some things. Show me how to get on a horse. Show me how people work on a ranch."

"Why don't you let them show you the ropes?" he asked, frustrated that she was so invested in the Hardwells.

Piper frowned and he regretted how harsh his words had sounded. "I don't want to embarrass myself," she confessed. "They've got ranching in their blood, and I don't want to look like a clumsy oaf. I'd like to know some basics before I even go out with them. YouTube can't teach me everything."

He sighed, curious why the family's opinion was so important to her. "Is impressing the Hardwells, or writing this story on them, really that important?"

She paused for a moment before nodding. "Yes," she said. "It is."

Maverick hadn't wanted Piper on his land, and knowing that she was asking around about his family, he knew he shouldn't want to get close to her at all, but as she stood in front of him, he knew he couldn't refuse her. Plus, the temptation of getting her alone again was too great to resist. "Sure," he said. "I'll show you some basics."

She let out a small squeal. "Thank you! You're a lifesaver!" A voice came over the loudspeaker announcing the beginning of the pie competition. Maverick noted that no one in the vicinity reacted and he wondered how many years would pass before the town would put an end to the event. "I've got to get over there, I guess. I've got your card. I'll give you a call tomorrow and we can set up a time."

"No problem. I'll see you later." Maverick stood by as Piper breezed through the crowd to get to the pie judging. His entire conversation with Piper had knocked him off guard. There was just something about the woman that he couldn't stay away from. No matter how much trouble she might be.

A few hours later, Piper found herself at her desk in the *Applewood Tribune* office. She'd just put the finishing touches on her story about the pie-baking competition. While it was a technically sound article, the content didn't exactly set the world on fire. She looked over the contributions from the other reporters, town council meeting notes, social announcements, a report on the latest innovations in leather saddle technology… The newspaper could surely use a little more spice.

A quick peek at the numbers had confirmed what she'd thought. Local newspapers were facing a declining readership and the *Applewood Tribune* was no different. It needed something else, something to boost interest in subscriptions. The *Tribune* could use a more personal touch, a little spice, something for the readers to connect with. She thought about what was missing from the paper. At the magazine where she'd worked, she'd created a fairly popular fashion advice column. That might not swing in a small town in Texas, but maybe she could give people advice. An "Ask Piper" column might be just the thing.

The only problem was that she didn't have any current questions to get her started. For the first week, she realized, she might have to write something about herself. She could use it to drum up interest in a reader-submitted section. She could introduce herself, discuss her feelings on the town, why she was there... Well, not the real reason she was there, of course. She wasn't about to air the Hardwells' laundry until they were all ready to tell people who she was. Until then, she wouldn't rock the boat.

Nine

The next morning, Piper pulled on a pair of jeans and an old T-shirt. She'd been at the office, putting together the final version of the weekly newspaper; it had been more work than she could have imagined, and she was tired.

This morning, she wasn't going to the *Tribune* office, like she had done bright and early the past couple of days since she'd gotten the job there. She was heading to Maverick Kane's ranch to learn some ranching basics. Sure, she could have learned them from the Hardwells—they'd been willing to show her—but as she'd told Maverick the day before, she didn't want to embarrass herself in front of the people who claimed that *ranching was in their blood*. Her goal was to fit in with the family, and if she could make it *look* like she belonged, it was a good first step. More importantly, however, it was never a bad day when she got to spend it with a man as sexy and electric as Maverick.

She descended the stairs at the inn, where she saw that Willa was standing behind the check-in desk. She hadn't crossed paths with the woman in a few days and smiled in greeting.

"Good morning, Piper."

"Morning," she said, walking over to the desk to join Willa. She noticed that the *Tribune* was open to her column introducing herself to the town.

Willa saw her eyeing it. "That was a great piece," she told her.

"Thanks. I'm always a little self-conscious writing about myself."

"You shouldn't be. I noticed you didn't say anything about the family," she noted.

"I didn't think it was the place or time to get that in-depth," Piper told her.

"Probably for the best. But soon—" she lowered her voice "—I'm sure Elias will want to tell everyone who you are."

"I think we should all talk about and agree on a time-line for that. It'll come."

"I'm sorry I haven't seen you in a while to check in with you," she said. "I hope everything is okay so far?"

"Yeah—the room is perfect. I don't think I've ever stayed anywhere so comfortable. And it's so quiet and tranquil, I've never slept better. Thank you so much for everything."

"It's my pleasure," Willa told her. "Anything for family."

Piper laughed. "I'd live here if I could." She leaned in closer. "And I really appreciate the *deal* you've given me on the room. Speaking of which, given my new job, it seems like my stay in Applewood will be a little longer than I'd originally anticipated. I have to stop taking advantage of your generosity. Do you know of any rooms for rent in town?"

"Don't be silly," Willa told her. "You are family, and I wouldn't even think of charging you for a room. Plus, we haven't been open long and we're not exactly filled up every night."

"But—" Piper interjected.

"If this makes you feel better, you can keep the room for now. If we somehow get a lot of reservations, then we can talk price. But don't count on it."

"I really appreciate it," Piper insisted. "That's very kind. True small-town hospitality."

"Consider it a reward for how boorish the guys were to you the other night," she said with a wink.

"It's fine," Piper told her. "It must have been a pretty big shock. I know how I felt when Elias contacted me." Piper laughed. "But I met with Garrett and Wes yesterday. They were great. They must have come around."

"Daisy and I had a talk with them after you left that night. They promised they'd be on their best behavior. Just don't write a tell-all exposé about them," she finished, laughing.

Piper's grin was small. She knew that Willa had meant no harm, but it told her that the easy day she'd spent with the men was only because they had been told by their wives to be nice.

"There's little chance of that," Piper said. With the exception of the skeptical glances Garrett and Wes had thrown her way when they'd first met—and who could blame them?—they'd been nothing but kind, courteous and accommodating.

An idea came to her. She wasn't a charity case, and as long as Willa wasn't going to budge on not charging her, Piper would repay her in any way she could. "Well, you know, I have a decent social media following and a blog. I'll definitely feature your inn in my posts."

"Don't go to any trouble."

"It's no trouble at all. I'm happy to do it."

"Well, thank you. That's a pretty good trade. I checked out your website last night. You do a lot of interesting things. How did you get into it?"

"My online life and the social media, including the blog, used to be my side work, just a hobby that brought in some money. But since I got let go from the magazine, I've been thinking about making it more of a full-time thing, along with the freelance work I've been doing."

"On top of your job at the *Tribune*? You're going to be pretty busy."

She shrugged. "I'm used to it. This type of job is feast and famine, and how much you can hustle, but I know it's a temporary thing. I won't be here forever, but it's good to fill the time. When there's work, you work. When there isn't, hopefully you've saved enough money to make it through. I was lucky enough to land a steady gig at the magazine. But in this economy, and with the changing news landscape, nothing lasts forever. Being editor at the *Tribune* will help fill the time and my bank account."

"So you don't think you'll settle here?"

"Probably not. I honestly never saw myself in Texas at all. But you know how it is—a girl watches one too many Sam Elliott movies and she heads out West to meet some cowboys of her own."

"So, it's all about finding a man?"

Immediately, Piper's brain flashed a picture of Maverick. "No, of course not. I'm here to get to know my family," she said. "A cowboy would be a nice extra benefit, though," she finished with a wink.

Piper was about to say her goodbyes when Willa's eyes

brightened with an idea. "We're going to Longhorn's to-night. For a girls' night. Want to join us?"

"Longhorn's? The bar?" She'd driven by it a couple of times, but it didn't look like the most glamorous place to have a girls' night.

"Yeah, believe it or not, it's the place to be in Apple-wood. It's always a good time. Join us. It'll be fun."

Piper thought about it. It had been a while since she'd gone out with the girls. "Yeah, thanks for the invite. I'd like that." She checked the time on her phone and saw that if she didn't leave now, she would be late getting to Maverick's ranch. And she didn't want to make him wait too long. "I've got to head out now," she told Willa. "But I'll be back later. Just let me know what time to be ready."

"Great. I'll get your phone number from Garrett, and I'll text you the time after I talk to Daisy."

Piper grinned, looking forward to getting out and having some fun with the girls in her family. "Can't wait. I'll see you then."

Clutching his coffee mug, Maverick stepped outside. It was quiet and the heat from the sun warmed him. He looked across the pasture and saw that his ranch hands were already at work, tending to the horses, feeding the chickens. He liked to roll up his sleeves and do the work alongside them, but this morning he didn't want to get dirty or sweaty before his company showed up. He was going to show Piper some of the basics when it came to horses and riding.

In the distance, he watched the environmental clean-up crews getting starting for the day. They would soon finish their latest section of land, plugging up the well that had been abandoned a few years back. Taking over the property from his grandfather had come with built-in work and the expense of cleaning up and reclaiming it after decades of oil exploration. It would be a long, drawn-out process, but once it was done, the land would start to heal. It would all be worth it.

Once the land was back to its natural state, Maverick's plan was to establish himself as a rancher. He was starting small but had big plans for the business, and he had the money and time to devote to it. He would gladly work the land until his dying day.

He sat on the wooden step and drank more of his coffee, taking in the morning, feeling the warmth of the sunshine on his face. He had to enjoy the solitude while it lasted. But even though Piper was on the way to his place, he still wasn't sure about her. She was clearly aligned somehow with the Hardwells, and he wondered why. Why did she care so much about their approval? And yet, she was still spending time with him. The Hardwells clearly hadn't told her about the rivalry between their families.

Several birds called in the distance and he smiled. Despite his problems with the Hardwells, he knew that settling in Applewood had been the right decision for him. If he kept to himself, the townspeople left him alone. Ranch life was quiet, serene, and that was the way he liked it… until the roar of an engine interrupted the peace. The noise got closer and closer to his home. Raising his hand over his eyes to shield them from the sun, he only saw a cloud of dust in the distance. But he didn't need to break out his binoculars to see what was causing the racket.

He stayed seated as the gorgeous driver brought the cherry-red convertible to a stop in front of the house.

Piper killed the engine and opened the door. "Morning," she called. She was smiling, but he couldn't bring himself to do the same at the moment.

He stood. "Mornin', Piper."

She hopped out of the car and then leaned over the side to reach for her bag. His eyes were glued to the way her denim jeans clung to her curves.

"Hey, there," she said brightly. "How's your morning going?"

It's better now, he thought to himself as he watched her move, the shape of her body highlighted by her casual clothing, but he settled on a "It's going well." Until he knew what she was doing with the Hardwells, he would be on edge and he would keep her at a distance. No matter how good she looked in a pair of blue jeans.

"Are you ready for my lesson?" she finally asked.

He could certainly teach her a lesson or two, he thought, distracted. Then he realized that he had a formidable foe in Piper Gallagher. "As ready as I'll ever be," he said. "I'll be honest, I didn't expect you."

"Why not? I told you that I need this. You said you would teach me. Why wouldn't I show?"

"Well, the ranch life is difficult," he started. "It's not the cushy life you likely had in Chicago—commuting, deskwork, happy hour with your girlfriends…"

"You make me sound like I'm a character from *Sex and the City,*" she scolded in a high tone that told him he'd made a mistake. "Just because I'm from a city, write at a desk and enjoy an occasional—okay, frequent—happy hour, that doesn't mean I'm some television caricature."

He held up his hands, laughing. "Fair enough. Sorry I was stereotyping. I probably shouldn't have."

"You've got that right." She slanted her gaze in his direction. "And as far as I remember, you were a city kid once upon a time."

He looked down at her. She had him there. Perhaps that

last bit had been a bit of projection on his part. His past was the last thing he wanted to talk about, and he should respect that maybe she didn't want to discuss hers, either. It nagged at him that despite her insistence to not be there to dig into his life, he couldn't help but think there was something to her blowing into town, bumping into him, getting a job at the paper... Her alliance with the Hardwells... Had they bring her here to get under his skin? Or was he just being paranoid? The more he considered it, the edgier it made him.

As far as why she was so interested in the Hardwells, she wasn't budging. He'd revealed more about himself to her than he'd have liked, and she'd given him nothing. Wes had told him that she was writing a story on the family. That might be true, he figured. So they might as well get on with their day. Maybe spending more time with her would get her talking about herself. He pointed in the direction of the stable. "Well, let's get on with it then."

"Sure. Where do we start?"

He dropped a guiding hand onto her lower back. He tried to ignore the frisson of electricity that danced along his fingers from the contact. He flattened his palm against the arch, and she looked up at him, a knowing grin on her lips. So she felt it, too. He cleared his throat. "Let's go to the stable," he told her. "I'll show you the horses first."

"Lead the way."

He kept his hand on her as they walked and he noted the way she moved closer to him. They came upon the fenced-in pasture and he saw that his few horses were already fed and trotting the perimeter.

They stopped at the fence and he reluctantly removed his hand. But the awed look on her face as she watched them made him smile. "They're beautiful."

He paused beside her. "They sure are. I don't have a big operation over here like the Hardwells do," he told her. "Just these six. We're not in the business, so to speak. I just do this for myself."

"So, what do you do here?"

"Didn't you google me?" he teased.

"Not since you made it clear that you didn't like it. I didn't get that in-depth with it."

"My grandfather was in oil and gas," he told her. "He found some very lucrative deposits on this land, and from there, he built his own energy company, which my father and his siblings run. I used to work with them there. As much work as I did, going in at noon, hungover as hell." He thought back to his days as a money-hungry younger man who'd barely lifted a finger and was spoiled with anything he could have ever wanted. It had been a lucky day when he'd realized that he didn't want to live like the others in his family. He'd wanted more. "When my grand-dad passed away, I left the company. I realized that I was wasting my life and I turned it around. I didn't want anything to do with the business. All I wanted was this land."

"So, you're rich and don't need to make money is what you're saying?"

He laughed. While leaving the energy company had caused him to forfeit his stock options, which would have made him extremely wealthy, he had his trust, and the land and ranch he'd inherited from his grandfather. "I'm pretty comfortable."

"I'll bet you are. Are you still involved with the oil in-dustry?"

"No," he said with an emphatic shake of his head. "Def-initely not."

She pointed to the equipment in the distance. "What's all that?"

"Since I moved back, I've been restoring the land. They're the crew that's reclaiming the land. Cleaning up the damage done by decades of exploration."

She smiled. "That's really great."

"It's a lot of work, but it's worth it."

After several quiet beats, she turned to face him. "Are you going to teach me how to ride?" she asked.

"Yeah, I will. But not yet. There's work to do first."

"Like what?"

He moved away and pulled open the large double doors of the stable.

She followed behind.

He picked up a three-pronged pick and handed it to her, while he grabbed a shovel. "First we have to muck these stalls."

"Mucking," she said, her voice low, looking at the pick in her hand.

"That's right."

"Do *you* do much mucking?" she asked.

Truthfully, he didn't. His ranch hands took care of most of the hard, disgusting work. But he wanted to show Piper that there was a lot more to him that the spoiled oil heir the media portrayed him as. "I do my share," he answered vaguely.

"I'm sure you do."

He folded his arms across his chest and looked at her. Gesturing to the first stall, he nodded. "Okay, go ahead."

"What?"

"Get to work. You want to know about the work that goes into a ranch to impress the Hardwells for your little story? You go first."

* * *

"I don't think the Hardwells are going to be impressed with my ability to rake out a stall," Piper told Maverick, looking over her shoulder. She scowled when one corner of Maverick's mouth twisted upward, but he said nothing. She sighed. "Fine."

She turned to the open stall and dug her pitchfork into the hay. "How exactly do I do this?" She pushed the hay aside and saw that it wasn't as soiled as she'd thought it might be. "Wait a minute," she said, turning the hay over. "This is clean."

Maverick chuckled. "Yeah, the guys already cleaned the stalls. They start pretty early in the morning."

Piper turned to face Maverick and kicked some hay in his direction. "I can't believe you."

He held up his hands. "Sorry, I was just playing with you." He headed out of the stall, clearly assuming that she would just follow him. "Come on."

They walked out of the stable to the fenced-in field where the horses were already frolicking and running together. He led her over to a light fawn-colored mare. He reached up to scratch the horse's ear. "This is Peach," he told her.

"She's gorgeous."

"She was my first horse," he told her. "I learned to ride when I was a kid but, after a while, granddad never kept animals here, so I gave it up. When I came back here and started looking at horses for myself, Peach was the first I saw. I bought her and got back in the saddle, literally."

She brushed her fingers over Peach's side. Her short bristly hair was surprisingly smooth to the touch. "Will I be riding Peach?"

"Afraid not," he said as he waved to someone over her

shoulder. Piper turned and saw a man walking a brown horse over to them. He handed the reins to Maverick before putting a small wooden step stool next to the horse's left side. "Thanks, Doug."

"Send me a message when you're done, and I'll take care of them for you."

"Will do." He turned back to her. "You're taking Cupid out. He's a little better with beginner riders. Peach has a bit of a stubborn temperament." As if in response, Peach snuffled and rubbed her muzzle against Maverick's cheek. His smile was playful as he stroked her.

"Stubborn," Piper repeated. "Good for her."

"She's like someone else I know."

"Because you're doing me a favor, I'll let that one slide."

"Have you ever been on a horse before?"

"Never. That's why I need your help."

"Okay, let's start then."

He cupped her elbow with his hand, his strong fingers guiding her around to the other side of the horse. Just the touch of his hand shot heat throughout her entire body. Sure, she was attracted to him—she'd been attracted to lots of men in her life—but with just a simple touch, Maverick was able to set her ablaze.

"First, you have to make sure the horse is comfortable," he told her. "Horses can easily feel claustrophobic, so it's important to make sure she has plenty of room." Piper started making mental notes, trying her best to commit everything to memory, to not screw anything up, despite the fact that Maverick's closeness was doing things to her body and hormones. Big things. The last thing she wanted to do was to hurt or stress his horse.

"Make sure the mounting block is sturdy on the ground," he continued, using a hand to wriggle the stool back and forth. It was solid. He took her elbow again and handed her the reins. "Now, hold these, and step up on the block."

As she did as she was told, a nervous energy traveled through her, and she wasn't sure if it had more to do with mounting the beautiful creature beside her—or if it was the creature's owner getting under her skin.

He came up behind her and put his hands on her waist, and the move startled her. "Sorry," he said, quickly removing his hands.

"It's okay. I'm okay," she assured him. "I'm just a little nervous."

"It's okay to be nervous. You have to put your trust into this animal. But if he feels that you're stressed, it'll stress him out."

"Okay," she told him. "I'm fine. I'm relaxed." He put his hands back on her waist. She knew that he was just helping to guide her onto the horse, but she couldn't help but ascribe an intimate emotion to the touch, and she almost let herself fall into that feeling. *Don't be dumb*, she told herself. *You asked him to help you, and he is.*

"Put your left foot in the stirrup," he told her next. When she did, he gave her a small push. "And pull your body up. Swing your right leg over his back, and then just let yourself sink into the saddle."

Piper settled into the leather saddle and looked down at Maverick. He was looking up at her, smiling. "How do I look?" she asked.

He gave her a once-over, and she felt her temperature rise—more because of him than the Texas heat. "You look great."

She gave him what she hoped was a sultry smirk. "I'm talking about how I'm doing."

His eyes flared in response but his attention went back

to the horse. Her stomach was a swirl of nerves. There was no doubt they had chemistry, and Piper wondered just how far it would take them. "You're a natural. Just make sure you keep your balance. Keep your back straight."

She followed his command, knowing that the movement pushed her breasts out. She caught the moment his eyes dipped to her chest. Piper cleared her throat, getting his attention. "Okay. What now?" she asked.

He dragged his palm over the lower half of his face. "Right," she heard him say under his breath. "Okay, turn your legs inward slightly, not squeezing tightly, just kind of hug him with your thighs." He waited until she got into position, and, as predicted, his gaze lingered briefly on her thighs.

Piper was fully dressed, in jeans and a T-shirt, but his gaze made her feel as if she were naked. She squeezed her thighs, but it had nothing to do with riding the horse. She was trying to concentrate on the task at hand, but Maverick was making her forget all about that. She wanted to jump off the horse and onto him. "Like this?" she asked.

He took a step closer to her. "Yeah, like that," he said, his voice husky.

"What now?"

He cleared his throat and she could tell that he was having just as difficult a time as she was. "You take the reins in a firm hold with two hands," he instructed. "But still make sure to leave them loose."

Piper nodded and fumbled with the reins for bit, but he stood next to her on the mounting block and took her hands in his, adjusting them. "Like that. Remember. Firm, but still loose."

Piper raised her eyes from looking at their hands together and saw that his face was close to hers. They stayed like that for several beats. She was unsure if he was going to kiss her; she barely caught the small twitch in his lips. Meanwhile, hers ached. But instead of moving closer, his throat bobbed as he swallowed and looked away, stepping off the mounting block.

She took a moment to steady her breathing. "So, how do I make him go?"

With an ease that she hadn't exhibited, Maverick mounted Peach. "Just squeeze your thighs against him. He's well-trained. He'll obey."

Piper did as he'd instructed and was thrilled and terrified when the horse began to trot. She held on to the reins, and when she looked up, she saw that Maverick was right beside her. "You're doing great," he assured her.

She squeezed her thighs again and her horse took that as a sign to go faster. But instead of increasing the speed a little, Cupid took off in a quick run. Piper had no idea how to control the horse as he sped across the field. She pulled up on the reins and lost her balance, almost falling, then dropped them. Maverick rode up beside her and grasped the reins in his hands, stopping her.

"Jesus, are you okay?"

"Yeah, I'm fine," she told him, trying to catch her breath. "I'm just a bit shaken up. I'm not sure what happened."

"You could have gotten yourself killed is what."

"I'm sorry."

"I know you are. And it isn't your fault. You probably weren't ready to go on by yourself. I should have been more careful." Maverick dismounted and went around to her. He raised up and grasped her by the waist, this time helping her down.

"Thanks," she said, glancing up at him. The adrenaline from almost falling from the horse wore off and was replaced by an energy of a different kind as Maverick's eyes connected with hers. "Thank you for teaching me how to ride."

"I think you still need a bit of practice," he pointed out.

"Yeah, no kidding. I was just hoping not to embarrass myself in front of my family," she said absently. The words were out there before she could take them back. She hadn't meant to tell a stranger—albeit a sexy, charming one— why she was in town. Especially since she hadn't yet told the Hardwells.

"What's that?" he asked. "Your *family*? The Hardwells?"

She shook her head. "I shouldn't have said anything," she said. "It was a mistake."

"I'm going to want some clarification here. Are you a Hardwell?"

She chewed her bottom lip and looked past him into the horizon. Maybe she could trust him. "Can you keep a secret?"

"I suppose I can."

She didn't know Maverick well, but she knew that he wasn't a gossip. Still, it didn't feel right telling her family business to an outsider without clearing it with Elias and the rest of the Hardwells. She hesitated.

"What is it?" he asked.

"I'm Elias Hardwell's daughter."

"Daughter…" he repeated. "I didn't know he had any younger children. You can't be older than his grandchildren."

"I'm not. We're about the same age."

"You know, I was wondering why you were so closely involved with them. It makes sense. So you're not doing a story on them?"

She shook her head. "Well, I am a journalist, as you

know. I did just happen to get a job at the newspaper office. But I'm not writing a story about them. Since that seemed to be what you believed, I wasn't sure what else to say." She went on to tell him about how Elias had tracked her down and brought her to Applewood to surprise the family.

"Does that even happen in real life?" he asked. "Sounds like something straight from a daytime talk show."

"Try living it," she added. "But, seriously, I don't know where this is going to go. The family and I have been keeping it quiet since I came to town. We haven't told anyone else yet. So, I'm begging that you keep this secret."

"You don't have to worry," he told her. "I don't have any time or energy to start more drama with the Hardwells. Your secret is safe with me."

She exhaled, grateful that he wasn't going to cause any trouble for her. "Thank you."

She gazed over at Maverick, who seemed distracted, deep in thought. After several beats, he snapped out of it and looked her over again. "Are you sure you're not hurt? That ride looked pretty rough."

"No, I'm good."

"I shouldn't have let you go off on your own," he said again, his voice husky. His hand still cupped her low on her waist, and she was only aware of his touch.

He leaned down and grazed his lips against hers. It shocked her, but she parted her lips underneath his. He tasted of coffee and peppermint gum, and she grasped his neck, pulling him closer, desperately wanting more. He pressed against her, his firm chest flattening her breasts. His lips moved from hers, the contact stoking a fire so deep within her that she would burn to death just to feel more. But instead of bringing the kiss deeper, he pulled back.

"That's probably enough for today," he said.

"Are you sure?" she asked, breathless, as if he'd pulled the air from her lungs. In the few days since their first meeting, she'd thought about Maverick—touching him, kissing him. She was infatuated by him. She thought she'd outgrown schoolgirl crushes but, clearly, she was wrong.

"Am I sure? Not at all. But it's probably best if we end this now before my ranch hands walk up on something embarrassing."

Piper didn't want to end the kiss at all. In fact, she would face any embarrassment head-on. "We could find some-where more private," she suggested hopefully—shame-lessly—wanting to keep touching him.

"Don't tempt me," he told her, his voice rough.

"Fine," she said, biting back the unfulfilled lust that boiled inside her. "I guess our lesson is over, huh?"

"Yeah. We can walk the horses back."

Piper exhaled raggedly. Her heart rate had returned to normal but she was still disappointed in herself. She'd looked like an idiot in front of Maverick. And if she couldn't figure out how to sit on a horse, she would do the same in front of her new family.

They walked side by side in silence, Maverick leading both horses. She was embarrassed and, despite their kiss, she couldn't help but wonder if he was angry for putting his horse in danger. When they returned to the stable, she looked at her cell phone. "Oh, damn, look at the time. I should be getting out of here anyway."

"You have a busy afternoon ahead?"

"Yeah, I have some things to take care of, and some work to do before it gets too late."

"Working on a big story, or a revealing tell-all about your relationship with the Hardwells?"

"Oh, yeah, they would love that," she said, rolling her

eyes. "I've got to make sure all of my work is done before this evening," she explained. "Willa Hardwell has invited me out to a bar tonight."

"Getting to know the family," he said.

"Hopefully."

"You must be going to Longhorn's."

"How'd you know?"

"Well, there aren't many places in Applewood where people can go socially, so I took a guess."

"Will I see you there then?"

He shook his head. "Probably not. It's not really my scene."

She sidled a little closer. "That's right. I forgot you were the town recluse," she teased.

She leaned toward him and smoothed her hands up his chest, feeling the twitch of his firm muscles underneath his shirt. "Even if I'm going to be there?"

He blew out a ragged breath. "That's a mighty strong argument, but I wouldn't count on it."

"I'm not really into the country-western scene, either," she told him. "But it could be fun if you were there," she said, taking a chance on buttering him up.

"You're going with Willa?" he scoffed. "I don't think Garrett will take kindly to me socializing with his wife."

"I think you're being ridiculous. You're not that bad of a guy, are you?"

"I'm afraid you'll have to ask them."

"Do you guys not get along, or something?" she asked. She thought back to some of the comments that she'd heard from Garrett and Wes about what they and Elias thought of the Kanes. She hadn't dwelled too much on them at the time. She couldn't reconcile that image of Maverick or his family with the man in front of her. Elias hated him because of his family, but perhaps if they got to know him for him and forgot about the bad blood between the families… "Maybe I will." They stood in silence for a bit, each stroking their horses. Then a ranch hand approached and he and Maverick removed the saddles and halters. "How do you think the place will compare to my *big-city happy hours*?" she asked.

Maverick laughed and looked down at her tennis shoes, which were already caked with mud from their ride. "I'm guessing you didn't bring your cowboy boots."

"You guessed correct."

"I'm guessing you don't even *own* cowboy boots."

"Ding, ding, ding," she said. She considered the clothing she'd packed. Not much of her wardrobe would work for a country-western bar. She typically stuck with bright colors, flowing materials and fabulous patterns. "I guess I don't really have anything that might work for a place called Longhorn's."

"There's a place in town that sells Western wear if you want to fit in."

She shook her head. She could go to the Western store, but given how people in town already craned their heads to check her out when they passed her in the street, she decided against it. "I don't think I need to go shopping." She shrugged and cast a sideways glance up at Maverick. "If I can't fit in, I might as well stand out."

When Maverick walked into Longhorn's, he knew he'd made a mistake. Attending the Applewood Days Festival was one thing, but country bars had never been his thing. As a younger man, he'd opted for nightclubs that played dance and house music. Kicking up your boots to country music had never appealed to him. But as he looked around the crowded bar, he wondered just what it was about Piper Gallagher that made him do the unexpected.

First things first—he needed a drink. He walked over to the bar and ordered a beer. Then he found a somewhat quiet corner and stood awkwardly at a high table, looking through the crowd, until he saw the woman he'd come to see walking toward him.

And stand out, she did. Her red hair was knotted into an intricate bun, and she was wearing a multicolored, striped jumpsuit. It was loud, almost garish, but on her, like everything he'd seen Piper wearing, it looked amazing. It clung to her body in all the right places and was low-cut, showing off her more than ample cleavage.

"Thought this wasn't your scene," Piper said before taking a sip from her drink.

"It's been a while. I thought I'd check it out." He looked her up and down. "And it's safe to say you didn't stop at the Western store on your way back to your room."

Piper laughed and sipped her drink. Maverick's eyes were drawn again to the way her full lips closed around the straw. "I just happened to find this old thing in my bag. Do you like it?"

"I do. You're definitely making a statement."

She looked down at her outfit. "That's me."

He looked past her, not seeing Willa or Daisy. "Shouldn't you be on your girls' night?"

"They aren't here yet. Daisy was running late at work. So, I saw you and decided to come and talk to my friend."

"Are we friends?"

"Well, we've shared a meal and spent the afternoon together, didn't we?"

"I was just helping you out."

"I'm sure. In my book, that makes us friends."

"If you say so. But every time I turn around, you're there," he said. "You keep inserting yourself in my life."

With one finger, she tapped the brim of his hat. "You've got me there, cowboy. Maybe I can't stay away. Although, between here and the Applewood festival," she started, "I feel like you're the one following me around town."

"Just because you and I show up at the same events, doesn't mean I'm following you around." He shook his head.

"Sure," she said, laughing. "Don't think I'm not grateful to you. I'm here in a new town. I want to meet new people. I want to get to know you. Have adventures. I've never known a cowboy before. It's sometimes hard for me to make friends here. People are nice, but they aren't looking to get close to me. I guess I'm a bit of an oddity. Some people just want the gossip that they can bring back to their friends— Who am I? Where am I from? Why am I here?" she finished, her lips pursing upward. "But I don't feel like that around you. We have a good time together."

He thought back to the kisses that they'd shared and how his entire body still yearned to be near her. But she was Elias Hardwell's daughter. He knew that Piper was her own woman, but based on her desire to learn the ropes earlier that day, she was also desperate for the approval of her family. There was no way the old man would approve of her seeing him. It didn't matter that Maverick, personally, had done nothing to wrong Elias, his last name was Kane, and that was bad enough. "It was a fun day," he admitted.

"Until I almost fell off the horse."

"Could happen to anyone."

She frowned. "How's Cupid?"

It impressed him that she cared about the horse. "He's fine. No trouble."

"Good," she said. "I was worried."

"How are you? Any bruises or soreness from the rough ride?"

He raised his drink to his lips and saw how, in the low light of the bar, her eyes twinkled with mischief. "Maverick, if you think that was a rough ride, I've had rougher."

Maverick choked on his drink, coughed and eventually swallowed, the liquor turning to jagged glass in his throat.

"Sorry, I couldn't help myself. But, seriously, I feel like I used muscles today that I haven't used in ages. My boiling-hot shower felt heavenly, though."

Maverick's throat dried at the image of her standing in her shower, hot water and soap running off her body. He drank from his beer while her brown eyes bore into his, as if she could read his thoughts.

"Are you going to the festival ball next weekend?"

He hadn't thought about it. He only went to elaborate functions when it was absolutely necessary or required of him by the family. Putting on a tuxedo and attending a ball didn't exactly equate to keeping a low profile. "I wasn't planning on attending."

"Oh, come on." She pushed his shoulder playfully. "I have an extra ticket."

"You have tickets?"

"As the editor of the town paper, I apparently get all kinds of perks, I guess, in lieu of any sort of decent salary," she said with a laugh. "I've got to get the inside scoop on all of the social events. You never know when breaking news will occur."

"That's always a risk in Applewood, isn't it?"

"But, really, do you want to come to the ball with me? Maybe you'll find out. You wanted to take me out on a date," she reminded him. "Why not have it there?"

He sighed. "Okay, fine. I'll go with you."

"Geez, make it seem like a hardship."

"You haven't gone to an Applewood social event." Her smile was smug and he glowered at her. "You're trouble."

"With a capital T," she said, the smirk on her lips telling him it was a promise.

Her phone chirped in her purse and she pulled it out. She looked at the screen and frowned.

"Everything okay?" he asked.

"It's Willa. Daisy had an emergency at the vet clinic and Willa isn't feeling well." She looked up at him. "I guess the girls' night is canceled."

"That's too bad," he told her. "I guess you're stuck with me."

She took a step closer and looked up at him. "Are you afraid of getting into trouble?"

He chuckled. "It's not me I'm worried about. You have no idea the amount of trouble I can get into."

She didn't take her eyes off him as she brought her straw to her lips again. She sipped from her drink and, when she pulled the straw away, a droplet of liquid clung to her lower lip; the lights from the club emphasized it. He reached out and swiped it away with his thumb. She looked up at him and her lips turned up in a grin. "Why don't you show me?"

Ten

When Maverick grabbed her waist and pulled her close, Piper dropped her glass to the ground and barely heard it as it shattered at their feet.

He lowered his mouth to hers and his lips took hers in a rough, commanding kiss. His stubble rubbed against her chin and it sent chills down her spine. His tongue ran against hers, twining, exploring her mouth. When he pulled away, she was breathless. She'd kissed the man before, but they'd managed to pull themselves away from one another before they'd lost control. This time, she knew there was no way they would separate. There was too much fire between them to snuff it out now.

After quickly informing the bartender of the broken glass, he pulled her close. "My truck's in the parking lot," he told her. "Let's go."

"Where?"

"The inn is closer than my ranch."

"Sounds good to me."

She didn't argue as he tugged her, leading her to his truck. He opened the passenger's-side door and helped her step up into the cab.

He walked around and sat behind the wheel. "We'll be there soon."

True to his word, they arrived at the inn in just a couple of minutes. She said nothing to him as they walked carefully through the lobby, not wanting to get attention for bringing a man—especially Maverick—to her room at Willa Hardwell's inn.

They headed up the stairs and she led him to her room. She opened the door and walked in. He followed and, with her back turned to him, she heard the click of the door behind her as Maverick closed it. He came to her and pushed her hair off her shoulder and leaned in, skimming his lips along the sensitive skin of her neck. She moaned. Maverick put his hands on her shoulders and she leaned back against him. She could feel the heat of his firm chest and his strong hands as he dragged his palms down her arms until they came to rest at her waist.

Maverick pushed on her gently, walking her to the nearby wall, and in a couple of quick steps, Piper was pressed lightly into it, her back to his chest. She could feel his arousal, thick and hard against her spine. With his warm lips, he again found the sensitive spot on the side of the column of her neck, kissing her, and nipping her lightly with his teeth, while his hands smoothed their way up and down the curve of her hips to her waist. He took her hands in his and raised them over her head caging her in, between the wall and his chest. She closed her eyes and leaned back into him, where he continued to kiss the side of her neck, her jawline and her shoulders. Piper turned her head to the side, allowing him to take her mouth with his.

He kissed her with the same fire as he did before, his lips strong and firm against her own. And when her lips parted, his tongue swept in, finding hers, stroking it, stoking the fires of need that curled low in her stomach and shot upward throughout her body. It shocked her when he pulled away. She was barely able to catch her breath before his large hands took her hips again, and in one swift movement, he turned her so that she was facing him.

Her cheek still burning from the rasp of his five-o'clock shadow, she looked up at him and took in his features—high, sharp cheekbones and firm jawline, his wicked smile, that showed a cocky, white smile—Maverick's was a face she could look at forever.

He cupped her cheek and leaned in. Again, his mouth took hers, dominating and owning it. She could vaguely taste the beer that still clung to his breath, but, mostly, his taste was completely unique to him. She needed more, and frankly couldn't imagine a life when she wouldn't crave it, she wrapped her arms around his neck and pulled him closer. The man could kiss, and she moaned appreciatively.

In response, Maverick slid his hands past her hips to settle on her backside before making his way to the backs of her thighs. With seemingly no effort, he lifted her, bringing his lips to her chest, to the curve of her breast.

Piper wrapped her thighs around his hips, as he held her against the wall.

"You good?" he asked, his voice rough.

"Everything is fine."

"Just fine?" he said, smiling, showing that devastating flash of teeth. "I'm going to have to do a lot better than that."

Piper was at Maverick's mercy as he held her to the wall, his hands and lips all over her. She reached out for him, touching his face, pushing her fingers through his hair, the strong muscles of his neck and shoulders. And when he leaned against her, pressing his hard length against her core, she moaned in anticipation of what was to come.

They were both still dressed and their clothes proved to be a frustrating barrier. Maverick pulled at the buttons on the low neckline of her jumpsuit, exposing the lacy cups of her black bra, and he cupped her. When his large hands molded to her full breasts, she thought she might explode.

With her legs still wrapped tightly around his waist, Maverick pushed away from the wall and carried her to the bed. He lowered her gently and they worked together to rid her of her jumpsuit. When she was free of it, he tossed it over his shoulder. Keeping his eyes on her, he unbuttoned his shirt and then discarded his jeans. His body was just as spectacular as she'd imagined it would be. Finely chiseled muscles were covered by a thin layer of soft, dark hair. She reached for him again. She needed to touch him. Everywhere.

Without warning, Maverick pushed away from her, leaving the mattress. He reached for his pants and withdrew a condom from a pocket. Ripping the foil, he rolled the condom over his length before he returned to her, regaining his position on the mattress.

"If we don't do this right now, I might explode," Piper warned him through heavy breaths.

"Is that right?" He trailed his fingers down her stomach, tickling her, teasing, toying with her.

"Mav, please."

"Well, as long as you're asking nicely..." His voice rumbled as he spoke and kissed her briefly once more on the mouth before he thrust into her.

Piper parted her lips, but no sound came out as Maverick had taken control of every part of her, each of her senses. Her entire essence, her mind, her body, now belonged to him.

Planting his lips in the crook of her neck, Maverick groaned roughly, and the primal sound reverberated through her and she sighed. He continued his controlled, slow technique until she panted and begged him for more.

"Maverick, faster. Please."

He chuckled in triumph against her cheek then he obliged, quickening his pace. She matched his thrusts with her own, shifting her hips upward. With their wild, frenetic movements, they shifted the bed, so that the headboard slammed against the wall with every push.

Briefly, she wondered how soundproof the walls of the old inn were. But when she remembered that the room next door was thankfully empty, she forgot all of that when she felt her climax approaching, and everything else in the room fell away, leaving only the two of them. When Maverick's lips came to rest on the sweet, sensitive spot in the dip of her collarbone, it was all she needed, and she rocketed over the edge and came with a loud shriek, crying out Maverick's name. Maverick's body tensed above her then he pushed inside her one final time, and with a harsh shout, he followed her.

Eleven

The next morning, Piper headed down the stairs to the main lobby of the inn. It was early and she was tired, her head heavy, her body spent, not from cocktails—she'd had just the one before she'd seen Maverick at the bar—but from her night with Maverick.

The man, who'd gone back to his ranch early that morning, had left her completely sated; he'd paid attention to every inch of her. In the light of day, however, her encounter left her confused. She liked Maverick, and she didn't regret their night together, but the words of Garrett and Wes rang in her head and she knew that Elias wouldn't approve of her spending any time with him. Would she give up seeing him to appease her father…the man she'd met only a few days ago?

That theory was about to be tested because she'd been invited back to the Hardwell ranch today and, this time, Elias would be there.

She hadn't meant to seek Maverick out the night before.

She hadn't meant to bring him back to her room. She hadn't meant to spend hours with him in bed. But once she'd gotten in front of him, she'd been unable to do anything else.

Willa sat behind the desk in the lobby, smiling at her. "Morning, Piper. I'm really sorry about flaking last night. I got home and just felt a migraine coming on. Then Daisy called with the emergency. I'm sorry I texted you so late."

"It's perfectly fine," Piper told her. "I had fun. I got to see Longhorn's. Albeit briefly, before I left."

"Did you get up to anything after?"

Piper thought back to the ways that Maverick had brought her to the heights of pleasure, over and over, the night before, but given what she knew about the apparent rivalry between the Hardwells and the Kanes, she wasn't about to tell Willa that she'd spent the night with him. "You know, I just stayed in bed," she told the other woman. It wasn't a lie. She'd just omitted part of the truth—the *Maverick* part of it. "You know, it's been a bit of a wild week for me." Between Elias reaching out to her, coming to Applewood, meeting her family, who hadn't even known she was who she was, getting a job, Maverick…

"Yeah, a lot has happened for you." *She had no idea.* "So, Garrett tells me that you're heading up to the ranch again today?" Piper was grateful for the change of topic.

"Yeah, Garrett and Wes are showing me the parts of the ranch I haven't seen yet. They want me to see the kinds of things that go into working the ranch. I'm looking forward to getting out on the land again. And Elias is back today, so it'll be nice to talk with him."

"Do you know how to ride?"

She thought back to her afternoon with Maverick, when she'd made a fool of herself riding one of his horses. "Not so well. But I learned a few pointers… From Maverick."

Her voice had taken on a careful tone, as if she were testing the waters to glimpse how Willa would react to her seeing him.

"Maverick Kane?" Willa asked, her interest clearly piqued.

"Yeah. I'm such a city girl. But I was talking to him and he showed me my way around a horse. I'm not great, but I know the basics now, at least."

"I'm surprised that Maverick agreed to help you out. You should have just come to one of us."

"Really?" she asked. Maverick had been nothing but open and helpful to her. As far as she could see, the feud was one-sided...on the Hardwell side, in fact. "Yeah, the guys told me that there isn't any love lost there." She decided to test the waters further. "Do you think it'll be a problem that I've spent time with him?"

Willa raised an eyebrow and leaned in conspiratorially. "How much time?"

Piper had no idea how to answer. She was hoping to count Willa as a friend, but she didn't know how much she could trust her with the news of her attraction to her family's sworn enemy. She looked around the lobby and saw that there were people lingering around the counter. "Maybe we can talk about it later."

Willa grinned. "That means there's a story."

"I'm just concerned that being friends with Maverick will cause problems with Elias, because the way Garrett tells it, he's still pretty mad about what went down decades ago."

"I wish I knew what to tell you. I know Elias is a tough, stubborn man, but he loves his family. Get to know him more and you'll see that. Then, if your *friendship* with

Maverick is something that you want to pursue, maybe he'll come around."

"Thanks for the chat. I should be going."

"See you later. We'll have to reschedule that girls' night for another time," Willa said.

"Definitely. That sounds great. Between the *Tribune* office and my room upstairs, you know where to find me."

"And if you're not there, maybe I'll find you at Maverick's ranch."

Piper felt the heat rise in her cheeks. Willa had been able to read between the lines of her relationship with Maverick. "Maybe," she said. "Have a good day."

More than an hour later, Piper dismounted the horse that Garrett had provided. Thankfully, it was one of the more manageable horses, and her meager riding skills hadn't been tested too hard. Along with Elias, Piper, Garrett and Wes had ridden across just a small portion of the massive ranch.

Before she'd arrived in Texas, she'd had no concept of how big the wide-open spaces of these plots of land were. Looking around, she was amazed by the expanse of scenic landscape around her. The rolling green hills, the thick stand of trees all around them, a calm breeze blowing through the branches. Even the air smelled sweeter on the ranch. Maybe there really was something to this way of life. Maybe when she finally revealed to the family her growing feelings for Maverick—if they didn't banish her—part of her wondered if she might be happy making Applewood her home.

"How many acres do you have here?" She had barely known what an acre was before she'd arrived in Applewood, but she was becoming a quick study.

"A few shy of one million," Garrett answered in a far-too-casual manner.

"What sorts of animals do you herd?"

"Mainly cattle and horses," Wes told her. "In all, we've got about twenty thousand cows of different types. But the main focus are the horses."

"We breed, raise and train them here and at our facilities around Texas," Garrett finished.

"That's a lot of animals to keep going."

"It's a lot of work, but we have good people working here. We put a lot of trust into them. That's what means the most to us—trust."

Piper felt a pang of emotion—regret?—tighten her chest. If they discovered the truth about her and Maverick, would they be unable to trust her? "Yeah, trust is everything," she said weakly. She'd already begun to feel connected to the family. How would they feel when they found out that she was seeing their rival?

Elias came up to her. "You ride pretty well for someone with no experience on a ranch," he told her. "You know the basics already. Pretty soon you'll be galloping off on your own," he said with a look of pride that made her chest clench.

"Thanks. Maverick certainly didn't think so," she said casually. She'd been so distracted trying to stay on the horse, that his name had just come flying out. She hadn't meant to let it slip.

Garrett stopped walking. "Maverick? Really?"

"Maverick Kane?" Elias asked, the previous look of pride replaced with anger.

Dammit, Piper thought. She considered lying again, but she just couldn't. If she got too caught up with too many lies, there was no way she'd ever be able to find her way out of them. "Yeah, he offered to help me out. He showed me few things about riding."

"You should be more careful and stay away from him," her father told her.

She stilled. "Why? Is he dangerous?" She'd never gotten any sort of those kinds of vibes from Maverick, but a woman couldn't be too sure.

"Of course he isn't," Wes answered. "He's just being dramatic."

"I'm not being dramatic. The history between our family and his goes back generations."

"With Harlan, right?" she asked.

Elias raised an eyebrow. "You've done your homework."

"Not really. When reporting is your job, people are always willing to talk. Especially in a small town like this. I've learned that word travels quickly here."

"It sure does."

"Well, I don't like talking about it," Garrett muttered.

"Why not?" she pushed, her own stubbornness getting in the way of trying to win them over. She was her own worst enemy sometimes. "If it's such a long-ago story?"

"Everyone in this town works hard," Elias said. "They've earned their riches and their prominence. Not Maverick, though. He came about his money from his family. He barely even works the land."

Piper opened her mouth. It would have been a prime time to mention the Hardwell inheritance and the fact that Garrett and Wes had many people who worked the ranch for them. But it wouldn't have been her place. If she'd been close enough to poke at him, like an actual family member, perhaps... But they weren't there yet. So, she said nothing.

Piper knew that pushing the topic wouldn't get her very far, so she relented. She'd get to the bottom of it later.

"Okay, fair enough. Let's drop it. I'm sure you have your reasons."

"And we do."

"Understood."

They were quiet for a moment before Wes spoke. "You really didn't have to go to him for riding lessons. We have some great teachers here."

Piper considered the way Maverick's hands had felt on her hips. The kiss he'd given her when she'd fallen. She certainly wouldn't have had those feelings with any of their trainers. "I appreciate that, but I didn't want to look like a complete rookie in front of you guys."

Wes laughed. "Just so you know, you don't have to worry about not knowing how to ride. Trust me. I came back here last year after a...hiatus from the ranch, you could say. I didn't know what I was doing, but my loving brother gave me a hard enough time about being a city boy that I eventually learned the ropes."

"I don't believe that you never fit in here."

"Oh, believe it. I lived in London for years. Coming back was certainly an adjustment for me."

"I just helped the transition," Garrett supplied.

"Yeah, sure you did. We didn't always get along. But we're doing better now."

"That's good to hear." Knowing that the brothers hadn't always gotten along but had been able to mend their rift anyway lightened some of her dread. Maybe they would also forgive her for her dalliance with Maverick. However, she was a stranger to them. They had no long history between them. What were the odds that they would forgive her for her lies once they discovered the truth? *Not great.*

They walked quietly for a while, up a hill, to a high point on the ranch. A fence ran along the top of the hill.

She looked in the distance and was able to see the next property over, which, she realized, was Maverick's ranch. It was too far away for her to see details, so she retrieved her binoculars from her saddlebag and brought them to her eyes. Through them, she saw Maverick talking with some of his ranch hands. The sleeves of his black shirt were rolled up over strong, tanned forearms, and his hands rested above his trim hips. She lost herself for a moment; allowed herself to think about their night together; to think about everything she would like to do to him next time…

Garrett cleared his throat. "If you're about ready," he started. When she lowered the binoculars, she saw that Garrett was frowning at her. "We can head back."

They'd been having a nice ride, but Piper knew that she'd made a faux pas in even mentioning Maverick's name. The rivalry between the two families was indeed a deep one, and she knew there would be no easy way to keep seeing Maverick and also be a member of her new family.

When they arrived at the main house, there was much more activity there than when they'd started their ride. There were several cars parked out front, and a black SUV was pulling into the driveway beside them. "You've got company?"

"Now that Elias is back in town," Garrett told her, "we're having a big family dinner." He pointed to a silver luxury vehicle. "That's my dad's car. The red truck belongs to Aunt Carmen. Uncle Darryl owns the motorcycle."

Elias came up behind her. "I know our previous attempt at a family dinner didn't work out. Tell me you'll stay this time. You are family, after all."

Piper smiled. She'd been worried that they had been angry with her, but the way they still included her in their family plans, even though they'd just shared a tense moment, made her feel warm inside. Maybe that's what family was—they loved you despite how much you might like their rival. But she wasn't sure how far she could push that. "It must be nice to have the family so close that you can all get together so regularly," she said. Her mother had given her a happy life, but it had always been just the two of them. Maybe a large, loving family was in the cards for her.

Wes grimaced playfully. "It is. I missed it when I was away. But sometimes it's nothing but chaos and opinionated people in your business." From inside, they could hear laughter from the people who had already gathered. "But mostly there's a lot of laughter."

"That sounds perfect." She smiled and they got closer to the ranch house. She was filled with such anticipation that she wondered if it would even be worth it to screw up her relationship with her family to continue seeing Maverick. This was everything she'd ever wanted.

She looked toward the front door, where Stuart stood, raising his hand. "Piper, howdy."

After almost a week in Applewood, she might be feeling more comfortable in the Southern town, but she doubted that she would ever feel comfortable enough to utter the word "howdy" to another human being.

"Hi," she said, raising an arm in return.

Elias touched her arm in a surprisingly gentle way. "Before we go in, Piper, can we talk in private?" he asked.

"Yeah, of course," she told him. "I'd like that." With Elias's leaving Applewood to go to Arizona so soon after she'd arrived, she welcomed the chance to spend more time with him.

They took a seat on the swing on the front porch, facing the setting sun.

"I apologize that I've been away. Cathy had helpfully

reminded me that she had a social event in Tucson, and I had to accompany her. I'd completely forgotten about it."

"It's fine," she said, looking at him. "I've been checking out the town. People have been pretty nice and welcoming."

He smiled at her. "I heard you've been busy. Congratulations on the new job."

"Thank you."

"Does that mean you have plans to move here?"

She shook her head. "I don't do well with plans," she told him. "I just like to see where life takes me. It's brought me here so far," she said. "I'll stay for a while and then, when it's time to move on, I will."

"You're a free spirit," he noted with a nod. "Like your mother."

"I learned from the best."

"How's the car?" he asked, glancing at the vintage cherry-red convertible parked nearby.

"It's a dream. I always wanted a car like this."

"And now you have one."

She looked off into the distance and saw that Wes and Garrett were watching them. Elias followed her gaze, and now that Elias was also looking at them, both men took the hint and walking by them, they went into the ranch house.

"I don't know why your mother didn't tell me about you, but I'm glad I found you. I didn't know it before, but our family wasn't quite complete. I'm looking forward to getting to know you."

"I'm looking forward to getting to know you, as well."

Piper took a deep breath to calm her nerves. It felt odd, opening up to her father like this. "I asked her about you when I was younger, but she never told me anything about you, except that you were a businessman in Texas. I guess she thought it would just make all of our lives more complicated. We had our lives in Chicago. She was finishing school and starting her own life. The fewer complications the better, I guess."

"I still wish that I'd known about you."

"Me, too."

"I didn't know anything until I received the letter she'd sent before she died. It had been delivered to one of my other properties and I didn't see it until it was too late."

"I didn't know she'd sent you a letter."

He nodded. "She wanted to come clean about having a daughter—you."

"Well, I guess we'll just have to make up for lost time."

She looked over at Elias. She knew that he was her father, but he was still very much a stranger. Piper could tell that she wanted to be closer to him, but was holding herself back. Maybe closeness would come with time, but, for now, she forced herself to keep her emotional distance. "Why don't we go inside?"

Together, they walked through the front door. Elias reached the door and held it open for her as she walked inside. Garrett and Wes, along with their father, mother-in-law and their aunt and uncles, were in the kitchen, socializing and catching up over coffee. When Piper and Elias entered the kitchen, they strangely quieted and looked in their direction. Piper caught her reflection in a nearby decorative mirror and saw that they were both wearing frowns. The rest of the family was probably looking at them with curiosity because they looked like people with unpleasant news to deliver.

"Hey, Dad," Stuart said. "How was Arizona?"

Elias put an easy smile on his face. "Lovely, as usual. Cathy sends her regards. She wanted to come back, too, but she has to put the finishing touches on decorating our place there before she gets too caught up with the final details of the wedding." He moved to the bar area off the kitchen, and poured himself a drink.

He turned to his grandsons. "Are your lovely wives joining us for dinner this evening?" he asked.

Wes was first to answer. "Daisy will be here after work," he told him.

"Willa is working late at the inn," Garrett added.

Darryl, Elias's younger son, and his daughter Carmen smiled and moved toward her. "Piper, it's great to see you again," Darryl said, coming to stand before her.

"I'm happy to be here." She hugged her brother and sister, and when she was handed a glass of wine, she sipped as her new family came around her, welcoming her into the fold. Her cell phone vibrated in her pocket, and she almost ignored it to talk to her family, but she didn't want to risk the chance it was an emergency, or breaking news at the paper.

She stepped outside to check the caller ID, and, despite herself, and the way she was feeling, she smiled and answered it. "Hello?"

"Hey," Maverick responded.

His deep voice was enough to stir up memories from the night before, causing a wave of desire to crash over her. "I didn't expect you to call."

"Well, I'm a gentleman. A gentleman always calls the next day."

She grinned. "You weren't very gentlemanly last night."

His chuckle on the other end almost made her knees buckle. "Sorry about not calling earlier," he said. "I got caught up out on the ranch, and the day got away from me. I just wanted to say that last night was great."

"Yeah, it was."

"And I was wondering—"

Piper looked up and into the house and saw that Garrett and Wes were talking with Elias. They didn't look happy. Elias raised his hand to her and gestured for her to join them. They couldn't know that she was talking to Maverick. "I'm sorry, have to go," she said, quickly cutting him off.

She walked into the house and followed the men into the study. Elias closed the door behind her.

"Please sit down."

She did just that, sinking slightly into the plush furniture. When she looked from Garrett to Elias, she wondered why she'd been summoned. "What's up?" she asked.

"Piper. You're a part of the family, so we need to discuss what that means financially."

She shook her head. "I swear, I'm not here for your money, or any part of that inheritance you talked about before. I'm not here to screw anyone over or take anyone's money." She noticed that Wes and Garrett were quiet.

"We all know that," Elias said carefully, though the look on his grandsons' faces told her that perhaps they weren't so sure.

"Do you guys believe that?" she asked them. "I thought we were having a great day together."

"We are," Wes told her. "But when it comes to the family and the business, and all of our assets, there's a lot at stake."

"Is this about the car?" she asked. "If it is, I'll leave the keys right here."

"It's not about the car," Garrett told her. "But there is an inheritance to consider."

Elias stepped forward. "When I retired from the business, neither of my children were interested in continuing it, so I left controlling interest to Garrett, and shares to the rest of my grandchildren. My children, however, received considerable payments. If you'll accompany me to the bank on Monday morning, I can transfer the same amount to you."

She held up her hands. "I told you, I'm not interested in the money. I grew up with just my mom and my grandma. I had a happy childhood, but it was lonely. When you contacted me and told me that I had a big family down here, I decided to come because I want to get to know all of you, and that's all I'm interested in."

All three men were quiet until Garrett spoke up. "I don't think I can fault you there," he said. "Everyone deserves family." She could see that both Garrett and Wes had softened in her presence.

Wes frowned. "I understand that, Piper. I was away from the family for so long. Now that I'm back, I can't ever imagine leaving again. The timing is awful convenient, though, don't you think? Just when Elias announces his retirement, and that the inheritance is up for grabs, you suddenly appear."

"We're just protective," Garrett added. "Of him and the rest of the family."

"I'm not some senile old man," Elias protested. "With the guidance of my lawyer, I reached out to Piper and brought her here."

Piper looked at Wes and then Garrett. "I'm not here to bamboozle or manipulate an old man, if there was any doubt. I think that Elias completely understands what it looks like, but he reached out to me first, remember? I know you guys are confused, but whether we all like it, or not, I'm here. We are family." They both nodded. But neither spoke. She couldn't blame them. They were right. She could easily have just rolled into town and claimed to be one of them to take a share of their inheritance. It had never been about the money for her. And she hoped that she could convince them of that someday.

"But on that note," she continued, "there's something else I wanted to discuss with you." The thought just occurred to her. If she wanted to be a Hardwell—and, more importantly, gain their trust—she had to join them. "Back on my first night in town, Elias asked me to stay here. I didn't want to do it at the time because I wanted to give you all some space after our announcement. I don't want to pressure anyone, but, with your blessing, I'd like to stay here and continue to bond with you all." Staying at the ranch would help her become closer to new family, but she thought about what it would do to her growing relationship with Maverick.

Again, they were quiet. Until Wes looked at her. "You said it—you're family. Family stays in the house. Of course you're welcome here."

Piper smiled. "Thank you. I'll bring my things by in the next couple of days. I'll give you a little time before I move in. I feel like I've completely turned your lives upside down."

"Yeah, just a little." Garrett held up his thumb and forefinger, an inch separating them.

"The table is set. Get on out here," Elias called to them.

"You're welcome to come back tonight after dinner, of course. But if you would like take some time to pack up your room at the inn, that's fine," Garrett said, as they walked out of the study and towards the dining room. They table was set and the food looked delicious.

Elias held out a hand, gesturing to the chair next to the one he took at the head of the table. "Piper, please sit."

"Thank you," she said, looking around at everyone—

her family. They all smiled back, showing her acceptance that she never thought she'd needed.

Once dinner was finished and the table cleared, Piper made her way out of the house. She got in her car and drove away from the ranch. She was headed back to her room at the inn, where she would pack her bags. She was going to be living—no, *staying*—at the family home. At least until she could get her own place. She'd come to Applewood on a temporary basis, but as she drove down the road toward town, the path growing increasingly familiar, she realized that she was coming to like the small-town life. It was quiet, serene, and if her personal family life wasn't such a mess at the moment, she might say she was more relaxed than she'd ever felt. Maybe she wouldn't be leaving any time soon. She had a job here, family here, and that was more than she had anywhere else.

She came upon the turn in the road that would take her to Maverick's ranch, and she fought the urge to take it. It had been such an intense day that she had barely had time to think about the fact that she'd spent the night before with him. He was her family's rival. That was another complication. She had to go about earning the trust of Wes and Garrett. If they knew that she was attracted to their enemy, it might be tougher than she'd thought.

That was part of her reasoning for staying at the ranch with them. If she was with the Hardwells, then it might be easier to keep her distance from Maverick. Maybe. Hopefully.

She parked her car outside Applewood Inn and walked inside. Saying hello to Taylor, the desk agent, she headed upstairs to her room. She had put the Do Not Disturb sign on the door before she'd left that morning, and she saw that her bedsheets were still tousled from her night with Maverick. Away from the drama she'd created at the Hardwell house, she was now able to put herself back to the night before. What it had felt like to be in his arms. She had never had a lover like Maverick, and she knew she never would again, because, thanks to the family rivalry, she knew the time had come to pick a side.

Twelve

It was just past nine in the morning. Maverick, already finished with most of his morning tasks, and having checked in on his capable ranch hands, sat on his bedroom's balcony. It had been more than a day since he'd last seen Piper, when he'd left her near sleep in her rumpled bed at the inn. And about every half hour, he had to talk himself out of texting or calling her. The one time he had called, she hadn't been able to get off the phone quickly enough. He wasn't going to put himself out there again. If she was interested in talking to him, she would have to come to him, and she knew exactly where to find him.

He sighed heavily. He was helpless to resist her. He'd wanted to stay away from her, to keep to himself. But she'd gotten under his skin. There was something compelling about her—her humor, her brashness, the way she wouldn't compromise who she was because she was in Applewood. Not to mention that fact that she was likely the sexiest woman he'd ever met.

He sipped his coffee and checked his watch. He wished it was just going to be another quiet day on the ranch, but he wouldn't have any such luck. His parents were coming for a visit, and he knew what the topic of conversation would be—what it was every time—getting him to go back to the energy business.

He'd received word from his parents' driver that they were on their way from the landing strip. He headed inside and walked downstairs. The ranch house was a grand thing. Part of it was still considered the original building. His grandfather had built many additions to the place over the years, bringing the square footage just over ten thousand. It was far too much house for him. It was too much for any one person—except his grandfather, of course, who'd wanted the biggest, shiniest, most extravagant things money could buy. That was also a quality that Harlon had passed on to his son Edward, Maverick's father.

He walked outside in time to see the black SUV pull up the driveway to stop in front of the entrance. The driver came around and opened the door, escorting his mother, Sylvia out of the car. His father, Edward, followed behind her, then sent the driver off instead of removing any luggage from the back.

Maverick greeted his mother with a hug and his father with a firm handshake, as was customary for them. He stepped back and took in their appearance. With the exception of his mother's purse and the small attaché case that his father carried, they had no other bags. "Traveling light?"

"Yes, we won't be here long," his father told him.

"Just a quick visit, dear," his mother added.

Maverick nodded. "Would you like to go inside?"

"That would be lovely."

"So, what brings you by for such a quick visit?" he asked, pouring them each a cup of coffee.

"There's no reason to beat around the bush, son. We want you back in the company."

Maverick shook his head. "No, not a chance." He had a good thing going on at the ranch. He was cleaning up the land, living a simpler life, enjoying the solitude. Well, when he wasn't entertaining mysterious women from the rival family. "I like it here."

"We'll make you a vice president in new exploration. Or something else, if that doesn't work. We're expanding. There are more openings."

"New exploration?"

"There's another thing."

His father's serious tone caught his attention. "What is it?"

"Since your grandfather passed, we've been going through the old records. We went through the safe, his desk, his computer, but in a shoebox in his beach house, we discovered something."

"What is it?"

His father reached into the attaché case and removed some papers, yellowed with age. On them were crudely drawn scrawls that looked like a map of his ranch. "If you can't read this, it's a depiction of the oil wells that were discovered on the land." He pointed to a colored-in mass. "This is another well. One that we haven't explored. Before he passed, he had it seismically tested—" he handed over another paper "—and he found oil. And quite a bit of it."

Maverick shook his head. "That's why you want me back in the company? So you can exploit my land for even more oil?"

"We want you back because you're family."

"Right."

"You like the life you have here, right?"

"You know I do."

"You would have none of it if it wasn't for your family. We pulled you out of a self-destructive spiral, got you away from those old *friends* of yours," his father said with a grimace. "We got you into rehab and into an Ivy League college. Gave you a position in the family business. And you threw it all away to work on a ranch."

"I'm happy, and you just want me back at the company because you think if you can keep me under your thumb, then I'd happily let you drill for oil."

"That's not true," his mother interjected.

"You've taken all you will from this land, and it's my land now."

"Son. Think of the family. We need this exploration."

Maverick scoffed. "You don't *need* anything."

"We've had a tough couple of years. Your grandfather made some questionable investments. The company is hemorrhaging money. We need something to bring to the shareholders."

"You flew here in a private jet," he noted. "You're not hurting."

"Not yet. But once people get wind of the losses, we could be in some serious trouble."

"Maybe you should learn to budget a little better," he told them. "Skip the lattes and the avocado toast."

"This isn't a time for joking, Maverick," his mother said sharply.

Maverick sighed. "Let me think about it." He knew then that he wasn't going to let them extract any more oil from his land. But he also didn't want to see his family, or his grandfather's legacy, suffer. The way his father presented it, Kane Energy was in serious trouble. He didn't want them to lose everything. Maverick just wanted his land, his own thing. He didn't want to return to the corporate work. But, like it or not, he was a Kane, and he was obligated to help his family. He looked a little closer at the map. Though crudely drawn, he knew the dimensions and property values of his land. "This isn't right," he said.

"What isn't?" his father asked, leaning in.

"This property line," he explained. "I know this is just a rough drawing, but the property line between us and Hardwell Ranch is right here." He traced his finger along an imaginary line to the right of the one his grandfather had drawn in black pen. "That oil is on Hardwell land. Is this map dated?"

His father flipped over the paper. "June, 1950."

"Just after the falling out," Maverick mused. "The land survey I have clearly shows that as Hardwell land when they divided it back then."

"Unless there was a problem with the survey," his mother chimed in.

"Are you suggesting that part of our land is sitting on Hardwell Ranch?" Edward asked.

Maverick didn't bother to correct his father and tell him that it was *his* land. He let it slide. He was busy looking at the map. Maverick knew that the map had been hand-drawn by his grandfather many decades ago, but if there was one thing Harlan Kane had been, it was meticulous when it came to his assets. If Harlan had thought the land was his that long ago, Maverick wondered what had happened to make it part of Hardwell Ranch.

When the paper was printed and the stacks were distributed all around town shops, the café, the diner and homes,

Piper sat back in her chair and put her feet up on the desk. Now that she had a week as editor under her belt, she realized that maybe running the town newspaper wasn't so hard after all. Between her excelling at her new job, moving into the Hardwell home and getting to know her new, large, extended family, life was really coming together for her.

She even had plans to attend the annual festival ball tonight, courtesy of the *Tribune*. Cynthia had sent one of her dresses over for the occasion—after lamenting at length on a video chat that she couldn't join her.

There was just one problem—the tall, dark and handsome Maverick Kane. What was she going to do about the fact that she was attracted to a man her father would never accept? She looked at her phone. He hadn't called or texted her since last night, when she'd been at the Hardwell Ranch and blown him off. She wasn't sure where she would end up with the decision, but she hoped that she hadn't driven him away.

Having been awake since the early hours of the morning to the get the paper out, Piper needed a caffeine boost. She pushed up from her desk and walked next door to the café. Before she could get in line for her double espresso, she found something else that was capable of boosting her heart rate.

"Maverick," she said. "Fancy seeing you here. You must be following me again?"

"It's the best café in town," he said with a sexy grin that made her clothing want to fall off. "Actually, I'm pretty sure it's the only café in town."

"Then all the more reason why I should be here."

"I'm not following you. It's just a coincidence."

"It just so happens to be in the same building as my office?"

He shrugged. "I didn't build it here."

"I'll keep that in mind," Piper said with a smile. It seemed that bantering with Maverick was almost as much fun as being in bed with him. *Almost.* They both entered the line. With just one look at him, all of her trepidation about going against her family was gone. She wanted Maverick, and she was just going to have figure it out.

"I'm sorry I didn't call you back last night," she told him. "I got caught up."

He frowned. "Family stuff with the Hardwells?" he asked. "Don't worry about it."

The playful mood between them shifted. "Okay."

It was their turn in line and they both ordered. Maverick paid before she had a chance to reach into her purse. "Thanks," she said to him as she picked up her short cup. They both walked to the door and she knew she should say something else before they parted ways. "Was there something you were going to ask me when you called?"

"I was just doing that calling-the-next-day thing you ladies like."

She nodded a little sadly because, secretly, she'd been hoping he was going to ask to see her again soon. "Yeah, of course. Appreciate it."

"I had a really good time the other night."

"I did, too."

Neither of them said anything for bit. The air between them went from electrically charged to awkward. She needed to focus on winning over her new family, and she surely couldn't do that if she turned into a melting puddle whenever Maverick was around her. "I guess we're off for the Applewood Festival ball? Given how we're supposed to be sworn enemies?" She scrunched her nose. "That sounded a bit dramatic, didn't it?"

He laughed. "Yeah, just a little, though. But I guess you're right. Why complicate matters any further?"

At least he agreed. It would definitely help her keep her distance from him if he was on the same page. "Thanks." She turned to leave and head back to work, but Maverick tapped her gently, stopping her.

"So, I'll see you at the ball tomorrow night then?"

She smiled. The thought of seeing him in a tuxedo in person sent her heartbeat ratcheting up, and she realized that maybe they were on the same page after all. But not the one her family would approve of.

Thirteen

Piper walked into the main house at Hardwell Ranch with her bags in tow. The house's full-time occupants, Daisy and Wes, led her, not up the grand staircase, as she'd expected, but to the left of it, which led to a double door. Piper opened both doors to reveal another sitting room, but it was lighter than the main part of the house, more feminine.

"You should be comfortable here," Daisy said, leading her into the space.

"Cathy had this wing built and decorated to her liking," Wes explained. "She felt the rest of the house had too masculine of a feel."

"And she was right. Stuck here with all that testosterone," Daisy added.

Piper looked around the sitting area. The cream-colored furniture looked inviting, and there was a rocking chair positioned in the center of a bay window, where she could just imagine herself curled up, reading a good book. "This looks amazing."

"There's a bedroom through here." Daisy gestured, bringing her attention across the room to a short hallway.

As they made their way down that hallway, Piper thought that she would just find a bedroom, but when they walked past a room that was filled with books on floor-to-ceiling shelves, she stopped. "Whoa."

"Cathy's library. She's got a lot of different things in there—romance, thrillers, history, true crime. If you want to read it, you'll probably find it in there. This is her sanctuary, at least when she's on the ranch."

"Are you sure she won't mind me crashing here?"

"She insisted on it," Wes said. His face was unreadable and left her unsure where she stood with him. "Said her stepdaughter is always welcome to the space."

Stepdaughter. Just a few weeks ago, she'd only known of her mother and grandmother, who had both passed on. Now she also had a father, stepmother, siblings, nephews—who were older than she. Emotion choked her throat and moistened her eyes. Piper blinked back the tears. "Well, I'll have to call her and thank her. And I thank all of you. This has all been so surreal."

"We're more than glad to have you," Daisy told her. Piper shifted her eyes to Wes, who was no longer quite as welcoming to her, but still not outright hostile. She'd have to work a little more on Wes and Garrett.

"This is the bedroom," Wes said, pushing open another door.

"This one was mostly used when Cathy's girlfriends or other family stayed over."

Piper entered the room and her eyes widened. The bedroom was large, bright, every piece of furniture, bedding, tapestry put together in a way that made the entire space look and feel like a luxurious cloud.

She walked into the bathroom en suite to see the large soaker tub that sat in front of a wall of glass.

"Just so you know, the other side of that glass is reflective. You can look out, obviously, but no one on the outside will be able to see you."

She ran her fingers along the cool, smooth lip of the tub. "Thanks for telling me that. I think I'll be pretty comfortable here for as long as I'm here."

"You aren't staying long-term?" Wes asked.

"I'm not sure what my plans are. I'll be here for a while, at least. But I am really enjoying myself here. I never thought I was cut out for the small-town life."

"Coming from the city, it's definitely a big change," Wes said. "When I moved back from London, it took a while to love it."

"I believe it."

"Well, I guess we'll let you get settled," he said.

"You're going to the ball tonight, as well, right?"

"Yeah, I am. The festival committee gave the *Tribune* a couple of tickets and nobody else wanted them."

Daisy's smile crinkled her eyes. "I can't imagine why not."

"I just really like an opportunity to dress up," she told them.

"Did you find a dress in town?"

"I had one of my own shipped from Chicago," she said, gesturing to the garment bag that she'd hung over the handle of her rolling suitcase. "Thank God we live in the twenty-first century, right?"

Daisy laughed. "Well, we'll leave you to it. The limo will be here at seven thirty."

It hadn't occurred to her that she would be going to the event with the Hardwells. It was probably for the best that she hadn't made plans to go with Maverick. How would her new family have reacted to that?

Now alone, Piper looked around the room, marveling at how everything about her life had changed. Just over a week ago, she'd been a laid-off peon who'd worked for a fashion magazine, but now she was the editor of a small-town paper, part of one of the richest ranching families and moving into her own *wing* of a gigantic home. Life came at you fast.

She went back to the bathroom. She sat on the edge of the tub and turned on the hot water. But life also had a way of working out.

Fourteen

Maverick tugged at the collar of his shirt as he walked into the Applewood Festival ball. Considering his family's status, he may have grown up wearing tuxedos and formal wear, but he still hated the things. He adjusted the black Stetson on his head—required wear for any social event in Applewood—and walked into the ballroom.

"Maverick Kane," he heard a woman say behind him. He turned, and saw Judy Arnold, one of the town counselors and member of the Applewood Society Circle, standing behind him.

"Hello, Judy," he said, tipping his hat. "How are you?"

"I'm well, honey," she told him. "I'd like to thank you for the donation you made to the society to make this gala happen."

He looked away. He didn't want to be noticed for what he'd given. "You're welcome," he told her. "I'm glad to do it."

"It's been nice having you in Applewood," she said sincerely. "You should come out to more events. Don't be such a stranger."

"Thank you," he said. Before, he would have scoffed, with no intention of going to any other events, if he didn't have to. But now, he'd started to find them... fun? Did Piper do that? It was something he'd have to unpack at a later time, so for now, he smiled politely. "It's been nice seeing you." He moved on from her.

He looked around the crowded ballroom—not looking for anyone in particular, of course, he told himself. But if Piper happened to show up, then maybe he'd go over and talk to her. Maybe. He chuckled to himself. Hell, when he saw Piper, he knew *exactly* what he'd want to do with her. And it had nothing to do with talking.

He turned toward the open double doors just as she was entering the room with the Hardwells. As she always seemed to do wherever she went, Piper garnered attention from the people of Applewood. She walked in with Garrett, Willa, Wes and Daisy, but he knew that all eyes were on her. Instead of the full-length formal gown that conservative Texan women normally donned at events like these, Piper had opted for an outfit that would make her stand out. Her dress was a deep emerald green; a miniskirt with long sleeves and cut so low he might have considered it indecent if she didn't look so incredible. Her red hair rolled over one shoulder in loose curls.

He watched her as she moved around the room with the Hardwells, waiting until she broke away from them before approaching her. He didn't have to wait long. She looked around until her eyes settled on him and, from across the room, they watched each other. Instead of coming to him, however, she looked away again and disappeared deeper into the crowd.

It was as if she'd hooked him with a lure and drawn him closer, and he was unable to turn away. His phone rang in his pocket. He grumbled, not appreciating the distraction. Checking the caller ID, he saw that it was his father. *Impeccable timing.*

He brought the phone to his ear. "Hello?"

"Son, how are you?"

"Fine. This isn't a great time—I'm out."

"Oh, really?" his father asked. "Busy night?"

"Applewood Festival ball."

"That isn't normally your cup of tea."

"What can I say, I'm trying new things."

"Your mother and I are flying out to Galveston tomorrow," he told him. "We're going on the boat. We'd like you to join us."

He thought about that. The ranch may be his home, but he loved being on the water, even without being on his family's luxury yacht. He had a meeting with his family there the next day, but with the exception of the crew, he'd have the night there alone. "Yeah, that'd be great. I'll leave here and get to Galveston tonight." Piper's loud laugh rose above the din of the room, capturing his attention. He paused and watched her for a moment. "Tell the deck crew to expect two of us."

Piper smoothed her hand down the side of her short dress and looked around the room. The people who looked away quickly as she spied them watching her made her smile. She was glad she'd had Cynthia overnight it to her. It definitely made the statement she was looking for.

She moved away from the people she'd been chatting with—the owners of a craft shop in town—and she stood on her own. Even though Piper was supposed to be using the night to get closer to her family, every time she looked up, there was someone new who was looking to meet the paper's new editor. People were curious about her, and she was happy to oblige them.

However, no matter how interesting the conversations she'd been having were, every time she looked up, her eyes automatically found Maverick, as if he had some sort of beacon on him. She finished her champagne and looked across the room. She saw that he had his phone to his ear and he was looking at her. He always seemed to do that—know exactly when she was watching him. He smiled and hung up. He looked in her direction, his grin downright rakish as he headed across the dance floor to her.

"Having fun?" he asked.

"Galas aren't normally my type of thing, but I am having fun. How about yourself?"

"It's okay," he said with a casual shrug. "Do you have any plans tomorrow?"

"No. I'm free until work on Monday." She narrowed her eyes. "Why? What are you getting at?"

"Do you want to get out of here?" he asked her.

She shook her head. "Not until you tell me what's going on."

"I've got something to show you."

"If you're going to keep being this vague, I'm not going anywhere."

"Fine. I want to take you somewhere. Get you out of this town for a bit."

"Where?"

"Galveston."

"As far as exotic locales go, it leaves something to be desired."

He chuckled. "I know it isn't very exotic, but I have some

things to take care of there. But, if you want to come with, I can show you a good time."

Even though Piper was coming to appreciate the small-town life, her sense of adventure nipped at her. She was intrigued and wanted to see what he had in mind. She looked around the room and saw that Willa was watching her curiously. But she thankfully didn't alert either Garrett or Wes to her conversation with Maverick—they probably wouldn't take kindly to her consorting with the enemy.

"I don't know..." she started. "That might not be a good idea."

"Are you worried about the Hardwells? You might be living at the ranch, but they don't own you. You can take a night away."

"How did you know I was living there?" she asked.

"Word travels fast," he told her, reminiscent of their earlier conservation.

"Yeah, I guess you're right."

"Would it help if I left first? You can meet me outside in a couple of minutes."

She thought about that. It was ridiculous to be living in such a secretive way. Her every instinct told her to live her life out loud, without any influence from others. But while she was trying to connect with her family, she had to be careful. She had to follow the letter of the Hardwell law. She looked up at Maverick, who was still staring at her with that cocky, lopsided grin. She couldn't say no to him. "Give me two minutes."

He smiled and tipped the brim of his hat at her. "I'll be at the valet stand."

When he was gone, Piper walked a casual lap around ballroom until she made her way back to the Hardwells.

She stopped in front of them. "Hi, I think I'm going to take off. I'm feeling tired."

"Oh, really?" Willa asked, her eyebrow raised.

Piper knew that Willa was sharp and probably knew she was leaving with Maverick. But bless her for not saying anything in front of the rest of the family. "Yeah. I'm going to head back home to the ranch," she said again.

"Okay, well, we'll see you tomorrow," Garrett said.

"Actually, I'm heading out of town tomorrow for the day. Do some exploring around Texas." Thankfully, they didn't question her about who she was going with, or how.

"That's nice," Willa said. "I guess we'll see you again when you get back."

Piper said goodbye and quietly left. She walked outside and, just as Maverick had promised, he was standing next to the valet stand when a charcoal-gray Aston Martin pulled up. She whistled at the luxury car. "Wow. Nice ride."

He opened her door and she slid inside. The butter-smooth leather seat cupped her body. "What? Did you think I was going to arrive in the ranch truck?"

"Well, you never know. I know how much you boys love your trucks."

"Trucks are functional to me," he said. "It helps for hauling gear and feed at the ranch, and that's about it." He sat behind the wheel. In his fitted tuxedo, he matched the luxurious interior of the car so well, that she believed it must have been tailored to him. "This—" he smoothed his hands over the wheel "—is a real ride."

"You're not wrong," she said.

"Buckle up," he told her before peeling out of the parking lot, kicking up dust with his rear tires.

After they drove a distance, Maverick passed a highway sign showing the miles to nearby Austin. Piper took out her phone to consult the maps app and saw that they were headed in the opposite direction of their destination. "Austin? I thought we were going to Galveston."

"Galveston is a ways away," he told her. "What, did you think we were driving to the Gulf Coast?"

"Well, we got into a car, didn't we? It's not exactly a wild assumption."

He laughed. "I guess you're right. But just wait."

"For what?"

"You'll see."

After around thirty minutes, they drove into Austin and didn't stop until they arrived at a private airport. The "you'll see" he'd mentioned turned out to be a waiting helicopter. He stopped the car and an attendant came and opened her door. Piper turned to Maverick. "Are you serious?"

He chuckled. "It's the only way to travel."

Less than two hours later, they were touching down on a helipad in Galveston. He whisked her into a waiting SUV, and again, they were off. Piper felt like a princess in a fairy tale. But Maverick Kane was no prince. He was the rival of her new family. She'd worry about the fallout later.

"So, where to now—private jet to a space shuttle, to the stratosphere?"

"You'll see. We're almost there."

They stopped at the marina. The driver opened her door first and escorted her from the SUV. Maverick got out, too, and, together they walked down the pier to a large yacht. The journey so far had already been unreal, but she was struck by the size of the yacht. "Wow. Is this yours?"

"Yeah," he told her without even a hint of arrogance.

As if it was just a basic fact. "It belongs to the family. But you've seen nothing yet."

"You know, all this time I thought you were just a guy who just happened to be rich and chose a humble life on your ranch. This whole night is showing me that I was wrong."

"I'm still the same guy who feeds the chickens and cleans out the silos. I just have access to luxury when I want it."

The waiting crew greeted them and took their shoes before she and Maverick stepped onto the teak deck.

"Why don't we show you to your room, and you can get comfortable?" one of the stewards asked.

At that moment, Piper realized that she was still wearing her evening dress. She clearly wasn't prepared for this impromptu adventure. She held out her hands and looked at Maverick. "I don't have anything with me. I don't have clothes or any of my toiletries."

"It's all taken care of," Maverick said behind her. "Go to your cabin. I'll be waiting on the upper deck."

The female attendant said, "Why don't I show you around? We have everything you'll need in your personal cabin."

Piper followed the attendant as she showed her all of the amenities aboard the boat. *Boat* was a misnomer, of course. They yacht was massive, holding a gym, a formal dining room, an office and, finally, what the other woman had called *her personal cabin*. Meaning that Maverick wouldn't be joining her, even though it was clearly the master cabin. She opened the closet and saw that it had been stocked with clothing, bought for her, with the tags still attached. She turned to the steward. "Where did all of this come from?"

"We keep the vessel fully stocked for guests, but we ran out and bought a few things when we were told you were coming."

"Tell me something. Does Maverick do this a lot?"

"I'm not at liberty to discuss Mr. Kane's private life—" she leaned in "—but, to be honest, this isn't common."

She nodded. "Interesting."

The steward stepped back from her. "I'll let you change. If you'd like your dress cleaned, just let us know."

"Thank you."

Alone in the cabin, Piper sat on the bed. She may still be in Texas, but she was far away from the rolling acres of ranchland in Applewood. And she had no idea what she was doing there, or how she'd gotten there.

Reaching back, she unzipped her dress, allowing the satin to pool at her feet. In the closet, she selected a comfortable-looking, silky, two-piece lounge suit and put it on. The fine material of the designer outfit slid against her skin. She didn't know what the night had in store, but it was her first time on a yacht, and she was there with Maverick, no nosy townsfolk or sworn enemies in sight. She and Maverick could be themselves there. At least for one night. She might as well enjoy it while she could.

Maverick was on the upper deck, leaning his arms on the railing, looking out at the moonlit ocean. He raised the short glass of whiskey to his lips and drank. His parents would be there the next day, but at least he would have the night alone with Piper.

"What a nice night." He heard a voice behind him. Turning, he saw Piper, wearing some of the clothes he'd had picked up for her. "There are worse places to be kidnapped to, I guess."

"This isn't a kidnapping," he assured her. "Just say the word and you're on your way back to Applewood."

She looked out at the bay, her skin glistening in the moonlight. A slash of light reflecting from her collarbone caught his attention. "Nah, I like it here."

"Me, too," he told her.

"Champagne?" the steward behind the bar asked Piper.

"Yes, please."

"For you, sir?" he asked Maverick.

"I'd love one. Thank you." He took a drink from his glass. "We'll have some privacy here if we can. Leave the bottle."

"Yes, sir. Let us know if you need anything."

They both watched the steward depart then she looked up to take in the night sky. "Okay, this is incredible."

While the ranch was his first love, he also loved being on the water. On land or sea, the wide-open spaces and the cool breeze were a tonic for his soul. "Yeah, it's okay," he said with a shrug.

"'Okay'?" she repeated. "This is more than okay."

"How is your cabin?"

"It's great. But you already know that. Strange how it's been fully stocked with clothing in my size and toiletries. How many women have you done this for?"

"No others, I swear. I just got the crew to pick up a few things I'd hoped you might like."

"Sure, sure," she said in a skeptical tone. "You rich people sure do lead different lives than the rest of us."

"I don't know what to say to that," he told her.

"I don't want to sound like I'm not grateful," she said. "But you need to tell me why we're here. Last I thought, we were going to avoid each other. Being alone on a private yacht is hardly avoiding each other."

"Yeah, I know, but it's an excellent way to avoid other people."

"You mean the Hardwells?"

He shrugged. "They're part of it. But there's something else. Tomorrow, my mother and father are coming to discuss some business matters. I decided to come here tonight and stay on the boat, and I thought it might be nice to have a little company."

"Why didn't you tell me that your parents are coming here, too?"

"I didn't think it mattered."

"Of course you didn't. You're professionally laid-back."

"Didn't you call me an *insufferable grump* before?"

"It's possible to be both." She sipped her champagne and again looked out to the harbor. "Meeting the parents. That's a big step, don't you think?"

"You don't have to meet them if you don't want. The boat's big enough that you never have to see them, and they'll only be here for the afternoon."

"So, what kind of business are you doing out here with them?" she asked.

He paused, unsure of what to tell her. Even if she was new to the family, and to Applewood, she was a Hardwell, after all. How did he know she wouldn't go back and tell Elias what he shared with her?

"I'm meeting with my parents."

"'*Meeting with*'?" she asked. "That sounds pretty formal."

"We're a pretty formal family. We've got to have some discussions over what I'm doing with the ranch." He thought about it. "Or what I'm *not* doing, to be more accurate."

"What you're *not* doing?"

"Keeping up oil production, specifically. When I took over the land, I told them that it was done. And they don't like it." Neither of them liked that they were going to lose the oil revenue from new development, but as Maverick stood on the deck of a 70-million-dollar yacht, he knew that money was in full supply with him and his family. But what he didn't share with her was the fact that his parents believed the Hardwells were infringing on his land, or that he was interested in increasing his ranching capabilities. Even though he wouldn't be able to compete with the Hardwells right away, he could take a significant amount of profit in the coming years for himself. He liked Piper, but he also knew how much winning the approval of the Hardwells meant to her.

She nodded, as if she understood. "You've got to live your own life, though, right?" she asked.

"Yeah, absolutely. But I don't really want to talk about them anymore. Do you?"

"Not really, no."

He heard the low hum of the engines as they left the dock.

"We're moving," she said.

"Yeah, we aren't going far offshore. Is that okay?"

"Yeah, it's fine. It's been a while since I've been on the water."

He turned to her. The full moon reflected just as easily off her radiant skin as it did the surface of the ocean. "I'm glad you came with me. I wanted to get you out of Applewood for a little while. Seemed like it would be good for you."

"How did you know that?"

"This whole thing with the Hardwells and you working

overtime at the *Tribune* office. That sounds like it could be stressful. Tell me I'm wrong."

"I can't. It's been a lot."

"Why are you still in Texas? You could go back to Chicago if you wanted."

"Since I lost my job at the magazine, there's really no reason to keep paying so much rent in the city. I've always wanted a big family, and I have family here that I want to get to know. I found a new job. Part of me feels like maybe I could settle down here. I could put down some roots."

"In Applewood?" he scoffed. While part of him liked the idea of having her around permanently, her continued presence in Applewood would definitely complicate his future moves when it came to the Hardwells.

"You came back and stayed, didn't you?" she asked him. "Why is that so hard to believe I could do the same?"

"I guess it isn't," he conceded. "Although you're a little different from many of the women in town."

She laughed. "I stand out like a sore thumb, huh?"

"Not a sore thumb. But like a rose among thorns."

"That's mean to the other women."

He settled on "You're very noticeable."

"I'll take that one."

"How are you liking it so far at the Hardwell Ranch?"

"Elias and the Hardwells have been good to me. I mean they've been welcoming, but then the topic of money came up, and that complicates things. I told them firmly that I'm not interested in any part of an inheritance, and I'll pass over the keys to the car he gave me. Wes and Garrett have been nice to me, but I think they're a little apprehensive in that respect. They are going to take a little more convincing that I'm not just here to home in on their money."

"I think they'll come around," he said, unsure of what

that would mean for him and Piper. He wanted her to be closer to her family, because that was what she wanted, but the closer she got to the Hardwells, the bigger the wedge between them might get.

"The rest of the townsfolk, though? They're a different story," she said, and Maverick laughed. "They're nice, but still curious about me and my motives. I still get a lot of sideways glances, but it's nothing that I can't get past."

"Yeah, I know from experience that some people in Applewood don't much care for outsiders."

"Are you an outsider?"

"Seeing as how I don't take the time to kiss their asses, stick and all, they don't like it."

"I heard some folks talk about the check you left at the ball. You let your bank account do the kissing."

"Better than the alternative. If not submission, the only other way to their hearts is money. It keeps them off my back, and off my land."

"I was right before—you are an insufferable grump," Piper muttered with a good-natured shake of her head.

"Only sometimes."

They drank the rest of their champagne in silence as they moved farther out into the harbor.

"What else should we talk about?" she asked, gesturing to her empty glass flute.

"I don't know. I think we're done talking for the evening. Don't you?"

A bead of champagne clung to her lip as she smiled. "What do you suggest we do? I don't think the crew would appreciate it if we took a night swim."

"No, they certainly wouldn't." He bent his head and lowered his lips to hers. She tasted like champagne, and he wanted more.

He wrapped his arms around her waist and pulled her close, leaning her upper half slightly over the railing. Her long hair hung down and was being tossed around by the wind. Maverick wasn't sure about much, but the more time he spent with Piper, the more he needed her. He knew that things were complicated between them, but none of that mattered to him when he held her in his arms.

Piper pulled back and looked at the distance to the water. She gasped and he held her tighter.

"Don't worry," he told her. "You aren't in any danger."

"Aren't I?"

"Not from me." His hands on her waist, he lifted her, and her legs wrapped around his hips. He brought her to the padded chaise and lowered her.

He unfastened the buttons of her shirt, and when it opened, he was pleased to see that she'd done without a bra after changing out of her evening gown. He pushed the material aside, and her pink nipples pearled with the chill of the sea air. He lowered his head to take one between his teeth when she put her hands on his chest and pushed him away.

"What about your crew?"

"Don't worry. They're very discreet."

"That still doesn't mean I want them to walk up here and see us."

"They know to not disturb us. Don't worry."

"You're sure?"

"I'm positive." He lowered his head again and this time she didn't stop him. She arched her back against him, bringing her breasts closer to him, and he took them in his mouth.

He skimmed his hands down her sides to the waistband of her pants. She lifted her hips and he slid them down her legs. She kicked them away and was naked beneath him. She shivered.

"You cold?"

"A little."

"We can go inside," he suggested.

"Why don't you warm me up instead?"

"I can do that."

Maverick shrugged off his jacket and tossed it aside. She reached up and unbuttoned his shirt with quick, efficient fingers. He pulled off his shirt and it joined the expensive jacket on the teak deck. He looked down at her, the orange glow of the deck lights making her skin look golden under the night sky, and smoothed his hands over her body.

He lowered himself between her legs and keeping his eyes on hers, he placed a kiss near her navel before venturing lower. She parted her thighs and he took full advantage of the access, dropping a line of kisses down to her sweet core. She sighed and he went deeper. Using his lips, tongue and fingers, he tasted her, enjoyed her, savored her, listening to her breathing hitch, until she grew tight underneath him, and she stiffened and cried out.

He raised over her, working his way up her body, then he kissed her lips as he unbuckled his belt and lowered his pants. He reached in his back pocket for his wallet and withdrew a condom. Sheathed, he couldn't wait any longer, and he pushed inside her. She was warm, waiting, molding around him like exquisite silk. It confirmed that their first night together, the explosive chemistry between them, hadn't been a fluke, a one-time thing. There was something about her. They fit together, and he knew that a lifetime full of nights with her wouldn't be close to enough.

He thrust in and out of her slick heat, sliding against her, his pace matched by the rolling of the yacht over the gentle waves, until the feeling hit a crescendo and he came with a rough groan against her shoulder. He excused himself to get rid of the condom, and when he returned to her, he picked up his discarded jacket and laid it over her naked body. He lay against her and pulled her close. She hummed and stroked his back. They didn't exchange words. Their caresses, their warmth, were enough as they lay back in the chaise, feeling the movement of the water, watching the stars shimmer against the inky night sky.

Fifteen

Piper wasn't sure if it was the squawking of a seabird, the rolling of the boat, or the cool Gulf air that woke her up. Another birdcall rang out and several more birds returned it. Piper stirred. The chilled air prickled her skin and she pulled her covering closer. She realized that it was Maverick's jacket and she pressed her nose to the collar and inhaled. The warmth of Maverick's naked chest against her back was pleasant and she snuggled in tighter. Out here, on Maverick's luxury megayacht, they were a long way from his ranch in Applewood—and the prying eyes of her newfound family—and the freedom felt amazing.

Holding Maverick's jacket to her chest, she opened her eyes and saw that the sky was a golden orange. She sat up, watching as the sky went from orange to blue as the sun rose, and the seabirds came to life, starting their own days.

It was barely dawn and, around them, the world came awake with a flourish. The water rocked them lightly, and she could feel the energy surround her. There was something so primal about spending a night under the stars; she felt so in tune with the world around her. She shifted and turned to face Maverick, whose strong arms were still wrapped around her. His eyes were still closed but soon fluttered open. It had been an incredible night, even more incredible than their first—which she hadn't even believed to be possible.

"Mornin'," he said with a sleepy, satisfied grin on his face.

"Morning," she said, snuggling into his chest. "I don't know if I've slept that good in a long time."

"Yeah, there's really something about sleeping under the stars."

"On the deck of a megayacht."

He grinned. "Especially when you've got a beautiful woman in your arms."

"I'll have to take your word for it. Thanks again for last night," she said. "It was fabulous. You really know how to surprise me."

"In what way?"

"You have a reputation as a grumpy recluse because you spend most of your time on your ranch. But this is our second time together, and you're so passionate and spontaneous. Romantic."

"What, an old ranch hand can't be romantic?"

She laughed. "Look around. You're more than an old ranch hand," she said.

He pulled her tighter and kissed her. "If you say so. But I could say the same about you. You have this tough, prickly exterior, but underneath it all, you're soft, warm."

Lying on his chest, Piper twirled the short hairs there with her fingernails while he stroked her back absently. Enjoying the quiet contentment that spread throughout her body, she felt more relaxed that she had in a long time. In that moment, she was fully satisfied. Maverick satisfied her sexual appetite, but he also filled her emotional needs. She liked being around him and being in his space.

But as the time went on, despite his warmth, Piper grew cold and shivered in his arms. "We'd better get dressed and inside before the crew comes looking for us."

"Yeah, breakfast should be ready soon."

He passed Piper her discarded clothing and she quickly pulled it on, and he did the same with his pants, leaving his shirt off. Together, they walked inside. Heading for the cabins, they passed an attendant.

"Good morning, Mr. Kane."

"Mornin', Lisa."

"How did you sleep last night?"

When Maverick looked down at her in response, Piper felt a flush spread across her cheeks. "Very well, thank you."

"Will you take your coffee in your cabin?"

"Yes, please. I'll take mine in the second master. Ms. Gallagher will be in the first." He turned to her and put his hand on her lower back. "What would you like?"

Piper wasn't used to being fussed over. It made her uncomfortable. "Uh, just black coffee is fine," she told the attendant.

"Very good. I'll be right back with them."

"Thank you. And we'll have breakfast on the aft deck."

"Are your parents joining us today?"

He grimaced. "Yes. They'll be boarding before lunch."

Lisa smiled and walked away.

"What time are we heading to the dock?" Piper asked. "I'd like to go back up for the trip in."

"We're not going anywhere. They're meeting us here."

"How—"

"There's a helipad up top."

She nodded. How could a man say something like that in such a casual manner? "Of course there is."

"If you'd like to meet them, you could join us for lunch. Or you could take your lunch elsewhere."

"I can join you. I'd feel awkward if they knew I was here and didn't join you all."

"Great."

"Meeting the parents is a pretty huge step and, as far as I remember, we're barely even friends."

"I think that going to bed together puts us in a different category than just friends, don't you?"

"So, what is it then? You think we're going steady, or something? Gonna get married?" she asked. "Unlikely. You're a Kane and I'm a Hardwell."

"We've got a real Capulet and Montague thing going on here, don't we?" he joked. "I don't know what this is, Piper." He stretched his back dramatically. "The only thing I do know is that the next time I make love to you, it's going to be in an actual bed."

Piper smiled at the thought of a *next time*. "I look forward to it." She turned to go into her room to get ready for the day, but he smacked her sharply on her butt, causing her to scream out in surprise. "Hey!"

"Sorry," he said with a smile that told her he wasn't sorry at all. "I couldn't resist."

"Incorrigible," she said.

"But am I still a grump?" he asked with a smile.

She shook her head and walked into the stateroom, closing the door, putting a barrier between them. Away from him, in her room, which was clearly his own master cabin, she was able to think about what had happened the night before. He'd whisked her away in a helicopter and brought her to his yacht, where they'd spent the night under the stars. Her life had certainly taken a few turns in the past several months. But this was one she hadn't expected. She'd come to Applewood to find her family, but she hadn't expected to find love. *No!* she told herself. *That's just a figure of speech.* Whatever was going on between Maverick Kane and herself was not love. Infatuation, chemistry maybe—but definitely not love.

She went to the closet and looked through the clothing that hung there. In terms of size and style, they'd supplied her with some great items. He must have been paying more attention to her than she'd realized. She picked out a light blue sundress and pulled it on.

A knock on the door surprised her. She'd expected it to be Maverick, but when she opened the door, she saw that the attendant had arrived with her coffee, in a steaming French press, and a mug on a tray. The woman set the tray on the nearby table.

"Thank you so much," Piper said gratefully. She inhaled the aroma, and her mouth watered, as she was generally unable to function without her morning coffee.

"You're welcome," Lisa responded. "Can I bring you anything else?"

"No, everything is perfect. This is too much really."

"I'm sorry?"

She shook her head. "I'm not used to any of this. It's all so strange."

Lisa smiled. "You'll get used to it."

Piper's smile faded. She didn't know if she would. She may be sticking around in Applewood for a while, but there was no way she could expect to spend much time with Maverick. Not if she wanted to get closer to her family.

* * *

While Piper was down below, Maverick greeted his parents, who had just arrived—unexpectedly early—via helicopter. As usual, he hugged his mother, shook his father's hand and walked them down to the deck, where the crew had set the breakfast table for them.

Noticing the extra place setting, and after a brief interrogation, his mother's interest was piqued. "You said someone would be joining us," she said. "Where are they?"

"Yes, my friend, Piper, is here. She's getting ready, and will be up here soon."

"So, you brought a woman here?" his mother asked, intrigued. "Tell me more—who is she?"

"Her name is Piper Gallagher. She's new in Applewood, from Chicago."

His father casually took a sip from his coffee mug. "I've heard about her. She's the editor at the *Tribune*," he said simply.

"That's right."

"And she's just moved on to Hardwell Ranch."

"How did you know that?"

"You know I keep tabs on the people around my son. Someone spotted you two together in town, and I had her looked into."

"You had her investigated?"

"Of course."

"I'd prefer if you didn't look into my friends like that again."

"I'm trying to protect you and the business."

"Edward," his mother admonished, buttering a piece of toast. She had always been closer to him than his father. Constantly trying to find out information about his love life, she was also digging to see if he was seeing anyone, if there were wedding bells in the future, the pitter patter of tiny feet, etc… Honestly, between that and his father's coldness and sole focus on business, he wasn't sure which he preferred. "We need to mind our own business when it comes to Maverick's personal life."

"That's right," Maverick seconded.

"Even when his personal life is tied to the Hardwells?"

"How did you know about that?"

"What is going on?" his mother asked.

"Our son brought Elias Hardwell's daughter to our boat."

"What? Is that true?"

"What does she know about the land dispute we're looking into? Or why the families parted ways?" his father asked.

Maverick pushed his plate away, suddenly not hungry. He expected a lot of things from his parents, but their spying on him was not one of them. "I don't believe she knows anything. How would she? She just got here. She barely knows anything about the family, and I doubt she's researching their history."

"But we don't know that for sure," his father said. "I want you to keep an eye on her."

"I'm not with her to keep an eye on anything. We met before it had even come out that she was a Hardwell," Maverick returned.

"So she says."

Maverick slammed his fist down on the table, rattling the dishes. "What's that supposed to mean?"

"It means that it's awful convenient that she shows up, starts a relationship with you, and it turns out that she's part of the family that's always been out to get ours."

"That's not who she is."

"Maybe she's a spy."

"What?" Maverick almost jumped up from the table. "That's the most ridiculous thing I've ever heard."

"Maybe she's here to pump you for information to take back to Elias and Garrett."

"That is not what's happening."

"No? How do you know? If anyone finds out about the land, it could mean serious consequences for us. Especially if we continue drilling."

"We're not continuing the drilling." His parents had no idea he wanted to expand his ranching operations.

"Son, the revenues alone—"

"If you're so concerned about revenues, sell the goddamn yacht, get rid of the helicopters, why don't you?" he snapped, grateful the topic was off Piper and her lineage.

"Whether or not Kane Energy fails, the family will still have money. This is about preserving your grandfather's legacy, the business."

"The legacy is his land. I'll protect that. If I'd known about the drama that would come with owning this land, I wouldn't have even taken it over. I would have let it all go to ruin."

"Don't say that," his mother said.

"It's true. Coming back here, the last thing I wanted was to be caught up in some longstanding family drama with the Hardwells."

"Hi, there," came a voice from behind him. It was Piper. How much of their disagreement had she heard?

"Piper, hi. Mom, Dad, this is Piper."

"Nice to meet you, dear."

"Thank you."

Piper took a seat next to him at the table. She was quiet. Almost too quiet. He looked at his parents, who were making polite conversation. But he knew their tells. He knew that, like him, they were wondering what she'd heard. Piper was smart and, with her journalism experience, knew how to research. There's no telling how much she had looked into the backgrounds of both families. Had she learned that the Kanes had a potential land feud brewing with the Hardwells? Would she bring that information back to the Hardwells?

He draped his arm over the back of her chair and she looked up at him with a smile. Instantly, he knew that that wasn't what was happening at all. She wasn't there to spy on him for the Hardwells.

"We hear you're the new editor at the *Applewood Tribune*," his mother said.

"Yes, that's right."

"And you're relatively new to town?"

"That's also right. You've studied me as Maverick's new friend, I see." She heard Maverick snort next to her.

Mrs. Kane gave her a withering smile. Maverick's father cleared his throat. "But, you being a Hardwell, I have to wonder what you're doing here with my son."

"Dad."

She looked up to face Maverick. "Did you tell them?" she asked.

"Sorry, it slipped out," he lied, knowing it would require less of an explanation than telling her his father had had her investigated. Let her be pissed off at him. At least he wouldn't have to explain anything more sinister than that.

"To be honest," she started, "I'm really not sure why I'm here on your yacht. Maverick invited me. We're friends."

"But you've been seen around town with Maverick. It's no secret that you've been romantic."

"So, you've taken this spying to the next level, huh?" Maverick asked.

"We just want to know what you get up to at that ranch by yourself."

"You could just ask," he said.

"Not like you would tell us," his father responded.

"What do you want from me?" Maverick asked, raising his voice.

His father put up his hands.

"Maverick, Edward, let's not argue," his mother said. "Especially in front of company. Why don't we take advantage of the beautiful day and enjoy our breakfast?"

"Fine." Maverick turned to Piper. "I'm sorry."

"It's okay." He watched as she picked up a fork. She seemed quiet, pensive, likely because of the scene he and his family had just created. But he still wondered if she'd heard any of the previous conversation about the land dispute, and if she had, how much of it?

Sixteen

Piper had come back to Applewood with Maverick the night before, and he'd dropped her off at Hardwell Ranch. They had never recovered the blissful mood they'd shared on the yacht before that horribly awkward breakfast with his parents. She'd walked in on an intense conversation, of which she'd only heard pieces. There was something to the long-standing feud between the families. Something about the land division, and she was going to find out what.

She'd driven the cherry-red convertible into town and was now walking into the library. She'd learned that municipal records were kept in a section in the back, so she made her way past the librarians at the front and the patrons sitting at tables, reading the *Tribune* and other newspapers, reference books and fiction, or using the bank of computers.

Clarice, the aging records clerk, smiled at her. They'd become acquainted during one of Piper's earlier visits.

"Piper, what a surprise to see you back here. I don't get a lot of company."

"Hi, Ms. Clarice. I was wondering if you could help me find something."

"And what's that?"

"I'm looking to do a title search on the Kane and Hardwell ranches." Clarice looked at her skeptically. "I'm just doing a little research on the town," she explained. There was much more to it than that, however. She knew that she was missing a key part about the rivalry between the two families. She knew that Harlan Kane and Elias had once been business partners. She had no idea when or why the rivalry had started, so the land titles might tell her something useful.

Instead of questioning her motives, that response seemed good enough for Clarice. "You wait right here and I'll see what I can find."

"Thanks." Piper took a seat and waited.

Less than fifteen minutes later, Clarice came back to the desk holding a folder. "I think I have everything you might need here."

"Thank you so much."

"No problem—just make sure none of my secrets end up in that column in the *Tribune*, okay?" she asked, winking.

Piper smiled. She couldn't imagine what gossip she could ever dig up on the kindly older woman. "I'll see what I can do." She took the folder and walked out of the library.

She headed back to Hardwell Ranch and sat at the desk next to the bed in her temporary bedroom. Thumbing through the documents, she noticed that Clarice had also helpfully included a map of the area. It didn't take long to see that there was a discrepancy in the land as it had been divided by the Kanes and Hardwells years ago and where the property lines had been recently drawn.

Looking closer, she pictured the land as it currently was. She looked up a satellite image and saw that the new training facility had been built on what should have been Maverick's land. Did Maverick know? Surely, it would have come up or he would have done something to take it back. It didn't seem likely that anyone knew of this development. She leaned back in her chair.

Then it hit her: given the rivalry between the Kanes and the Hardwells, she wondered if perhaps Maverick was using her? What if, after she'd told him about her relationship to the family, he'd decided to use her for information, or to get back at the Hardwells for taking some of his land? The thought of it made her sick, and she couldn't reconcile the man with whom she was falling in love with as a man who might deceive her. That thought stopped her. She'd been falling for him all this time. But when she considered it, there was no doubt that she was in love with Maverick. No matter how difficult it would make her life in the long run.

The sharp peal of her cell phone ringing broke the silence of the room, startling her. She picked it up and checked the screen. *Maverick.* As if he were in the room with her, she shoved the papers back into the folder before answering. "Hello?"

"Hi, Piper." His voice rumbled over the phone.

"Hi, Maverick."

"I, uh, just wanted to call to make sure you're okay, and to apologize again for how my family and I acted yesterday."

"It's okay. A little family drama doesn't bother me too much."

He chuckled. "Good to know. I want to see you tonight. Do you have any plans?"

"I don't."

"Why don't I pick you up at dusk? Dress warm."

"Why don't I meet you a little farther down the road?" she suggested. That way the family wouldn't see him or hear his vehicle, as ridiculous as that was. She was a grown woman and should be able to see any man she wanted. "This feud thing is getting pretty old."

"You're telling me," he said.

Briefly, she wondered if she should get both families together, and tell Maverick and Garrett about the land, to see if they could reconcile their problems. But she didn't. She didn't know how much that would solve. But this was a new wrinkle, and between connecting with her new family and falling for Maverick, she had no idea on which side of the fence she would end up.

Maverick hung up the phone and replaced it into his front shirt pocket. He smiled, satisfied with the knowledge that Piper was still interested in seeing him again, and he had quite a night planned for them. But first, he had some work to do.

He got out of his truck and jogged up the steps of the library entrance. He stopped at the main desk. "Hi, there, could you tell me where I would find historical title searches and deeds?"

"That would be in the back room," the librarian told him. "Clarice will be back there, and she'll be able to help you."

"Thank you, ma'am," he said and headed for the back room of the library, where, as promised, Clarice was at the desk.

"Hi, there. I'm looking for a title search and survey

for Kane Ranch." He had to figure out where the official boundary of his land was, and he couldn't get a surveyor in for more than a month. The sooner he could put the matter to bed, the better.

"Oh, dear, I'm sorry. I don't have that. A woman just came by this morning looking for that information. I gave her the only copy we have. And we don't loan out the originals."

Why would someone come and take the information from the library? A woman? He smiled at Clarice. "Thank you for your help."

"Want me to give you a call when she brings it back?"

"No, that won't be necessary," he told her.

When he left, he wondered who would have cared enough about the land boundary between his ranch and Hardwells—then it hit him. Piper might have a reason.

Seventeen

The sun was setting, and Piper pulled a long-sleeved shirt over her tank top. She didn't have a lot of warm clothing, so layering would have to do. She checked her appearance in the mirror and smoothed down her hair. She was ready to go.

She walked through the wing where she'd been staying and into the main area, where Daisy, Wes, Willa and Garrett were sitting in the living room.

"Hey, guys," Piper said.

"Hi, Piper," Garrett said. "Heading out?"

"Yeah, just going to meet a friend."

"Maverick?" Wes quipped. To which Daisy smacked him on the chest.

"What?" she asked. How did everyone seem to know that she was seeing Maverick? Maybe she wasn't as slick in hiding her attraction to him as she thought she was.

"Why are you acting like she's in high school?" Willa asked. "She's a grown woman, and she doesn't have to report to you where she's going."

"Thank you, Willa, and, in fact, not only am I a grown woman, but I'm also actually your aunt," she teased.

"Have fun out with your *friend*," Daisy said.

"I definitely will."

Garrett stood. "I'll see you out."

When they got to the door, she was about to leave but Garrett touched her arm. "You've been hanging out with Maverick Kane, right?"

She didn't see the point in lying. "Yeah, he's my friend."

"I want you to be careful," he said.

"Why? Why is everyone so caught up in this family feud? Maverick hasn't done anything to any of you."

"You know that our families have not gotten along in decades." He stepped closer. "We can't just ignore the history there."

"And you're going to discount Maverick because of what went down between your grandfathers? Maybe that shows that you have a little growing up to do. And just so you know, Mav owns his grandfather's ranch now and he's started making changes. You might know that if you bothered to get to know him."

She heard Garrett sigh, and he leaned in. "I haven't told anyone, but I received a tip that he's ordered a survey on the boundary of our two ranches," he said, his voice low. "The only reason he'd do that is if he were going to make a claim to my land."

Piper looked away. She knew exactly why Maverick had done that, but she wondered what had tipped him off at this particular time. She thought back to the conversation she'd had with Maverick and his parents. Maverick had mentioned his parents spying on him. Is that what was happening? Was there someone watching her, as well?

"I don't know anything about that," she said, choosing to hold back on what she'd discovered about the land. "How about I ask him?"

"I'd appreciate if you didn't," Garrett said, glowering.

"Don't worry. I won't. It isn't my business."

"You're a Hardwell," Garrett told her. "It is your business." He turned away, leaving her alone at the door.

You're a Hardwell. The words rattled in her head. It was the first time that Garrett had called her a Hardwell, or even insinuated that she was part of the family. That stuck with her. She was finally being accepted, and she was now heading out to meet with their enemy.

Eighteen

The sun had set and the sky was dark as Maverick parked the truck in the middle of a field. She looked around and saw nothing but flat land and darkness around them. Her conversation with Garrett was still fresh in her head. All she had wanted was to be included in the family, and being called a Hardwell had done something to her. In that case, just being this close to Maverick was a betrayal to the family.

"You're quiet over there," he said.

She smiled faintly. "I'm just a little tired."

"Okay, stay right there," he told her, getting out of the truck and coming around to her side. He opened her door and helped her from the truck.

"What are we doing out here?"

He took her hand in a firm hold and they came around the back of the truck. He dropped the tailgate and she saw that he'd constructed what looked like one of the coziest beds she'd ever seen, made of an air mattress, blankets and pillows. He helped her up into the back of the truck, and she settled down onto it, and he followed.

"What is this?" she asked.

"You've never gone truck-bed camping?"

"Can't say I have."

He pulled a bottle of champagne from the nearby ice bucket and filled two glasses, handing her one.

"You've thought of everything."

"I try."

"All we do is drink champagne and look at the sky, it seems."

"There's no better way to spend a night, I reckon."

"You're right." She looked around. "Shouldn't we be scared of bears or coyotes or something?"

"Don't worry. We keep tight reins on predator protection. Nothing gets into the ranch. We're as close to bear-and-coyote proof as we could be."

"I'll have to trust you on that, but how do you know you aren't missing a part of the perimeter."

"Don't worry about that," he said. "I know every boundary of this land," he said with an undefinable slant in his voice.

She looked up at him, but his face was impassable. "Well, that's good."

"Let's just lie back and enjoy the evening."

She looked up at the sky. "You know, I'm really starting to love this place. I don't know how I could ever go back to the city after this."

"Yeah, it's pretty special, right?"

The night was warm, but the breeze still held a little chill. Maverick pulled a blanket over them, and Piper snuggled tighter against him. Her warmth permeated him. He'd meant to ask her if she'd withdrawn the files from the library. But with her settled in his arms, he couldn't. In that moment, he didn't even want to know the answer. It didn't matter that he was a Kane and she was a Hardwell; he was starting to fall for her, and he couldn't help himself now.

"This is incredible," she told him.

"It is, isn't it?"

She scoffed. "I'm sure you bring all of your women here."

"Honestly, I never have," he said with a shake of his head. What Maverick had left unsaid was that, while they'd only known each other for a short time, he'd never felt that kind of connection with another woman.

"No? This is an automatic way to assure you get laid."

"Is it now? Think it'll work tonight?"

"I think it might."

That was the sign Maverick needed. He gripped the back of her neck with his fingers and pulled her to him, taking her mouth in a blistering kiss. She moaned and rolled her hips against him, rubbing his length with her body. He needed her, and that need for her grew every time they were together. He wanted to take his time with her, to experience every part of her, but there would be time for that again next time, and he just couldn't wait. With her help, he pushed down her jeans until she kicked them off. Then came her shirt.

He was still fully clothed, and Piper, her nimble fingers working quickly, unbuckled his belt and pushed his jeans down over his hips. Pausing only for a moment, long enough to reach for the strategically placed condom he'd left nearby, she wrapped him in it, and he pushed inside her.

Piper cried out in the night, and he groaned into her

shoulder before bringing his mouth back to hers, tasting her sweetness, which mingled with the champagne. He kissed her, tasting her lips, her tongue, but it wasn't enough. He kissed his way across her jaw, stopping to gently nip her earlobe between his teeth. They moved as one, and then, together, they soared.

After she stilled in his arms, he followed her over the edge with a groan of his own. He rolled over and pulled her with him, holding her close to his chest. Feeling her heart beat rapidly then steadily against his, he realized then that, no matter how he felt about Piper's family, he couldn't get enough of her—and never would.

Nineteen

Maverick woke before his alarm went off, so as to not wake Piper. Sunlight was streaming into the room, and he found his clothing items scattered where he'd left them the night before. Despite his best intentions to keep them warm in the truck bed, Piper had suggested they go back to her room at Hardwell Ranch. He hadn't loved the idea, but with Wes and Daisy, and Garrett and Willa out for a night on the town, there was much less chance he'd run into anyone who might be upset at his presence. Sure, he mostly got along with Wes, but with his relationship with Piper growing and becoming more intense, he wondered if it had the power to shatter their uneasy peace.

So, against his better judgment, he'd parked his truck down the road and vowed to be up early enough to leave without being noticed. It was ridiculous, the hoops they had to jump through to be together as grown adults. He wanted Piper to be happy and get to know her family. But Maverick didn't hide from anyone.

He buttoned his shirt and glanced down at the folders on the desk. One caught his attention. It was stamped "Property of the Library of Applewood," and it had the name "Kane" written along the top.

He chanced a glance over his shoulder at Piper, who was still sleeping soundly, facing away from him. He picked up the folder and shuffled through the papers.

What he saw surprised him, and it confirmed what he had long suspected: Garrett had built one of his facilities on land that belonged to the Kanes. He looked at Piper again. The woman he'd fallen for had known about it, and not only had she kept it from him, she had also taken it from the library so he couldn't have found out on his own. Luckily, she'd made copies, so he took one of each and put the others back in the folder, and left the room quietly, without waking Piper. He had to pay a visit to Garrett Hardwell.

Later that day, and after a visit to his lawyer, Maverick parked his truck and got out in front of Garrett's house on Hardwell Ranch. His plan was to knock on the door, but Garrett must have heard him coming and met him before he even reached the door.

"Can I help you?"

"Yeah," he said, passing over the envelope. "Take a look at this."

"What is it?"

"I'm sure Piper has shown you anyway, but they're the original titles and surveys for our ranches."

"And?" Garrett looked closer.

"And that's an aerial shot of your new training facility. The one you bulldozed a large section of land and spent millions to build."

"That's right. What about it?"

"It might interest you to know that you've built it on land that belongs to me."

Garrett paused. "That's not true."

"I've got a new surveyor coming in a few weeks. I had a hunch, but as these documents prove, the land should have been divided equally between our grandfathers, but Elias took it for himself instead."

"Hardwell land starts with the fence and the patch of sycamore trees."

"Not according to this."

"Impossible."

Maverick knew that Garrett was thinking about the amounts of time and money that had gone into building the facility, but there was no way he was going to let anyone take advantage of him like that. "Afraid not."

Garrett looked up and faced him. "I'll contest it."

"I know you will, and I wish you luck, because it's my land, and it'll come back to me."

"Will you take a buyout?" he asked. It was a sign that Garrett was desperate.

"We can discuss it. It won't be cheap."

"How did you find this out? And what does it have to do with Piper?"

"It doesn't matter. Talk to your people, and we'll see if we can't come to an understanding."

Piper knew that the mood was off at the Hardwell Ranch when she walked into the ranch house after spending some time at the *Tribune* office. Add that to the way Maverick had left her calls and texts unanswered after their night together in her room at the ranch. Something strange was happening. Through the partially opened door of the study, she could see Garrett and Wes, along with Elias, huddled together.

Willa and Daisy were sitting in front of the fire, both wearing frowns. "What's going on?" she asked almost in a whisper.

"There's some land disagreement with Maverick," Willa responded.

Piper's mouth dropped. She'd found out about that only the day before. She hadn't even had a chance to figure out what she was going to do with the information. But she knew that the shift had something to do with the dispute.

"Apparently, there's some kind of land boundary issue with the Kane land. The guys are on the phone with their lawyers now, trying to figure out how to deal with it."

"How can they deal with it?"

"I don't know. They've been in there for a while."

The men finally emerged.

"What's going on?"

Before Garrett answered, he looked at Piper. As if he knew she was the one who'd uncovered the damning information. "It's a private matter. But we'll figure it out."

"We're all family here, Garrett," Willa reminded him.

"Apparently, the state-of-the-art facility that we've just built that's worth millions is built on Maverick Kane's land."

"How did you find that out?" Daisy asked.

He looked at Piper again. "Maverick came by with some interesting documents. I called the town records office and discovered that Piper here had taken out copies of the title searches. And that's how Maverick found them."

"Oh," Willa said quietly.

"Yeah, our new aunt is behind the information making its way to Maverick," Wes said.

Piper opened her mouth, even though she had no idea what to say. "I... I didn't mean to."

"Then explain this, please," Elias said, his expression a little softer than that of his grandsons.

"I just wanted to know where the rivalry came from. I thought a title search would provide some helpful information."

"Information that you then passed on to your boyfriend, Maverick Kane," Garrett said.

"I didn't tell him anything! Sure, I didn't quite know what to do with what I'd learned. But I swear to you that I didn't say anything." She could tell that neither of them was on her side, so she stood. "Maybe I should leave."

Her face heated as she walked past all of them without looking up. She heard Willa call, "Piper, wait," but she didn't stop. She couldn't.

In the room she'd been using, she quickly packed her bag. She didn't know where she was going, but with all of the Hardwells hating her, and Maverick not returning her calls, she knew it was connected. There was nothing left for her here.

She walked out to her car. But it wasn't her car. It was the one Elias had given her. There was no other way to get to the airport, so she had no choice but to drive it to the airport in Austin and leave it for someone to pick up.

Without the Hardwells, without Maverick, what did she have left in Applewood? She would go back to Chicago. Her mom was buried there, Cynthia and her other friends were there, and she'd never made a mess of her life there. She could go find Maverick and see what happened between him and Garrett, but she wasn't sure she would like the answer. His announcement that he was making a claim on the land had come at a suspicious time, when she had only just discovered it herself. Had he snooped in her files while she'd slept? Would he have done that? Could she trust him?

As if he knew she was thinking about him, her phone came to life, vibrating in her hand, his name displayed across the screen. "Hello?" she answered.

"Piper. Where are you?"

"I'm just outside the Hardwell Ranch, wondering where I should go from here."

"Why? What's wrong? What's going on?"

"Why didn't you answer my calls earlier?"

"Because I was thinking. I wasn't sure I wanted to answer."

She rolled her eyes. "That's great."

"Is this about the land dispute?" he asked.

"It seems like you already know."

"Why don't we talk?" he suggested. "Come to my ranch."

She sighed. "Sure. I'll be there soon."

Maverick was waiting for her when she arrived. She walked past him into his house.

"Hello to you, too," Maverick muttered. She glared in response.

"Why are you pissed at me?" he asked her.

"Did you go through the folders on my desk? When I was sleeping?"

"Just the one that had my name on it."

"And?"

"And I saw that you knew that Garrett had encroached on my land and didn't tell me."

"Did you think I was hiding it from you?"

"You weren't?"

Piper opened her mouth to speak but couldn't form the words. "I didn't mean to," she said after a few beats of silence. "I'd just discovered it myself. I didn't know what to do with the information, who to tell, you or my family?" She crossed her arms defiantly and looked up at him. "Why did you go to the Hardwells instead of talking to me about it?"

"I went to them because it was the right thing to do. Garrett built on land that is rightfully mine and I want it back."

"You know it'll cost them millions of dollars."

He shrugged. "They have it."

"That's not the point."

"Then what is?"

"You know they're my family."

He held up his hands. "That has nothing to do with me."

"You purposefully drove a wedge between us. They think I tipped you off, and that I'm responsible for you coming after them. *I* did nothing wrong. *You* were spying on me."

"Why didn't you tell me what you found out? I thought we had something. We slept together. Or is that all it was? Just sex?"

"It meant more to me than just sex," she insisted. "Everything is so confusing for me right now. I was falling for you, Maverick, but you betrayed my trust."

"*I* betrayed *your* trust?" he asked. "I was falling in love with you, and you discovered this huge secret and didn't tell me."

It was Piper's turn to stay silent. She had no idea how to respond. "It's not that easy. I didn't know what to do."

"You didn't tell me and sided with your family."

"No, I said that I didn't know what to do with the information, and I meant it. I knew that no matter what I did, it would affect someone close to me. It tore me up to not tell you that last night, but something stopped me. I've never had a big family, and the Hardwells have given me that."

"Everything you wanted. Sorry that couldn't be me."

"Don't do this, Maverick. What we have is special."

"I just can't count on you to have my best interest at heart in a matter that also involves the Hardwells."

"I can't choose between you and my family."

"How about I take the choice away?" he asked.

"What do you mean?"

"You don't need to worry about me, or my land, anymore." He opened the door, his meaning clear. He was asking her to leave. "I'll see around, Piper."

She walked past him and out of his life. "No, you won't."

Twenty

Piper got back in the car. But she knew she couldn't leave town without seeing the Hardwells again. For what was most likely the last time, she was heading back to Hardwell Ranch. When she got there a few minutes later, she walked up the steps to the main house and knocked on the door. Daisy opened it. "Piper, hi. I'm glad you came back."

"I'm only here for a minute," she said. "Can I come in?"

"Of course," she said, moving aside.

Piper walked into the living room and saw that, thankfully, everyone was still there. "Hi. I promise I'll be gone soon. I just wanted to say to you all that I'm sorry. I betrayed you with Maverick, and then again when I found out about the land dispute. I made a mistake—several mistakes. I'm sorry."

"Thank you," Garrett said.

"I just came back to thank you all for everything. For allowing me to be a part of your family, for letting me stay here. I had a great time getting to know you, and I wanted to say goodbye."

"Where are you going?" Elias asked. "You just got here."

"I'm going to head back to Chicago. I'll leave the car at the airport in Austin."

"It's your car," Elias told her. "We'll ship it to you in Chicago if you really want to go."

"Thank you."

"But we hope you'll stay," he finished.

No one else in the room disputed that they wanted her to stay. "I—"

Elias walked toward her and pulled a piece of paper out of his wallet. He handed it to her. "This is for you, Piper."

She took the envelope. "What is it?"

"You've shown us that you're a member of the family. So, this is your share of the business."

She looked down at the substantial check she held in her hands. "What's this for?"

"You're my daughter. If you promise to stick around, I want us to have the chance to get to know each other, but this is a family business, and everyone gets their piece."

"I can't accept this. I know that Garrett and Wes were concerned I was here for the family money. That's not true. I don't want anyone to think that. I found a job here and I've always paid my own way. I'm comfortable from what I make at the *Tribune* and my freelance work. I don't need this. I'm not here to take away from anyone else's inheritance."

"Dear, after choosing the family today, for coming back to us, you've shown to all of us that you belong here. You're a Hardwell, and you deserve what comes with it."

"Elias, I'm stunned."

He patted her on the shoulder. "I'll give you some time with it then. Go get your bags and get unpacked again."

Twenty-One

Arriving at the stable, Maverick dismounted his horse. He removed the leather saddle and Peach nuzzled his cheek. He smiled. He had grown up with so many luxuries, but he was quickly learning that it was the simple things that made him happiest. Piper had taught him that. He had done so many things in his life; his money had bought him so much. Being with Piper, however, riding horses, watching the stars, just holding her, had made him the happiest he'd ever been in his life.

Normally, a long ride cleared his mind, but he seemed more confused than ever. The ride had lasted so long, given he'd covered acres and acres of his vast plot of land. He had so much, and while he knew he wanted to expand a little more into ranching, perhaps he didn't need all of the land. He was one person. Why did he need it all?

And none of it mattered much if he didn't have Piper at his side. Even though he knew it could never work between them, he'd allowed himself to fall in love with her;

he just hadn't been able to help himself. Coming in second to her family hurt more than he wanted to admit, and he wondered if there was some way to endear himself to them. Perhaps they could get past the rivalry and land dispute. At least, he hoped they could.

Maverick came to Hardwell Ranch with a knot in his stomach. It was time to put the land matter to rest. If Piper could come here and take the chance to tell them that she was family, he was certainly brave enough to have a frank conversation with his neighbor.

He saw Garrett, who stood glowering at him.

"What are you doing here?" he asked.

"I just want to talk."

Garrett nodded. "Let's go inside." He led Maverick into the study of the main house, where, despite living next door, he'd only ever been once before, when he'd spent the night with Piper. His heart thudded in his chest—just like it always did when he thought about the woman. "Office is through here," he told him.

Maverick took a seat at the chair in front of the imposing desk, while Garrett sat behind it. "Nice office."

"Thanks. What did you want to talk about? Piper?"

At mention of her name, his gut clenched. He'd been doing his best not to think about her, but he hadn't been very successful. "No," he managed to say while keeping his voice even. "I don't want to talk about Piper. Not yet.

"I know that there's a portion of Hardwell Ranch that technically belongs to me. We discussed this when I came to your place before."

That got Garrett's attention and Maverick expected him to argue, but the other man nodded instead. "I know. What do we intend to do about it?"

"I'll buy the land from you." Garrett knew nothing about the potential for oil on the land, which, if it was as fruitful as every other well discovered on Kane property, had the potential to increase the value of the acreage twenty times over. He knew that Garrett would never explore it, though, so he remained confident in the decision he'd made the night before.

"It's rightfully mine," Maverick continued, "but you've already built your facility over it." He paused. "The land is yours."

"What?"

"I have enough land for what I need. And I don't want to cause any problems for you." Maverick slid the contract across the desk. "Here's the paperwork, take a look. Get back to me."

"What's in it for you?" Garrett asked.

"I need your help to get Piper back."

Twenty-Two

Elias and Cathy's wedding ceremony had been a beautiful, intimate affair. People were now dancing and toasting the couple, drinks were flowing and a wonderful time was being had by everyone in attendance.

Piper took her seat next to Willa at the family table. *The family table*. It was such a thrill for her. She'd never had a big family, but now each of the chairs was occupied by one of her siblings or nephews—although they hated it when she called them that—and their respective partners. It had taken her a while, and had cost her a great deal of heartache, but she now felt comfortable with them, at ease. As if she was part of the family.

Being a part of this family, however, had come at one hell of a cost. She'd been in love with Maverick, and she missed him every day. Everywhere she turned, she saw something that reminded her of Maverick—the diner, the café, the road leading to his ranch, the parking lot at Longhorn's. She missed him so much, but she'd made her choice and she had to live with the consequences.

"It was such a beautiful day," Piper told Willa, who had planned the nuptials and the reception. "You're amazing at what you do."

"Thank you. Cathy had a very specific vision. All I did was make it happen. Oh, I've got something for you." She placed the newest issue of the *Applewood Tribune* on the table in front of her. "Did you read today's paper?"

"I made the paper," Piper said. "I don't normally make a habit of reading the physical edition."

"Maybe you should read this one."

Piper didn't know or understand what Willa was getting at. "Why?"

"Just do it."

Piper opened the newspaper. And saw what Willa had wanted her to see. It was a full-size advertisement. She was certainly happy for the ad revenue, but it was the content that made her smile. It was a full-page spread, printed black with white lettering.

Which insufferable grump is miserable without his attention-grabbing, trouble-making city girl? it read. *He'd do anything to make it up to her, even bury a longtime family feud for her.*

Piper had to the read it three times before the meaning sank in. "What? Where did this come from?" she asked Willa.

Willa shrugged. "I don't know. You might want to ask that guy, though," she suggested, gesturing over Piper's shoulder.

When Piper turned her head to look, she saw Maverick

standing at the bar with Garrett and Wes. They were smiling and laughing—having apparently buried the hatchet.

He saw her looking at him and broke away from the men. When he approached the table, he held out his hand. "Can I have this dance?"

She put her hand in his. "Of course." Her heart was pounding in her chest as he led her to the dance floor. She hadn't seen Maverick in over a week, and her heart had ached every second. But now that he was in front of her, she couldn't help but experience him using every one of her senses. He held her close, his warm hand stroking her lower back. His touch sent tingles up her spine.

"Did you read anything interesting in the paper?" he asked, his voice rumbly.

"I did. There was an interesting ad in the latest edition." She paused. "How'd you do that?"

"I just contacted one of your reporters. They snuck it in before it went to print."

"I can't believe you did that."

"It's true," he told her. "I really missed you."

"I missed you, too. I'm really surprised to see you here."

"No more surprised than I am. I still can't believe that Elias and Garrett let me in here."

"How did you convince them?"

"We settled the land dispute, but I told them how much I loved you and I wanted to make it right with the family. I don't want the land that their facility is built on. I just want you."

"Are you serious?"

"Yeah, for now," he teased. "But I need to make it right with you. I'm so sorry I went through your desk. I had no right to do that."

"And I had no right to keep the survey from you."

"None of that matters now. I love you."

She smiled, feeling tears of relief and happiness build in the corners of her eyes. "I love you, too."

She asked, hopeful, "Do you think we can start over?"

He spun her around the dance floor. "I know we can."

She gasped as he dipped her back slightly to kiss her. When his lips found hers, she knew that, between her new family and Maverick, she'd found every kind of love she'd once sought. She was finally at home in Applewood.

* * * * *

COMING SOON!

OUT NOW!

Available at
millsandboon.co.uk

MILLS & BOON

OUT NOW!

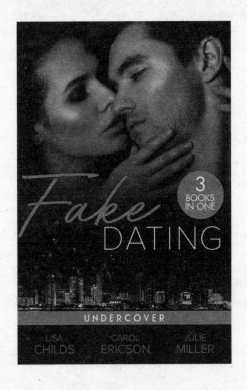

Available at
millsandboon.co.uk

MILLS & BOON

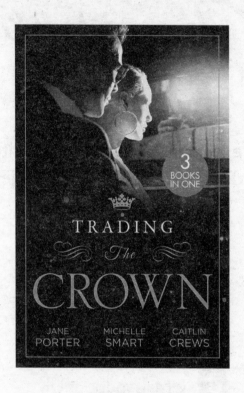

LET'S TALK
Romance

For exclusive extracts, competitions and special offers, find us online:

f MillsandBoon

𝕏 @MillsandBoon

⊙ @MillsandBoonUK

♪ @MillsandBoonUK

Get in touch on 01413 063 232